Sanditon

Jane Austen
and Another Lady

D0858095

Boston

HOUGHTON MIFFLIN COMPANY

1975

A PORTION OF THIS BOOK HAS APPEARED IN *REDBOOK*.

FIRST PRINTING V

Library of Congress Cataloging in Publication Data
Austen, Jane, 1775-1817.
Sanditon.

I. Another lady. II. Title.
PZ3.A93San8 [PR4034]   823'.7   74-20584
ISBN 0-395-20284-1

PRINTED IN THE UNITED STATES OF AMERICA

SANDITON

CHAPTER 1

A GENTLEMAN AND A LADY travelling from Tunbridge towards
that part of the Sussex coast which lies between Hastings and
Eastbourne, being induced by business to quit the high road and
attempt a very rough lane, were overturned in toiling up its long
ascent, half rock, half sand.

The accident happened just beyond the only gentleman's house
near the lane — a house which their driver, on being first required
to take that direction, had conceived to be necessarily their object
and had with most unwilling looks been constrained to pass by.
He had grumbled and shaken his shoulders and pitied and cut his
horses so sharply that he might have been open to the suspicion
of overturning them on purpose (especially as the carriage was
not his master's own) if the road had not indisputably become
worse than before, as soon as the premises of the said house were
left behind — expressing with a most portentous countenance that,
beyond it, no wheels but cart wheels could safely proceed.

The severity of the fall was broken by their slow pace and the
narrowness of the lane; and the gentleman having scrambled out
and helped out his companion, they neither of them at first felt
more than shaken and bruised. But the gentleman had, in the
course of the extrication, sprained his foot; and soon becoming
sensible of it, was obliged in a few moments to cut short both his
remonstrances to the driver and his congratulations to his wife and
himself and sit down on the bank, unable to stand.

"There is something wrong here," said he, putting his hand to his ankle. "But never mind, my dear," looking up at her with a smile, "it could not have happened, you know, in a better place. Good out of evil. The very thing perhaps to be wished for. We shall soon get relief. *There*, I fancy, lies my cure," pointing to the neat-looking end of a cottage, which was seen romantically situated among wood on a high eminence at some little distance. "Does not *that* promise to be the very place?"

His wife fervently hoped it was; but stood, terrified and anxious, neither able to do or suggest anything, and receiving her first real comfort from the sight of several persons now coming to their assistance.

The accident had been discerned from a hayfield adjoining the house they had passed. And the persons who approached were a well-looking, hale, gentlemanlike man of middle age, the proprietor of the place, who happened to be among his haymakers at the time, and three or four of the ablest of them summoned to attend their master — to say nothing of all the rest of the field, men, women and children, not very far off.

Mr. Heywood, such was the name of the said proprietor, advanced with a very civil salutation, much concern for the accident, some surprise at anybody's attempting that road in a carriage, and ready offers of assistance.

His courtesies were received with good breeding and gratitude, and while one or two of the men lent their help to the driver in getting the carriage upright again, the traveller said,

"You are extremely obliging, sir, and I take you at your word. The injury to my leg is, I dare say, very trifling. But it is always best in these cases, you know, to have a surgeon's opinion without loss of time; and as the road does not seem in a favourable state for my getting up to his house myself, I will thank you to send off one of these good people for the surgeon."

"The surgeon!" exclaimed Mr. Heywood. "I am afraid you will find no surgeon at hand here, but I dare say we shall do very well without him."

"Nay sir, if *he* is not in the way, his partner will do just as well — or rather better. I would rather see his partner. Indeed I would prefer the attendance of his partner. One of these good people can be with him in three minutes, I am sure. I need not ask whether I see the house," looking towards the cottage, "for excepting your own, we have passed none in this place which can be the abode of a gentleman."

Mr. Heywood looked very much astonished.

"What, sir! Are you expecting to find a surgeon in that cottage? We have neither surgeon nor partner in the parish, I assure you."

"Excuse me, sir," replied the other. "I am sorry to have the appearance of contradicting you, but from the extent of the parish or some other cause you may not be aware of the fact — stay — can I be mistaken in the place? Am I not in Willingden? Is not this Willingden?"

"Yes, sir, this is certainly Willingden."

"Then, sir, I can bring proof of your having a surgeon in the parish, whether you may know it or not. Here, sir," taking out his pocket book, "if you will do me the favor of casting your eye over these advertisements which I cut out myself from the *Morning Post* and the *Kentish Gazette* only yesterday morning in London, I think you will be convinced that I am not speaking at random. You will find in it an advertisement of the dissolution of a partnership in the medical line — in your own parish — extensive business — undeniable character — respectable references — wishing to form a separate establishment. You will find it at full length, sir," offering the two little oblong extracts.

"Sir, if you were to show me all the newspapers that are printed in one week throughout the kingdom, you would not persuade me of there being a surgeon in Willingden," said Mr. Heywood with a good-humoured smile. "Having lived here ever since I was born, man and boy fifty-seven years, I think I must have known of such a person. At least I may venture to say that he has not much business. To be sure, if gentlemen were to be often attempting this lane in post-chaises, it might not be a bad speculation for a surgeon to get a house at the top of the hill. But as to that cottage, I can assure you, sir, that it is in fact, in spite of its spruce air at this distance, as indifferent a double tenement as any in the parish, and that my shepherd lives at one end and three old women at the other."

He took the pieces of paper as he spoke, and, having looked them over, added,

"I believe I can explain it, sir. Your mistake *is* in the place. There are two Willingdens in this country. And your advertisements must refer to the other, which is Great Willingden or Willingden Abbots, and lies seven miles off on the other side of Battle. Quite down in the weald. And *we*, sir," he added, speaking rather proudly, "are not in the weald."

"Not *down* in the weald, I am sure," replied the traveller pleasantly. "It took us half an hour to climb your hill. Well, I dare say it is as you say and I have made an abominably stupid blunder. All done in a moment. The advertisements did not catch my eye till the last half hour of our being in town — everything in the hurry and confusion which always attend a short stay there. One is never able to complete anything in the way of business, you know, till the carriage is at the door. So satisfying myself with a brief inquiry, and finding we were actually to pass within a mile or two of *a Willingden*, I sought no farther. . . . My dear" (to his wife) "I am very sorry to have brought you into this scrape. But do not be alarmed about my leg. It gives me no pain while I am quiet. And as soon as these good people have succeeded in setting the carriage to rights and turning the horses round, the best thing we can do will be to measure back our steps into the turnpike road and proceed to Hailsham, and so home without attempting anything farther. Two hours take us home from Hailsham. And once at home, we have our remedy at hand, you know. A little of our own bracing sea air will soon set me on my feet again. Depend upon it, my dear, it is exactly a case for the sea. Saline air and immersion will be the very thing. My sensations tell me so already."

In a most friendly manner Mr. Heywood here interposed, entreating them not to think of proceeding till the ankle had been examined and some refreshment taken, and very cordially pressing them to make use of his house for both purposes.

"We are always well stocked," said he, "with all the common remedies for sprains and bruises. And I will answer for the pleasure it will give my wife and daughters to be of service to you in every way in their power."

A twinge or two, in trying to move his foot, disposed the traveller to think rather more than he had done at first of the benefit of immediate assistance; and consulting his wife in the few words of "Well, my dear, I believe it will be better for us," he turned again to Mr. Heywood.

"Before we accept your hospitality sir, and in order to do away with any unfavourable impression which the sort of wild-goose chase you find me in may have given rise to — allow me to tell you who we are. My name is Parker, Mr. Parker of Sanditon; this lady, my wife, Mrs. Parker. We are on our road home from London. My name perhaps — though I am by no means the first of my family holding landed property in the parish of Sanditon — may be unknown at this distance from the coast. But Sanditon itself — everybody has heard of Sanditon. The favourite — for a young and rising bathing-place — certainly the favourite spot of all that are to be found along the coast of Sussex; the most favoured by nature, and promising to be the most chosen by man."

"Yes, I have heard of Sanditon," replied Mr. Heywood. "Every five years, one hears of some new place or other starting up by the sea and growing the fashion. How they can half of them be filled is the wonder! Where people can be found with money and time to go to them! Bad things for a country — sure to raise the price of provisions and make the poor good for nothing — as I dare say you find, sir."

"Not at all, sir, not at all," cried Mr. Parker eagerly. "Quite the contrary, I assure you. A common idea, but a mistaken one. It may apply to your large, overgrown places like Brighton or Worthing or Eastbourne — but *not* to a small village like Sanditon, precluded by its size from experiencing any of the evils of civilization; while the growth of the place, the buildings, the nursery grounds, the demand for everything and the sure resort of the very best company — those regular, steady, private families of thorough gentility and character who are a blessing everywhere — excite the industry of the poor and diffuse comfort and improvement among them of every sort. No sir, I assure you, Sanditon is not a place — "

"I do not mean to take exception to any place in particular," answered Mr. Heywood. "I only think our coast is too full of them altogether. But had we not better try to get you — "

"Our coast too full!" repeated Mr. Parker. "On that point perhaps we may not totally disagree. At least there are *enough*. Our coast is abundant enough. It demands no more. Everybody's taste and everybody's finances may be suited. And those good people who are trying to add to the number are, in my opinion, excessively absurd and must soon find themselves the dupes of their own fallacious calculations. Such a place as Sanditon, sir, I may say was wanted, was called for. Nature had marked it out, had spoken in most intelligible characters. The finest, purest sea breeze on the coast — acknowledged to be so — excellent bathing — fine hard sand — deep water ten yards from the shore — no mud — no weeds — no slimy rocks. Never was there a place more palpably designed by nature for the resort of the invalid — the very spot which thousands seemed in need of! The most desirable distance from London! One complete, measured mile nearer than Eastbourne. Only conceive, sir, the advantage of saving a whole mile in a long journey. But Brinshore, sir, which I dare say you have in your eye — the attempts of two or three speculating people about Brinshore this last year to raise that paltry hamlet — lying as it does between a stagnant marsh, a bleak moor and the constant effluvia of a ridge of putrefying seaweed — can end in nothing but their own disappointment. What in the name of common sense is to *recommend* Brinshore? A most insalubrious air — roads proverbially detestable — water brackish beyond example, impossible to get a good dish of tea within three miles of the place. And as for the soil — it is so cold and ungrateful that it can hardly be made to yield a cabbage. Depend upon it, sir, that this is a most faithful description of Brinshore — not in the smallest degree exaggerated — and if you have heard it differently spoken of — "

"Sir, I never heard it spoken of in my life before," said Mr. Heywood. "I did not know there was such a place in the world."

"You did not! There, my dear," turning with exultation to his wife, "you see how it is. So much for the celebrity of Brinshore! This gentleman did not know there was such a place in the world. Why, in truth, sir, I fancy we may apply to Brinshore that line of the poet Cowper in his description of the religious cottager, as opposed to Voltaire — '*She*, never heard of half a mile from home.' "

"With all my heart, sir — apply any verses you like to it. But I want to see something applied to your leg. And I am sure by your lady's countenance that she is quite of my opinion and thinks it a pity to lose any more time. And here come my girls to speak for themselves and their mother." Two or three genteel-looking young women, followed by as many maid servants, were now seen issuing from the house. "I began to wonder the bustle should not have reached *them*. A thing of this kind soon

7

makes a stir in a lonely place like ours. Now, sir, let us see how you can be best conveyed into the house."

The young ladies approached and said everything that was proper to recommend their father's offers, and in an unaffected manner calculated to make the strangers easy. As Mrs. Parker was exceedingly anxious for relief — and her husband by this time not much less disposed for it — a very few civil scruples were enough; especially as the carriage, being now set up, was discovered to have received such injury on the fallen side as to be unfit for present use. Mr. Parker was therefore carried into the house and his carriage wheeled off to a vacant barn.

CHAPTER 2

THE ACQUAINTANCE, thus oddly begun, was neither short nor unimportant. For a whole fortnight the travellers were fixed at Willingden, Mr. Parker's sprain proving too serious for him to move sooner. He had fallen into very good hands. The Heywoods were a thoroughly respectable family and every possible attention was paid, in the kindest and most unpretending manner, to both husband and wife. *He* was waited on and nursed, and *she* cheered and comforted with unremitting kindness; and as every office of hospitality and friendliness was received as it ought, as there was not more good will on one side than gratitude on the other, nor any deficiency of generally pleasant manners in either, they grew to like each other in the course of that fortnight exceedingly well.

Mr. Parker's character and history were soon unfolded. All that he understood of himself, he readily told, for he was very openhearted; and where he might be himself in the dark, his conversation was still giving information to such of the Heywoods as could observe. By such he was perceived to be an enthusiast — on the subject of Sanditon, a complete enthusiast. Sanditon, the success of Sanditon as a small, fashionable bathing place, was the object for which he seemed to live.

A very few years ago, it had been a quiet village of no pretensions; but some natural advantages in its position and some accidental circumstances having suggested to himself and the other principal landholder the probability of its becoming a profitable speculation, they had engaged in it, and planned and built, and praised and puffed, and raised it to something of young renown; and Mr. Parker could now think of very little besides.

The facts which, in more direct communication, he laid before them were that he was about five and thirty, had been married — very happily married — seven years, and had four sweet children at home; that he was of a respectable family and easy, though not large, fortune; no profession — succeeding as eldest son to the property which two or three generations had been holding and accumulating before him; that he had two brothers and two sisters, all single and all independent — the eldest of the two former indeed, by collateral inheritance, quite as well provided for as himself.

His object in quitting the high road to hunt for an advertising surgeon was also plainly stated. It had not proceeded from any intention of spraining his ankle or doing himself any other injury for the good of such surgeon, nor (as Mr. Heywood had been apt to suppose) from any design of entering into partnership with him; it was merely in consequence of a wish to establish some medical man at Sanditon, which the nature of the advertisement induced him to expect to accomplish in Willingden. He was convinced that the advantage of a medical man at hand would very materially promote the rise and prosperity of the place, would in fact tend to bring a prodigious influx; nothing else was wanting. He had *strong* reason to believe that *one* family had been deterred last year from trying Sanditon on that account — and probably very many more — and his own sisters, who were sad invalids and whom he was very anxious to get to Sanditon this summer, could hardly be expected to hazard themselves in a place where they could not have immediate medical advice.

Upon the whole, Mr. Parker was evidently an amiable family man, fond of wife, children, brothers and sisters, and generally kind-hearted; liberal, gentlemanlike, easy to please; of a sanguine turn of mind, with more imagination than judgement. And Mrs.

10

Parker was as evidently a gentle, amiable, sweet-tempered woman, the properest wife in the world for a man of strong understanding but not of a capacity to supply the cooler reflection which her own husband sometimes needed; and so entirely waiting to be guided on every occasion that whether he was risking his fortune or spraining his ankle, she remained equally useless.

Sanditon was a second wife and four children to him, hardly less dear, and certainly more engrossing. He could talk of it forever. It had indeed the highest claims; not only those of birthplace, property and home; it was his mine, his lottery, his speculation and his hobby horse; his occupation, his hope and his futurity.

He was extremely desirous of drawing his good friends at Willingden thither; and his endeavours in the cause were as grateful and disinterested as they were warm. He wanted to secure the promise of a visit, to get as many of the family as his own house would contain to follow him to Sanditon as soon as possible; and, healthy as they all undeniably were, foresaw that every one of them would be benefited by the sea.

He held it indeed as certain that no person could be really well, no person (however upheld for the present by fortuitous aids of exercise and spirits in a semblance of health) could be really in a state of secure and permanent health without spending at least six weeks by the sea every year. The sea air and sea bathing together were nearly infallible, one or the other of them being a match for every disorder of the stomach, the lungs or the blood. They were anti-spasmodic, anti-pulmonary, anti-septic, anti-billious and anti-rheumatic. Nobody could catch cold by the sea; nobody wanted appetite by the sea; nobody wanted spirits; nobody wanted strength. Sea air was healing, softening, relaxing — fortifying and bracing — seemingly just as was wanted — sometimes one, sometimes the other. If the sea breeze failed, the sea-bath was the certain corrective; and where bathing disagreed, the sea air alone was evidently designed by nature for the cure.

His eloquence, however, could not prevail. Mr. and Mrs. Heywood never left home. Marrying early and having a very numerous family, their movements had long been limited to one small circle; and they were older in habits than in age. Excepting two journeys to London in the year to receive his dividends, Mr. Heywood went no farther than his feet or his well-tried old horse could carry him; and Mrs. Heywood's adventurings were only now and then to visit her neighbours in the old coach which had been new when they married and fresh-lined on their eldest son's coming of age ten years ago.

They had a very pretty property; enough, had their family been of reasonable limits, to have allowed them a very gentlemanlike share of luxuries and change; enough for them to have indulged in a new carriage and better roads, an occasional month at Tunbridge Wells, and symptoms of the gout and a winter at Bath. But the maintenance, education and fitting out of fourteen children demanded a very quiet, settled, careful course of life, and obliged them to be stationary and healthy at Willingden. What prudence had at first enjoined was now rendered pleasant by habit. They never left home and they had gratification in saying so.

But very far from wishing their children to do the same, they were glad to promote *their* getting out into the world as much as possible. They stayed at home that their children *might* get out; and, while making that home extremely comfortable, welcomed every change from it which could give useful connections or respectable acquaintance to sons or daughters.

When Mr. and Mrs. Parker, therefore, ceased from soliciting a family visit and bounded their views to carrying back one daughter with them, no difficulties were started. It was general pleasure and consent.

Their invitation was to Miss Charlotte Heywood, a very pleasing young woman of two and twenty, the eldest of the daughters at home and the one who, under her mother's directions, had been particularly useful and obliging to them; who had attended them most and knew them best.

Charlotte was to go: with excellent health, to bathe and be better if she could; to receive every possible pleasure which Sanditon could be made to supply by the gratitude of those she went with; and to buy new parasols, new gloves and new brooches for her sisters and herself at the library, which Mr. Parker was anxiously wishing to support.

All that Mr. Heywood himself could be persuaded to promise was that he would send everyone to Sanditon who asked his advice, and that nothing should ever induce him (as far as the future could be answered for) to spend even five shillings at Brinshore.

CHAPTER 3

EVERY NEIGHBOURHOOD should have a great lady. The great lady of Sanditon was Lady Denham; and in their journey from Willingden to the coast, Mr. Parker gave Charlotte a more detailed account of her than had been called for before. She had been necessarily often mentioned at Willingden — for being his colleague in speculation, Sanditon itself could not be talked of long without the introduction of Lady Denham. That she was a very rich old lady, who had buried two husbands, who knew the value of money, and was very much looked up to and had a poor cousin living with her, were facts already known; but some further particulars of her history and her character served to lighten the tediousness of a long hill, or a heavy bit of road, and to give the visiting young lady a suitable knowledge of the person with whom she might now expect to be daily associating.

Lady Denham had been a rich Miss Brereton, born to wealth but not to education. Her first husband had been a Mr. Hollis, a man of considerable property in the country, of which a large share of the parish of Sanditon, with manor and mansion house, made a part. He had been an elderly man when she married him, her own age about thirty. Her motives for such a match could be little understood at the distance of forty years, but she had so well nursed and pleased Mr. Hollis that at his death he left her everything — all his estates, and all at her disposal.

After a widowhood of some years, she had been induced to marry again. The late Sir Harry Denham, of Denham Park in the neighbourhood of Sanditon, had succeeded in removing her and her large income to his own domains, but he could not succeed in the views of permanently enriching his family which were attributed to him. She had been too wary to put anything out of her own power and when, on Sir Harry's decease, she returned again to her own house at Sanditon, she was said to have made this boast to a friend: "that though she had *got* nothing but her title from the family, still she had *given* nothing for it." For the title, it was to be supposed, she had married; and Mr. Parker acknowledged there being just such a degree of value for it apparent now as to give her conduct that natural explanation.

"There is at times," said he, "a little self-importance — but it is not offensive — and there are moments, there are points, when her love of money is carried greatly too far. But she is a good-natured woman, a very good-natured woman — a very obliging, friendly neighbour; a cheerful, independent, valuable character — and her faults may be entirely imputed to her want of education. She has good natural sense, but quite uncultivated. She has a fine active mind as well as a fine healthy frame for a woman of seventy, and enters into the improvement of Sanditon with a spirit truly admirable. Though now and then, a littleness *will* appear. She cannot look forward quite as I would have her and takes alarm at a trifling present expense without considering what returns it *will* make her in a year or two. That is, we think *differently*. We now and then see things *differently*, Miss Heywood. Those who tell their own story, you know, must be listened to with caution. When you see us in contact, you will judge for yourself."

Lady Denham was indeed a great lady beyond the common wants of society, for she had many thousands a year to bequeath, and three distinct sets of people to be courted by: her own relations, who might very reasonably wish for her original thirty thousand pounds among them; the legal heirs of Mr. Hollis, who must hope to be more indebted to *her* sense of justice than he had allowed them to be to *his*; and those members of the Denham family whom her second husband had hoped to make a good bargain for.

By all of these, or by branches of them, she had no doubt been long, and still continued to be, well attacked; and of these three divisions, Mr. Parker did not hesitate to say that Mr. Hollis's kindred were the *least* in favour and Sir Harry Denham's the *most*. The former, he believed, had done themselves irremediable harm by expressions of very unwise and unjustifiable resentment at the time of Mr. Hollis's death; the latter had the advantage of being the remnant of a connection which she certainly valued, of having been known to her from their childhood and of being always at hand to preserve their interest by reasonable attention.

Sir Edward, the present baronet, nephew to Sir Harry, resided constantly at Denham Park; and Mr. Parker had little doubt that he and his sister, Miss Denham, who lived with him, would be principally remembered in her will. He sincerely hoped it. Miss Denham had a very small provision; and her brother was a poor man for his rank in society.

"He is a warm friend to Sanditon," said Mr. Parker, "and his hand would be as liberal as his heart, had he the power. He would be a noble coadjutor! As it is, he does what he can and is running up a tasteful little cottage orné on a strip of waste ground Lady Denham has granted him, which I have no doubt we shall have many a candidate for before the end even of *this* season."

Till within the last twelvemonth, Mr. Parker had considered Sir Edward as standing without a rival, as having the fairest chance of succeeding to the greater part of all that she had to give; but there were now another person's claims to be taken into account — those of the young female relation whom Lady Denham had been induced to receive into her family. After having always protested against any such addition, and long and often enjoyed the repeated defeats she had given to every attempt of her relations to introduce this young lady or that young lady as a companion at

Sanditon House, she had brought back with her from London last Michaelmas a Miss Brereton, who bid fair by her merits to vie in favour with Sir Edward and to secure for herself and her family that share of the accumulated property which they had certainly the best right to inherit.

Mr. Parker spoke warmly of Clara Brereton, and the interest of his story increased very much with the introduction of such a character. Charlotte listened with more than amusement now; it was solicitude and enjoyment, as she heard her described to be lovely, amiable, gentle, unassuming, conducting herself uniformly with great good sense, and evidently gaining by her innate worth on the affections of her patroness. Beauty, sweetness, poverty and dependence do not want the imagination of a man to operate upon; with due exceptions, woman feels for woman very promptly and compassionately. He gave the particulars which had led to Clara's admission at Sanditon as no bad exemplification of that mixture of character — that union of littleness with kindness and good sense, even liberality — which he saw in Lady Denham.

After having avoided London for many years, principally on account of these very cousins who were continually writing, inviting and tormenting her, and whom she was determined to keep at a distance, she had been obliged to go there last Michaelmas with the certainty of being detained at least a fortnight.

She had gone to a hotel, living by her own account as prudently as possible to defy the reputed expensiveness of such a home, and at the end of three days calling for her bill that she might judge of her state. Its amount was such as determined her on staying not another hour in the house, and she was preparing — in all the anger and perturbation of her belief in very gross imposition and her ignorance of where to go for better usage — to leave the hotel at all hazards, when the cousins, the politic and lucky cousins, who seemed always to have a spy on her, introduced themselves at this important moment; and learning her situation, persuaded her to accept such a home for the rest of her stay as their humbler house in a very inferior part of London could offer.

She went, was delighted with her welcome and the hospitality and attention she received from everybody; found her good cousins the Breretons beyond her expectation worthy people; and finally was impelled by a personal knowledge of their narrow income and pecuniary difficulties to invite one of the girls of the family to pass the winter with her.

The invitation was to *one*, for six months, with the probability of another being then to take her place; but in *selecting* the one, Lady Denham had shown the good part of her character. For, passing by the actual daughters of the house, she had chosen Clara, a niece, more helpless and more pitiable of course than any — a dependent on poverty — an additional burden on an encumbered circle; and one who had been so low in every worldly view as, with all her natural endowments and powers, to have been preparing for a situation little better than a nursery maid.

Clara had returned with her and by her good sense and merit had now, to all appearance, secured a very strong hold in Lady Denham's regard. The six months had long been over and not a syllable was breathed of any change or exchange. She was a general favourite. The influence of her steady conduct and mild, gentle temper was felt by everybody. The prejudices which had met her at first, in some quarters, were all dissipated. She was felt to be worthy of trust, to be the very companion who would guide and soften Lady Denham, who would enlarge her mind and open her hand. She was as thoroughly amiable as she was lovely; and since having had the advantage of their Sanditon breezes, that loveliness was complete.

CHAPTER 4

"AND WHOSE very snug-looking place is this?" said Charlotte as, in a sheltered dip within two miles of the sea, they passed close by a moderate-sized house, well fenced and planted, and rich in the garden, orchard and meadows which are the best embellishments of such a dwelling. "It seems to have as many comforts about it as Willingden."

"Ah," said Mr. Parker. "This is my old house, the house of my forefathers, the house where I and all my brothers and sisters were born and bred, and where my own three eldest children were born; where Mrs. Parker and I lived till within the last two years, till our new house was finished. I am glad you are pleased with it. It is an honest old place; and Hillier keeps it in very good order. I have given it up, you know, to the man who occupies the chief of my land. He gets a better house by it, and I, a rather better situation! One other hill brings us to Sanditon — modern Sanditon — a beautiful spot. Our ancestors, you know, always built in a hole. Here were we, pent down in this little contracted nook, without air or view, only one mile and three quarters from the noblest expanse of ocean between the South Foreland and Land's End, and without the smallest advantage from it. You will not think I have made a bad exchange when we reach Trafalgar House — which by the bye, I almost wish I had not named Trafalgar — for Waterloo is more the thing now. However, Waterloo is in reserve; and if we have encouragement enough this year for a little crescent to be ventured on (as I trust we shall) then we shall be able to call it Waterloo Cresent — and the name joined to the form of the building, which always takes, will give us the command of lodgers. In a good season we should have more applications than we could attend to."

"It was always a very comfortable house," said Mrs. Parker, looking at it through the back window with something like the fondness of regret. "And such a nice garden — such an excellent garden."

"Yes, my love, but *that* we may be said to carry with us. It supplies us, as before, with all the fruit and vegetables we want. And we have, in fact, all the comfort of an excellent kitchen garden without the constant eyesore of its formalities or the yearly nuisance of its decaying vegetation. Who can endure a cabbage bed in October?"

"Oh dear, yes. We are quite as well off for gardenstuff as ever we were; for if it is forgot to be brought at any time, we can always buy what we want at Sanditon House. The gardener there is glad enough to supply us. But it was a nice place for the children to run about in. So shady in summer!"

"My dear, we shall have shade enough on the hill, and more than enough in the course of a very few years. The growth of my plantations is a general astonishment. In the meanwhile we have the canvas awning which gives us the most complete comfort within doors. And you can get a parasol at Whitby's for little Mary at any time, or a large bonnet at Jebb's. And as for the boys, I must say I would rather *them* run about in the sunshine than not. I am sure we agree, my dear, in wishing our boys to be as hardy as possible."

"Yes indeed, I am sure we do. And I will get Mary a little parasol, which will make her as proud as can be. How grave she will walk about with it and fancy herself quite a little woman. Oh, I have not the smallest doubt of our being a great deal better off where we are now. If we any of us want to bathe, we have not a quarter of a mile to go. But you know," still looking back, "one loves to look at an old friend, at a place where one has been happy. The Hilliers did not seem to feel the storms last winter at all. I remember seeing Mrs. Hillier after one of those dreadful nights, when *we* had been literally rocked in our bed, and she did not seem at all aware of the wind being anything more than common."

"Yes, yes, that's likely enough. *We* have all the grandeur of the storm with less real danger because the wind, meeting with nothing to oppose or confine it around our house, simply rages and passes on; while down in this gutter, nothing is known of the state of the air below the tops of the trees; and the inhabitants may be taken totally unawares by one of those dreadful currents, which do more mischief in a valley when they *do* arise than an open country ever experiences in the heaviest gale. But, my dear love, as to gardenstuff, you were saying that any accidental omission is supplied in a moment by Lady Denham's gardener. But it occurs to me that we ought to go elsewhere upon such occasions, and that old Stringer and his son have a higher claim. I encouraged him to set up, you know, and am afraid he does not do very well. That is, there has not been time enough yet. He *will* do very well beyond a doubt. But at first it is uphill work, and therefore we must give him what help we can. When any vegetables or fruit happen to be wanted — and it will not be amiss to have them often wanted, to have something or other forgotten most days; just to have a nominal supply, you know, that poor old Andrew may not lose his daily job — but in fact to buy the chief of our consumption from the Stringers."

"Very well, my love, that can be easily done. And cook will be satisfied, which will be a great comfort, for she is always complaining of old Andrew now and says he never brings her what she wants. There — now the old house is quite left behind. What is it your brother Sidney says about its being a hospital?"

"Oh, my dear Mary, merely a joke of his. He pretends to

advise me to make a hospital of it. He pretends to laugh at my improvements. Sidney says anything, you know. He has always said what he chose, of and to us all. Most families have such a member among them, I believe, Miss Heywood. There is someone in most families privileged by superior abilities or spirits to say anything. In ours, it is Sidney, who is a very clever young man and with great powers of pleasing. He lives too much in the world to be settled; that is his only fault. He is here and there and everywhere. I wish we may get him to Sanditon. I should like to have you acquainted with him. And it would be a fine thing for the place! Such a young man as Sidney, with his neat equipage and fashionable air. You and I, Mary, know what effect it might have. Many a respectable family, many a careful mother, many a pretty daughter might it secure us to the prejudice of Eastbourne and Hastings."

They were now approaching the church and neat village of old Sanditon, which stood at the foot of the hill they were afterwards to ascend — a hill whose side was covered with the woods and enclosures of Sanditon House and whose height ended in an open down where the new buildings might soon be looked for. A branch only of the valley, winding more obliquely towards the sea, gave a passage to an inconsiderable stream, and formed at its mouth a third habitable division in a small cluster of fishermen's houses. The original village contained little more than cottages; but the spirit of the day had been caught, as Mr. Parker observed with delight to Charlotte, and two or three of the best of them were smartened up with a white curtain and "Lodgings to let"; and farther on, in the little green court of an old farm house, two females in elegant white were actually to be seen with their books and camp stools; and in turning the corner of the baker's shop, the sound of a harp might be heard through the upper casement.

Such sights and sounds were highly blissful to Mr. Parker. Not that he had any personal concern in the success of the village itself; for considering it as too remote from the beach, he had done nothing there; but it was a most valuable proof of the increasing fashion of the place altogether. If the *village* could attract, the hill might be nearly full. He anticipated an amazing season. At the same time last year (late in July) there had not been a single lodger in the village! Nor did he remember any during the whole summer, excepting one family of children who came from London for sea air after the whooping cough, and whose mother would not let them be nearer the shore for fear of their tumbling in.

"Civilization, civilization indeed!" cried Mr. Parker, delighted. "Look, my dear Mary, look at William Heeley's windows. Blue shoes, and nankin boots! Who would have expected such a sight at a shoemaker's in old Sanditon! This is new within the month. There was no blue shoe when we passed this way a month ago. Glorious indeed! Well, I think I *have* done something in my day. Now, for our hill, our health-breathing hill."

In ascending, they passed the lodge gates of Sanditon House and saw the top of the house itself among its groves. It was the last building of former days in that line of the parish. A little higher up, the modern began; and in crossing the down, a Prospect House, a Bellevue Cottage and a Denham Place were to be looked at by Charlotte with the calmness of amused curiosity, and by Mr. Parker with the eager eye which hoped to see scarcely any empty houses. More bills at the windows than he had calculated on, and a smaller show of company on the hill — fewer carriages, fewer walkers. He had fancied it just the time of day for them to be all returning from their airings to dinner; but the sands and the Terrace always attracted some, and the tide must be flowing — about half-tide now. He longed to be on the sands, the cliffs, at his own house, and everywhere out of his house at once. His spirits rose with the very sight of the sea and he could almost feel his ankle getting stronger already.

Trafalgar House, on the most elevated spot on the down, was

a light, elegant building, standing in a small lawn with a very young plantation round it, about a hundred yards from the brow of a steep but not very lofty cliff, and the nearest to it of every building, excepting one short row of smart-looking houses called the Terrace, with a broad walk in front, aspiring to be the Mall of the place. In this row were the best milliner's shop and the library; a little detached from it, the hotel and billiard room. Here began the descent to the beach and to the bathing machines. And this was therefore the favourite spot for beauty and fashion.

At Trafalgar House, rising at a little distance behind the Terrace, the travellers were safely set down; and all was happiness and joy between Papa and Mama and their children; while Charlotte, having received possession of her apartment, found amusement enough in standing at her ample Venetian window and looking over the miscellaneous foreground of unfinished buildings, waving linen and tops of houses, to the sea, dancing and sparkling in sunshine and freshness.

CHAPTER 5

WHEN THEY MET before dinner, Mr. Parker was looking over letters.

"Not a line from Sidney!" said he. "He is an idle fellow. I sent him an account of my accident from Willingden and thought he would have vouchsafed me an answer. But perhaps it implies that he is coming himself. I trust it may. But here is a letter from one of my sisters. *They* never fail me. Women are the only correspondents to be depended on. Now, Mary," smiling at his wife, "before I open it, what shall we guess as to the state of health of those it comes from — or rather what would Sidney say if he were here? Sidney is a saucy fellow, Miss Heywood. And you must know, he will have it there is a good deal of imagination in my two sisters' complaints. But it really is not so — or very little. They have wretched health, as you have heard us say frequently, and are subject to a variety of very serious disorders. Indeed, I do not believe they know what a day's health is. And at the same time, they are such excellent useful women and have so much energy of character that where any good is to be done, they force themselves on exertions which, to those who do not thoroughly know them, have an extraordinary appearance. But there is really no affectation about them, you know. They have only weaker constitutions and stronger minds than are often met with, either separate or together. And our youngest brother, who lives with them and who is not much above twenty, I am sorry to say is almost as great an invalid as themselves. He is so delicate that he can engage in no profession. Sidney laughs at him. But it really is no joke, though Sidney often makes me laugh at them all in spite of myself. Now, if he were here, I know he would be offering odds that either Susan, Diana or Arthur would appear by this letter to have been at the point of death within the last month."

Having run his eye over the letter, he shook his head and began,

"No chance of seeing them at Sanditon I am sorry to say. A very indifferent account of them indeed. Seriously, a very indifferent account. Mary, you will be quite sorry to hear how ill they have been and are. Miss Heywood, if you will give me leave, I will read Diana's letter aloud. I like to have my friends acquainted with each other and I am afraid this is the only sort of acquaintance I shall have the means of accomplishing between you. And I can have no scruple on Diana's account; for her letters show her exactly as she is, the most active, friendly, warm-hearted being in existence, and therefore must give a good impression."

He read:

My dear Tom, we were all much grieved at your accident, and if you had not described yourself as fallen into such very good hands, I should have been with you at all hazards the day after the receipt of your letter, though it found me suffering under a more severe attack than usual of my old grievance, spasmodic bile, and hardly able to crawl from my bed to the sofa. But how were you treated? Send me more particulars in your next. If indeed a simple sprain, as you denominate it, nothing would have been so judicious as friction, friction by the hand alone, supposing it could be applied instantly. Two years ago I happened to be calling on Mrs. Sheldon when her coachman sprained his foot as he was cleaning the carriage and could hardly limp into the house; but by the immediate use of friction alone steadily perservered in (and I rubbed his ankle with my own hand for six hours without intermission) he was well in three days.

Many thanks, my dear Tom, for the kindness with respect to us, which had so large a share in bringing on your accident. But pray never run into peril again in looking for an apothecary on our account, for had you the most experienced man in his line settled at Sanditon, it would be no recommendation to us. We have entirely done with the whole medical tribe. We have consulted physician after physician in vain, till we are quite convinced that they can do nothing for us and that we must trust to our own knowledge of our own wretched constitutions for any relief. But if you think it advisable for the interest of the place to get a medical man there, I will undertake the commission with pleasure, and have no doubt of succeeding. I could soon put the necessary irons in the fire. As for getting to Sanditon myself, it is quite an impossibility. I grieve to say that I dare not attempt it but my feelings tell me too plainly that, in my present state, the sea air would probably be the death of me. And neither of my dear companions will leave me or I would promote their going down to you for a fortnight. But in truth, I doubt whether Susan's nerves would be equal to the effort. She has been suffering much from the headache, and six leeches a day for ten days together relieved her so little that we thought it right to change our measures; and being convinced on examination that much of the evil lay in her gum, I persuaded her to attack the disorder there. She has accordingly had three teeth drawn, and is decidedly better, but her nerves are a good deal deranged. She can only speak in a whisper and fainted away twice this morning on poor Arthur's trying to suppress a cough. He, I am happy

*to say, is tolerably well though more languid than I like —
and I fear for his liver. I have heard nothing of Sidney since
your being together in town, but conclude his scheme to the
Isle of Wight has not taken place or we should have seen him
in his way.*

*Most sincerely do we wish you a good season at Sanditon,
and though we cannot contribute to your beau monde in
person, we are doing our utmost to send you company worth
having and think we may safely reckon on securing you two
large families: one a rich West Indian from Surrey, the other
a most respectable Girls Boarding School, or Academy, from
Camberwell. I will not tell you how many people I have
employed in the business — wheel within wheel. But success more than repays. Yours most affectionately — etcetera.*

"Well," said Mr. Parker, as he finished. "Though I dare say
Sidney might find something extremely entertaining in this letter
and make us laugh for half an hour together, I declare I, by myself,
can see nothing in it but what is either very pitiable or very credit-
able. With all their sufferings, you perceive how much they are
occupied in promoting the good of others! So anxious for
Sanditon! Two large families — one for Prospect House probably, the other for Number two Denham Place or the end house
of the Terrace, with extra beds at the hotel. I told you my sisters
were excellent women, Miss Heywood."

"And I am sure they must be very extraordinary ones," said
Charlotte. "I am astonished at the cheerful style of the letter,
considering the state in which both sisters appear to be. Three
teeth drawn at once — frightful! Your sister Diana seems almost
as ill as possible, but those three teeth of your sister Susan's are
more distressing than all the rest."

"Oh, they are so used to the operation — to every operation —
and have such fortitude!"

28

"Your sisters know what they are about, I dare say, but their measures seem to touch on extremes. I feel that in any illness I should be so anxious for professional advice, so very little venturesome for myself or anybody I loved! But then, *we* have been so healthy a family that I can be no judge of what the habit of self-doctoring may do."

"Why to own the truth," said Mrs. Parker, "I do think the Miss Parkers carry it too far sometimes. And so do you, my love, you know. You often think they would be better if they would leave themselves more alone — and especially Arthur. I know you think it a great pity they should give *him* such a turn for being ill."

"Well, well, my dear Mary, I grant you, it *is* unfortunate for poor Arthur that at his time of life he should be encouraged to give way to indisposition. It *is* bad that he should be fancying himself too sickly for any profession and sit down at one and twenty, on the interest of his own little fortune, without any idea of attempting to improve it or of engaging in any occupation that may be of use to himself or others. But let us talk of pleasanter things. These two large families are just what we wanted. But here is something at hand pleasanter still—Morgan with his 'Dinner on table.'"

CHAPTER 6

THE PARTY were very soon moving after dinner. Mr. Parker could not be satisfied without an early visit to the library and the library subscription book; and Charlotte was glad to see as much and as quickly as possible where all was new.

They were out in the very quietest part of a watering-place day, when the important business of dinner or of sitting after dinner was going on in almost every inhabited lodging. Here and there might be seen a solitary elderly man, who was forced to move early and walk for health; but in general, it was a thorough pause of company. It was emptiness and tranquillity on the Terrace, the cliffs and the sands. The shops were deserted. The straw hats and pendant lace seemed left to their fate both within the house and without, and Mrs. Whitby at the library was sitting in her inner room, reading one of her own novels for want of employment.

The list of subscribers was but commonplace. The Lady Denham, Miss Brereton, Mr. and Mrs. Parker, Sir Edward Denham and Miss Denham, whose names might be said to lead off the season, were followed by nothing better than: Mrs. Mathews, Miss Mathews, Miss E. Mathews, Miss H. Mathews; Dr. and Mrs. Brown; Mr. Richard Pratt; Lieutenant Smith R.N.; Captain Little — Limehouse; Mrs. Jane Fisher, Miss Fisher, Miss Scroggs; Reverend Mr. Hanking; Mr. Beard — Solicitor, Grays Inn; Mrs. Davis and Miss Merryweather.

Mr. Parker could not but feel that the list was not only without distinction but less numerous than he had hoped. It was but July, however, and August and September were the months. And besides, the promised large families from Surrey and Camberwell were an ever-ready consolation.

Mrs. Whitby came forward without delay from her literary recess, delighted to see Mr. Parker, whose manners recommended him to everybody, and they were fully occupied in their various civilities and communications; while Charlotte, having added her name to the list as the first offering to the success of the season, was busy in some immediate purchases for the further good of everybody as soon as Miss Whitby could be hurried down from her toilette, with all her glossy curls and smart trinkets, to wait on her.

The library, of course, afforded everything: all the useless things in the world that could not be done without; and among so many pretty temptations, and with so much good will for Mr. Parker to encourage expenditure, Charlotte began to feel that she must check herself — or rather she reflected that at two and twenty there could be no excuse for her doing otherwise — and that it would not do for her to be spending all her money the very first evening. She took up a book; it happened to be a volume of *Camilla*. She had not Camilla's youth, and had no intention of having her distress; so she turned from the drawers of rings and brooches, repressed further solicitation and paid for what she had bought.

For her particular gratification, they were then to take a turn on the cliff; but as they quitted the library they were met by two ladies whose arrival made an alteration necessary: Lady Denham and Miss Brereton. They had been to Trafalgar House and been directed thence to the library; and though Lady Denham was a great deal too active to regard the walk of a mile as anything requiring rest, and talked of going home again directly, the Parkers knew that to be pressed into their house and obliged to take her tea with them would suit her best; and therefore the stroll on the cliff gave way to an immediate return home.

"No, no," said her Ladyship. "I will not have you hurry your tea on my account. I know you like your tea late. My early hours are not to put my neighbours to inconvenience. No, no, Miss Clara and I will get back to our own tea. We came out with no other thought. We wanted just to see you and make sure of your being really come — but we get back to our own tea."

She went on however towards Trafalgar House and took possession of the drawing room very quietly without seeming to hear a word of Mrs. Parker's orders to the servant, as they entered, to bring tea directly. Charlotte was fully consoled for the loss of her walk by finding herself in company with those whom the conversation of the morning had given her a great curiosity to see. She observed them well.

Lady Denham was of middle height, stout, upright and alert in her motions, with a shrewd eye and self-satisfied air but not an unagreeable countenance; and though her manner was rather downright and abrupt, as of a person who valued herself on being free-spoken, there was a good humour and cordiality about her — a civility and readiness to be acquainted with Charlotte herself and a heartiness of welcome towards her old friends — which was inspiring the good will she seemed to feel.

And as for Miss Brereton, her appearance so completely justified Mr. Parker's praise that Charlotte thought she had never beheld a more lovely or more interesting young woman. Elegantly tall, regularly handsome, with great delicacy of complexion and soft blue eyes, a sweetly modest and yet naturally graceful address, Charlotte could see in her only the most perfect representation of whatever heroine might be most beautiful and bewitching in all the numerous volumes they had left behind on Mrs. Whitby's shelves. Perhaps it might be partly owing to her having just issued from a circulating library but she could not separate the idea of a complete heroine from Clara Brereton. Her situation with Lady Denham so very much in favour of it! She seemed placed with her on purpose to be ill-used. Such poverty and dependence joined to such beauty and merit seemed to leave no choice in the business.

These feelings were not the result of any spirit of romance in Charlotte herself. No, she was a very sober-minded young lady, sufficiently well-read in novels to supply her imagination with amusement, but not at all unreasonably influenced by them; and while she pleased herself the first five minutes with fancying the persecution which *ought* to be the lot of the interesting Clara, especially in the form of the most barbarous conduct on Lady Denham's side, she found no reluctance to admit from subsequent observation that they appeared to be on very comfortable terms. She could see nothing worse in Lady Denham than the sort of old-fashioned formality of always calling her *Miss Clara*; nor anything objectionable in the degree of observance and attention which Clara paid. On one side it seemed protecting kindness, on the other grateful and affectionate respect.

The conversation turned entirely upon Sanditon, its present number of visitants and the chances of a good season.

It was evident that Lady Denham had more anxiety, more fears of loss, than her coadjutor. She wanted to have the place fill faster and seemed to have many harassing apprehensions of the lodgings being in some instances underlet. Miss Diana Parker's two large families were not forgotten.

"Very good, very good," said her Ladyship. "A West Indy family and a school. That sounds well. That will bring money."

"No people spend more freely, I believe, than West Indians," observed Mr. Parker.

"Aye, so I have heard; and because they have full purses fancy themselves equal, maybe, to your old country families. But then, they who scatter their money so freely never think of whether they may not be doing mischief by raising the price of things. And I have heard that's very much the case with your West-injines.

And if they come among us to raise the price of our necessaries of life, we shall not much thank them, Mr. Parker."

"My dear Madam, they can only raise the price of consumable articles by such an extraordinary demand for them and such a diffusion of money among us as must do us more good than harm. Our butchers and bakers and traders in general cannot get rich without bringing prosperity to *us*. If *they* do not gain, our rents must be insecure; and in proportion to their profit must be ours eventually in the increased value of our houses."

"Oh! well. But I should not like to have butcher's meat raised, though. And I shall keep it down as long as I can. Aye, that young lady smiles, I see. I dare say she thinks me an odd sort of creature; but *she* will come to care about such matters herself in time. Yes, yes, my dear, depend upon it, you will be thinking of the price of butcher's meat in time, though you may not happen to have quite such a servants' hall to feed as I have. And I do believe those are best off that have fewest servants. I am not a woman of parade as all the world knows, and if it was not for what I owe to poor Mr. Hollis's memory, I should never keep up Sanditon House as I do. It is not for my own pleasure. Well, Mr. Parker, and the other is a boarding school, a French boarding school, is it? No harm in that. They'll stay their six weeks. And out of such a number, who knows but some may be consumptive and want asses' milk; and I have two milch asses at this present time. But perhaps the little Misses may hurt the furniture. I hope they will have a good sharp governess to look after them."

Poor Mr. Parker got no more credit from Lady Denham than he had from his sisters for the object which had taken him to Willingden.

"Lord! my dear sir," she cried. "How could you think of such a thing? I am very sorry you met with your accident, but upon my word, you deserved it. Going after a doctor! Why, what should we do with a doctor here? It would be only encouraging our servants and the poor to fancy themselves ill if there was a doctor at hand. Oh! pray, let us have none of the tribe at Sanditon. We go on very well as we are. There is the sea and the downs and my milch asses. And I have told Mrs. Whitby that if anybody inquires for a chamber-horse, they may be supplied at a fair rate — poor Mr. Hollis's chamber-horse, as good as new — and what can people want for more? Here have I lived seventy good years in the world and never took physic above twice — and never saw the face of a doctor in all my life on my *own* account. And I verily believe if my poor dear Sir Harry had never seen one neither, he would have been alive now. Ten fees, one after another, did the man take who sent *him* out of the world. I beseech you Mr. Parker, no doctors here." The tea things were brought in. "Oh, my dear Mrs. Parker, you should not indeed — why would you do so? I was just upon the point of wishing you good evening. But since you are so very neighbourly, I believe Miss Clara and I must stay."

CHAPTER 7

THE POPULARITY of the Parkers brought them some visitors the very next morning; amongst them, Sir Edward Denham and his sister who, having been at Sanditon House, drove on to pay their compliments; and the duty of letter writing being accomplished, Charlotte was settled with Mrs. Parker in the drawing room in time to see them all.

The Denhams were the only ones to excite particular attention. Charlotte was glad to complete her knowledge of the family by an introduction to them; and found them, the better half at least (for while single, the *gentleman* may sometimes be thought the better half of the pair) not unworthy of notice.

Miss Denham was a fine young woman, but cold and reserved, giving the idea of one who felt her consequence with pride and her poverty with discontent, and who was immediately gnawed by the want of a handsomer equipage than the simple gig in which they travelled, and which their groom was leading about still in her sight.

Sir Edward was much her superior in air and manner — certainly handsome, but yet more to be remarked for his very good address and wish of paying attention and giving pleasure. He came into the room remarkably well, talked much — and very much to Charlotte, by whom he chanced to be placed — and she soon perceived that he had a fine countenance, a most pleasing gentleness of voice and a great deal of conversation. She liked him. Sober-minded as she was, she thought him agreeable and did not quarrel with the suspicion of his finding her equally so, which *would* arise from his evidently disregarding his sister's motion to go, and persisting in his station and his discourse.

I make no apologies for my heroine's vanity. If there are young ladies in the world at her time of life more dull of fancy and more careless of pleasing, I know them not and never wish to know them.

At last, from the low French windows of the drawing room which commanded the road and all the paths across the down, Charlotte and Sir Edward as they sat could not but observe Lady Denham and Miss Brereton walking by; and there was instantly a slight change in Sir Edward's countenance — with an anxious glance after them as they proceeded — followed by an early proposal to his sister, not merely for moving, but for walking on together to the Terrace, which altogether gave a hasty turn to Charlotte's fancy, cured her of her half-hour's fever, and placed her in a more capable state of judging, when Sir Edward was gone, of *how* agreeable he had actually been. "Perhaps there was a good deal in his air and address; and his title did him no harm."

She was very soon in his company again. The first object of the Parkers, when their house was cleared of morning visitors, was to get out themselves. The Terrace was the attraction to all. Everybody who walked must begin with the Terrace; and there, seated on one of the two green benches by the gravel walk, they found the united Denham party; but though united in the gross, very distinctly divided again: the two superior ladies being at one end of the bench, and Sir Edward and Miss Brereton at the other.

Charlotte's first glance told her that Sir Edward's air was that of a lover. There could be no doubt of his devotion to Clara. How Clara received it was less obvious, but she was inclined to think not very favourably; for though sitting thus apart with him (which probably she might not have been able to prevent) her air was calm and grave.

That the young lady at the other end of the bench was doing

penance was indubitable. The difference in Miss Denham's countenance, the change from Miss Denham sitting in cold grandeur in Mrs. Parker's drawing room, to be kept from silence by the efforts of others, to Miss Denham at Lady Denham's elbow, listening and talking with smiling attention or solicitous eagerness, was very striking — and very amusing or very melancholy, just as satire or morality might prevail. Miss Denham's character was pretty well decided with Charlotte.

Sir Edward's required longer observation. He surprised her by quitting Clara immediately on their all joining and agreeing to walk, and by addressing his attentions entirely to herself. Stationing himself close by her, he seemed to mean to detach her as much as possible from the rest of the party and to give her the whole of his conversation. He began, in a tone of great taste and feeling, to talk of the sea and the sea shore; and ran with energy through all the usual phrases employed in praise of their sublimity and descriptive of the *undescribable* emotions they excite in the mind of sensibility. The terrific grandeur of the ocean in a storm, its glass surface in a calm, its gulls and its samphire and the deep fathoms of its abysses, its quick vicissitudes, its direful deceptions, its mariners tempting it in sunshine and overwhelmed by the sudden tempest — all were eagerly and fluently touched; rather commonplace perhaps, but doing very well from the lips of a handsome Sir Edward, and she could not but think him a man of feeling, till he began to stagger her by the number of his quotations and the bewilderment of some of his sentences.

"Do you remember," said he, "Scott's beautiful lines on the sea? Oh! what a description they convey! They are never out of my thoughts when I walk here. That man who can read them unmoved must have the nerves of an assassin! Heaven defend me from meeting such a man unarmed."

"What description do you mean?" said Charlotte. "I remember none at this moment, of the sea, in either of Scott's poems."

"Do you not indeed? Nor can I exactly recall the beginning at this moment. But — you cannot have forgotten his description of woman —

Oh! Woman in our hours of ease —

Delicious! Delicious! Had he written nothing more, he would have been immortal. And then again, that unequalled, unrivalled address to parental affection —

> *Some feelings are to mortals given*
> *With less of earth in them than heaven — etcetera.*

But while we are on the subject of poetry, what think you, Miss Heywood, of Burns's lines to his Mary? Oh! there is pathos to madden one! If ever there was a man who *felt*, it was Burns. Montgomery has all the fire of poetry, Wordsworth has the true soul of it, Campbell in his pleasures of hope has touched the extreme of our sensations —

Like angels' visits, few and far between.

Can you conceive anything more subduing, more melting, more fraught with the deep sublime than that line? But Burns — I confess my sense of his pre-eminence, Miss Heywood. If Scott *has* a fault, it is the want of passion. Tender, elegant, descriptive — but *tame*. The man who cannot do justice to the attributes of woman is my contempt. Sometimes indeed a flash of feeling seems to irradiate him, as in the lines we were speaking of —

Oh! Woman in our hours of ease —

But Burns is always on fire. His soul was the altar in which lovely woman sat enshrined, his spirit truly breathed the immortal incense which is her due."

"I have read several of Burns's poems with great delight," said Charlotte as soon as she had time to speak. "But I am not poetic enough to separate a man's poetry entirely from his character; and poor Burns's known irregularities greatly interrupt my enjoyment of his lines. I have difficulty in depending on the *truth* of his feelings as a lover. I have not faith in the *sincerity* of the affections of a man of his description. He felt and he wrote and he forgot."

"Oh! no, no," exclaimed Sir Edward in an ecstasy. "He was all ardour and truth! His genius and his susceptibilities might lead him into some aberrations — but who is perfect? It were hyper-criticism, it were pseudo-philosophy to expect from the soul of high-toned genius the grovellings of a common mind. The coruscations of talent, elicited by impassioned feeling in the breast of man, are perhaps incompatible with some of the prosaic decencies of life; nor can you, loveliest Miss Heywood," speaking with an air of deep sentiment, "nor can any woman be a fair judge of what a man may be propelled to say, write or do by the sovereign impulses of illimitable ardour."

This was very fine — but if Charlotte understood it at all, not very moral; and being moreover by no means pleased with his extraordinary style of compliment, she gravely answered,

"I really know nothing of the matter. This is a charming day. The wind, I fancy, must be southerly."

"Happy, happy wind, to engage Miss Heywood's thoughts!"

She began to think him downright silly. His choosing to walk with her, she had learnt to understand. It was done to pique Miss Brereton. She had read it, in an anxious glance or two on his side; but why he should talk so much nonsense, unless he could do no better, was unintelligible. He seemed very sentimental, very full of some feeling or other, and very much addicted to all the newest-fashioned hard words, had not a very clear brain, she presumed, and talked a good deal by rote. The future might explain him further.

But when there was a proposition for going into the library, she felt that she had had quite enough of Sir Edward for one morning and very gladly accepted Lady Denham's invitation of remaining on the Terrace with her. The others all left them, Sir Edward with looks of very gallant despair in tearing himself away, and they united their agreeableness; that is, Lady Denham, like a true great lady, talked and talked only of her own concerns, and Charlotte listened, amused in considering the contrast between her two companions. Certainly there was no strain of doubtful sentiment nor any phrase of difficult interpretation in Lady Denham's discourse. Taking hold of Charlotte's arm with the ease of one who felt that any notice from her was an honour, and communicative from the influence of the same conscious importance or a natural love of talking, she immediately said in a tone of great satisfaction and with a look of arch sagacity,

"Miss Esther wants me to invite her and her brother to spend a week with me at Sanditon House, as I did last summer. But I shan't. She has been trying to get round me every way with her praise of this and her praise of that; but I saw what she was about. I saw through it all. I am not very easily taken in, my dear."

Charlotte could think of nothing more harmless to be said than the simple enquiry of —

"Sir Edward and Miss Denham?"

"Yes, my dear. *My young folks*, as I call them sometimes, for I take them very much by the hand. I had them with me last summer, about this time, for a week; from Monday to Monday; and very delighted and thankful they were. For they are very good young people, my dear. I would not have you think that I *only* notice them for poor dear Sir Harry's sake. No, no; they are very deserving themselves or, trust me, they would not be so much in *my* company. I am not the woman to help anybody blindfold. I always take care to know what I am about and who I have to deal with before I stir a finger. I do not think I was ever overreached in my life. And that is a good deal for a woman to say

41

that has been married twice. Poor dear Sir Harry, between ourselves, thought at first to have got more. But," with a bit of a sigh, "he is gone, and we must not find fault with the dead. Nobody could live happier together than us — and he was a very honourable man, quite the gentleman of ancient family. And when he died, I gave Sir Edward his gold watch."

She said this with a look at her companion which implied its right to produce a great impression; and seeing no rapturous astonishment in Charlotte's countenance, added quickly,

"He did not bequeath it to his nephew, my dear. It was no bequest. It was not in the will. He only told me, and *that* but once, that he should wish his nephew to have his watch; but it need not have been binding if I had not chose it."

"Very kind indeed! Very handsome!" said Charlotte, absolutely forced to affect admiration.

"Yes, my dear, and it is not the *only* kind thing I have done by him. I have been a very liberal friend to Sir Edward. And poor young man, he needs it bad enough. For though I am *only* the *dowager*, my dear, and he is the *heir*, things do not stand between us in the way they commonly do between those two parties. Not a shilling do I receive from the Denham estate. Sir Edward has no payments to make *me*. He don't stand uppermost, believe me. It is *I* that help *him*."

"Indeed! He is a very fine young man, particularly elegant in his address." This was said chiefly for the sake of saying something, but Charlotte directly saw that it was laying her open to suspicion by Lady Denham's giving a shrewd glance at her and replying,

"Yes, yes, he is very well to look at. And it is to be hoped that some lady of large fortune will think so, for Sir Edward *must* marry for money. He and I often talk that matter over. A handsome young fellow like him will go smirking and smiling about and paying girls compliments, but he knows he *must* marry for money. And Sir Edward is a very steady young man in the main and has got very good notions."

"Sir Edward Denham," said Charlotte, "with such personal advantages may be almost sure of getting a woman of fortune, if he chooses it."

This glorious sentiment seemed quite to remove suspicion.

"Aye my dear, that's very sensibly said," cried Lady Denham. "And if we could but get a young heiress to Sanditon! But heiresses are monstrous scarce! I do not think we have had an heiress here — or even a co- since Sanditon has been a public place. Families come after families but, as far as I can learn, it is not one in a hundred of them that have any real property, landed or funded. An income perhaps, but no property. Clergymen maybe, or lawyers from town, or half-pay officers, or widows with only a jointure. And what good can such people do anybody? Except just as they take our empty houses and, between ourselves, I think they are great fools for not staying at home. Now if we could get a young heiress to be sent here for her health — and if she was ordered to drink asses' milk I could supply her — and, as soon as she got well, have her fall in love with Sir Edward!"

"That would be very fortunate indeed."

"And Miss Esther must marry somebody of fortune too. She must get a rich husband. Ah, young ladies that have no money are very much to be pitied! But," after a short pause, "if Miss Esther thinks to talk me into inviting them to come and stay at Sanditon House, she will find herself mistaken. Matters are altered with me since last summer, you know. I have Miss Clara with me now which makes a great difference."

She spoke this so seriously that Charlotte instantly saw in it the evidence of real penetration and prepared for some fuller remarks; but it was followed only by,

"I have no fancy for having my house as full as an hotel. I should not choose to have my two housemaids' time taken up all the morning in dusting out bed rooms. They have Miss Clara's room to put to rights as well as my own every day. If they had hard places, they would want higher wages."

For objections of this nature, Charlotte was not prepared. She found it so impossible even to affect sympathy that she could say nothing. Lady Denham soon added, with great glee,

"And besides all this, my dear, am I to be filling my house to the prejudice of Sanditon? If people want to be by the sea, why don't they take lodgings? Here are a great many empty houses — three on this very Terrace. No fewer than three lodging papers staring me in the face at this very moment, Numbers three, four and eight. Eight, the corner house, may be too large for them, but either of the two others are nice little snug houses, very fit for a young gentleman and his sister. And so, my dear, the next time Miss Esther begins talking about the dampness of Denham Park and the good bathing always does her, I shall advise them to come and take one of these lodgings for a fortnight. Don't you think that will be very fair? Charity begins at home, you know."

Charlotte's feelings were divided between amusement and indignation, but indignation had the larger and the increasing share. She kept her countenance and she kept a civil silence. She could not carry her forbearance farther, but without attempting to listen longer, and only conscious that Lady Denham was still talking on in the same way, allowed her thoughts to form themselves into such a meditation as this:

"She is thoroughly mean. I had not expected anything so bad. Mr. Parker spoke too mildly of her. His judgement is evidently not to be trusted. His own good nature misleads him. He is too kind-hearted to see clearly. I must judge for myself. And their very *connection* prejudices him. He has persuaded her to engage in the same speculation, and because their object in that line is the same, he fancies she feels like him in others. But she is very, very mean. I can see no good in her. Poor Miss Brereton! And she makes everybody mean about her. This poor Sir Edward and his sister — how far nature meant them to be respectable I cannot tell — but they are *obliged* to be mean in their servility to her. And I am mean, too, in giving her my attention with the appearance of coinciding with her. Thus it is, when rich people are sordid."

. . .

The two ladies continued walking together till rejoined by the others, who, as they issued from the library, were followed by a young Whitby running off with five volumes under his arm to Sir Edward's gig; and Sir Edward, approaching Charlotte, said,

"You may perceive what has been our occupation. My sister wanted my counsel in the selection of some books. We have many leisure hours and read a great deal. I am no indiscriminate novel reader. The mere trash of the common circulating library I hold in the highest contempt. You will never hear me advocating those puerile emanations which detail nothing but discordant principles incapable of amalgamation, or those vapid tissues of ordinary occurrences from which no useful deductions can be drawn. In vain may we put them into a literary alembic; we distil nothing which can add to science. You understand me, I am sure?"

"I am not quite certain that I do. But if you will describe the sort of novels which you *do* approve, I dare say it will give me a clearer idea."

"Most willingly, fair questioner. The novels which I approve are such as display human nature with grandeur; such as show her in the sublimities of intense feeling; such as exhibit the progress of strong passion from the first germ of incipient susceptibility to the utmost energies of reason half-dethroned; where we see the strong spark of woman's captivations elicit such fire in the soul of man as leads him — though at the risk of some aberration from the strict line of primitive obligations — to hazard all, dare all, achieve all to obtain her. Such are the works which I peruse with delight and, I hope I may say, with amelioration. They hold forth the most splendid portraitures of high conceptions, unbounded views, illimitable ardour, indomitable decision. And even when the event is mainly anti-prosperous to the high-toned machinations of the prime character — the potent, pervading hero of the story — it leaves us full of generous emotions for him; our hearts are paralysed. It would be pseudo-philosophy to assert that we do not feel more enwrapped by the brilliancy of his career than by the tranquil and morbid virtues of any opposing character. Our approbation of the latter is but eleemosynary. These are the novels which enlarge the primitive capabilities of the heart; and it cannot impugn the sense or be any dereliction of the character of the most anti-puerile man, to be conversant with them."

"If I understand you aright," said Charlotte, "our taste in novels is not at all the same."

And here they were obliged to part, Miss Denham being much too tired of them all to stay any longer.

The truth was that Sir Edward, whom circumstances had confined very much to one spot, had read more sentimental novels than agreed with him. His fancy had been early caught by all the impassioned and most exceptionable parts of Richardson's. And such authors as had since appeared to tread in Richardson's steps (so far as man's determined pursuit of woman in defiance of every opposition of feeling and convenience was concerned) had since occupied the greater part of his literary hours, and formed his character.

With a perversity of judgement which must be attributed to his not having by nature a very strong head, the graces, the spirit, the sagacity and the perserverance of the villain of the story outweighed all his absurdities and all his atrocities with Sir Edward. With him such conduct was genius, fire and feeling. It interested and inflamed him. And he was always more anxious for its success, and mourned over its discomfitures with more tenderness, than could ever have been contemplated by the authors. Though he owed many of his ideas to this sort of reading, it would be unjust to say that he read nothing else or that his language was not formed on a more general knowledge of modern literature. He read all the essays, letters, tours and criticisms of the day; and with the same ill-luck which made him derive only false principles from lessons of morality, and incentives to vice from the history of its overthrow, he gathered only hard words and involved sentences from the style of our most approved writers.

Sir Edward's great object in life was to be seductive. With such personal advantages as he knew himself to possess, and such talents as he did also give himself credit for, he regarded it as his duty. He felt that he was formed to be a dangerous man, quite in the line of the Lovelaces. The very name of Sir Edward, he thought, carried some degree of fascination with it.

To be generally gallant and assiduous about the fair, to make fine speeches to every pretty girl, was but the inferior part of the character he had to play. Miss Heywood, or any other young woman with any pretensions to beauty, he was entitled (according to his own views of society) to approach with high compliment and rhapsody on the slightest acquaintance.

But it was Clara alone on whom he had serious designs; it was Clara whom he meant to seduce — her seduction was quite determined on. Her situation in every way called for it. She was his rival in Lady Denham's favour; she was young, lovely and dependent. He had very early seen the necessity of the case, and had now been long trying with cautious assiduity to make an impression on her heart and to undermine her principles. Clara saw through him and had not the least intention of being seduced; but she bore with him patiently enough to confirm the sort of attachment which her personal charms had raised. A greater degree of discouragement indeed would not have affected Sir Edward. He was armed against the highest pitch of disdain or aversion. If she could not be won by affection, he must carry her off. He knew his business.

Already had he had many musings on the subject. If he *were* constrained so to act, he must naturally wish to strike out something new, to exceed those who had gone before him; and he felt a strong curiosity to ascertain whether the neighbourhood of Timbuctu might not afford some solitary house adapted for Clara's reception.

But the expense, alas! of measures in that masterly style was ill-suited to his purse; and prudence obliged him to prefer the quietest sort of ruin and disgrace for the object of his affections to the more renowned.

CHAPTER 8

ONE DAY, soon after Charlotte's arrival at Sanditon, she had
the pleasure of seeing, just as she ascended from the sands to the
Terrace, a gentleman's carriage with post horses standing at the
door of the hotel, as very lately arrived and by the quantity of
luggage being taken off bringing, it might be hoped, some respectable family determined on a long residence.

Delighted to have such good news for Mr. and Mrs. Parker,
who had both gone home some time before, she proceeded to
Trafalgar House with as much alacrity as could remain after having
contended for the last two hours with a very fine wind blowing
directly on shore. But she had not reached the little lawn when
she saw a lady walking nimbly behind her at no great distance;
and convinced that it could be no acquaintance of her own, she
resolved to hurry on and get into the house if possible before her.
But the stranger's pace did not allow this to be accomplished.
Charlotte was on the steps and had rung but the door was not
open when the other crossed the lawn; and when the servant
appeared, they were just equally ready for entering the house.

The ease of the lady, her "How do you do, Morgan?" and
Morgan's looks on seeing her were a moment's astonishment; but
another moment brought Mr. Parker into the hall to welcome
the sister he had seen from the drawing room; and Charlotte
was soon introduced to Miss Diana Parker.

There was a great deal of surprise but still more pleasure in
seeing her. Nothing could be kinder than her reception from

both husband and wife. How did she come? And with whom? And they were so glad to find her equal to the journey! And that she was to belong to *them* was taken as a matter of course.

Miss Diana Parker was about four and thirty, of middling height and slender; delicate looking rather than sickly; with an agreeable face and a very animated eye; her manners resembling her brother's in their ease and frankness, though with more decision and less mildness in her tone.

She began an account of herself without delay. Thanking them for their invitation but "*that* was quite out of the question for they were all three come and meant to get into lodgings and make some stay."

"All three come! What! Susan and Arthur! Susan able to come too! This is better and better."

"Yes, we are actually all come. Quite unavoidable. Nothing else to be done. You shall hear all about it. But my dear Mary, send for the children — I long to see them."

"And how has Susan borne the journey? And how is Arthur? And why do we not see him here with you?"

"Susan has borne it wonderfully. She had not a wink of sleep either the night before we set out or last night at Chichester, and as this is not so common with her as with *me*, I have had a thousand fears for her. But she has kept up wonderfully — no hysterics of consequence till we came within sight of poor old Sanditon — and the attack was not very violent — nearly over by the time we reached your hotel — so that we got her out of the carriage extremely well with only Mr. Woodcock's assistance. And when I left her she was directing the disposal of the luggage and helping old Sam uncord the trunks. She desired her best love with a thousand regrets at being so poor a creature that she could not come with me. And as for poor Arthur, he would not have been unwilling himself, but there is so much wind that I did not think he could safely venture for I am *sure* there is lumbago hanging about him; and so I helped him on with his great coat and sent him off to the Terrace to take us lodgings. Miss Heywood must have seen our carriage standing at the hotel. I knew Miss Heywood the moment I saw her before me on the down. My dear Tom, I am so glad to see you walk so well. Let me feel your ankle. That's right; all right and clean. The play of your sinews a *very* little affected, barely perceptible. Well, now for the explanation of my being here. I told you in my letter of the two considerable families I was hoping to secure for you, the West Indians and the seminary."

Here Mr. Parker drew his chair still nearer to his sister and took her hand again most affectionately as he answered,

"Yes, yes, how active and how kind you have been!"

"The West Indians," she continued, "whom I look upon as the *most* desirable of the two, as the best of the good, prove to be a Mrs. Griffiths and her family. I know them only through others. You must have heard me mention Miss Capper, the particular friend of *my* very particular friend Fanny Noyce. Now, Miss Capper is extremely intimate with a Mrs. Darling, who is on terms of constant correspondence with Mrs. Griffiths herself. Only a *short* chain, you see, between us, and not a link wanting. Mrs. Griffiths meant to go to the sea for her young people's benefit, had fixed on the coast of Sussex but was undecided as to the where, wanted something private, and wrote to ask the opinion of her friend Mrs. Darling. Miss Capper happened to be staying with Mrs. Darling when Mrs. Griffiths' letter arrived and was consulted on the question. *She* wrote the same day to Fanny Noyce and mentioned it to her; and Fanny, all alive for *us*, instantly took up her pen and forwarded the circumstance to me — except as to *names*, which have but lately transpired. There was but *one* thing for *me* to do. I answered Fanny's letter by the same post and pressed for the recommendation of Sanditon. Fanny had feared your having no house large enough to receive such a family. But I seem to be spinning out my story to an endless length. You see how it was all managed. I had the pleasure of hearing soon afterwards by the same simple link of connection that Sanditon *had been* recommended by Mrs. Darling, and that the West Indians were very much disposed to go thither. This was the state of the case when I wrote to you. But two days ago — yes, the day before yesterday — I heard again from Fanny Noyce, saying that *she* had heard from Miss Capper, who by a letter from Mrs. Darling understood that Mrs. Griffiths had expressed herself in a letter to Mrs. Darling more doubtingly on the subject of Sanditon. Am I clear? I would be anything rather than not clear."

"Oh, perfectly, perfectly. Well?"

"The reason of this hesitation was her having no connections in the place, and no means of ascertaining that she should have good accommodations on arriving there; and she was particularly careful and scrupulous on all those matters more on account of a certain Miss Lambe, a young lady — probably a niece — under her care than on her own account or her daughters'. Miss Lambe has an immense fortune — richer than all the rest — and very delicate health. One sees clearly enough by all this the *sort* of woman Mrs. Griffiths must be: as helpless and indolent as wealth and a hot climate are apt to make us. But we are not born to equal energy. What was to be done? I had a few moments' indecision, whether to offer to write to you or to Mrs. Whitby to secure them a house; but neither pleased me. I hate to employ others when I am equal to act myself; and my conscience told me that this was an occasion which called for me. Here was a family of helpless invalids whom I might essentially serve. I sounded Susan. The same thought had occurred to her. Arthur made no difficulties. Our plan was arranged immediately, we were off yesterday morning at six, left Chichester at the same hour today — and here we are."

"Excellent! Excellent!" cried Mr. Parker. "Diana, you are unequalled in serving your friends and doing good to all the world. I know nobody like you. Mary, my love, is not she a wonderful creature? Well, and now, what house do you design to engage for them? What is the size of their family?"

"I do not at all know," replied his sister, "have not the least idea, never heard any particulars; but I am very sure that the largest house at Sanditon cannot be *too* large. They are more likely to want a second. I shall take only one, however, and that but for a week certain. Miss Heywood, I astonish you. You hardly know what to make of me. I see by your looks that you are not used to such quick measures."

The words "unaccountable officiousness!" "activity run mad!" had just passed through Charlotte's mind, but a civil answer was easy.

"I dare say I do look surprised," said she, "because these are very great exertions, and I know what invalids both you and your sister are."

"Invalids indeed. I trust there are not three people in England who have so sad a right to that appellation! But my dear Miss Heywood, we are sent into this world to be as extensively useful as possible, and where some degree of strength of mind is given, it is not a feeble body which will excuse us — or incline us to excuse ourselves. The world is pretty much divided between the weak of mind and the strong; between those who can act and those who cannot; and it is the bounden duty of the capable to let no opportunity of being useful escape them. My sister's complaints and mine are happily not often of a nature to threaten existence *immediately*. And as long as we *can* exert ourselves to be of use to others, I am convinced that the body is the better for the refreshment the mind receives in doing its duty. While I have been travelling with this object in view, I have been perfectly well."

The entrance of the children ended this little panegyric on her own disposition; and after having noticed and caressed them all, she prepared to go.

"Cannot you dine with us? Is not it possible to prevail on you to dine with us?" was then the cry. And that being absolutely negatived, it was,

"And when shall we see you again? And how can we be of use to you?" And Mr. Parker warmly offered his assistance in taking the house for Mrs. Griffiths.

"I will come to you the moment I have dined," said he, "and we will go about together."

But this was immediately declined.

"No, my dear Tom, upon no account in the world shall you stir a step on any business of mine. Your ankle wants rest. I see by the position of your foot that you have used it too much already. No, I shall go about my house-taking directly. Our dinner is not ordered till six; and by that time I hope to have completed it. It is now only half past four. As to seeing *me* again today, I cannot answer for it. The others will be at the hotel all the evening and delighted to see you at any time; but as soon as I get back I shall hear what Arthur has done about our own lodgings, and probably the moment dinner is over shall be out again on business relative to them, for we hope to get into some lodgings or other and be settled after breakfast tomorrow. I have not much confidence in poor Arthur's skill for lodging-taking, but he seemed to like the commission."

"I think you are doing too much," said Mr. Parker. "You will knock yourself up. You should not move again after dinner."

"No, indeed you should not," cried his wife, "for dinner is such a mere *name* with you all that it can do you no good. I know what your appetites are."

"My appetite is very much mended, I assure you, lately. I have been taking some bitters of my own decocting, which have done wonders. Susan never eats, I grant you; and just at present

I shall want nothing. I never eat for about a week after a journey. But as for Arthur, he is only too much disposed for food. We are often obliged to check him."

"But you have not told me anything of the *other* family coming to Sanditon," said Mr. Parker as he walked with her to the door of the house. "The Camberwell Seminary. Have we a good chance of *them?*"

"Oh, certain. Quite certain. I had forgotten them for the moment. But I had a letter three days ago from my friend Mrs. Charles Dupuis which assured me of Camberwell. Camberwell will be here to a certainty, and very soon. *That* good woman — I do not know her name — not being so wealthy and independent as Mrs. Griffiths, can travel and choose for herself. I will tell you how I got at *her*. Mrs. Charles Dupuis lives almost next door to a lady, who has a relation lately settled at Clapham, who actually attends the seminary and gives lessons on eloquence and belles lettres to some of the girls. I got this man a hare from one of Sidney's friends; and he recommended Sanditon. Without my appearing however— Mrs. Charles Dupuis managed it all."

CHAPTER 9

IT WAS NOT A WEEK since Miss Diana Parker had been told by
her feelings that the sea air would probably, in her present state,
be the death of her; and now she was at Sanditon, intending to
make some stay and without appearing to have the slightest recollection of having written or felt any such thing.

It was impossible for Charlotte not to suspect a good deal of
fancy in such an extraordinary state of health. Disorders and
recoveries so very much out of the common way seemed more
like the amusement of eager minds in want of employment than of
actual afflictions and relief. The Parkers were no doubt a family
of imagination and quick feelings, and while the eldest brother
found vent for his superfluity of sensation as a projector, the
sisters were perhaps driven to dissipate theirs in the invention of
odd complaints. The *whole* of their mental vivacity was evidently
not so employed; part was laid out in a zeal for being useful. It
would seem that they must either be very busy for the good of
others or else extremely ill themselves.

Some natural delicacy of constitution, in fact, with an unfortunate turn for medicine, especially quack medicine, had given
them an early tendency at various times to various disorders;
the rest of their sufferings was from fancy, the love of distinction
and the love of the wonderful. They had charitable hearts and
many amiable feelings; but a spirit of restless activity and the
glory of doing more than anybody else had their share in every
exertion of benevolence; and there was vanity in all they did, as
well as in all they endured.

Mr. and Mrs. Parker spent a great part of the evening at the hotel; but Charlotte had only two or three views of Miss Diana posting over the down after a house for this lady whom she had never seen and who had never employed her. She was not made acquainted with the others till the following day when, being removed into lodgings and all the party continuing quite well, their brother and sister and herself were entreated to drink tea with them.

They were in one of the Terrace houses; and she found them arranged for the evening in a small neat drawing room with a beautiful view of the sea if they had chosen it; but though it had been a very fair English summer day, not only was there no open window, but the sofa and the table and the establishment in general was all at the other end of the room by a brisk fire.

Miss Parker, whom, remembering the three teeth drawn in one day, Charlotte approached with a peculiar degree of respectful compassion, was not very unlike her sister in person or manner, though more thin and worn by illness and medicine, more relaxed in air and more subdued in voice. She talked, however, the whole evening as incessantly as Diana; and excepting that she sat with salts in her hand, took drops two or three times from one out of several phials already at home on the mantelpiece and made a great many odd faces and contortions, Charlotte could perceive no symptoms of illness which she, in the boldness of her own good health, would not have undertaken to cure by putting out the fire, opening the window and disposing of the drops and the salts by means of one or the other.

She had had considerable curiosity to see Mr. Arthur Parker; and having fancied him a very puny, delicate-looking young man, materially the smallest of a not very robust family, was astonished to find him quite as tall as his brother and a great deal stouter, broad made and lusty, and with no other look of an invalid than a sodden complexion.

Diana was evidently the chief of the family — principal mover and actor. She had been on her feet the whole morning, on Mrs. Griffiths' business or their own, and was still the most alert of the three. Susan had only superintended their final removal from the hotel, bringing two heavy boxes herself, and Arthur had found the air so cold that he had merely walked from one house to the other as nimbly as he could, and boasted much of sitting by the fire till he had cooked up a very good one.

Diana, whose exercise had been too domestic to admit of calculation but who, by her own account, had not once sat down during the space of seven hours, confessed herself a little tired. She had been too successful, however, for much fatigue; for not only had she — by walking and talking down a thousand difficulties — at last secured a proper house at eight guineas per week for Mrs. Griffiths; she had also opened so many treaties with cooks, housemaids, washerwomen and bathing women that Mrs. Griffiths would have little more to do on her arrival than to wave her hand and collect them around her for choice. Her concluding effort in the cause had been a few polite lines of information to Mrs. Griffiths herself, time not allowing for the circuitous train of intelligence which had been hitherto kept up; and she was now regaling in the delight of opening the first trenches of an acquaintance with such a powerful discharge of unexpected obligation.

Mr. and Mrs. Parker and Charlotte had seen two post chaises crossing the down to the hotel as they were setting off, a joyful sight and full of speculation. The Miss Parkers and Arthur had also seen something; they could distinguish from their window that there *was* an arrival at the hotel, but not its amount. Their visitors answered for two hack chaises. Could it be the Camberwell Seminary? No, no. Had there been a third carriage, perhaps it might; but it was very generally agreed that two hack chaises could never contain a seminary. Mr. Parker was confident of another new family.

When they were all finally seated, after some removals to look at the sea and the hotel, Charlotte's place was by Arthur, who was sitting next to the fire with a degree of enjoyment which gave a good deal of merit to his civility in wishing her to take his chair. There was nothing dubious in her manner of declining it and he sat down again with much satisfaction. She drew back her chair to have all the advantage of his person as a screen and was very thankful for every inch of back and shoulders beyond her preconceived idea.

Arthur was heavy in eye as well as figure but by no means indisposed to talk; and while the other four were chiefly engaged together, he evidently felt it no penance to have a fine young woman next to him, requiring in common politeness some attention; as his brother, who felt the decided want of some motive for action, some powerful object of animation for him, observed with considerable pleasure. Such was the influence of youth and bloom that he began even to make a sort of apology for having a fire.

"We should not have had one at home," said he, "but the sea air is always damp. I am not afraid of anything so much as damp."

"I am so fortunate," said Charlotte, "as never to know whether the air is damp or dry. It has always some property that is wholesome and invigorating to me."

"*I* like the air too, as well as anybody can," replied Arthur. "I am very fond of standing at an open window when there is no wind. But, unluckily, a damp air does not like *me*. It gives me the rheumatism. You are not rheumatic, I suppose?"

"Not at all."

"That's a great blessing. But perhaps you are nervous?"

"No, I believe not. I have no idea that I am."

"*I* am very nervous. To say the truth, nerves are the worst part of my complaints in *my* opinion. My sisters think me bilious, but I doubt it."

"You are quite in the right to doubt it as long as you possibly can, I am sure."

"If I were bilious," he continued, "you know, wine would disagree with me, but it always does me good. The more wine I drink — in moderation — the better I am. I am always best of an evening. If you had seen me today before dinner, you would have thought me a very poor creature."

Charlotte could believe it. She kept her countenance, however, and said,

"As far as I can understand what nervous complaints are, I have a great idea of the efficacy of air and exercise for them — daily, regular exercise — and I should recommend rather more of it to *you* than I suspect you are in the habit of taking."

"Oh, I am very fond of exercise myself," he replied, "and I mean to walk a great deal while I am here, if the weather is temperate. I shall be out every morning before breakfast and take several turns upon the Terrace, and you will often see me at Trafalgar House."

"But you do not call a walk to Trafalgar House much exercise?"

"Not as to mere distance, but the hill is so steep! Walking up that hill, in the middle of the day, would throw me into such a perspiration! You would see me all in a bath by the time I got there! I am very subject to perspiration, and there cannot be a surer sign of nervousness."

They were now advancing so deep in physics that Charlotte viewed the entrance of the servant with the tea things as a very fortunate interruption. It produced a great and immediate change. The young man's attentions were instantly lost. He took his own cocoa from the tray, which seemed provided with almost as many teapots as there were persons in company — Miss Parker drinking one sort of herb tea and Miss Diana another — and turning completely to the fire, sat coddling and cooking it to his own satisfaction and toasting some slices of bread, brought up ready-prepared in the toast rack; and till it was all done, she heard nothing of his voice but the murmuring of a few broken sentences of self-approbation and success. When his toils were over, however, he moved back his chair into as gallant a line as ever, and proved that he had not been working only for himself by his earnest invitation to her to take both cocoa and toast. She was already helped to tea — which surprised him, so totally self-engrossed had he been.

"I thought I should have been in time," said he, "but cocoa takes a great deal of boiling."

"I am much obliged to you," replied Charlotte. "But I *prefer* tea."

"Then I will help myself," said he. "A large dish of rather weak cocoa every evening agrees with me better than anything."

It struck her, however, as he poured out this rather weak cocoa, that it came forth in a very fine, dark-coloured stream; and at the same moment, his sisters both crying out, "Oh, Arthur, you get your cocoa stronger and stronger every evening," with Arthur's somewhat conscious reply of "'*Tis* rather stronger than it should be tonight," convinced her that Arthur was by no means so fond of being starved as they could desire or as he felt proper himself.

He was certainly very happy to turn the conversation on dry toast and hear no more of his sisters.

"I hope you will eat some of this toast," said he. "I reckon myself a very good toaster. I never burn my toasts. I never put them too near the fire at first. And yet, you see, there is not a corner but what is well browned. I hope you like dry toast."

"With a reasonable quantity of butter spread over it, very much," said Charlotte, "but not otherwise."

"No more do I," said he, exceedingly pleased. "We think quite alike there. So far from dry toast being wholesome, I think it a very bad thing for the stomach. Without a little butter to soften it, it hurts the coats of the stomach. I am sure it does. I will have the pleasure of spreading some for you directly, and afterwards I will spread some for myself. Very bad indeed for the coats of the stomach — but there is no convincing *some* people. It irritates and acts like a nutmeg grater."

He could not get command of the butter, however, without a struggle; his sisters accusing him of eating a great deal too much and declaring he was not to be trusted, and he maintaining that he only ate enough to secure the coats of his stomach, and besides, he only wanted it now for Miss Heywood. Such a plea must prevail. He got the butter and spread away for her with an accuracy of judgement which at least delighted himself. But when her toast was done and he took his own in hand, Charlotte could hardly contain herself as she saw him watching his sisters while he scrupulously scraped off almost as much butter as he put on, and then seizing an odd moment for adding a great dab just before it went into his mouth.

Certainly, Mr. Arthur Parker's enjoyments in invalidism were very different from his sisters' — by no means so spiritualised. A good deal of earthy dross hung about him. Charlotte could not but suspect him of adopting that line of life principally for the indulgence of an indolent temper, and to be determined on having no disorders but such as called for warm rooms and good nourishment. In one particular, however, she soon found that he had caught something from *them*.

"What!" said he. "Do you venture upon two dishes of strong green tea in one evening? What nerves you must have! How I envy you. Now, if I were to swallow only one such dish, what do you think its effect would be upon me?"

"Keep you awake perhaps all night," replied Charlotte, meaning to overthrow his attempts at surprise by the grandeur of her own conceptions.

"Oh, if that were all!" he exclaimed. "No. It acts on me like poison and would entirely take away the use of my right side before I had swallowed it five minutes. It sounds almost incredible, but it has happened to me so often that I cannot doubt it. The use of my right side is entirely taken away for several hours!"

"It sounds rather odd to be sure," answered Charlotte coolly, "but I dare say it would be proved to be the simplest thing in the world by those who have studied right sides and green tea scientifically and thoroughly understand all the possibilities of their action on each other."

Soon after tea, a letter was brought to Miss Diana Parker from the hotel.

"From Mrs. Charles Dupuis," said she, "some private hand," and having read a few lines, exclaimed aloud, "Well, this is very extraordinary! Very extraordinary indeed! That both should have the same name. Two Mrs. Griffiths! This is a letter of recommendation and introduction to me of the lady from Camberwell — and *her* name happens to be Griffiths too."

A few more lines, however, and the colour rushed into her cheeks and with much perturbation, she added,

"The oddest thing that ever was! A Miss Lambe too! A young West Indian of large fortune. But it *cannot* be the same. Impossible that it should be the same."

She read the letter aloud for comfort. It was merely to introduce the bearer, Mrs. Griffiths from Camberwell, and the three young ladies under her care to Miss Diana Parker's notice. Mrs. Griffiths, being a stranger at Sanditon, was anxious for a respectable introduction; and Mrs. Charles Dupuis, therefore, at the instance of the intermediate friend, provided her with this letter, knowing that she could not do her dear Diana a greater kindness than by giving her the means of being useful. "Mrs. Griffiths' chief solicitude would be for the accommodation and comfort of one of the young ladies under her care, a Miss Lambe, a young West Indian of large fortune in delicate health."

It was very strange! Very remarkable! Very extraordinary!

But they were all agreed in determining it to be *impossible* that there should not be two families; such a totally distinct set of people as were concerned in the reports of each made that matter quite certain. There *must* be two families. Impossible to be otherwise.

"Impossible" and "Impossible" were repeated over and over again with great fervour. An accidental resemblance of names and circumstances, however striking at first, involved nothing really incredible; and so it was settled.

Miss Diana herself derived an immediate advantage to counterbalance her perplexity. She must put her shawl over her shoulders and be running about again. Tired as she was, she must instantly repair to the hotel to investigate the truth and offer her services.

CHAPTER 10

IT WOULD NOT DO. Not all that the whole Parker race could say among themselves could produce a happier catastrophe than that the family from Surrey and the family from Camberwell were one and the same. The rich West Indians and the young ladies' seminary had all entered Sanditon in those two hack chaises. The Mrs. Griffiths who, in her friend Mrs. Darling's hands, had wavered as to coming and been unequal to the journey, was the very same Mrs. Griffiths whose plans were at the same period (under another representation) perfectly decided, and who was without fears or difficulties.

All that had the appearance of incongruity in the reports of the two might very fairly be placed to the account of the vanity, the ignorance or the blunders of the many engaged in the cause by the vigilance and caution of Miss Diana Parker. *Her* intimate friends must be officious like herself; and the subject had supplied letters and extracts and messages enough to make everything appear what it was not.

Miss Diana probably felt a little awkward on being first obliged to admit her mistake. A long journey from Hampshire taken for nothing, a brother disappointed, an expensive house on her hands for a week must have been some of her immediate reflections; and much worse than all the rest must have been the sensation of being less clear-sighted and infallible than she had believed herself. No part of it, however, seemed to trouble her for long. There were so many to share in the shame and the blame that probably, when she had divided out their proper portions to Mrs. Darling, Miss Capper, Fanny Noyce, Mrs. Charles Dupuis and Mrs. Charles Dupuis's neighbour, there might be a mere trifle of reproach remaining for herself. At any rate, she was seen all the following morning walking about after lodgings with Mrs. Griffiths as alert as ever.

Mrs. Griffiths was a very well-behaved, genteel kind of woman, who supported herself by receiving such great girls and young ladies as wanted either masters for finishing their education or a home for beginning their displays. She had several more under her care than the three who were now come to Sanditon, but the others all happened to be absent. Of these three, and indeed of all, Miss Lambe was beyond comparison the most important and precious, as she paid in proportion to her fortune. She was about seventeen, half mulatto, chilly and tender, had a maid of her own, was to have the best room in the lodgings, and was always of the first consequence in every plan of Mrs. Griffiths.

The other girls, two Miss Beauforts, were just such young ladies as may be met with in at least one family out of three throughout the kingdom. They had tolerable complexions, showy figures, an upright decided carriage and an assured look; they were very accomplished and very ignorant, their time being divided between such pursuits as might attract admiration, and those labours and expedients of dexterous ingenuity by which they could dress in a style much beyond what they ought to have afforded; they were some of the first in every change of fashion. And the object of all was to captivate some man of much better fortune than their own.

Mrs. Griffiths had preferred a small, retired place like Sanditon on Miss Lambe's account; and the Miss Beauforts, though naturally preferring anything to smallness and retirement, having in the course of the spring been involved in the inevitable expense of six new dresses each for a three-days visit, were constrained to be satisfied with Sanditon also till their circumstances were retrieved.

There, with the hire of a harp for one and the purchase of some drawing paper for the other and all the finery they could already command, they meant to be very economical, very elegant and very secluded; with the hope, on Miss Beaufort's side, of praise and celebrity from all who walked within the sound of her instrument, and on Miss Letitia's, of curiosity and rapture in all who came near her while she sketched; and to both, the consolation of meaning to be the most stylish girls in the place.

The particular introduction of Mrs. Griffiths to Miss Diana Parker secured them immediately an acquaintance with the Trafalgar House family and with the Denhams; and the Miss Beauforts were soon satisfied with "the circle in which they moved in Sanditon," to use a proper phrase, for everybody must now "move in a circle" — to the prevalence of which rotatory motion is perhaps to be attributed the giddiness and false steps of many.

Lady Denham had other motives for calling on Mrs. Griffiths besides attention to the Parkers. In Miss Lambe, here was the very young lady, sickly and rich, whom she had been asking for; and she made the acquaintance for Sir Edward's sake and the sake of her milch asses.

How it might answer with regard to the baronet remained to be proved but, as to the animals, she soon found that all her calculations of profit would be vain. Mrs. Griffiths would not allow Miss Lambe to have the smallest sympton of a decline or any complaint which asses' milk could possibly relieve. Miss Lambe was "under the constant care of an experienced physician," and his prescriptions must be their rule. And except in favour of some tonic pills, which a cousin of her own had a property in, Mrs. Griffiths never deviated from the strict medicinal page.

The corner house of the Terrace was the one in which Miss Diana Parker had the pleasure of settling her new friends; and considering that it commanded in front the favourite lounge of all the visitors at Sanditon, and on one side whatever might be going on at the hotel, there could not have been a more favourable spot for the seclusion of the Miss Beauforts. And accordingly, long before they had suited themselves with an instrument or with drawing paper, they had, by the frequency of their appearance at the low windows upstairs in order to close the blinds, or open the blinds, to arrange a flower pot on the balcony, or look at nothing through a telescope, attracted many an eye upwards and made many a gazer gaze again.

A little novelty has a great effect in so small a place. The Miss Beauforts, who would have been nothing at Brighton, could not move here without notice. And even Mr. Arthur Parker, though little disposed for supernumerary exertion, always quitted the Terrace in his way to his brother's by this corner house for the sake of a glimpse of the Miss Beauforts — though it was half a quarter of a mile round about and added two steps to the ascent of the hill.

CHAPTER 11

CHARLOTTE had been ten days at Sanditon without seeing Sanditon House, every attempt at calling on Lady Denham having been defeated by meeting with her beforehand. But now it was to be more resolutely undertaken, at a more early hour, that nothing might be neglected of attention to Lady Denham or amusement to Charlotte.

"And if you should find a favourable opening, my love," said Mr. Parker, who did not mean to go with them, "I think you had better mention the poor Mullins's situation and sound her Ladyship as to a subscription for them. I am not fond of charitable subscriptions in a place of this kind — it is a sort of tax upon all that come. Yet as their distress is very great and I almost promised the poor woman yesterday to get something done for her, I believe we must set a subscription on foot, and, therefore, the sooner the better; and Lady Denham's name at the head of the list will be a very necessary beginning. You will not dislike speaking to her about it, Mary?"

"I will do whatever you wish me," replied his wife, "but you would do it so much better yourself. I shall not know what to say."

"My dear Mary," he cried. "It is impossible you can be really at a loss. Nothing can be more simple. You have only to state the present afflicted situation of the family, their earnest application to me, and my being willing to promote a little subscription for their relief, provided it meet with her approbation."

"The easiest thing in the world," cried Miss Diana Parker, who happened to be calling on them at the moment. "All said and done in less time than you have been talking of it now. And while you are on the subject of subscriptions, Mary, I will thank you to mention a very melancholy case to Lady Denham which has been represented to me in the most affecting terms. There is a poor woman in Worcestershire, whom some friends of mine are exceedingly interested about, and I have undertaken to collect whatever I can for her. If you would mention the circumstance to Lady Denham! Lady Denham *can* give, if she is properly attacked. And I look upon her to be the sort of person who, when once she is prevailed on to undraw her purse, would as readily give ten guineas as five. And therefore, if you find her in a giving mood, you might as well speak in favour of another charity which I and a few more have very much at heart — the establishment of a Charitable Repository at Burton on Trent. And then there is the family of the poor man who was hung last assizes at York, though we really *have* raised the sum we wanted for putting them all out, yet if you *can* get a guinea from her on their behalf, it may as well be done."

"My dear Diana!" exclaimed Mrs. Parker, "I could no more mention these things to Lady Denham than I could fly."

"Where's the difficulty? I wish I could go with you myself. But in five minutes I must be at Mrs. Griffiths' to encourage Miss Lambe in taking her first dip. She is so frightened, poor thing, that I promised to come and keep up her spirits and go in the machine with her if she wished it. And as soon as that is over, I must hurry home, for Susan is to have leeches at one o'clock — which will be a three hours' business. Therefore I really have not a moment to spare. Besides that, between ourselves, I ought to be in bed myself at this present time for I am hardly able to stand; and when the leeches have done, I dare say we shall both go to our rooms for the rest of the day."

"I am sorry to hear it, indeed. But if this is the case I hope Arthur will come to us."

"If Arthur takes my advice, he will go to bed too, for if he stays up by himself he will certainly eat and drink more than he ought. But you see, Mary, how impossible it is for me to go with you to Lady Denham's."

"Upon second thoughts, Mary," said her husband. "I will not trouble you to speak about the Mullinses. I will take an opportunity of seeing Lady Denham myself. I know how little it suits you to be pressing matters upon a mind at all unwilling."

His application thus withdrawn, his sister could say no more in support of hers, which was his object, as he felt all their impropriety and all the certainty of their ill effect upon his own better claim. Mrs. Parker was delighted at this release and set off very happy with her friend and her little girl on this walk to Sanditon House.

It was a close, misty morning and, when they reached the brow of the hill, they could not for some time make out what sort of carriage it was which they saw coming up. It appeared at different moments to be everything from a gig to a phaeton, from one horse to four; and just as they were concluding in favour of a tandem, little Mary's young eyes distinguished the coachman and she eagerly called out, "It is Uncle Sidney, Mama, it is indeed."

And so it proved. Mr. Sidney Parker, driving his servant in a very neat carriage, was soon opposite to them, and they all stopped for a few minutes. The manners of the Parkers were always pleasant among themselves; and it was a very friendly meeting between Sidney and his sister-in-law, who was most kindly taking it for granted that he was on his way to Trafalgar House.

This he declined, however. He was "just come from Eastbourne proposing to spend two or three days, as it might happen, at Sanditon"; but the hotel must be his quarters. He was expecting to be joined there by a friend or two.

The rest was common enquiries and remarks, with kind notice of little Mary, and a very well-bred bow and proper address to Miss Heywood on her being named to him. And they parted to meet again within a few hours. Sidney Parker was about seven or eight and twenty, very good-looking, with a decided air of ease and fashion and a lively countenance.

This adventure afforded agreeable discussion for some time. Mrs. Parker entered into all her husband's joy on the occasion and exulted in the credit which Sidney's arrival would give to the place.

The road to Sanditon House was a broad, handsome, planted approach between fields, leading at the end of a quarter of a mile through second gates into grounds which, though not extensive, had all the beauty and respectability which an abundance of very fine timber could give. These entrance gates were so much in a corner of the grounds or paddock, so near to one of its boundaries, that an outside fence was at first almost pressing on the road, till an angle *here* and a curve *there* threw them to a better distance. The fence was a proper park paling in excellent condition, with clusters of fine elms or rows of old thorns following its line almost everywhere. *Almost* must be stipulated, for there were vacant spaces, and through one of these, Charlotte, as soon as they entered the enclosure, caught a glimpse over the pales of something white and womanish in the field on the other side. It was something which immediately brought Miss Brereton into her head; and stepping to the pales, she saw indeed—and very decidedly, in spite of the mist — Miss Brereton seated not far before her at the foot of the bank which sloped down from the outside of the paling and which a narrow path seemed to skirt along — Miss Brereton seated, apparently very composedly, and Sir Edward Denham by her side.

They were sitting so near each other and appeared so closely engaged in gentle conversation that Charlotte instantly felt she had nothing to do but to step back again and say not a word. Privacy was certainly their object. It could not but strike her rather unfavourably with regard to Clara; but hers was a situation which must not be judged with severity. She was glad to perceive that nothing had been discerned by Mrs. Parker. If Charlotte had not been considerably the taller of the two, Miss Brereton's white ribbons might not have fallen within the ken of *her* more observant eyes.

Among other points of moralising reflection which the sight of this tete-a-tete produced, Charlotte could not but think of the extreme difficulty which secret lovers must have in finding a proper spot for their stolen interviews. Here perhaps they had thought themselves so perfectly secure from observation — the whole field open before them; a steep bank and pales never crossed by the foot of man at their back, and a great thickness of air to aid them as well! Yet here she had seen them. They were really ill-used.

The house was large and handsome. Two servants appeared to admit them and everything had a suitable air of property and order. Lady Denham valued herself upon her liberal establishment and had great enjoyment in the order and importance of her style of living. They were shown into the usual sitting room, well proportioned and well furnished, though it was furniture rather originally good and extremely well kept than new or showy. And as Lady Denham was not there, Charlotte had leisure to look about her and to be told by Mrs. Parker that the whole-length portrait of a stately gentleman which, placed over the mantelpiece, caught the eye immediately, was the picture of Sir Henry Denham; and that one among many miniatures in another part of the room, little conspicuous, represented Mr. Hollis. Poor Mr. Hollis! It was impossible not to feel him hardly used: to be obliged to stand back in his own house and see the best place by the fire constantly occupied by Sir Henry Denham.

Lady Denham's brisk style of greeting on entering made it plain that, though she regarded their visit as a necessary piece of civility, she had no intention of exercising equal civility in being inconvenienced by it herself.

"Very fortunate indeed you find me at home, Mrs. Parker," she said in her abrupt way. "I was on the point of setting out for the library and in a few minutes we may all walk back that way together. Hodges has it from Mrs. Whitby that Mrs. Griffiths has actually been enquiring about a chamber-horse. The wonder of it is she mentioned no such thing when I called on her the day before yesterday. And if Miss Lambe is not to be benefited by asses' milk, how am I to guess that daily indoor exercise on a chamber-horse is exactly what this physician of hers recommends? I have no patience with invalids who spurn one aid to health and clutch at another. But no matter — the ill wind is still blowing in my direction. Mr. Hollis's chamber-horse is in excellent condition and we may have it delivered to the Terrace this very day, as soon as I have gone round and settled the terms. I am only waiting now for Miss Clara to return from the Jacksons'; and their cottage is not a quarter of a mile across the park."

Charlotte, suspecting Lady Denham might have to wait rather longer than she intended, wondered how a formal call could be indefinitely prolonged after so unpromising a beginning; the more especially as their hostess, making no move to sit down herself and lending only half an ear to Mrs. Parker's polite remarks, showed no readiness for any conversation which did not advance her own immediate plans.

But in her quiet, unassuming fashion, Mrs. Parker persevered steadily on, enquiring after the health of old Mrs. Jackson, mentioning Mr. Sidney Parker's arrival in Sanditon, and commenting on a fine display of irises and roses in one alcove.

A pause succeeded for a few moments while Lady Denham
fidgeted impatiently about the room. Neither Charlotte nor Mrs.
Parker had disarranged anything there; but little Mary, having
seated herself first on one chair and then on another, had hollowed
several cushions, slightly rumpled their seat covers, shifted a
footstool and disturbed a small hearthrug. It was apparent that
Lady Denham could not endure waiting till her guests had gone
before restoring each item of furniture to its exact and appointed
place, and Charlotte watched in amazement as the minor modi-
fications Mary had made to the room were fussily adjusted.

"I wonder what can have detained Miss Clara?" Lady Denham
said at last, patting a final cushion back into shape. "It was
only the usual pail of soup we send across whenever cook has it
on hand — beef soup, you know. But she cannot be wasting the
whole day on such errands — and *my* day as well, she might
consider. Hiring out the chamber-horse is a great deal more to
the point this morning, and Miss Clara could be supervising
Betsy removing the dust covers up in the garret."

Disconcerted by so self-centred a train of thought being voiced
aloud, Charlotte decided Lady Denham was put out by their call
and trying to discourage them from staying. Beginning to feel
extremely uncomfortable herself, she wished Mrs. Parker would
make some movement to speed their departure. But Mrs. Parker,
who knew their hostess rather better, continued seated and made
several more of her gentle, commonplace observations. Over
a period of years, she had come to understand that this discourtesy towards casual visitors did not arise from any unwilling-
ness to entertain them, any deficiency in the appointment or
arrangement of the household, nor even any real lack of
hospitality. The truth lay more in a failure of mental resilience,
an unfortunate but inevitable result of Lady Denham's declining
years; she preferred everything and everybody about her to
remain comfortably settled in their proper places.

Charlotte could only think her very impolite. But Mrs. Parker, restraining Mary from further movement, could recognise the selfishness but still excuse it from the circumstances of Lady Denham's having had rather too much her own way all her life, and being too old to change those ways now.

So she set herself out to be as pleasant as possible; and having decided in advance how long their call was to last, refused to be provoked into curtailing it.

CHAPTER 12

AFTER CONTINUING in this uneasy manner a quarter of an hour, they heard quick steps across the hall, Miss Brereton appeared and Charlotte's interest in the visit immediately revived. She now saw Clara's white ribbons at closer quarters, was struck once again by so much beauty and elegance, but found a new spice added to the fascination in trying to decide whether there was the least appearance of guilt or deceit on that lovely countenance.

Miss Brereton apologised calmly to the visitors with a brief explanation for the length of her absence: she would have hurried back had she known of Mrs. Parker's intention to call, but she had been all this time sitting with old Mrs. Jackson; and to Charlotte's observant eye, her cheeks suffered no variation in colour as she offered this as her sole excuse.

Mrs. Parker, already rising, was beginning to suggest they should now all walk back in the direction of the Terrace, when Lady Denham suddenly and perversely summoned the servants to bring refreshment. Charlotte, agreeably surprised by the variety of hot-house fruit which Sanditon House could produce at a moment's notice, wondered why this gesture had been withheld when most needed to fill a void, and made when the importunate guests were on the point of departure; and she followed Mrs. Parker's lead to the buffet table, her orderly mind still trying to grapple with the kindly intentions, shrewd calculations and capricious behaviour which combined to form the character of their hostess.

Their visit, however, soon afforded further exercise for her powers in summing up an even more complex situation. The entrance of Sir Edward Denham was apparently quite unexpected by everyone except herself — and presumably Miss Brereton; but Charlotte, scrutinising him closely throughout his opening speech, could at least feel some astonishment in the complete self-possession with which he accounted for his appearance. He had been speaking with Mrs. Whitby that very morning and, hearing of Miss Lambe's need for a chamber-horse, had hurried to pass on the news to Lady Denham — with earnest assurances of perpetual regard for her concerns, delivered with all the flourish of which Sir Edward was capable; he had come to Sanditon House *direct* from the library, he said.

There was not the slightest embarrassment in his manner as he told this shameless lie; and Charlotte knew not what to infer. She moved her eyes to Clara and saw that, with an air of indifference towards Sir Edward, she was entertaining little Mary and helping her to a bunch of grapes.

Charlotte had observed this studied lack of interest in Sir Edward on previous occasions but now it occurred to her that these had all taken place in Lady Denham's presence. That Clara encouraged his addresses and listened to Sir Edward more favourably in private meetings seemed equally obvious. The connection between them was as ambiguous in some respects as it was plain in others; and Lady Denham, listening to Sir Edward very complacently, accepting both his exaggerated deference and his insistence on calling as her due, was clearly being deceived quite systematically by them both. For Charlotte had seen enough in this one instance to convince her that their secret encounter that morning had been neither by chance nor the first of its kind. Unless Sir Edward and Miss Brereton were practised conspirators, she could scarcely believe they would carry through their duplicity in so normal a fashion.

"Miss Brereton is certainly at fault in concealing her meetings with Sir Edward from Lady Denham," she decided. "But she is in a difficult position, no doubt. If she were more open about his courtship, who knows how Lady Denham might react? *She* expects Sir Edward to marry an heiress — and although *he* might equally expect Miss Brereton to become an heiress in time, his calculations on this point and Lady Denham's might not exactly coincide." To be continually at the mercy of such an old lady's whims struck Charlotte as being particularly hard upon a young couple. But it did not alter her original judgement in condemning their deceit and in resolving to be very circumspect over her own dealings with both of them in the future.

So engrossed was she in these thoughts and the various interpretations she could suggest for Miss Brereton's conduct, that she was taken by surprise in finding herself addressed by her directly. In a most cordial manner, Miss Brereton seemed to be trying to further their acquaintance. She was asking Charlotte about sea-bathing. Whether she intended to bathe while at Sanditon and whether she had ever done so before?

"I should like it very much," replied Charlotte. "And Mrs. Parker has been kind enough to suggest she will come with me the first morning we can arrange it."

"Ah, I have been hoping you will accept my company on just such an expedition. I am sure sea-bathing must be delightful and have longed to try it; but the weather up till now has not been much in favour and besides, Lady Denham has not liked me to venture into a bathing machine on my own."

"Oh pray, let us not be starting again on such nonsense, Miss Clara," cried Lady Denham. "All this to-do with bathing machines was not the fashion of *my* youth, let me tell you; and I now heartily regret allowing Mr. Parker to talk me into introducing them at Sanditon!"

"But my dear ma'am, *every* resort must have its bathing

machines these days," protested Mrs. Parker. "They are a great attraction. And you must surely agree ours are most conveniently placed — so sheltered a cove for the very purpose just westward of the main beach."

"Oh aye, spare me all the arguments in favour of them. If I heard them from Mr. Parker once, I heard them a thousand times. But the only one that came uppermost with me was the lack of expense. They're among the few of Mr. Parker's improvements that haven't cost me a penny, I'll say that for them," conceded Lady Denham. "The applications he had from people wanting to run them! Everyone in the village seemed to believe their fortunes could be made by starting up bathing machines. And yet I hear their terms are moderate. One shilling for each gentleman, Mrs. Whitby tells me, and one and sixpence for ladies — with the price decreasing for regular customers. But some people are great fools. Why pay even that to ruin their complexions? You young ladies will only make yours rude and coarse by exposing them to salt water. But there, I suppose young people must always be trying out anything new and never mind how the wind may show their legs when they climb into them."

Here Mrs. Parker again interposed, and placidly interpreting Lady Denham's last grudging sentence as sufficient approval, advised Charlotte to accept Miss Brereton's invitation. She herself was happy to concur with any suggestion which offered some prospect of pleasure for her young friend and she was a faithful enough accomplice of her husband's to resist any slander that sea water could ever be harmful.

"As to the complexion, I never heard of such a thing myself. Wind and sun perhaps have done the damage and salt water has been given the blame. I really believe that sea bathing in itself can do nothing but good," said she, "where moderation is shown and provided certain care is exercised."

"Oh, certainly," agreed Sir Edward, who had been trying to

encourage the bathing party for some time without actively opposing Lady Denham. "Saline immersion should not be prolonged if depression and languor are to be avoided. And then take, for instance, the *hour* of bathing. This must be selected with particular circumspection. It should be postponed till past noon if possible or at least some hours after breakfast, when the digestion of that meal may be supposed to be terminated. And a degree of exercise should always be taken previous to entering the water and also on leaving it."

He went on at such length, interspersing his lecture with such minute instructions to the young ladies as to the exact time they should take their bathe, and the distance they should walk before and after it, that Charlotte began to suspect he was smoothing the way for his next assignation with Clara — almost choosing the time and place — in Lady Denham's own hearing.

The conjecture took away much of her inclination for the bathing excursion; but though publicly agreeing to join Miss Brereton on the following morning, she privately resolved to be on the lookout for Sir Edward and do whatever she could to thwart his obvious intention of escorting Clara home.

"No doubt they are both hoping I shall be very useful to them; and Miss Brereton is trying to become friendly with me so she will have an excuse to escape more often from Sanditon House. But I want no part in such deceit and they will find me a very obstructive chaperone," were Charlotte's thoughts as the three of them fell into a natural grouping behind Lady Denham, Mrs. Parker and Mary in the walk back across the park.

Sir Edward, unaware of such meditated opposition to his plans and incapable of relegating any personable young woman to the role of chaperone, treated both Charlotte and Clara to equal excesses of gallantry as he walked between them. Still extolling the pleasures of bathing, he sought to entertain them with his longest syllables and most edifying sentences.

"To plunge into the refreshing wave and be wrapped round with the liquid element is indeed a most delightful sensation," he assured them. "But health and pleasure may be equally consulted in these salutary ablutions; and to many a wan countenance can the blush of the rose be restored by an occasional dip in the purifying surge of the ocean. Not," he hastened to add, trying to bow to them both at the same time, "that either of my fair listeners would need the rose *restored* to their lovely cheeks."

Charlotte could only gaze at him in astonishment; and even Clara's fair cheek showed so little sign of blushing that Sir Edward, had he been a reasonable man, might have felt abashed. He continued, however, much in this vein till their party was obliged to separate at the entrance drive to Trafalgar House.

Extremely happy to be relieved of his company, Charlotte watched him take up his new position between Lady Denham and Clara, deferring so assiduously to the former and treating the latter in so offhand a manner as her mere companion that the mystery of the exact relationship between all three of them puzzled her more than ever. It was so very clearly not what it appeared on the surface. But what could it all mean?

"It is very difficult for me to understand till I know more of both the people and the circumstances," said she to herself. "Lady Denham prides herself on being shrewd, but she is also very suspicious. And if she is always imagining hidden motives and anticipating deceit in everyone, perhaps other people should not be blamed for protecting themselves and not being entirely open with her."

Charlotte knew her own first impressions were not without their defects; she had already changed her mind once about both Sir Edward and Lady Denham, and felt she should reach no more false conclusions by forming too rapid and definite an opinion of Clara Brereton.

"But I do not *think* I will change my mind about Sir Edward again," she decided. "He *is* a very muddled and silly young man."

Such were her musings as she walked towards the house, listening only half-heartedly to Mrs. Parker, whose sweet-tempered remarks could usually be ignored or agreed to without serious damage to any discussion.

And Charlotte had said "Yes, yes" several times, "Oh, I agree, decidedly handsome, a very fine young man," and "Most elegant in his address," before she realised they were talking not of Sir Edward Denham but of Sidney Parker.

CHAPTER 13

EVEN SUCH TEMPORARY forgetfulness of the new arrival in Sanditon became an impossibility once they had crossed the threshold of Trafalgar House. Sidney Parker had already called there and his brother could talk of nothing else.

"Only think of it, Mary," he cried. "To have him with us at last! And two of his friends joining him tomorrow! So exactly the set of young people we want encouraged among us; they will lend a proper fashionable air to the place. Even for a few days it may do a great deal — but I wonder how long they *will* stay? They are sure to be most excellent young men if they are friends of Sidney's."

Charlotte had already noticed that Mr. Parker tended to judge people by their usefulness to Sanditon, the respectable tone they lent it or the admiration they expressed for it rather than on their own merits. She was not at all surprised when he continued his commendation of Sidney by repeating with strong delight his recent praise of Sanditon.

"He is all amazement at the improvements and developments since he was last here — so many new houses finished, our plantation growing up so quickly, such activity on the hill and the Terrace. But still he tends to make a joke of it. He will joke about everything, you know. He has been making me laugh most heartily for the past hour and is now gone off to call on Susan and Diana. He vows he will bring them all to dinner with us this evening. I hope, my love, that Reynolds will prove equal to providing a family dinner at short notice if Sidney can prevail with them? I told him we could always squeeze in another four without a doubt. *They* eat nothing, we know, but we must do our best to tempt them."

Mrs. Parker, who always kept a very good table, murmured something about a saddle-of-mutton which Mr. Parker would be carving himself, hesitated between adding a couple of birds or some well-filled corner dishes and ended by doubting whether the entire Parker family could ever be induced to take dinner with them.

"I am sure Diana will come if she is feeling up to it," she decided. "But not even Sidney could persuade Arthur or Susan to venture out in the evening air. They have never done so before."

"Nor have they," said Mr. Parker, much struck. "It is time they dined with us."

"Susan has not yet climbed our hill during the daytime."

"Depend upon it my dear, Sidney will persuade them all to come," Mr. Parker assured her with undiminished cheerfulness. "He will consider such objections as they make mere nonsense and will have his own way in the end."

And this optimism was soon justified. Shortly after midday, a message arrived from Miss Diana confirming the projected family dinner; and by five o'clock Sidney and Arthur could be observed from an upper window escorting their sisters up the hill.

The very real pleasure which the whole family then shared on being together could only be remarked by Charlotte with approval. Her own large family of brothers and sisters had scarcely ever been separated and she wondered if they would undergo such a great improvement in collective amiability as did the Parkers on their reunion. Diana, always active and talkative, was more mellow and good-humoured; Miss Parker less eccentric in her facial contortions; Mr. Parker more exuberant than ever; and

Arthur wore the look of complete satisfaction which he usually reserved for his food.

On their entering the drawing room amid all the early confusion of warm greetings, unanswered questions and unfinished sentences, Charlotte at first stood a little apart. But Arthur, finding nobody was listening to *him*, soon detached himself from the knot at the door and came towards her. Eager to communicate what he felt about the situation to someone he hoped would attend, he exclaimed,

"Well, Miss Heywood, did you ever know anything so delightful as this? Sidney is a capital fellow and makes us all lively. It always is so. He will be setting schemes afoot for the few days he is here and turning us all upside down."

The enthusiasm with which Arthur appeared to welcome this possibility convinced Charlotte that boredom rather than ill-health was his main problem. The constant company of his sisters must sometimes be irksome to a young man of one and twenty; and the regard he seemed to have for his brother was no doubt founded in part on a desire for occasional excitement and novelty.

But Miss Parker's voice could also be heard amid the babble at the entrance, predicting with complacence that "everything will be at sixes and sevens now Sidney is here." And Diana, issuing brisk directions to Morgan about the various packets of herb tea they had brought with them, made the tolerant exclamation: "There, I knew Sidney would forget to bring Susan's phials from the mantelpiece. Ah well, for one evening what does it matter? It is not often we can assemble in such a pleasant family group."

It was a group which could not but interest Charlotte. The peculiar licence which his brothers and sisters apparently extended to Mr. Sidney Parker had already attracted her attention; and long before she had an opportunity of talking with him herself, she was watching him and attending to his conversation with the others. There was a novelty in his character which to her was certainly pleasing. His person was uncommonly fine for he was the tallest of the family; his countenance, though not regularly handsome, was made nearly so by a pair of very alert and intelligent eyes; and his manners were at once so animated and yet so polished that she thought it must be impossible for him to be other than amiable, and was ready to give him the credit for being perfectly so.

"And what of these friends of yours, Sidney?" demanded Mr. Parker as soon as they were seated at dinner. "You have not yet given us an account of them or why they are joining you here. Will they stay long? Have you mentioned them to us before? I have been puzzling ever since this morning why you should be meeting them in Sanditon."

"You may have heard me speak of them — I have known them both some time. Reginald Catton and Henry Brudenall."

"Catton — the young man who is always buying curricles? Admired that yellow one of yours and had it copied? You stayed with him last year in Shropshire? And did you not once say he also had a town house? Not married yet, is he? Why should he be putting up at a hotel in Sanditon?"

Although Mr. Parker was the elder brother by some seven years, his quick curiosity and infectious enthusiasm about everything sometimes made him appear the younger of the two.

"Reginald will not be staying more than a night or two, if that," explained his brother, replying only to the most relevant of the questions. "His only purpose in coming is to drive our mutual friend down from London. And my purpose in meeting them here is to introduce Henry Brudenall among you. He will be remaining some few weeks on account of his health."

"His health?" cried Diana, her curiosity aroused now too. "What is the exact problem over Mr. Brudenall's health? Is he bilious? nervous? feverish?"

"Nothing our good sea air will not be able to cure, I hope," said Mr. Parker.

"Sea air may be beneficial for some complaints; but there are certainly many others — mine and Susans's and I am sure Arthur's too — which derive no value from the sea whatsoever. Any sort of nervous complaint, bile, lumbago, rheumaticky disorders should be kept well away from the sea. Bronchial conditions too. I trust Mr. Brudenall does not suffer from asthma? Sanditon will certainly kill him within his fortnight if he does."

Sidney, who appeared to Charlotte to have some earlier difficulty in maintaining complete composure, assured his sister with perfect gravity that Mr. Brudenall was not suffering from asthma.

"In fact there is nothing *seriously* the matter with Henry. When I spoke of his health, I was not referring to either its past or present state, but rather to the future," he said somewhat obscurely; he paused, apparently decided some further explanation was necessary, and continued: "The case is that Henry is soon to go out to India. Being the younger son of a respectable but impoverished family, there is not much future for him in England, and he is being sent off to make his fortune in Bengal. With a sea voyage of several months ahead of him, his family feel he should harden his constitution by some earlier exposure to the sea air."

"I see," said Mr. Parker doubtfully.

"You mean he is quite healthy otherwise?" demanded Diana, her disappointment overshadowing her judgement.

"It seems to me a singular manner of proceeding," Mrs. Parker had begun when Arthur, who had been staring fixedly at his brother, suddenly burst out laughing and said,

"Oh, but it is all a complete hum. Sidney is making up the whole story. I can tell by his face. It is nothing but one of his take-ins."

Sidney smiled at him.

"Let us say I only half expected you to be taken in by it," he admitted frankly. "And I must confess I had forgotten, when I so unwisely mentioned health, how you would all go plagueing Henry about asthma and bile and nervous disorders till you had diagnosed him to your satisfaction. On the spur of the moment my powers of invention failed me and I could hit upon no better story than that. It *is* quite true that he is going to Bengal. But now I suppose I must let you fully into the secret; though to all outsiders I think it best to maintain the fiction that Henry is here in Sanditon for his health. They at least should be too tactful to enquire the exact nature of his complaints."

He said this in a more serious tone than he had used previously and went on to explain that his friend's lack of spirits, which called for some weeks of retirement, resulted more from the state of the heart than that of the body. Mr. Brudenall had been for many years most warmly attached to a cousin and she to him. They had always intended to marry before setting out for India, which his family indeed had in mind for him from a very early age. Their betrothal, although a close family secret, had been approved by both sets of parents; but on *her* side it was felt that she should be given the enjoyment of a season in London before entering upon the long and no doubt cheerless exile in Bengal.

Next year had been the time fixed for their marriage and departure. And what had been Henry's dismay when he had heard — only last month — of his cousin's public engagement to another. Sidney Parker believed it impossible for a man to be more attached to a woman than Henry had been to his cousin. Even now he uttered no word of reproach towards *her*. He felt *his* future was a dismal one and he did not blame her for choosing a better match and a more comfortable existence. But his father was now truly anxious to hasten his departure from England as a means of providing some new direction for his thoughts, to remove him from past associations and settle him as early as possible in the circle where he would spend the rest of his life. Preparations for his journey were now well in hand, but his cousin's wedding would be taking place within the next fortnight; and as their assembled families would be expected to attend, it was thought more convenient for Henry to absent himself from London.

Sidney and his friend, Reginald Catton, being consulted over the problem, had decided Reginald would drive Henry to Sanditon on his own way to Brighton; and Sidney would ensure his introduction there among strangers, who would know nothing and ask nothing about him during this very delicate period.

"I do not object to taking my own family into my confidence over this; but what I have told you must go no further than this table," he warned them. "Henry is a most sensitive young man and would be deeply upset if he felt everyone he met in Sanditon was pitying him on his cousin's wedding day."

The sympathy and good will which Sidney had now excited towards his friend was very great.

"Poor young man," said Diana. "But you have done very well in telling us this, Sidney. It is very bad that his prospects have been blighted by a thoughtless young woman, but who knows what unguarded remarks we might have let fall had we not known the full circumstances?"

"Indeed yes," agreed Mrs. Parker. "It is always better to tell the truth."

Arthur, who was still watching his brother intently, appeared quite satisfied this time. And Sidney, after a quick glance round the dinner table which confirmed his impression that Henry Brudenall would meet with only tact and kindness in Sanditon, was content to drop the subject and turn the conversation on other matters.

CHAPTER 14

AFTER DINNER, Charlotte was given an opportunity for studying Sidney Parker a little more closely as, stationing himself by her, he claimed her attention in the most friendly manner.

"I am persuaded you will prove an ally of mine, Miss Heywood. I am always on the lookout for one on these occasions," he said, pulling up a chair next to hers. "Till the tea tray is brought in, nobody else will talk of anything but the value of various herbs in digesting what they have just eaten."

"For shame, Sidney, you do exaggerate," protested Mr. Parker as he joined them.

"Then go and see for yourself whether I do," replied Sidney waving him away. "I grant there may be an occasional digression on the advantages of one medicine over another in further digesting the herb tea; and perhaps a minor disagreement on the exact temperature at which both should be taken to settle the stomach completely. But I do assure you, Miss Heywood, I have sometimes sat for over an hour without wedging another subject into our family discussions."

"An hour! What nonsense!" cried Diana, interrupting her own conversation at the far end of the room with an ease which showed her quite capable of listening and talking at the same time. "I would be the last person to deny we are all sad invalids and you give us no sympathy. But, Miss Heywood, you must not believe everything Sidney says. His high spirits often run away with him and he frequently speaks without thinking. I am sure it is impossible for *anyone* to talk less of their health than we do in general with so much cause."

"And I am sure Miss Heywood has already suffered just such ordeals as I have described," retorted Sidney, "and will be ready to join forces with me in repelling them."

"Phoo, phoo. Now you are being quite ridiculous."

"Let him be, Diana," Mr. Parker advised her. "It is only his usual way of talking himself into doing just as he wishes. But we will let him sit next to Miss Heywood if he is so determined on it." And he turned away with great good humour to settle down between his two sisters on the sofa.

"Every member of a family thinks he knows the other's faults," said Sidney, laughing. "But now I *have* got my own way, I will share the victory by allowing you to choose the topic of our conversation, Miss Heywood."

Charlotte was quite ready to talk on any subject and suggested books; and they were soon engaged in comparing their opinions on those *she* had read; for she did not doubt that he had read a great many more.

No one was more calculated to shine in such a conversation than Sidney, who was so far from having any fixed opinion that he could alter it whenever he chose, sometimes agreeing and sometimes dissenting, according to whichever view he decided would provide most entertainment for the moment. He could, therefore, always take either side and always argue with temper. They continued conversing together on a variety of subjects for Sidney seldom dwelt long on any but had something to say on all; and Charlotte was soon convinced that, both in natural abilities and acquired information, he was infinitely superior to the rest of his family.

He talked well and with a great deal of sense; and she could not help contrasting his manner and the subject matter he chose with that of the two other young men she had met and conversed with recently. Sir Edward Denham, displaying quotations like framed certificates of culture in his talk, had been a sad disappointment as an amiable acquaintance. And as for Arthur Parker — he had not the slightest idea how to make himself agreeable to any young lady, believing his diet and his symptoms must be as paramount an interest to all women as they were to his two sisters. Mr. Sidney Parker's ready address and well-bred ease of manner made him a much more entertaining companion than either of them; and Charlotte found the evening passing more swiftly and delightfully for her than any she had known since her arrival in Sanditon.

But having heard his opinion on many topics, she remained doubtful of his real tastes; for though his mind was clearly well-informed, he frequently surprised her by a lack of conformity and by contradicting one idea with another. In his indifference over maintaining any uniform attitude, Sidney was certainly very unlike his companion, whose judgement had been guided by her parents from an early age and who always adopted a restrained and consistent standpoint.

"I see there is absolutely no shaking your common sense, Miss Heywood, and will stop teasing you and let you have your tea," he said, rising at last; and Charlotte was surprised to discover the tea tray had been in the room for some time and could not credit how the interval had passed so quickly. She now felt she had been insensible in monopolising Sidney's attention in this family circle where all wished to talk to him, and reproached herself for such thoughtlessness in consulting nobody's pleasure but her own during the last hour.

Fearful of being considered negligent of others, she immediately rose too, determined to rectify such selfish behavior. But he protested against this, begging her to remain where she was while he brought their tea; and though approving his civility she still insisted on a slight adjustment of her position which would bring them more into the general discussion. This he acknowledged with a smile as he helped her to the tea things, only adding a cheerful warning.

"Perhaps we have managed to escape the worst, but from what I have just overheard, their favourite topic is by no means exhausted."

And Charlotte, turning her attention back to the main party and picking up the threads of the conversation, soon realised his sisters had indeed discovered a new hazard to their health. Miss Parker, replying to a polite enquiry from her sister-in-law and acknowledging they were *fairly well* settled in their new lodgings on the Terrace, had just startled her audience by remarking, in the same languid tones, that she suspected their new scullery maid was, however, slowly poisoning them all.

"Poison?" exclaimed Mr. Parker, rather aghast. "My dear Susan, you cannot be serious. What is this you are saying?"

"Yes, Tom, it is only too true," agreed Miss Diana more energetically. "I am always running to the kitchen every possible second to try to prevent it. But I fear we are being poisoned — oh, unintentionally, I suppose. The fact is we are convinced this new scullery maid we have hired never rinses the dishes; and soap, as you know, is *highly* poisonous. But nothing I say seems to convince her of the seriousness of the situation. Would you believe it — she actually laughed at me — said her last employers never insisted on rinsing dishes and never knew a day's illness. Oh, Sally is a good-hearted, pleasant enough girl but I am afraid she will have to go or poor Susan will never be in good health here. And Arthur is now beginning to suffer almost identical symptoms — spent the most wretched night, scarcely closing his eyes for one minute. Both Susan and I tried everything we could to get him off — hot bricks and weak cocoa — though he will never try my favourite concoction for sleeplessness. Warm water steeped with the second rind of an alder stick — have I recommended that to you before, Mary? But last night poor Arthur begged only for a small glass of port wine; and after a while, I could see none of us would get any sleep unless I gave in, so I judged it best to let him have it. Port wine, after all, seldom does great harm and I do believe he spent the rest of the night fairly comfortably. At all events Susan and I got off and heard no more. But today, as a result, we have all been in very poor shape. Had it not been for Sidney's arrival, I am sure we would have all gone to bed this evening long before dinner."

During this account of Arthur's recent indisposition, Charlotte had turned her eyes towards him where he sat, sipping his cocoa and eating his toast beside his sister-in-law. Beyond a little sleepiness and a great deal of indolence, she could not detect that he had passed such an uncomfortable night as Miss Diana described. Following her gaze and surmising her thoughts, Sidney Parker murmured in a quiet undertone.

"Arthur's health has always been an obsession of theirs. My eldest brother and I had the advantage of being sent away to school before our parents died and thus escaped falling into our sisters' care. Arthur, as you see, was not so lucky. They have cossetted him and pandered to him for so long that he positively enjoys being an invalid now."

There was such an air of good humour and frankness in Sidney that Charlotte, though feeling herself unauthorised to speak of his family with so much familiarity, could not but respond to it and speak to him at that moment as he spoke to her.

"But surely it is very dreadful for so young a man to take no interest in anything except his health? Cannot something be done to *make* him adopt a profession? Or at the very least develop some enthusiasm which might take up more of his time?"

"I tried my best to take him abroad with me last year, but he had very little eagerness for travel himself; and Susan and Diana between them soon convinced him he would be most uncomfortable moving about from one foreign city to another."

"Perhaps if he had some property," said Charlotte, rather

hesitantly, "he might bestir himself in trying to improve it."

"He has a small competence, quite sufficient for his needs and offering him no great excitement in enlarging it. But discussing money with Arthur is more than uphill work — I long ago came to the conclusion that no prospect of financial reward would ever push *him* into exertion. The best we can hope is that he will develop some harmless interest of his own — an over-riding passion for collecting butterflies, watching birds or breeding dogs; these are the sort of activities which I believe Arthur could enter into with great success, but they are not the sort a brother can guess or force on him. Some chance encounter with an enthusiast or some buried inclination of his own must provide the stimulus. Our family are not usually lacking in enthusiasm after all. On the contrary, my sisters' whims and oddities frequently run away with them."

Deciding Sidney's discussion of his family was now becoming rather too outspoken for her to encourage, Charlotte made no reply and, turning slightly, directed her attention back to the group. But the rest of the Parkers being still engaged on the failings of temporary servants, their resistance to training and the possible recruits at present available from Sanditon village, no immediate opening presented itself for her to join in.

Mr. Parker, having run through the list of candidates for Sally's place, soon began trying to persuade his sisters that the bracing effects of sea air alone would be sufficient to counteract any dire results they expected from the soap poisoning. And, after sitting for some little time, listening to him expound on this well-worn theme, Charlotte heard a chuckle at her elbow and Sidney Parker speaking again in a low voice.

"You know, in some ways Tom is the worst of them all. *His* fancy for medicine takes a different turn. He places all his blind reliance in Dr. Sanditon, which is just as foolish and even more wayward than my sisters' faith in quack remedies."

While she did not censure these opinions, Charlotte felt all the

impropriety of his making them known to her, who was little more
than a stranger. And yet Sidney Parker's manners were so
obviously those of the fashionable world that she also felt both
priggish and provincial for daring to criticise them. His ease
and openness and the delight with which he seized on anything
which might contribute to his own amusement or that of others —
all these, she conceded, were perfectly allowable in someone who
spent the greater part of his time in the wider society of London.
But in her narrow and limited experience, which so far had extended little beyond her own comfortable and well-regulated
family circle, a very different style of behaviour was practised
and a very different set of values the only acceptable ones. The
exercise of continual restraint in all social meetings, a proper
consideration of both neighbours and relations, and a tactful forbearance in censuring the foibles of others were the principles she
had always been taught to respect. She recognized their importance in maintaining good relations among people who were
destined to meet each other every day of their lives, but could
perceive their drawbacks where any contribution of wit or
liveliness might be expected in the gaieties of small talk; and
though she envied Sidney Parker his freedom of saying whatever
came into his head to whoever he happened to be near, she made
no attempt to follow his example.

But with some surprise at her continued silence, he pressed even
more pointedly for her opinion till Charlotte realised there was
no avoiding a reply.

"You cannot really expect me to agree with you, Mr. Parker,"
she said with evident reluctance and in a tone of mild seriousness.
"For although there may be no harm in your speaking of your own
family in such terms, it would be the greatest impertinence for me
to do the same."

It was said and she could not regret it. She felt some mortifica-
tion in having been forced to reveal her own sober standards of

conduct and even more in reflecting that he would probably find her both dull and slow-witted beside his usual companions. But the reproof which had cost her such deliberation to deliver was met only with a shout of delighted laughter.

"Oh sensible, prudent Miss Heywood, how very correct in you to rebuke me," said he, very much amused. "You are already so well acquainted with my family that I had forgotten how short a while *we* have known each other. I should, of course, have waited at least a month before trying to compare our opinions on all my relations."

"I very much doubt that a month would bring any great change in my outlook," replied Charlotte, quite firmly. "Very few of us lack superficial faults and we must rely on each other's kindness to overlook them."

"But people take such trouble with their faults and go to such lengths to make them fascinating to others that it is really very *unkind* to overlook them," protested Sidney. "They would much rather be laughed at on their own merits than politely ignored as members of a community."

Charlotte could not help smiling at so light-hearted a defence of his own forthright methods in conversation; but very satisfied to have made her own point while exciting so little ill-will, she was now quite determined to end any private discussion between them; and pretending the general talk among the others had absorbed her full attention, she managed to shift her chair by almost imperceptible movements towards the larger circle.

He saw what she was about and good-naturedly let her have her way, making only one last attempt to provoke another smile from her before rising to surrender his position.

"Here comes Arthur. I am sure you will find conversation with him less of an effort. No need at all to ponder over the correct reply to any of his statements," he said. "I can tell by the look on his face that he intends to explain in great detail how and why the cranberry custard at dinner did not make him *quite* bilious."

She tried to look disapprovingly at him as he moved off to occupy the vacated chair by his sister-in-law but found it harder to repress the smile when Arthur, having taken the seat beside her in exchange, began in almost the exact style his brother had predicted. It was the roast duckling he selected to illustrate his point and not the cranberry custard, but Charlotte had great difficulty in keeping her countenance as she listened. Indeed, once when she looked up and noticed Sidney's eyes on her as he leaned forward to enjoy Arthur's recital himself, she had to turn away quickly on the pretext of finding her workbox and sorting a fringe of Mrs. Parker's.

It was only after she had picked it up that she remembered her promise of having it ready soon after dinner. She had been so well entertained ever since that she had completely forgotten Mrs. Parker's fringe. She busied herself with it now, resolving to do penance for the very real enjoyment the evening had already afforded her.

The others were soon engaged in discussing the arrival of Sidney's friends; and he was very willing to outline the many schemes he had in mind for their entertainment.

"I doubt whether Reginald will remain more than a day in Sanditon — probably not more than a few hours — so we need not plan much on his behalf unless he decides to drive over again from Brighton. But with Henry, no effort will be too great. I know I can rely on you to make him feel welcome; but it occurs to me that more is required to keep his mind off his own problems. If he could be constantly moving among an entirely new set of people — and we could organise some little excursions and parties for his benefit —"

"Excursions, parties! What can you be thinking of, Sidney? Here are Susan and I quite worn out with settling ourselves down in Sanditon! What can you mean us to do for your friend?"

"We could all take walks in pleasant groups, go for drives to local beauty spots," Sidney suggested with alacrity. "And I am not only referring to *us* but to the neighbouring families in general," throwing his arms wide to include the whole of Sanditon. "There are Mrs. Griffiths and her party you have been speaking of this evening. And I remember Tom saying on my last visit that the Denhams were a presentable young couple — and then there is that niece or cousin or whoever it is Lady Denham has with her —"

"Miss Brereton," supplied Mr. Parker. "She and Lady Denham are often with us as a matter of course in our comings and goings."

"Indeed she and Miss Heywood are to bathe together for the first time tomorrow," said Mrs. Parker. "But Lady Denham herself has become so very settled in her ways that I doubt she would welcome more contact with her neighbours. And my dear Sidney, beyond these daily meetings we have with our friends, what can you want us to be attempting?"

"A ball or a dance or something of that sort," Sidney told her promptly.

"A ball! A dance!"

"Well at least there are young ladies enough in Sanditon —"

"Impossible!" cried Mr. Parker, shrugging his despair at this suggestion. "Only last year we tried to arrange a few fortnightly assemblies during the season and the project was abandoned for want of support."

"But am I not now pointing out you will find more support this season?" Sidney persisted. A little discouragement to be overcome was apparently no evil to him. He rather derived spirits from it and, always confident of success, began demanding to know where last year's assemblies would have been held.

"To be sure there is a capital set of assembly rooms close by the hotel," Mr. Parker told him with some pride and more vexation. "I am telling you the only difficulty is that there is nobody to fill them. Be reasonable, Sidney. This is not Brighton, you know."

"Not Brighton perhaps. But what is that other resort you are forever mentioning? Bridley or Brincombe?"

"You mean Brinshore?"

"Brinshore. The very place. I am convinced they have more by way of entertainment in Brinshore. In fact, I would be extremely surprised to learn that Brinshore had no fortnightly assemblies."

Charlotte saw directly that Sidney Parker was now trying to assail his brother on his most vulnerable side. He probably knew nothing whatsoever about what went on in Brinshore but as a lever for persuasion he realised its value; and his perseverance in his own schemes, which had not been damped by any objections, redoubled as he saw the way he could achieve them. By skilfully throwing Brinshore into the discussion at the opportune moment, he had soon awakened eager speculation on what Sanditon could also offer its visitors in the matter of entertainment.

And Charlotte, watching and listening to all of this, decided Sidney's exertions on behalf of his friend were going to prove quite equal in scope to anything his sister Diana ever attempted.

CHAPTER 15

As IT HAPPENED, Charlotte was able to witness the arrival of Sidney Parker's friends in Sanditon the following morning. She and Clara Brereton had just left Trafalgar House for their descent to the sands when a very handsome barouche swept past the end of the driveway and continued at a smart pace downhill to the hotel. They were too far off to determine the occupants with any certainty. Charlotte, guessing whom the barouche might contain, thought she perceived two young men; but Miss Brereton, a more impartial observer, could distinguish nothing beyond a vague number of heads, two splendidly conspicuous black horses and a vast deal of shiny paintwork glittering in the sun.

"What people of fashion can these be? Does Mr. Parker know anything of them? I am sure Lady Denham has heard of no such party arriving!" were her first exclamations of surprise.

"In a small resort like Sanditon, I suppose someone usually hears something in advance?" said Charlotte, still straining her eyes and unwilling to be definite.

"Oh yes. People nearly always write ahead. Friends recommend the place after being here themselves, you know. A Mr. and Mrs. Marlowe — visitors last year — wrote only this week to Lady Denham mentioning a family they *believed* might be coming to Sanditon for the season. The daughter, poor thing, has been having severe attacks of the migraine and her parents hope sea air might relieve them a little. Could it be these Fletchers indeed arriving so soon?"

The barouche had now drawn up in the coach yard of the hotel and Charlotte tried to discern the occupants descending from it; she was sure there were only two but the strong sunlight was blurring rather than assisting her vision.

"Mr. Sidney Parker is also expecting some friends in Sanditon today."

"Well, whoever they may be, this is at least some news I can carry back to Lady Denham," said Miss Brereton with satisfaction. "She is always accusing me of being unobservant and incurious; and I must admit I am usually the last to learn of anything that happens in Sanditon."

This placid view of her own defects of temperament struck Charlotte as containing a good deal of truth. So far as her own observation went, Miss Brereton's disposition was indeed of a withdrawn, daydreaming and secretive nature. And as they walked on down the hill, she heightened this impression by falling into a sudden reverie. With a pensive and wholly preoccupied air, she ignored all Charlotte's further attempts at conversation and stared fixedly ahead at the distant inn yard and the bustle the arrival of the barouche was occasioning. That her thoughts were pleasant was evident from the slight smile flitting now and then across the beautiful face; but what they could be remained a mystery to Charlotte. Clara Brereton had clearly forgotten both her companion and their conversation and was indulging in some happy train of introspection as though she were quite alone.

Charlotte, who could never have allowed her own thoughts to absorb her to such an extent — to the almost complete exclusion of her surroundings — was more fascinated than ever as the conviction grew on her that the air of secrecy which clung about Miss Brereton was quite unstudied. Nothing seemed to be feigned. On the contrary, Miss Brereton appeared genuinely contrite, genuinely apologetic when at last roused from her fit of abstraction.

When Charlotte decided to end this interlude of silence, she judged it best to check their walk and stand still for a moment.

"I have now been in Sanditon long enough to realise what enthusiasm there is for new arrivals and their requirements," she remarked rather more loudly than necessary and stopping to confront Miss Brereton; but the blank expression on the face turned towards her was sufficient confirmation that Miss Brereton had heard not one word of this very prosaic sentence either. She tried afresh.

"Everyone takes such an interest in visitors here," she said with a smile. "They are all competing with each other to spread any news there is."

Miss Brereton at last seemed to recollect herself. Her recent admission that Lady Denham frequently scolded her for being inattentive, Charlotte now decided, was probably a very useful illustration of both their characters. Lady Denham, so sharp and practical herself, must often become rather irritated with her Miss Clara, while the latter would need to exercise considerable forbearance, patience and self-control to remain on comfortable terms with her; and Charlotte, observing the very real exertions her companion was making to suppress what remained of her own private musings, was much inclined to give Miss Brereton all the credit for the fact that they lived together in such continued harmony.

"Oh dear, yes — the Sanditon news." She sighed. "And I am facing the strongest competition of all. You must know, Miss Heywood, that the gardener from Sanditon House is a great collector of local news, both from the village and from the hill. He delivers our extra gardenstuff round Sanditon every day and brings back all the gossip in return; but perhaps this is one occasion where I can be ahead of Hodges. If you do not dislike it, when we have finished our bathe, I should like to call at the hotel and find out the particulars from Mrs. Woodcock."

Charlotte, positive she had just seen a figure in a blue coat, like Mr. Sidney Parker's, welcoming the newcomers into the hotel, was now convinced she could identify them.

"I have no objection but I am sure I can save you that trouble," she replied. "They *are* Mr. Parker's friends — a Mr. Reginald Catton and a Mr. Henry Brudenall."

"Reginald Catton — and Henry Brudenall," echoed Miss Brereton, as though dutifully memorising the names for later repetition to Lady Denham. "And — " she appeared uncertain what further particulars might be demanded from her — "and will they be staying here long?"

"Mr. Catton, I believe not. But Mr. Brudenall has come for his health and, I understand, will remain some weeks."

Unlike the Parkers, Miss Brereton showed no interest at all in Mr. Brudenall's health; and accepting this statement without query, seemed satisfied that the names alone — which she repeated to herself several times — were sufficient information to have collected ahead of Hodges.

Only too willing to avoid further discussion of the new arrivals, Charlotte led the way down to the Terrace; and after several minutes, deciding to take advantage of another long pause to drop the subject completely, she observed,

"What a beautiful day we have chosen for our bathe. I have not seen such a clear sky all summer." And she looked about her with pleasure at the blue sky, the green downs and the sparkling sea. "I am looking forward to it immensely — are you not too? But I still cannot quite imagine what it must feel like to be in the sea. Do you think the water will be very cold?"

Receiving no immediate answer, she glanced back at Miss Brereton and saw that her eyes were again roving eagerly on ahead with a look of animation — almost, Charlotte would have said, of anticipation. The unwelcome suspicion that she was already watching for Sir Edward could not fail to intrude, but

Charlotte tried to repress it and make herself believe that Miss Brereton was merely enjoying the prospect of their bathe and the beauty of the open scenery spread out before them under a bright midday sun. Headland after weathered headland could be seen stretching into the distance beyond the beach of polished pebbles edging a tidy blue sea. A few clouds hung on the horizon and a few gulls went wheeling and crying overhead, but otherwise the shore was deserted.

Charlotte determined to make no more efforts at conversation; and by the time they had passed the Terrace, leaving the more spectacular view from the hillside behind them, Miss Brereton had become quite talkative herself. Lady Denham had told her that Mrs. Gunn's was the bathing machine they must patronise; and afterwards they must certainly drink tea and eat bread and butter in the thatched tea rooms which Lady Denham and Mr. Parker had constructed just above the beach the season before.

"Mr. Parker also advised us to do that," said Charlotte.

"Oh yes, the seaside tea rooms are entirely his own idea. He never heard of the innovation from any other resort. And Lady Denham did not think them necessary at all. The building is very simple — there, you can see it now, just below us, at the top of the shingle — but Lady Denham finds it too large and elaborate. She would have preferred a more temporary structure and fears this will never show a return for the money invested."

"I have no doubt Mr. Parker considers permanent tea rooms part of the amenities of Sanditon, a convenience to bathers, which helps attract visitors. And the profit must be looked for in the rents they receive from their houses."

"Ah — you hear all Mr. Parker's views on his improvements — and I, Lady Denham's. It would be interesting for us to compare them sometimes because I am sure they do not always coincide," said Miss Brereton with a smile and a more open and encouraging manner than she had yet shown; and Charlotte, feeling their conversation was at last becoming natural, smiled back her agreement. For in spite of Miss Brereton's inconsistent behaviour and her own resolution of observing caution towards any friendship between them, she was still prepared to like and admire her so long as Sir Edward remained out of sight.

"Lady Denham tries to encourage everyone to use the tea rooms — the walkers as well as the bathers," continued Miss Brereton. "But as she has never found it very convenient to walk so far herself just to drink tea, I hardly think she will succeed in persuading anyone else."

Another of her friendly, half-rueful smiles made Charlotte like her even better; and though they were only discussing tea rooms, she could not regret that their acquaintance was already advancing some way towards intimacy.

They had now reached the edge of the shingle bank which shelved quite steeply towards the sea, bordered by a strip of sand. When the tide was out, this strip widened; and as it was now almost at low water, considerable spaces of fine hard sand were visible — particularly at the far end of the beach, near the rocks and bathing machines. They walked on towards them along the natural rampart of pebbles, which formed the upper part of the shore line, and were soon taken in charge by Mrs. Gunn, a large and somewhat intimidating personage.

She directed the young ladies into her bathing machine, had the horse put to while they changed into bathing garments, and guided it out into deep water. She then let down the green hood at the front of the caravan, hooked a ladder into position and supervised their descent into the water, issuing very sensible directions and maintaining such a constant flow of talk that any apprehensions they may have felt were very soon dispelled.

It was all so novel and interesting to Charlotte that she could not have said which sensation impressed her most: the heat inside the bathing machine as the sun beat down on its roof, the sudden tingling cold of the sea water, or the rather terrifying surge and movement as it lapped past her. The brilliant shimmer of the sun on the sea was at first so dazzling, and her eyes so full of this reflected light, that for several moments she could see nothing. She was not even very sure she was enjoying herself. But when she grew more accustomed and could distinguish all the separate features, had time to look around her — at the sunlight sparkling on the water, at the ripples and shadows as the sea responded to every change in that sunlight, and at the gulls, flying to and fro, now vanishing into the white of the waves, now standing out in contrast to sea and sky — she suddenly found herself smiling at she knew not what: the smell of the salt air, the soft freshness of the fine southerly breeze, the rhythmic flow of the water, the pure joy of the day.

"Walk a little and move around constantly," advised Mrs. Gunn sternly. "But do not go pivotting and prancing about like that. The practise of some females in jigging and jumping up and down in the water has no value whatsoever, medicinal or artistic."

Charlotte, who had been doing a little gentle jumping herself, looked round enquiringly, unable to understand why such a dictum should be either issued or obeyed; and discovered to her surprise that Miss Brereton with far more liveliness had been splashing and leaping, her face quite radiant with pleasure in discovering so delightful a sensation. They smiled at each other with such a lack of constraint, such happy, open enjoyment in sharing that shining sea that Charlotte felt sure Miss Brereton could only be a normal girl like herself — more beautiful and bewitching perhaps, but essentially simple and unaffected — and certainly not the deceitful conspirator she had sometimes been imagining.

All too soon, Mrs. Gunn was ordering them back into the machine; and although they begged to stay longer in the sea, she insisted that fifteen minutes was more than enough for the first time and would hear of no extension.

The two girls, having stood on Mrs. Gunn's footwarmers, been vigorously towelled to restore their circulation and ordered to change their dress quickly to avoid chills, were then advised by Mrs. Gunn to take gentle exercise and the prescribed cup of tea which all Sanditon seemed determined to recommend to everyone else.

Still in perfect charity with each other, the young ladies did all these things, discussing only the pleasure they had felt in their bathe and seeming to forget everything that did not increase this new bond between them. Charlotte, in fact, was beginning to hope they could often share such innocent morning expeditions when, suddenly looking up towards the Terrace, she saw Sir Edward Denham walking purposefully in their direction.

"Here comes Sir Edward," she said with cold vexation. "I had no notion he intended to walk this way today. However there is no need for *that* to delay *us*."

"No, no, of course not," cried Miss Brereton, but she flushed nevertheless. "I suppose — I suppose some business or other brings him here. No doubt he will soon tell us what it is."

"It can be no concern of mine," said Charlotte with indifference. "Unless he wishes to accompany us the short distance to Trafalgar House. Mrs. Parker is hoping you will give us the rest of your morning. And I am quite ready to walk back there now if you are agreeable."

"Yes — no. That is — were we not going to call in to see Mrs. Woodcock at the hotel?"

"But surely you decided that was unnecessary?" said Charlotte with surprise. "I hardly thought — "

"Oh well — perhaps we had best see what Sir Edward suggests," said Miss Brereton, looking even more embarrassed. "Possibly he has — he may — " She stopped in some confusion and Charlotte could only stare at her incredulously, feeling she was confronted by some mysterious heroine, whose actions were unpredictable, and not the companionable friend she had been learning to like for the last hour. Clara Brereton must be as capable as she was of forming a just opinion of Sir Edward; and judging from her own reactions, Charlotte imagined such attentions as his would rather irritate than gratify; and yet here was Miss Brereton willing to wait about and encourage them.

They said no more on the subject and an uneasy silence replaced their former friendly chatter; for Charlotte, not even troubling to hide her annoyance, was determined to be as unhelpful and mute as possible within the bounds of common politeness; and Miss Brereton, glancing anxiously towards the Terrace, seemed divided between making apologies over this delay and trying to discover if the meeting were being observed by any but the three it involved. Sir Edward alone appeared in full command of his usual loquacity.

"How fortunate I am in finding both fair charmers of Sanditon still by the sea shore, just as in my most sanguine expectations," he began with one of his flourishing bows. "It were fallacious of me to pretend I am not come by design for I am presuming to hope I may accompany you on your necessary exercise."

"I am afraid you have come too late, Sir Edward," Charlotte said firmly. "We have walked enough already and were on the point of returning home."

"Ah, but you have underestimated the amount of exercise one must take after saline immersion," cried Sir Edward. "And naturally, one cannot walk forever along the beach. But I hope I can persuade you to perambulate as far as my precious little cottage orné, which is now so nearly finished that I prognosticate prevenient tenants. Your comments will be of such ineffable use. The cottage needs a woman's discrimination to tell me what is now lacking there."

For Charlotte the prospect was one of unrelieved boredom in listening to Sir Edward. And although she suspected Miss

Brereton was very eager to go — nay, had even planned this meeting with Sir Edward so she could see over his building venture without any impropriety — she had no inclination to accompany them.

"Your sister's comments must surely be of greater value than ours? She has had far more practice in running a house," she pointed out. "And if you want outside opinions, Miss Diana Parker would be the very person to advise you. Some day you must arrange a little viewing party to see over your cottage, Sir Edward. This morning, I am afraid, Mrs. Parker is already expecting us back at Trafalgar House."

"But the cottage is no more than a step down the length of the beach — nestling into that craggy cliff you see jutting out by the river. The delay will be a mere nothing. Come now, you cannot refuse."

"I would not be so *very* disinclined — " began Miss Brereton.

"But I am already beginning to feel unreasonably tired," said Charlotte quite untruthfully and in no very cordial tones. "I have now just strength enough left to climb our hill."

But Sir Edward was not to be deflected as easily as this. He continued to urge and to persist, with sentences almost too elaborate for his powers, till Charlotte began to be both angry and resentful at so selfish a perseverance in waving aside all her objections.

"Depend upon it, Mrs. Parker cannot miss you for half an hour, even an hour. And your present fatigue is not to be regarded, merely unfamiliar sensations in exchanging one element for another — but all exactly suited to produce only the most healthful stimulation of mind and body."

Charlotte looked towards Miss Brereton and realised she would receive no support from that averted face and guarded silence; and, as always, she was unable to decide the exact state of their owner's feelings towards Sir Edward. The calm reserve of manner showed none of Charlotte's own distaste but no positive admiration either. Perhaps she considered his title, his handsome good looks and their combined prospects as Lady Denham's favourites and possible heirs would outweigh all his defects and make him an acceptable suiter? Whether Miss Brereton could sacrifice every better feeling to worldly advantage, Charlotte was hardly in a position to decide. She would not have believed it possible of the joyful young woman who had been dancing among the waves an hour since, but the circumspect stranger who had now replaced her might indeed be capable of it.

There was obviously great caution and great resolution in Miss Brereton somewhere, for while she avoided meeting Charlotte's eye and appeared insensible to her wishes, she gave no marked encouragement to Sir Edward's proposals either: it was all prudence, reticence and indecision.

This inconclusive style of conduct was not at all to Charlotte's liking and made her more determined than ever to escape the role of chaperone being forced upon her. If Miss Brereton wished to inspect Sir Edward's cottage, she would have to make some other opportunity; she herself had reached the conclusion that her own best course of action was to face their joint displeasure by flatly announcing her intention of returning forthwith to Trafalgar House.

She was on the point of carrying out this decision when, chancing to look towards the hotel, she perceived Sidney Parker and one of his friends to be crossing the threshold. She was certain they had seen the group by the shore; they seemed to be hesitating, to be conferring, and then to be moving towards them; and on a sudden impulse, deciding such an addition to their party might help her to separate Sir Edward and Miss Brereton, she abruptly changed her mind.

"Very well then, I agree to come," she said. "But first of all here is a pebble lodged in my shoe which must be removed before we set out. It is quite impossible for me to walk on it."

And so saying, she sat down on a ridge of shingle and proceeded to spend as much time as she could locating and removing this irritating, non-existent pebble.

CHAPTER 16

SIDNEY PARKER'S COMPANION must be Mr. Reginald Catton, Charlotte decided, though for no better reason than that he would seem the less likely of the two expected friends to sit gloomily indoors on a pleasant sunny day. She watched them approach, trying to determine when a meeting between the two groups would become inevitable, and finally rejoined Sir Edward and Miss Brereton only in time to say,

"Here are Mr. Sidney Parker and one of his friends walking towards us. I do not think you are yet acquainted?" and then turned her back on any attempt Sir Edward could have made to hurry them away at the last moment.

The stranger was undoubtedly the taller and more handsome of the two advancing but it was Sidney Parker's alertness of manner which claimed the greater share of Charlotte's attention; and when, while still beyond hailing distance, he waved to her gaily with a pleased air of encounter, she felt she had neither seen him the night before nor thought of him since with an admiration he did not merit. By contrast, his friend's less vital appearance made very little impression till Sidney surprised her by introducing him as Mr. Brudenall — Reginald Catton being so little inclined to sit indoors and so much more active and high-spirited that he had already set off for Brighton to keep a pressing evening engagement.

Henry Brudenall then appeared just as he ought: as romantic, as sombre and as sensitive as she could have imagined. But she scarcely had time to adjust her ideas and begin to appreciate this interesting melancholy she had expected in Mr. Brudenall before the opportunity was lost in the universal smiling and polite introductions of a party merging together; and she could only note he had an unassuming and slightly diffident manner but seemed very willing to make all the acquaintance and fall in with every plan his more forceful friend had in mind for them.

"As you see, we are taking the earliest opportunity to benefit from your famous sea breezes," said Sidney Parker, addressing Sir Edward with easy civility. "And where would you suggest we now walk to enjoy them?"

Sir Edward immediately waved his hand towards the cliffs above the cove which sheltered the bathing machines.

"That is undoubtedly the most favoured walk for all new-comers to Sanditon, sir. The prospect from the headland is certainly the most highly favoured situation for observing the beauty and diversity of the surrounding scenery and the limitless expanses of the ocean in all its sublimity."

"Well, that is quite a long climb to those cliffs, Miss Heywood," said Sidney, smiling and offering his arm to Charlotte. "Perhaps you and Miss Brereton will be glad of more assistance."

"No, no, you have quite mistaken me, sir," cried Sir Edward, slightly disconcerted by this very natural misunderstanding. "My companions and I are, in fact, taking the opposite direction. As you will observe, the colour is already distinctly wrought upon their cheeks and speaks eloquently of their fatigue, as those im-mortal lines of Cowper bring so vividly before us — "

"Perhaps you mean Donne?" suggested Sidney, one of his mobile eyebrows seeming to rise up of its own accord. "Though I am not sure he was referring to fatigue —

> *Her pure and eloquent blood*
> *Spake in her cheeks and so distinctly wrought*
> *That one might almost say her body thought.*"

115

"Exactly, sir. They have already been indulging in a contest with the sea's stimulating effects this morning and would by no means be equal to such energetic exercise as I have been recommending to you. We intend to make only a gentle promenade along the shore where I will show my fair companions over a small project of mine, a simple cottage orné. Our little excursion would only bore yourself and Mr. Brudenall."

Here Charlotte, seeing a convenient opening, interrupted with the suggestion which, however unwelcome to Sir Edward, might prove acceptable to Sidney Parker. A solitary climb along the cliffs was not, after all, the most ideal way of introducing his dispirited friend to Sanditon.

"Indeed, Sir Edward, it might be very useful for you to hear their opinions on your cottage as well as ours," she said eagerly. "And I am sure Mr. Parker must know a great deal about architecture."

"Miss Heywood does me too much honour," was Sidney's answer, with a bow of mock gravity. "However, we shall certainly be delighted to accompany you."

This prompt acceptance of an invitation he had never issued took Sir Edward completely unawares; but as Sidney Parker and Henry Brudenall both immediately turned in the direction he had been indicating as their proposed route, and Charlotte and Miss Brereton fell into step beside them, there was very little he could do beyond looking extremely annoyed and turning to follow them.

Somewhat surprised by the ease she had encountered in manipulating the company, Charlotte was even more pleased by the grouping which developed quite naturally in its passage along the beach. Sidney Parker devoted his attention exclusively to Sir Edward, pausing so frequently to comment on the new buildings and admire the surrounding scenery that their progress was necessarily slowed down a good deal; while Mr. Brudenall belied his languid appearance by proving a fast walker and marched silently on ahead with Miss Brereton, who, as his companion at the outset, had little alternative but to be separated from the others by an ever-widening gap. Every now and then, when Sir Edward looked towards these retreating figures, his good manners underwent a severe test and he tried to increase their own speed. But Sidney Parker soon slowed them down again.

"You must tell me more of your cottage orné, Sir Edward," he said encouragingly. "I am not well acquainted with the style but have heard it spoken of as a most original one."

And as Sir Edward was a boundless talker, by the time they were half way along the beach, he was expounding on gables and barge-boarding, fancy leading, curved canopies and wrought-iron balustrades; and when they arrived at the far end, where Miss Brereton and Mr. Brudenall stood composedly waiting for them, he had become so engrossed in his subject that he almost ignored them.

"You will see, you will see," he cried, rushing on ahead. "My cottage is tucked away just beyond the stream there — over that arborescent cliff. I will proceed directly in advance to effect ingress. You cannot fail to behold it when you attain the crest — *and having climbed the steep-up heavenly hill* — as the poet says — "

Sir Edward went bounding across the shingle and vanished up a steep path overhung with bushes and creepers.

"Shakespeare, I imagine," said Sidney Parker. "But is our friend ever precise in these matters? I never in my life came across a man so intent on using nonsensical words and inappropriate quotations. Does he always talk like that?"

Although she agreed with this swift verdict on Sir Edward, Charlotte was mainly struck by the rashness with which it had been uttered. Mr. Sidney Parker was a young man who carried frankness a great deal too far, in her opinion; and she looked quickly towards Miss Brereton to discover if this latest piece of indiscretion had been overheard. Fortunately, both she and Mr. Brudenall, though only a few yards distant, were engaged in quiet conversation themselves; and their attention being directed at that very moment to the course of the stream, they moved off to examine it more closely from the bank.

"Sir Edward has not perhaps a very strong understanding," she replied, lowering her voice with a significant glance after them. "But he is generally considered a very fine young man among his acquaintance in Sanditon."

"Oh? A suitor of Miss Brereton's, is he?" demanded Sidney, with an instant display of interest. "But surely she does not return his regard? Let us find a nice place to sit down here in the sun and discuss all these curious particulars."

There was no denying he had penetration; but he was so quick to pursue the slightest hint that Charlotte felt she might very soon find her tongue outrunning wisdom.

"Had we not best be starting after Sir Edward? I am sure he is expecting us to follow him immediately."

"I am sure he is too, but I feel Sir Edward's company is best partaken of sparingly, in small doses — say at half-hour intervals." He inspected an overturned fishing boat, carefully tested the dried paint and moved along to allow her the most comfortable position by the prow. "No rust, no dirt, quite dry, I assure you," he said, patting the white boards invitingly; and with a mixture of gaiety and authority peculiar to himself he persuaded Charlotte to join him, settled her to his own satisfaction and leaned against the side of the boat as though prepared for a long and confidential exchange.

"Well, where shall we begin? With Sir Edward? Now, Miss Heywood, does not your own observation of his character make you sometimes doubt whether he merits all this universal approbation?"

"On such a brief acquaintance as I have had, it would be

difficult to judge his character at all," replied Charlotte cautiously. "Manners are all that can safely be decided and Sir Edward's are generally accounted to be pleasing — "

"So are Miss Heywood's," agreed Sidney, shaking his head at her in disappointment. "Very pleasing indeed. I can see she is quite determined to make no adverse comment whatsoever on anyone in Sanditon. Tell me, do you never relax from this very correct behaviour?"

"I do not pretend people in general are without imperfections," Charlotte said stiffly. "All I am saying is that goodness and foolishness are so often combined to such an extent that it is sometimes impossible to separate them on a short acquaintance."

"Then you have perceived goodness as well as foolishness in Sir Edward?"

"I was speaking of people in general."

"Surely you have realised by now, Miss Heywood, that is a thing I never do if I can avoid it?" he reproved her. "People vary so much that I find it both dull and pointless to discuss them except as individuals. So having now assumed — from your scrupulous reluctance to discuss them — that your views on Sir Edward are the same as mine, let us pass on to Miss Brereton who, I must confess, interests me a great deal more." And he paused expectantly.

"I am not very well acquainted with Miss Brereton either." The reply seemed inadequate even to her; and not wishing to be considered similarly ungenerous with her praise in this direction, she added quickly, "She is certainly a most elegant young woman — and very beautiful — "

"Which I have, of course, seen for myself with no trouble at all," said Sidney with a smile. "But what I should like to know is why you think the lovely Miss Brereton should be unwise enough to encourage the foolish Sir Edward?"

This particular question had privately puzzled Charlotte the first time she had observed Sir Edward and Miss Brereton together. She already found it natural for Sidney Parker to be asking it publicly on his first meeting with them; but doubting her right to betray the vague and accumulated suspicions she had formed on each subsequent encounter with them — indeed discovering she was quite unable to sum them up to herself now with any coherence — she said only, and with perfect honesty,

"I am afraid I do not at all know the answer to that."

"But all the same you disapprove of such an attachment and disliked being forced into chaperoning them while they inspected Sir Edward's cottage?"

His astuteness was beginning to alarm Charlotte; and having at last succeeded in shaking her composure, he laughed triumphantly at the apprehensive look which confirmed this deduction of his.

"Come now, it was not so difficult to guess, after all. Sir Edward's obvious displeasure was in far too great a contrast to *your* pressing invitation to join the party."

"I did not have to press very hard," she said, defending herself with some resentment. "And you might also give me a little credit for considering yourself and Mr. Brudenall. You *said* you wanted him to be constantly mixing with new people."

"Oh yes. I was indeed grateful for your invitation," Sidney admitted handsomely. "I am quite as anxious to escape playing nursemaid to Henry as you could be over playing chaperone to Miss Brereton." And he looked across to where his friend stood in rather poetic fashion, frowning down at the waters of the stream. "Poor old Henry has never been very articulate — a romantic rather than a practical fellow, I am afraid; but according to Reginald the journey down from London was one long moody silence — glaring abstractedly at nothing, never hearing a question, thoroughly dismal the whole way. Reginald freely confessed to me another hour of it would have been more than he could himself endure; so he took refuge in Brighton as fast as he could. Well, I hope I may prove a stouter friend to the afflicted; but I have every intention of accepting any outside help I am offered."

"You may find outsiders can help him most," said Charlotte, observing that Mr. Brudenall was now listening with a show of attention to something Miss Brereton had said. "With his friends he might be excused occasional moods of depression; with strangers, he must make more effort to appear normal."

"Particularly with beautiful young women," agreed Sidney, watching Miss Brereton with approval himself. "I have been thinking much the same thing. Henry *is* a great favourite among your sex — always full of sentiment but never expressing any of it very clearly. Women seem to enjoy exerting themselves trying to understand that sort of vagueness; and Henry is usually grateful enough to be agreeable to them in return. I have not the slightest doubt he and Miss Brereton are very well pleased with each other — if they were not, they could easily have joined us long ago." He gave Charlotte a sideways glance. "However, perhaps you yourself would like to accept the role I am allotting to Miss Brereton?"

But this Charlotte firmly declined. She suspected that Sidney would not be averse to exchanging her company for Miss Brereton's, but preferred to avoid the exertion of consoling Mr. Brudenall by herself.

"I see no reason to allot such a role to anybody in particular. Surely your purposes will be just as well served if you contrive to make him one of a sociable group? Why should anyone be expected to deal with him single-handed?"

She had the greatest compassion for Mr. Brudenall but no wish to be responsible for his problems; and before Sidney Parker could involve her in them further, she moved away from the boat and again suggested they should all follow Sir Edward together.

However, instead of complying, he began to look about him

— at the other boats drawn up on the shore, the fishermen's cottages nearby with their nets spread out in the sun to dry, and the stream, which at this point appeared to come to an end at a high ridge of pebbles and to have no visible communication with the sea. In no haste at all to move their party on, Sidney tried to decide how the stream found its way underground between the stones; and after examining and exclaiming over this natural phenomenon, he appealed to Miss Brereton for enlightenment.

"It is called a chesil. I have just been explaining to Mr. Brudenall what I can understand of it myself," she said gravely.

"Yes, we have been deeply engaged in trying to solve that riddle," Mr. Brudenall agreed. "and have only concluded it must be a poor stream to creep between pebbles instead of driving them left and right in front of it."

"Have you indeed? Yes, a very poor stream, I grant you," Sidney decided after contemplating it himself quite earnestly for some time. "A really robust one would be bound to open up a good straight passage for itself. You think so, I am sure, Miss Brereton?"

Charlotte, who was not very interested in the stream, wandered out on to the pebble ridge without seeing anything remarkable in that either. The other three, remaining where she had left them, continued to stare down at the water and its shallow ripples among the shingle.

"The season of the year may have something to do with it," Miss Brereton said, after rather a long pause. "I believe in *some* months the stream can be more direct — or at any rate less encumbered." She hesitated again. "In winter for instance."

Surprised that she had taken so long in making so commonplace a reply, Charlotte glanced back at them to see a self-conscious look and a slight blush on Miss Brereton's face; and Sidney Parker regarding her with a degree of interest which probably accounted for it. There was no reason why he should not look so intently at Miss Brereton, Charlotte told herself sensibly. He had already owned that he thought her a very beautiful girl and the slight air of mystery and reserve added to her attractions. But nevertheless Charlotte sighed over her own fate in being always outshone in such company. Such desultory comments from *her* on a meandering stream could never have held two young men waiting so attentively for her to think them out.

"Ah, but these encumbrances do not appear so very great to me," cried Sidney, throwing a few more pebbles into the water. "Little stones like these can surely be ignored."

"There are rather more of them than you think," Mr. Brudenall said gloomily. And Charlotte's attention being immediately directed to him, she could not but pity the oppression of spirits she imagined he must constantly be struggling to overcome.

"Nature often takes a very long time to work decisive changes," she said reflectively. "Haste is too much to expect from it on these occasions."

Fortunately, Sidney Parker at last withdrew his fascinated gaze from Miss Brereton, caught sight of his friend and immediately began talking in a more animated style. The words had little importance in themselves but the tone was bracing and optimistic. Winter, he observed, was a long time ahead and they could hardly stand watching the stream till then; nor was there much point in discussing it if they could come to no better conclusions than that.

While honouring Sidney's real good nature in assisting his friend at this delicate time, Charlotte did not envy him his task; and she was thankful to observe that his chatter and determination to encourage his friend produced a gradual change on the present occasion.

Sir Edward now reappeared at the top of the hill, signalling to them impatiently; and they dutifully climbed up to him, skirted a group of trees and found themselves confronted by a small house of decided oddity, a cottage in size but a mansion in details. It had pointed Gothic windows, a double coach-house, wrought-iron verandah posts, lacy barge-boards of complex design and, to cap all this, a heavy and ornamental thatch. The result was a play-house, a pretence house, in which prospective tenants might perhaps believe themselves country people living in a kind of Arcadia.

Mr. Brudenall, Miss Brereton and Charlotte, having regarded it with awed astonishment, seemed equally doubtful what they could say about it; but Sidney Parker was more certain of his ground, both in praising the house and pleasing its owner.

"Perfect. Quite perfect of its genre," he said, standing well back in the minute carriage drive and running his eye over the proliferating detail. "You have achieved the perfect illusion of rustic simplicity — for I take it the effect you are actually aiming at is far from rustic and anything but simple?"

"Exactly, sir. You have it precisely," cried Sir Edward, highly delighted. "My aim throughout has been to radiate rurality. There are many who think they wish to escape from stilted and stately mansions to the homeliness of low ceilings and the intimacy of hole-and-corner rooms; but those who seek rustic peace do not always comprehend the drawbacks which appertain to the normal, genuine country cottage. Now in *my* cottage, they can be snug without such irritations. It also epitomises a certain seaside theme, do you not agree?"

Sidney Parker said that he did. And by agreeing a great many more times and interposing a flattering observation whenever Sir Edward paused and seemed to expect one, he managed to pilot them through a complete inspection of the house without anyone else being put to the inconvenience of making an untoward remark.

Miss Brereton and Mr. Brudenall seemed content to wander from room to room without taking part in the discussion at all.

And Charlotte, very relieved to be able to follow their example, wondered if they were as ignorant as she was over Sir Edward's actual aim — till it began to dawn on her that not even Sidney Parker had the remotest idea of there being any consistent overall plan in the building of this house.

Attending most carefully to their discussion herself, and hearing the solemn absurd nonsense Sir Edward talked as he tried to justify each separate feature, she began to suspect that his mind, when designing his cottage, was as muddled as it appeared to be on most other subjects; and Sidney, nimbly seizing the advantage and adopting the same principle, was merely replying with a similar amount of nonsense. After an hour, however, he felt he had earned another rest; and although Sir Edward, after locking up his cottage, was quite ready to go on discussing it, Sidney had no intention of humouring him further.

They chose a different route back down the hill, leaving the sea behind them and reaching the stream, where a stone bridge spanned it, taking the main road across to the toll-gate.

"A turret now — did you ever consider adding that?" Sidney was idly suggesting when he suddenly recognised their exact position. "Ah," he said, brightening considerably. "I seem to remember Denham Park lies a short distance along this turnpike road, does it not? Well, much as I am enjoying our discussion, I shall not press you to be continuing out of your way, Sir Edward. No, no, not at all," with his most civil bow, "how much time you have already given up to us today! We would not consider such a sacrifice for one minute. Miss Brereton and Miss Heywood are tired out by now, I dare say, and we will see them back to Trafalgar House. Directly on our own route. Not the slightest trouble, I assure you."

And despite all protests, he firmly directed the party across the bridge, leaving a disconsolate Sir Edward standing by the toll-gate, vaguely aware that he had just encountered someone a great deal more expert in getting his own way than he was himself. He frowned; and watching Miss Brereton being led away from him, tried to decide how much interference in his own plans he could expect from this new rival.

CHAPTER 17

THOUGH VERY WILLING to assume guidance over their party, Sidney Parker showed no inclination at all to conduct it back to Trafalgar House directly. Once clear of the bridge, he began inspecting paths branching off the main road; and finally selecting one to the right, he struck off across a broad meadow with the considerate remark that it should be dry enough for ladies underfoot but without consulting them whether it was in the direction they wished to go.

"Should we not perhaps have turned left towards the sea?" suggested Charlotte, when they were half-way across the expanse of grass without anyone else having raised an objection. "Or even continued along the road? I am almost certain this path must lead inland to old Sanditon."

"I dare say it does," agreed Sidney. "Had you any other object in mind for our walk?"

"None. I only thought we had already had our walk."

"Ambling along a beach and standing about in a cottage?" protested Sidney. "Unless you and Miss Brereton are worn out by such dawdling, I propose we now take some exercise."

"It must be two o'clock at least," she said doubtfully, looking towards Miss Brereton for support.

"Well, it certainly could not be three," Sidney argued, "so we have a clear two hours in hand for exploring old Sanditon."

"Two hours!" Charlotte had condemned Sir Edward's persistence in suggesting an expedition that required only one, and

127

she was certain Miss Brereton must feel all the inconsistency over such a change of plan. But Miss Brereton was as reticent and circumspect now as she had been then and gave Charlotte no indication of her real opinion; it was Mr. Brudenall who finally decided the matter, by coughing and saying,

"I own I should very much like to examine a real seaside village before it is changed and developed to fit in with the fashionable new pattern."

For Sidney, this was encouragement enough. His friend's wishes must be paramount; and taking it for granted that the rest of the opposition was negligible, he walked on down the path.

"Oh, you will find old Sanditon looks permanent enough," he said, talking as he went. "Much too neat a little place to leave room for improvements — what do you think, Miss Brereton? A cosy little village; there is something so cheerful about its air — do you not agree?" turning towards her and smiling slightly. "And I am persuaded you must wish to take advantage of this spell of fine weather. Are *you* not in favour of remaining out of doors as long as possible?"

They reached the edge of the meadow as he addressed these questions to her and it was natural they should enter the woodland on the other side of it together. The path here was not wide enough to admit a party of four walking abreast, and Charlotte, finding she had been relegated to the rear with Henry Brudenall, tried to decide the exact point when this grouping had become inevitable and whether Sidney had effected it on purpose. She had more than a suspicion that he was eager to seize an opportunity of becoming better acquainted with the beautiful Clara. He walked briskly on ahead, talking without pause as though making a special effort to be agreeable to his companion. Henry Brudenall, on the other hand, made no effort at all. He strode along moodily switching at bushes with a stick he had picked up, looking so abstracted that Charlotte readily forgave his incivility and merely pitied his affliction.

Twice he ignored remarks she made: the restful shade of summer trees and the pleasure of bird-song, both absent from the previous walk along the sands, were perhaps trite to comment on in themselves but reasonable enough, Charlotte felt, to show her own willingness for conversation.

And once, on the only marshy patch of the entire woodland path, he trampled through so heedlessly that the hem of her gown was liberally splattered with mud. If Mr. Brudenall was so preoccupied with his own problems that he failed to notice even this discourtesy, Charlotte decided she could be forgiven for lapsing into silence. And having stopped wondering how to embark on any sort of conversation with him herself, she could only marvel that Miss Brereton had managed it for over an hour without apparent strain. Beyond glancing at him nervously whenever the pathway produced any sort of obstacle, she disregarded him completely and allowed him to enjoy his misery in peace.

Exercise had been Sidney's avowed excuse for making this detour and he was setting a quick pace on ahead. Charlotte and her partner were also walking quite fast, though never sufficiently in reach of the others to overhear their conversation. They kept them well in sight, however; and with very little else to divert her, Charlotte found herself observing them both very intently and becoming extremely curious over what they were discussing so earnestly. That Clara herself should be grave and serious did not surprise her in the least; that she appeared to be doing most of the talking surprised her a good deal; but that Sidney's profile, so repeatedly turned towards his companion, should be equally solemn and unsmiling was the most difficult to explain of all. *Her* summing up of his character had been that he would usually contrive to keep his daily communication with people on a fairly light-hearted level.

The other definite characteristic she had associated with him — his easy manners — were altogether so much a part of him, she noted, that they showed no variation in this change of mood.

As she watched him holding back overhanging branches from Miss Brereton's path, now and then bending attentively towards her to catch something else she had said, she could not help feeling a small pang of something which could only be described as jealousy.

This was not an emotion Charlotte normally experienced; and she tried to occupy her mind in yet another direction by reasoning herself into a proper understanding of so extraordinary a symptom: Clara's beauty she had always acknowledged, and with the warmest admiration untinged by any suspicion of envy. Sidney Parker was a worthy admirer for such a perfect heroine, so the spectacle of them enjoying an earnest tête-a-tête should have been particularly satisfying to any unprejudiced observer.

Arriving at this very logical conclusion, Charlotte was then forced to admit, in common honesty, that she was at present far from an unprejudiced observer. She was both a reluctant and a resentful one. Any prospect of her own pleasure in this walk now seemed most unlikely; and she would gladly have exchanged a silent Henry Brudenall for an articulate Sidney Parker. But that surely was no foundation for jealousy? Dissatisfaction yes, assuredly. She felt justified in a feeling of general ill-usage; and she was still busily reasoning away the more disturbing emotion of jealousy into the purely transient sensations of dissatisfaction and disappointment, when they emerged from the wood.

Sidney appeared quite willing to keep their party intact for the moment and his own flow of spirits and ready chat were sufficient to lend conviviality to the entire group. Charlotte was thoughtful, and neither of the others replied to him with any marked enthusiasm, but he addressed his remarks impartially to all with a persistent good humour which she could not but admire.

"Now is this your idea of a genuine seaside village, Henry?" he asked as they reached the outskirts and stepped from worn track on to cobbles. "Here is old Sanditon proving a point I have often made to my brother. Here the sea is not only invisible — even its sound and smell are shut off in all but the worst of weathers. Sea views, I maintain, are only for urban folk who never experience its menace. The true sailor prefers to be land-locked rather than face the ocean."

"I would certainly agree with that," replied Mr. Brudenall. "The sea is an old enemy of his. Why should he wish to gaze on it? I can also understand that he would prefer to build his house like a ship. All of these," waving his hand along the street, "look as snug and cramped and battened down as any brigantine."

Charlotte had never heard him speak so normally before. She had begun to think he was incapable of talking pleasantly, of taking any interest in his surroundings and making sensible, dispassionate comments on them. She stared at him. But neither Sidney nor Miss Brereton seemed to find this present reasonable conduct any odder than his previous dejection.

"Yes, one can feel this is a village which has grown naturally over the centuries; that this has always been peopled by real sea-farers," said Miss Brereton, continuing the conversation without apparent effort.

They wandered on through the streets of the old village, narrow and winding against wind and storm, with their thick-walled haphazardly built cottages in complete antithesis to Mr. Parker's modern rules of design, deportment and situation. Even such inland farming towns as Charlotte knew were dependent on busy market days and could never have afforded to cramp themselves in the confined space of old Sanditon. She also noticed the houses boasted tidy shrubs in iron-bound barrels instead of gardens, brass ships' bells instead of door-knockers, more weather vanes on their rooves and more shutters at their windows than the usual village.

To Charlotte's surprise, Sidney fell into step beside her as they walked on down the street and persisted in addressing himself so pointedly in her direction as to make her suspect he was now intent on retaining *her* as his companion. She could hardly understand this conduct and warily eluded several attempts to detach her from the others.

On leaving the village behind, however, they faced quite a steep walk up the hill before crossing the down towards the new buildings; and though they were following the main road again and there was not the slightest need for any division into walking pairs, Sidney had soon effected it again. But this time Charlotte decided to let him know she realised what he was about; and when they reached the first outcrop of rocks on their ascent, she remarked drily,

"Surely we can now dispense with all these pauses to admire the scenery, the birds and the smoke curling up from chimneys? I cannot think we are any longer in danger of catching them up."

"Quite true," agreed Sidney, as ready to laugh at himself as at others. "I had just thought out a masterly halt to enjoy this fresh southerly breeze and the approaching tang of salt air now coming to us from over the hill. I believe I have neglected the wind so far, have I not? But I am willing to renounce it if you prefer to get on faster."

Rather disconcerted by this brazen admission, Charlotte said flatly, "Thank you, I do prefer it," and stalked on up the hill.

"How humiliating to discover my stage directions are not being appreciated," he said, keeping pace with her. "You could at least have pretended you were pleased by my singling you out to walk with. It is more natural for a young lady to be flattered into overlooking the actual steps by which such matters are arranged."

"But I see no necessity for arranging anything at all," replied Charlotte. "Mr. Brudenall is much less abstracted and more polite when we are all together in the same group. He is then forced to pay some slight attention to the general conversation instead of tramping about lunging at nettle heads with a stick."

Sidney was much amused by this character sketch of his friend.

"Did you find him so impossible on your walk through the woods?"

"I made no headway at all," she admitted. "I suppose there must be some way of communicating with him if one perseveres long enough," she added charitably, "but he never replied to any of *my* remarks."

He laughed outright at this.

"Is he also responsible for all that mud on your gown?"

"Oh, quite unintentionally, I am sure," said Charlotte, glancing down at her ruined hem. "They *are* most remarkable splashes, I agree. Too large, you would think, for anyone to ignore; but Mr. Brudenall never even noticed them."

"Oh dear. I hope they will wash out?"

"Of course they will wash out," she said with some asperity. "My gown is perfectly ordinary cambric."

"I am very relieved to hear it. But I was *almost* confident it must be so. I was sure you would never commit the folly of wearing impractical clothes. Fragile materials — such as taffeta — should be kept strictly for the evening, do you not agree? But some muslins are not very sensible for walking either — inclined as they are to snag and fray."

Charlotte had no intention of discussing the various merits of female clothing with Sidney; but she was beginning to realise he was capable of evading any issue unless confronted with it quite bluntly. She returned a few commonplace replies, waiting till he had exhausted his own knowledge of the subject, and then took advantage of the first pause to say resolutely,

"If you have no objection, I should now like to hear your reasons for dividing up our party so often. Why do you feel it is necessary to direct everyone about in this way?"

"Why do *you* feel it is necessary to study them?" said Sidney, smiling. "I suppose we each of us have our own methods of dealing with others — and our own special talents to exercise while enjoying their company. I direct. You observe. I have a certain sympathy with your point of view, you see. In its way, close observation of one's fellow men must be a most rewarding pastime — provided one fully understands everything one observes. So, if you tell me what you noticed during the course of our walk today, I will endeavour to explain my reasons for directing it along certain lines. Come, since we are having so free a discussion, let us go over all the odd points which may have puzzled you."

With such an invitation, Charlotte very nearly asked the questions which had been puzzling her most: What private understanding did he have with Clara Brereton? And to what extent were they already acquainted? But she hesitated; and finding herself unequal to such frank and personal enquiries, approached the same subject by a more roundabout route.

"I did find it slightly odd," she said slowly, "that you were holding such an earnest — no, perhaps that is inaccurate — such a very serious discussion with Miss Brereton, as you walked through the wood."

"Ah yes," agreed Sidney. "But surely you could guess what I was doing? You see, I decided to take her fully into my confidence over Henry's situation. I am sorry to have left you alone with him all that time. But indeed I had to make an opportunity — I felt I must have some private conversation with Miss Brereton and explain how very tactfully one must treat Henry at the moment."

"No, I must admit *that* had not occurred to me. After your statement yesterday that Mr. Brudenall's secret should go no farther than your own family, I naturally did not expect you would be divulging it to the first outsider you met."

"But Miss Brereton is such a very charming girl — such a warm,

134

sympathetic person — I was sure she would react entirely the way I hoped. She immediately offered her help in consoling and cheering him. And that," he added blandly, "is why I have divided up our party again now. I have a great deal of faith in *her* cooperation." He looked on ahead to where Miss Brereton was now deep in gentle converse with his friend. "It shows a very good impulse in her nature that *she* is willing to take trouble with Henry."

Charlotte felt this as a personal criticism, blushed, hastily swallowed a rather ill-judged retort, and again felt the stirrings of that strange emotion, jealousy.

"We do not all have the talent for drawing people out. Particularly those in distress," Sidney continued in a solemn but rather too plausible manner she recognized from some of his earlier speeches that day in Sir Edward's cottage. "I would be the first to admit my own failure in this direction. I can sometimes cheer but never console — and cheerfulness alone has a very limited effect in these cases. There are just a few gifted with the engaging mildness of disposition to know exactly how to deal with the afflicted. And *that* appears to be Miss Brereton's great talent."

Charlotte thought there was more than an element of mischief in this pompous little homily. She glanced quickly at him, and observing the trace of a smile, decided he was also exercising his own special talent for diverting her from the subject.

"I also observed during your walk through the woods," she said, returning to what she considered the main issue, "that Miss Brereton was doing a lot of talking too."

"She was telling me of a very similar case to Henry's which had occurred in her own family. That of course would account for the genuine interest she has shown. Sympathy usually has a foundation of — ah — common experience. Do you not find it so?"

135

"I know nothing of the matter at all," said Charlotte coolly. "Broken hearts, unrequited love and inconsolable misery are subjects which, most fortunately, I have only ever read about in books." She was suddenly conscious that she was in danger of sounding both peevish and ill-natured and of the very bad impression she must be creating.

But Sidney only laughed, agreed she was indeed fortunate and continued to elaborate on Miss Brereton's superior understanding — provocation so highly resented by Charlotte that she made no attempt to reply, resolving to allow him all his own way for the rest of their walk.

Sidney, who appeared to be unaware of either provocation or resentment, and could carry any conversation quite unaided, remained undeterred by her silence; but as Charlotte was usually more concerned with the impression a person created on her than the impression she might be giving to him, she found this new state of affairs most confusing; and she was uneasily aware of an odd distortion creeping somewhere into her field of vision.

Sidney Parker, she decided, was as meddlesome as his sister Diana. He might justify his interference and delude himself into thinking he was directing his friend about for his own good, but there was an officious streak of vanity in all this which she could not like. He might believe he was rendering Henry Brudenall a service by manipulating and regulating his relations with everyone he met into a tactful, considerate pattern; but to her there was something both repugnant and improper in trying to modify the course of other people's lives. She suspected that Sidney had been doing this for years — making all his friends behave in the way he directed them — till it had become a type of disease with him.

Like all the Parkers, he had a charitable heart and many amiable feelings; but he allowed himself to be misguided by an overweening conceit into believing he could manage everyone's affairs better than they could themselves. Only his high spirits, his charm of manner and his ready address saved him from being as ridiculous as his sister.

But even as she reached this conclusion and made up her mind to disapprove of him, Charlotte could admit the success of his efforts to entertain her on this walk. She was very conscious that Sidney continually exerted himself to please and a little ashamed of her own failure to do likewise.

CHAPTER 18

MODERN SANDITON possessed no church of its own. On Sundays, Mr. Parker had his horses put to for the drive to the parish church of old Sanditon. It was Lady Denham's proud boast that she always walked to church. But the Parkers knew she only liked to walk downhill, to settle herself in the manor house pew in good time for the service, and expected to be offered a place in their carriage every Sunday for the return journey uphill.

The following morning there was a variation in this weekly custom. Sidney Parker and Henry Brudenall made their public debut; and the turned heads and stifled whispers which greeted their appearance in church were sufficient indication of the general curiosity aroused.

In front of her, Charlotte saw Miss Denham craning her neck, touching her brother on the arm and looking a question. He gave one significant nod before returning to his prayer book as though they had already discussed these newcomers at some length. She could also hear the restless murmuring which had interrupted the Miss Beauforts' devotions behind her. And after the service there was more haste than usual for all to quit their pews and greet their friends in the sunshine outside.

It was, however, Lady Denham's privilege to lead the way down the aisle, with Miss Brereton a few paces behind her. In defiance of custom, Sidney Parker and his friend slipped out of their rear pew to join them; and when the rest of the congregation gained the porch, they were only in time to see Sidney handing the ladies into his carriage, taking over the reins from his groom, and driving them off in great style.

Mr. Parker was the first to recover from his surprise at the speed with which all this had been accomplished.

"Well, upon my word, my brother has stolen a march on us, eh, Sir Edward?" he said jovially. "If we have to compete with these town tricks of his, we shall soon find ourselves with no ladies to squire about in Sanditon at all. Barely here the one day and already he deprives me of my sole act of gallantry in the week!"

Charlotte thought Sir Edward's reply to this pleasantry a trifle forced; and the haste with which he bundled his sister into their own gig confirmed her suspicion that he was in no state of temper to linger exchanging courtesies. Miss Denham scarcely had time to enquire of Mrs. Parker which of the strangers was her brother-in-law, and to remark on the odd circumstance that he should be the only member of the Parker family as yet unknown to her.

The Miss Beauforts were also disappointed at being cheated of an early introduction; and they were certainly no longer content to remain on their balcony now these two personable young men were to be perceived strolling about admiring the Sanditon views. Indeed, they felt a definite obligation to improve the landscape for them immediately by dotting graceful feminine silhouettes wherever they should be most visible.

The very next day Miss Letitia carried her easel out of doors and began moving it from sand to shingle, from hill to Terrace with tireless and unselfish activity. No concern for completing her own sketches interfered with her sense of duty to adorn whatever vista might require her presence.

Miss Beaufort would have found her harp more of an impediment, but she maganimously abandoned it and devoted herself to making the district more select by a parade of what she considered the very latest in seaside fashions. She had recently finished contriving a remarkable headgear — a pattern of which had been sent by her particular friend, Miss Nicholls. This consisted of a Dunstable straw bonnet over a laced cap which boasted a detachable green silk eye-shade stiffened with wire. Miss Nicholls assured her this "seaside bonnet" was all the rage in Ramsgate — she believed it had even originated in Brighton — and although principally designed to protect the eyes from the sun and the hair from the wind, it had the further advantage of framing the face most becomingly.

When seen at close quarters, it was a most fetching creation; but unfortunately Sidney Parker and Henry Brudenall remained at a distance and could only observe a stylish and ubiquitous figure promenading about in every variety of material which could be depended upon to billow attractively in the slightest breeze.

All these sacrifices in the cause of the Sanditon scenery might have had little effect had the Miss Beauforts not luckily recollected being introduced to Miss Heywood on their first arrival. Her clothes being neat and tidy rather than fashionable and her social standing somewhat obscure, they had proceeded to ignore her — beyond an occasional condescending nod from Miss Beaufort and one half-smile from Miss Letitia on the balcony (mainly to improve the profile she was presenting at the time to Arthur Parker). They had never, in fact, spoken to her.

But after twice observing Charlotte being greeted by these interesting young men, they rapidly decided her company was what they had always wanted and only a very natural diffidence had deterred them from approaching her. Their scruples and shyness being now overcome, they waylaid her on her next visit to the library. Charlotte was invited to step into the drawing room of the corner house to inspect Miss Letitia's unfinished sketches, to listen to the neglected harp and to satisfy the curiosity of both sisters by replying to enquiries as indirect and artless as they could devise.

"We have been longing this age — oh, quite aching, I assure you, dear Miss Heywood — for some chance of furthering our acquaintance with you. We have been making the most delightful schemes for days past. But there! We both have the greatest horror of being thought *forward* or *pushing*! It is amazingly difficult for us to get to know *anybody at all*."

"Sanditon is a most charming place, we find — perhaps a little thin of company. But more people are beginning to arrive now, I dare say. The hotel seems to be filling up at all events . . ."

"Oh! I am dotingly fond of Sanditon already in spite of it being a little secluded," interrupted Miss Beaufort, feeling her sister was being a shade premature. "My particular friend, Miss Nicholls, a dear creature and most truly modish, tells me there is far more going on in Ramsgate. *There* one sees new faces every day — but *here* the stranger is quite a rarity."

"Lord yes, I always say these small, retired places are infinitely to be preferred to the bustling, popular resorts," agreed Miss Letitia. "When one comes from a largish inland town, one longs only for solitude in a seaside retreat. I must declare the view from our balcony quite delights us. Not a soul to be seen on the beach for hours at a time."

"Oh yes, we both rave about the peace — about the generally deserted air of Sanditon. Within a few days one knows virtually every face in the district — "

"Exactly. So I really could not help exclaiming to Lydia the other morning when I saw — nothing beyond the merest glimpse really, you know — *two*, no less than *two*, complete strangers."

"Ah! now you mention it, Letitia, I do remember them. They seem to be putting up at the hotel — some connection with the Parkers I did overhear — most genteel-looking young men, both of them so excessively well-dressed."

"The sort of people, one would imagine, more likely to be found patronising Brighton rather than Sanditon."

In this style they ran on, scarcely leaving time for Charlotte to supply all the particulars they so eagerly sought. In the first pause they allowed her, she most willingly did so. She was more diverted than deceived by the Miss Beauforts, and though civilly responding to their overtures of friendship, held her own reservations on the worth of this new acquaintance — or even on its chances of survival. She suspected that all attempts at intimacy would cease abruptly once she had proved her usefulness to her new friends by bringing them to the newcomers' notice.

Charlotte, however, had her own private reasons for enlarging the circle of female companions available for the consolation of Henry Brudenall. It had more than once crossed her mind that Sidney Parker's extravagant praise of Miss Brereton's talent for dealing with his friend had been intended to goad *her* into similar efforts on his behalf. And as Sidney had reiterated many times that he hoped their pleasant foursome would often be repeated, the suspicion had also crossed her mind that she would frequently find herself left coping with Mr. Brudenall while Sidney pursued some sort of pleasant flirtation with Clara. Any addition which might prevent such irritating divisions into awkward pairs would be welcome to Charlotte.

And on the very first opportunity which presented itself — as she sat on the Terrace the following morning with the two young men — she smiled invitingly at the hovering Miss Beauforts and handsomely performed the necessary introductions. She then had great amusement in calculating whether the determination of the Miss Beauforts to attach themselves to the party would prevail over Sidney's patent but polite efforts to repulse them.

Although nothing had been regularly decided and no definite appointment made, Charlotte knew Sidney was now awaiting the arrival of Miss Brereton to suggest forming one of his select walking parties. He had thrown out several hints, in Charlotte's own hearing, that he and Mr. Brudenall would enjoy longer and more energetic rambles and were not averse to Miss Brereton's company whenever Lady Denham could spare it. The Terrace at midday had certainly been mentioned as a convenient meeting place on any convenient day. And Charlotte discovered, in her case and on this particular day, Sidney had said enough about a definite engagement to his sister-in-law for Mrs. Parker to post her off with the utmost good will and a message for her to deliver to Miss Diana en route. They had been sitting patiently on the Terrace for ten minutes, waiting to discover whether Sidney's hints would prove equally effective in respect to Miss Brereton.

The two friends had been bathing earlier that morning themselves, and scoffing at the notion that twenty minutes spent in the sea could tire anyone under the age of forty, Sidney had just proposed that the cliffs, which had been summarily rejected on their first day, would be an ideal excursion path, when the Beaufort intrusion took place.

"Well! this Terrace is an amazingly delightful spot. I declare I could sit here for hours," observed Miss Beaufort, very satisfied with their new situation on it. "So thoughtful of Mr. Parker and Lady Denham to provide these comfortable benches — they turn it into quite the most charming outdoor lounge."

"Oh! yes, delightful. Lydia and I have the greatest dislike of sitting indoors when the sun is beckoning us out every second."

"Sitting indoors! Oh heavens! What a shocking idea, Letitia, when we have the Terrace on our very doorstep. I always say it is the perfect rendezvous for meeting with everyone in Sanditon."

"If one sits here long enough, I dare say it is," said Sidney, beginning to regret he had chosen such a public rendezvous himself. "We are, in fact, on the point of setting out on a fairly energetic walking expedition."

"Ah, such a heavenly day for a long, bracing walk," agreed Miss Letitia. "I too have quite a horror of being confined in the one spot for any length of time. Lydia and I have been exploring Sanditon very thoroughly, I can tell you."

"Lord yes. There is absolutely nothing we enjoy better than energetic walks!"

"And we know all the best paths along the shore line. What direction were you intending to take today?"

"We were just discussing a plan for exploring the cliffs," admitted Sidney. "But I am afraid your shoes would not prove stout enough for the strenuous work we have in mind. They look entirely too fragile to be clambering over stones and rocks. You would ruin them within five minutes; and Miss Beaufort's beautiful gown would very likely be torn on the bushes."

"Oh! I never think about my clothes," cried Miss Beaufort, flashing a coquettish glance from beneath her green eye-shade. "No indeed, I must protest against any such idea. I always say mere gowns are meant for one's comfort and convenience and should never get in the way of one's pleasure. You cannot conceive what a blessing it is that fashion now allows us poor females shorter petticoats; at ankle length, you know, they were positively hobbling on long walks. And as for a few little rents and stains, they do not matter greatly one way or the other. But Letitia, perhaps *you* should take Mr. Parker's advice and slip indoors to change those pink shoes. The nankin boots would really be more suitable for a cliff walk."

Miss Letitia, who had been congratulating herself on appropriating the seat of honour between the two young men and was rather reluctant to surrender it to her sister, protested that her kid shoes were perfectly stout and she never thought about clothes either. And they both emphatically decided finery was out of place in a secluded retreat like Sanditon.

Charlotte, content to remain almost as silent as Henry Brudenall and leave the effort of entertaining the Miss Beauforts to Sidney, had managed nevertheless to convey her perfect approbation of their plans to monopolise both young men on this and on any subsequent occasion they might meet. They were not particularly grateful to her for this. On the contrary, they wrote her down as a sweet-natured but simple country nobody without shrewd enough eyes in her head to distinguish a real beau from the uncouth rustic squires to whom she had no doubt long been accustomed.

Charlotte was seated — very much by her own design but very willing for the sisters to believe it was theirs — next to Miss Beaufort at the far end of the green bench; and as soon as Miss Letitia managed to wrest Sidney's attention away from her sister, Charlotte threw in a judicious word or two on the advantage of large parties and quietly encouraged her to join in their excursions.

"Oh! Miss Heywood, I do agree with you indeed," cried Miss Beaufort, highly delighted with her stupidity. "I always say no scheme comes to anything without numbers to secure enough variety. Do you not think that very true, Mr. Parker?" breaking in on a speech of her sister's. "Miss Heywood has been saying that one cannot have too large a party for any expedition. It provides amusement for all."

"Has she indeed? Miss Heywood's amusement is, of course, always a consideration with me."

"In a large party those who wish to talk are a decided asset," Charlotte remarked with a sturdy bid to let him know she held to her own independent view on the matter. "And those who wish to be silent may do so without risk of giving offence."

"True, very true," said Sidney. "And those who wish to observe may do so to their heart's content. Everyone has plenty of opportunity to behave exactly as he likes; except perhaps those who pride themselves on their ability to organise. A large party is much less manageable for *them*. But there is no arguing with Miss Heywood. She is always so full of common sense — always has such a ready grasp of the essential point. A very rational, cautious young woman; do you not find her so, Miss Beaufort?"

Charlotte would have been surprised if Miss Beaufort had had a really appropriate answer for this ironic little speech; but she was spared the necessity of anything beyond a slightly bewildered "Oh yes, we are both quite charmed with her acquaintance; delightful — " by the unexpected arrival of Sir Edward Denham on the Terrace. He had now had sufficient time to assess the nature of the opposition which confronted him in Sanditon and had driven his sister over from Denham Park in his gig.

A general rearrangement of positions was inevitable; and this was accompanied by various strategic movements on the part of the Miss Beauforts, aimed at securing for themselves the most favourable places. They had considered the two young men already on the Terrace their lawful property — and were only at cross purposes on how to divide up the spoil. But yet another claimant for their attention brought the dilemma of choice and indecision.

Henry Brudenall was certainly the most handsome of the three prepossessing candidates; on the other hand — even with all their powers for gay chatter to carry any awkward pauses — they both found him a little difficult to engage in conversation. Sidney Parker was personable, pleasant *and* modish. He would certainly do very well for one of them. But Sir Edward possessed the same qualifications — and a title into the bargain. It was a difficult decision and Charlotte watched their hesitant manoeuvres with interest.

Miss Denham, however, had no hesitation at all. Fortunate in having her choice limited by the exclusion of her brother, and likewise discouraged by Mr. Brudenall's evident lack of interest in anybody, she aimed her attentions directly at Sidney Parker and had buttonholed him, blockaded him and appeared determined to hold on to him while the Miss Beauforts were still making up their minds.

Charlotte saw it all and gave Sir Edward full credit for bringing his sister along to support him. Probably she had been given no very specific orders to engage Sidney's attention. But Miss Denham was quite calculating enough to sum up an eligible young man of independent means for herself. Sidney's decided air of fashion alone would have been sufficient to assure him of Miss Denham's consideration. She was likely to prove an invaluable ally in counteracting any interference Sir Edward expected in his determined pursuit of Miss Brereton.

And when the Sanditon House ladies did indeed join them on the Terrace soon afterwards, Sidney was too occupied in protecting himself to be in a position to direct them in any way at all. His present discomfiture was more than Charlotte had dared to hope. She was not surprised, however, when he extricated himself with considerable self-possession and earned Lady Denham's delighted approval as well by suggesting that, as they were now such a very large party, the best thing they could do was to stroll along to the tea rooms and seat themselves in more comfort there. Charlotte, remembering the tea room tables seated a maximum of four at each, decided Sidney was wisely endeavouring to restrict the scope of his activities; but he somewhat naturally advanced a different reason for his proposal.

"My brother tells me the tea rooms are rather neglected; and here is just the sort of pleasant, spontaneous gathering which would do justice to them."

"Aye, that's very well spoken," cried Lady Denham. "There is a great deal of sense in what you say, young man. And if more visitors like you would remember our tea rooms on such occasions, we would suffer no losses at all. To be sure, I was intending to call on Mrs. Griffiths. But that can wait. A very good notion of yours, Mr. Parker. I will certainly form one of your little party to our tea rooms."

This gave Sidney the opening he needed for walking away from Miss Denham.

"I shall be deeply honoured by your inclusion in the party, Lady Denham," he cried with unfeigned enthusiasm; and he proffered his arm most gallantly, accepting her in happy exchange for her niece. "I have been hoping for an opportunity of a longer conversation than we had on our short drive back from church last Sunday. You know it is only since becoming acquainted with Miss Brereton — and recollecting *then* that this was of course your maiden name — that I realise I have long been acquainted with another near relation of yours — Miss Elizabeth Brereton. My total ignorance of the connection must plead my apology in never mentioning her on previous visits to Sanditon."

Nothing could have been more proper, or more adroit, than this very civil speech of Sidney's. Charlotte might wonder why he had never found his acquaintance with Miss Elizabeth Brereton worth mentioning to anyone before; but Sidney's manners were always so designed to captivate that she could easily suppose he only remembered it now in an effort to recommend himself to Lady Denham; and that nothing more serious was intended than a wish of giving pleasure to her.

Lady Denham's reaction therefore came as a considerable surprise. She immediately withdrew her hand from Sidney's arm, looked him up and down suspiciously and frowned with sudden disapproval.

"Indeed! So you've met my niece, have you? Well, you can save your compliments and your breath and so I warn you," she said with one of her shrewdest glances. "No doubt she has been getting round you to see whether an invitation can be wheedled for her to Sanditon House! Lord bless me, I am not one who was born yesterday as the saying goes; and my front door is not ajar to every relation I possess. And so you may tell her when you go back to London."

Sidney looked his astonishment at this forthright speech.

"Does your niece wish to come to Sanditon?" he said blankly.

"I own myself very surprised. Of course it would be an excellent notion in its way," he added hastily, "But Miss Elizabeth Brereton is so competent, so highly valued, so indispensable in her own home, that I doubt her family could ever be persuaded to let her come to you. Perhaps we are talking at cross-purposes and you have some other niece in mind?"

"No, no. Miss Elizabeth is the one I mean. *She* may have made no direct application herself. But the Breretons have been pushing her at me forever. They wanted me to invite her right from the beginning instead of Miss Clara. Oh! you may depend upon it, I saw what they were about. I see through all these little schemes of all my relations. And as for Miss Clara declaring this same Elizabeth to be her favourite cousin and talking and talking for month after month of getting her to Sanditon some time — no wonder I am heartily sick of the name. Who am I to be bumping into nieces in every parlour I possess?"

Sidney had recovered from his astonishment by this time and appeared to be struck only by the unlucky coincidence of seeking to recommend himself by a name which Lady Denham could not bear and the ridiculous apprehensions it had aroused. Highly delighted at having unwittingly occasioned them himself, he seemed chiefly engrossed in deciding how he might increase them.

"How fortunate you are, Lady Denham, in having so many nieces to choose among. And I am sure it would be a capital scheme if you could persuade Miss Elizabeth to come to Sanditon. The last time I met her she did not appear to me in the best of health. Perhaps her family *might* be convinced sea-bathing would be of some advantage to her."

"But no advantage to me at all," retorted Lady Denham. "Oh, there are plenty of applicants for my spare rooms, I can tell you. But I am not one to be taken-in so easily. And so I told Miss Clara last time she raised the question."

Lady Denham's displeasure would have been vented a great

while longer; but Sidney was not inclined to practise his powers of address on anyone so completely insusceptible to them; and without much attending to the rest of her discourse, he soon hit upon an adequate means of escape and seized the very next pause in her complaints to say,

"You know, it has just occurred to me that my brother and sisters should not be neglected in our little expedition to the tea rooms. They are none of them great walkers. But this is an easy saunter they would enjoy. If you will excuse me for one minute, I will step across to Number Four and invite them to join us"; and he walked away from the entire Denham family with an air of considerable relief.

"Perhaps Mrs. Griffiths and Miss Lambe would like to come too?" suggested Charlotte innocently. "It does seem a great pity to be leaving them out."

"Of course, of course," said Sidney over his shoulder with a smile which said very intelligibly, "As you see, *my* little plan is now completely out-of-hand. I may as well settle for the whole of Sanditon."

The Miss Beauforts also greeted Charlotte's suggestion with alacrity; and with such professions of affection for Miss Lambe and such real indifference over her inclusion in the party, that Charlotte decided they were not unduly alarmed by competition from her either. But they were well-meaning enough girls; and had Charlotte's idea crossed either of their minds, they might even have taken the trouble to propose it themselves; for despite her large fortune, Miss Lambe's health, her half-mulatto inheritance and her reticence always kept her in the background on social occasions though she was the pivot around which their own household revolved.

The truth was that the Miss Beauforts were indebted to Miss Lambe for many small kindnesses and generous gifts and delighted by this unexpected opportunity to do something effortless for her in return; and they vied with each other to be the first to issue this invitation and give "dearest Adela" some pleasure.

Their application was successful, as was Sidney's at Number Four, and the whole unwieldy group set off towards the tea rooms with some minor skirmishing among the young ladies for possession of the most favoured arms. Sidney had managed to elude even Miss Denham by presenting both of his arms to his sisters as they crossed their own threshold; and Henry Brudenall stepped so very quickly between Lady Denham and Miss Brereton that Charlotte revised her opinion of him: he might *look* as though he overheard nothing and was indifferent to everybody, but when it came to evading compulsive talkers, he knew very well how to take care of himself.

The Miss Beauforts clung to Sir Edward, but had to content themselves with Arthur's homage alone as it never occurred to him that the offer of his arm might be more useful.

Charlotte was very well satisfied to attach herself to Mrs. Griffiths and Miss Lambe, being attracted to the former as a steady, sensible woman and interested in the latter by a certain shy wistfulness. But Miss Denham, who made a very ungracious fourth member of their group and found it highly inconvenient to be stumbling across shingle without a male arm to support her, seemed to intimidate Adela. She had hardly got beyond resolving some reply to Charlotte's remarks on the day, the sunshine and the sea gulls when a waspish interruption from Miss Denham deprived her of further courage.

"Yes, I love to watch the sea gulls — " she was saying.

"My brother is being most inconsiderate," snapped Miss Denham, glaring at his retreating back closely flanked by the Miss Beauforts. "He knows I cannot bear slithering about on pebbles."

Adela looked at her in wonder, shrank closer to Mrs. Griffiths, and not a word more could be extracted from her. Charlotte thought this excessive vulnerability most unfortunate but she pitied

Miss Lambe and forbore teasing her with any more questions. A desultory conversation between herself and Mrs. Griffiths carried them all the way to the tea rooms, where Miss Denham abandoned them immediately; and Charlotte, relieved to be rid of her, hoped to be speedily on better terms with her two chosen companions.

But it was not to be. She had scarcely begun threading a way for them towards a vacant table, when she became aware of the polite struggle over seating now taking place among the others. Sidney naturally had his own very definite ideas of how to settle each particular foursome. But his sister Diana was equally determined to organise the entire group. And Miss Denham, the Miss Beauforts and even Lady Denham were offering powerful resistance to being directed in any other way than they envisaged for themselves.

"I intended calling on Mrs. Griffiths this morning so now I shall sit next to her in the tea rooms," announced Lady Denham very decisively, moving away from the table already occupied by Miss Brereton and Henry Brudenall.

"You will be very comfortable here, Diana," Sidney said almost at the same time, trying to neutralise his sister's interference in his plans by swiftly seating her in Lady Denham's vacated place.

"Oh, I never think of my own comfort when I can be of use to others," maintained Miss Diana, hovering about. "Now where is everyone else going to sit? Susan, you can come here," offering her sister the chair next to Miss Brereton beside which Sidney had stationed himself. "Now let me think — and if Miss Denham and Sidney take this table with — "

"You are only tiring yourself unnecessarily, Diana. We can all find places for ourselves."

But harassed as he was by Diana, and shadowed by a tenacious Miss Denham, Sidney did not have luck with all his arrangements; and while he was settling everyone else to his satisfaction, Diana chose the last chair at Miss Brereton's table for herself and he and Miss Denham indeed seemed destined for a tête-a-tête at the only remaining table. This, however, was too much for him.

"Miss Heywood, will you not join Miss Denham and myself?" he cried promptly. "I discover we are being sadly overlooked and cannot join in with any of your gay foursomes."

The tone of voice was both appealing and commanding, and accompanied by so grateful a look when Charlotte obeyed it that she felt herself repaid for postponing her acquaintance with Miss Lambe. In any case, Lady Denham had now usurped their quiet little corner with so forthright an air of proprietorship and such direct and assertive statements that she was doubtful if she would have succeeded in drawing out the retiring Adela in such company either.

She found her new situation had its compensations — not least of which was in noting the startling change in Miss Denham's manner once she had succeeded in her own objective. Charlotte had observed such a transformation before, but now it was so marked as to be almost a caricature of the spoiled and selfish child, whose smiles follow tears and tantrums and whose self-centredness is transparent to all.

Miss Denham was now all complaisance and set herself out to captivate Sidney Parker most thoroughly. Smiling and exclaiming, listening eagerly to his every remark and keeping up a steady flow of flattering comments herself, she gave him little opportunity to watch what was going on at the other tables or even to exchange a word with Charlotte at their own.

Charlotte herself did not particularly mind being slighted, being sufficiently amused by Miss Denham's style of conversation to remain an appreciative listener.

"I really must compliment you on your carriage and your horses, Mr. Parker. You will laugh at my warmth on such a subject," with a gay sparkle. "It is one which gentlemen usually choose to regard as peculiarly their own province for enthusiasm. But I have always raved over a smart carriage. I assure you," rather archly, "I take more notice of a handsome carriage and pair than I do over who is driving it. My brother often laughs at me. He teased me very merrily yesterday morning when I was in raptures over your equipage as it overtook us on the toll road. Your groom exercises the horses every day in that direction, I believe?"

"I imagine so. I have not made much use of them myself since coming to Sanditon. But, Miss Heywood, it occurs to me — "

"Such a perfectly matched pair! I have the greatest dislike of unmatched horses! It is a source of continual amazement to me that people can often spend so much money on their carriages — and then try to skimp on their horses. Mr. and Mrs. Partridge of Halham Lodge are a case in point. They have a coach, a barouche and a curricle, and not one of their horses is worthy of being put in the shafts of my brother's gig. And such as they *do* have are never exercised."

"Yes, of course, exercise is very necessary. As I was just about to remark to Miss Heywood, I should give my horses more work and ourselves more pleasure by exploring farther afield. If I drive myself, the carriage could easily accommodate four — "

"And my brother could lead the way in our gig," interposed Miss Denham, being uncertain which four Sidney had in mind but determined to join the expedition in some capacity. "You would certainly need local guidance to find the most attractive spots to visit."

"Oh, I already know the exact spot I want to visit," said Sidney pleasantly. "I have always had a very great desire to see Brinshore."

Whether the name was the first which occurred to him or whether he had indeed formed an idea of provoking his brother by

154

visiting Brinshore, Charlotte was unable to decide. But the plan certainly succeeded in disconcerting Miss Denham.

"But, Mr. Parker, you could not have reckoned up the distance. Brinshore must be a good sixteen miles off. Horses could not go that far and return in the same day."

"I am sure my horses could," said Sidney. "Perhaps it might be a little far for Sir Edward to drive his gig. But there is something about the very name of Brinshore which I find — "

"What is all this talk about Brinshore?" broke in Diana from the adjacent table. "Who is going to Brinshore? I own I should very much like to see Brinshore myself. Our carriage does nothing but sit in the stables of the hotel. We have only to hire a pair of post horses from the Woodcocks and we can accommodate four. And even if Tom does not wish to come himself, he can lend us his travelling chaise. I must ask Lady Denham if she is interested in such a plan and how many her carriage could hold."

And away sped Diana, leaving Miss Denham with the happy conviction that she could not fail to be included in so large a projected party.

"What an excellent woman your sister is, Mr. Parker. She has everyone's concerns so much at heart — always promoting schemes for the enjoyment of others. If only *she* had been staying in Sanditon on your previous visits, I am sure *we* would be better acquainted."

"Yes, it is a great pity," agreed Sidney but there was a momentary expression of such artificial assent and a certain contemptuous glance of his bright eye which informed Charlotte he regarded it as more of a pity to be acquainted with Miss Denham at all. She was beginning to read Sidney Parker's thoughts fairly accurately and to find herself in agreement with a great many of them. She also found that life in Sanditon had become considerably more interesting since his arrival.

155

After only five days' residence, the difference he had made was of a most striking nature. And although Charlotte could not hold him directly responsible for all the changes which had taken place, his influence and his presence seemed to be everywhere felt; and a spirited bustle and sudden desire for company had now begun to transform that scattered little society into one well-knit community.

CHAPTER 19

THE EXCURSION to Brinshore was soon talked of as a settled thing.
When two people as intent on organising (or determined on meddling — whichever way you chose to regard it) as Sidney Parker
and his sister had once made such a proposal, the speedy arrangement of all minor details could be expected as a matter of course.

Lady Denham's indifference and Mr. Parker's antagonism to the
project were alike discounted; and their horses and their carriages
were assumed to be at the disposal of everyone in Sanditon who
did wish to see Brinshore.

These plans seemed likely to be thwarted at first by unsolicited
interference from Sir Edward. He was so determined he was not
going to be left out of the party by the inadequacy of his own gig
that he made repeated overtures for the loan of Lady Denham's
carriage — the surest method of arousing both her suspicions and
her opposition. But by the time her refusal had become quite
obdurate, the Parkers decided the problem merited their full
attention.

"For how are we all to be conveyed to Brinshore otherwise?"
cried Miss Diana. "Lady Denham's coach may seat four with
ease. It is far larger than ours. And she raised not the slightest
objection when I first made the suggestion to her. So what is
preventing its use now except selfishness? I have no patience
with these people who lack any consideration for others. And I
have a good mind to tell her so."

"You leave Lady Denham to me," advised Sidney. "She is

always very busy searching for hidden motives in the wrong direction and anticipating deceit where none exists; but I think I have her measure by now."

Sidney possessed an opinion of his own consequence and a perseverance in his own schemes which were not to be damped by the conduct or calculations of others; and with the happy conviction that he knew how to ingratiate himself with an elderly lady whose own comfort was her main preoccupation, he set about arranging a series of accidental encounters with Lady Denham.

He then took infinite pains over lulling her suspicions, encouraged her to talk about her domestic concerns, listened patiently to complaints about her household and her housemaids, sympathised over his brother's expensive projects for Sanditon and solemnly agreed with her that method and economy were essential in everything.

As a consequence, Lady Denham was immediately struck by his good sense and steady principles. By the end of the week, Sidney Parker and Henry Brudenall had become welcome and regular callers at Sanditon House; and Lady Denham had convinced herself that her coachman was becoming indolent, her horses growing sluggish and her carriage rusting away from lack of employment. There would certainly be no harm, she announced gleefully, in ordering them all out on an excursion.

Sidney considered he had exerted himself quite enough by this time and was very willing for Diana to complete the negotiations over borrowing Mr. Parker's carriage. A mere brother's objections, he implied, required no such delicate treatment and could be easily overborne by her usual domineering tactics.

Miss Diana, determined to order and contrive all the remaining details herself, set about the task with a great deal of flurried commotion and a series of dogmatic decrees. Even the weather she insisted must obey her commands. But when the fine spell held out and another day of sunshine greeted her for the Brinshore outing, she was so delighted with her success that she allowed Sidney some further share in the proceedings.

As the large party began assembling at Trafalgar House after an early breakfast, she even appealed for his help in rearranging some of her careful plans for the division of passengers among the four available carriages.

"Well! What is to be done now, Sidney? I find Mrs. Griffiths has entrusted Miss Lambe to my care and does not need a place for herself. And here is Tom saying he and Mary will not go to Brinshore either! If only I had known all that, we could have dispensed with one carriage."

"I knew they never intended to go," admitted Sidney. "But it is always best to have spare places in any expedition, you know, Diana. Henry, for instance, is a very bad traveller and likely to be queasy on any journey. It would be an excellent thing if he were to travel inside my carriage by himself."

"Oh? I had planned to invite him to share ours. Or perhaps we should take Miss Lambe? Susan is very slight and even with Arthur we have room for four — "

"Miss Denham will expect such a mark of attention should be paid to her first. You had best invite her," suggested Sidney. "And Sir Edward, of course, should be in charge of Lady Denham's coach. But we must be off to a quick start. We have thirty-two miles to cover. If we are to see as much as we want of Brinshore in between, one day will hardly suffice unless we leave now. We cannot afford to waste any more of it talking."

Indeed he communicated such a sense of haste to all concerned that they scarcely tried to contradict him; and he had bundled two carriages off on their way, each containing four people, before anyone realised the two remaining carriages were now left to accommodate only four people between them.

"That was very stupidly done of you, Sidney," observed his

brother, standing in his driveway. "There you have let the two Miss Beauforts and Miss Lambe go off all crowded together in Lady Denham's carriage with Sir Edward; and here is still plenty of room in both mine and yours. Only Miss Brereton and Miss Heywood left, you see."

"And they can be very comfortable in your chaise," replied Sidney. "It is only large enough for three at most. As for myself, I am quite determined to drive in the rear the whole way. You never know what accidents may occur in such a positive cavalcade. Come, let us be off. Well Tom, you may be sure we will tell you all about the beauties of Brinshore on our return!" And flourishing his whip, he signalled the remaining two carriages to set off down the driveway.

Charlotte, finding she and Clara Brereton were to be confined together in the Parkers' carriage, wondered how many polite sentences she would be expected to exchange over the next few hours. She felt no temptation to go beyond that. Clara's reserved and circumspect behaviour, combined with the determined but silent pressure she had exercised over their visit to Sir Edward's cottage, made Charlotte very wary of any further efforts towards intimacy. And the air of mystery she had always sensed about Miss Brereton had only increased with recent observation of her conduct. Once, for a fleeting moment on the day of their bathing excursion, Charlotte had had a glimpse of the sun's rays full upon her, and had felt she understood her. But she had passed from sight again, preferring to remain in the shadows, tantalising and intriguing.

Since Sidney Parker's arrival in Sanditon, moreover, Miss Brereton had been so preoccupied with either talking to him or earning his good opinion by talking to his friend that she had had very little time to spare for Charlotte. And though the subsequent coolness in their relationship was none of her own doing, Charlotte was not sorry for it.

She was surprised therefore when, after a short and thoughtful silence, Miss Brereton began their conversation on a markedly personal note.

"How very sorry I am we have had no opportunity to repeat our bathing excursion, Miss Heywood. I often remember it with great pleasure. Did you not find it very delightful too?"

"I enjoyed it very much," Charlotte said quite sincerely.

"The sea so sparkling, the sun warm, the day so perfect — oh! and our excitement adding to it all. I was grateful you seemed to feel everything with the same joy as myself," continued Miss Brereton as though determined to draw Charlotte's attention to some amicable bond existing between them. "And I have always thought of you since as a friend in whom I could trust."

Charlotte gave a circumspect smile and wondered what was coming next.

"So I am very glad we find ourselves unexpectedly together now," went on Miss Brereton. "In other circumstances I might not have dared to consult you. But I badly need advice — advice from someone like you — another woman close to my own age," hesitating a little. "I have so few female friends."

Charlotte bit back a retort that female friends generally required to be encouraged as well as male, and said coolly,

"But surely you have known Miss Denham a great deal longer than *we* have been acquainted?"

"Miss Denham! Oh no! Her brother — oh no, no! She would be the last person to understand."

Charlotte had some sympathy with this view of Miss Denham's compassionate possibilities and relented sufficiently to say,

"Perhaps you may soon have a visit from your cousin, Miss Elizabeth Brereton. From something that was said among the Parkers the other day, I gathered Lady Denham might now be considering such an invitation — " She hesitated. Mrs. Parker's actual words to her husband had been: "Well, Lady Denham's latest complaint is that Miss Brereton has lost interest in her household duties. She is thinking of inviting another niece, a Miss Elizabeth, to stay with them. According to her, Miss Elizabeth is very competent and efficient and will be able to show Miss Clara how to run the household more smoothly, if only her family can spare her for a visit at this time."

To Charlotte's ears, this had sounded far more as though it was according to Sidney Parker — indeed a striking example of his latest persuasive powers; and her chief interest in the conversation at the time lay in wondering why he should seek to influence Lady Denham in such a direction. What possible object could he have in securing her niece an invitation to Sanditon? She could not understand it at all, but as Miss Brereton seemed in so confidential a mood, she hoped she might now learn more about the situation from her.

"Lady Denham does seem more favourably inclined towards a visit from Elizabeth," agreed Miss Brereton. "But I know how long she could still take over inviting her. She hates disturbing any of her routine arrangements. And though she talks of the visit as a possibility now, months may elapse before anything is achieved. By the time Elizabeth arrives it may be too late for me to discuss all my problems with her."

"All your problems?" said Charlotte with some surprise. She suspected Miss Brereton of over-dramatising her situation; but one glance at the lovely, earnest face beside her was sufficient proof that Miss Brereton at least regarded her own problems as very serious indeed. And Charlotte generously tried to rid herself of the suspicion that this was mere play-acting.

"Oh Miss Heywood, I am so terrified of taking momentous decisions in a hurry! And everything seems to be happening so quickly! What I badly need is sensible advice from someone not so closely involved as I am in the outcome of this dreadful tangle."

Momentous decisions and dreadful tangles had rarely come Charlotte's way. Though still feeling she was being drawn into a rather melodramatic and unnatural conversation, she tried her best to be charitable.

"My advice would not be worth a great deal," she said slowly, "as my experience has been rather limited."

"Ah, but that would be no drawback at all," cried Clara eagerly. "Nobody could have had much experience of the situation which now confronts me. Indeed I am considering such a step as sometimes appals me. You know, I am sure, something of the difficulties of my position with Lady Denham. And Sir Edward and his sister — oh, dear Miss Heywood, only to tell someone of my problems would be a relief."

Miss Brereton's sudden leap from secrecy to openness had already bewildered Charlotte into an embarrassed silence. She waited very uncomfortably through the ensuing pause, uncertain what she could usefully say till the situation became a little clearer to her.

"But I see I must tell you straight out if I want your help — the fact is — in short — " somewhat incoherently, "I am considering an elopement."

This stumbling confession was so far from what Charlotte had expected that she was too astonished to be immediately able to reply. Miss Brereton's position in Lady Denham's household, the difficulties she mentioned, perhaps some small intrigue with Sir Edward — but she had always believed her hard-headed enough to stop short of this! And it *could* only be Sir Edward whom she meant.

The thought flashed through her mind, only to be instantly dismissed, that Clara Brereton might be intending to elope with Sidney Parker. Common sense immediately told her such an idea was absurd. A doubt might remain whether or not Sidney was entirely free from any peculiar attachment to Clara. But if he did indeed wish to marry her, why should he not do so in the normal way? He had independent means, good connections and no reason at all to flout convention. There could be no possible objections to the match from his family or from hers. So why should either of them upset their friends and alarm their relations by carrying through such an intention behind their backs? In what cause? Such an elopement would be merely romantic nonsense of a sort Charlotte did not believe existed in real life. She was positive she could exonerate Sidney Parker from such thoughtless behaviour and acquit him of any but the most trifling duplicity. He certainly had his faults, but they were those of levity and high spirits, not genuine lack of consideration for others.

With an effort of will, she swung her mind away from Sidney Parker and tried to concentrate instead on the connection between Clara Brereton and Sir Edward. Miss Brereton had mentioned Sir Edward more than once during this strange conversation. She had said his sister would be the last person to understand her problems; and she had talked of difficulties with Lady Denham. Such a marriage would certainly not meet with *her* approval. And surely her approval was vital if they hoped to inherit her fortune? But Lady Denham was so unpredictable, so full of odd whims and caprices — perhaps Clara and Sir Edward had decided they could no longer wait till one or the other of them became her heir? By marrying first and throwing themselves on her mercy later, they might hope to be jointly forgiven and inherit the fortune between them?

Charlotte conceded that reasoning similar to this could explain the purpose behind such an elopement. But it brought her no nearer to understanding Clara Brereton. How any sensible girl could consider an elopement with Sir Edward was beyond her comprehension; and she was beginning to feel a great reluctance even to listen to any explanation Miss Brereton might wish to give. She did not want to be involved in all these problems of hers; and she certainly had no intention of helping her to elope with Sir Edward.

"I am very sorry," she said at last. "I do not believe I can be of any help to you. I will of course respect the confidence you have just made. But I must make it quite plain from the outset that I disapprove of elopements and could advise in no way at all."

The silence which followed this stiff little speech of hers was to Charlotte's feelings very dreadful. Miss Brereton, looking crushed, turned her head towards the window and they both sat quite mutely, hearing for the first time the horses' steady trot and the rumble of the carriage wheels along the road.

A very few moments more, however, completed Charlotte's present embarrassment. She had only time to decide there could be another two hours of this uncomfortable silence to sit through, when she was conscious of a shout, a sudden jolt and that all motion had abruptly ceased.

"I hope you are not alarmed," said Sidney Parker, opening the door. "But it is a small inconvenience to the accident you might have had. A wheel of your carriage is in immediate danger of collapsing."

He helped them both to alight and they stood rather despondently in the road with Henry Brudenall and the Parkers' groom. Still bewildered by Miss Brereton's revelation and preoccupied in trying to understand the reason or object behind it, Charlotte did not at first take in the details of what Sidney was saying. A wheel might come off at any moment. The carriage should proceed no further till it was mended. Providence indeed he had had the presence of mind to drive behind them and that he should have noticed it! But how all this would affect them on their expedition to Brinshore, she had not yet had time to consider.

"I wonder my brother should not have remarked that weakening before," said Sidney, looking gravely at a back wheel. "It must date from the time he overturned the carriage."

Charlotte looked carefully at the wheel to which his attention was directed but could not perceive it was very different from any of the other wheels. She frowned in an effort of concentration.

"But I am almost certain he overturned the carriage on the other side."

"Ah, that would account for it completely then," cried Sidney, his brow lightening. "A jolt and crack on *this* side passing unnoticed when all attention was directed to the left wheels! And the fault shows up far more in motion," he added. "It is splaying badly, particularly on the corners and when it lurches over bumps. You do not know a great deal about coach-building, Miss Heywood?"

"No — how should I? I once saw the wheel come off one of our farm wagons."

"Well, briefly, the problem here is this: the spokes are made of oak and tenoned into the stock in a staggered fashion, one forward, one back, so as not to weaken it. They seem to be still true. But the mortises on the rim here are cut either of ash or beech and are no longer picking up all the spoke tenons firmly. There is too much play. Parsons and I both agree the carriage must be sent straight to the wheelwright."

"That's right, Mr. Sidney. Lucky Toomey's is hard by," asserted the groom but with some amusement in his voice, which made Charlotte look at him quickly and wonder if Sidney Parker knew any more about coach-building than she did herself.

"And we have to wait for it to be repaired?"

"No, no — that will be a day's job at least. We can all fit very easily into my chaise. Nothing simpler. But by now we are so far behind the main party, we should lose no further time. Miss Brereton, may I help you inside?"

Charlotte, with some reluctance to be closeted again with the same companion, was turning to follow very naturally when Sidney announced her place would now be beside him on the box.

166

"But will not Mr. Brudenall be sitting with you?"

"Oh, Henry could not possibly sit on the box. He is the most shocking traveller. Come along, Henry, in you get."

It was not only Charlotte who questioned his judgement on this matter. Though Clara Brereton could no longer have had any desire for Charlotte's company, she made a feeble protest on being deprived of it; and Mr. Brudenall, shocking traveller though he was, seemed to find the plan an ungentlemanlike one.

"But Sidney, there is really no need — such an odd appearance — "

"Will Miss Heywood be comfortable up there in the wind? Mr. Parker, let us discuss how best we can all sit."

"Perhaps there is room for me inside as well?"

"Dreadful squash. You would not like it at all with three," maintained Sidney. "No wind at all today. And Miss Heywood will have a much better view of the country. This way we shall all sit very comfortably."

He advanced his arguments in a manner which plainly showed he had scarcely a doubt of his opinion being complied with; appeared to consider their objections in opposition as given for mere formality, and concluded with,

"Well, we can settle all the points you raise as we go along. Fortunately it is of little consequence how we sit. We are in too great a hurry and an immediate discussion is unnecessary. Do get in, Henry."

And to Charlotte's amazement, accepting Sidney Parker's authority, the others began to climb into the chaise.

"I am sure there is some better solution — " she insisted, standing obstinately in the road.

But Sidney, unused to any contradiction and impatient to catch up with the rest of the party, would neither allow them to wait and discuss the situation, nor listen to what Charlotte was saying now; and forcibly seizing her hand in his, he pulled her up on to the box beside him, having overpowered the combined objections of the other three by the rapidity of his own actions.

Charlotte, half angry and half laughing, was obliged to sit beside him; and the chaise had moved off again before she had time to decide what they really should have done.

Surprise that Sidney had chosen *her* to sit beside him was not the least of her sensations. That he should have selected her for his companion on a two-hour drive in preference to Clara Brereton both puzzled and pleased her and at first she was too astonished to attempt to understand it.

Her new vantage point on the box was indeed a pleasant one and for some minutes she was content to look around her from the peak of the coast road they had now reached.

An occasional cloud dimmed the bright sunshine for a moment; but the day seemed the most perfect of that summer; and Charlotte's very position for enjoying it, perched up in the open air, with the high, beautiful sky above her and the sea constantly changing its colours as it dashed against the cliffs below her, made her altogether in charity with Sidney, who had chosen it for her.

But although everything was thus smiling, she could not feel completely easy for very long. Several anomalies in this situation continued to vex her. Why, if Henry Brudenall was such a bad traveller, would he ever have wanted to spend four hours in a closed carriage on a sunny summer day? The short interval he would be allowed to explore an unknown and possibly unattractive seaside resort seemed to her a very doubtful incentive. For while the name of Brinshore might be a powerful inducement to Sidney Parker, it was unlikely to have roused great enthusiasm in an apathetic stranger.

Then there was the wheel; and the groom's veiled amusement at Sidney's profuse explanations; and finally this unnecessary division of the party once more into arranged pairs. On a walk, she had allowed it to be permissible; on a drive, she recognised a certain lack of propriety in such deliberate contrivance. And after hesitating some little while, Charlotte decided to broach the matter again.

"Nonsense," said Sidney immediately. "I did not expect you to stand upon such ceremony. The family nature of our party renders all such prudery ridiculous. I have merely chosen positions for us all which are individually the most comfortable. Are you now telling me you are *not* comfortable?"

"Thank you," said Charlotte, remembering the acute discomfort of her place beside Miss Brereton. "I am perfectly comfortable."

"Then are you trembling for fear of being seen by some chance acquaintance with starched notions?"

"We shall certainly not meet with anyone I know."

"Then we will meet with nobody I know," Sidney assured her cheerfully. "And as Miss Brereton, who has a larger acquaintance in the district, is now safely hidden inside the carriage, there is nothing at all to worry us."

"You are very ridiculous," Charlotte said, laughing in spite of herself. "Your arguments only amuse me instead of convincing me."

"At least they may convince you I am a very agreeable young man, which after all is the happiest conviction for me," said Sidney gallantly. "I do not know how you rate such things, Miss Heywood. But I think that is the very least I can expect after all my efforts. I have really gone to a great deal of trouble to secure pleasant company for myself on this drive."

The smile on her face and the glow of mingled surprise and confusion on her cheeks were an instinctive reply to this urbane compliment. That such an explanation of Sidney's odd seating arrangements *had* suggested itself to her she could not deny: it would have been a very welcome interpretation of this incident if it were true; but she refused to believe he had no other purpose in view. By provoking, by flattering, by subtle manoeuvres or by high-handed insistence, she had watched Sidney Parker getting his own way often enough by now to recognise that in choosing *her*, in endeavouring to be pleasant to *her*, his conduct must be likewise influenced by some ulterior motive.

"That is a very pretty speech, Mr. Parker," she said with as much composure as she could muster. "But unfortunately I would prefer to hear the truth."

"What a difficult young woman you are. There is no bamboozling you at all," sighed Sidney.

"I do not think it is being difficult to consider lies unnecessary."

"Unnecessary? Oh no! Lies are often very useful. I am rather fond of them myself. However, let us not quarrel the point in this particular case. I have no real objection to telling you the truth."

But he stopped and stared at his horses' heads for so long that Charlotte wondered if he was now inventing a fresh set of lies for her benefit.

"Well?" she said encouragingly.

"Yes, of course I am going to tell you," he said with a smile. "I am only deciding where it is best to begin. Well then, so far as I know — and I know nothing at all about wheels — there was nothing the matter with my brother's carriage. In return for a small gratuity, Parsons has agreed to give the horses some milder exercise and meet us at the wheelwright's on our return. Henry is not a particularly shocking traveller. But today, of all days, I wanted to assure him of an agreeable companion. I will make some opportunity in Brinshore to thank Miss Brereton for her very great kindness in performing this service for me."

"What service?" enquired Charlotte suspiciously. She was not entirely convinced Sidney was speaking the truth now but her attention was assured and she was very willing to listen.

"Miss Heywood, as you are such a sensible — such a logical person, I owe you some little explanation of the deceit I have been practising over this whole excursion. The day for our drive to Brinshore may seem to you — and to everyone else — to have been chosen by my sister Diana. But, in fact, I had a very particular reason for fixing on today out of any others. Today is the wedding day of Henry's cousin; and it is my very great wish that he should survive it as effortlessly as possible. I can neither leave him to mope by himself nor to be irritated by strangers.

"At breakfast, yesterday morning, Henry actually emerged from his fit of abstraction over his cousin long enough to establish Miss Brereton as a charming girl. I had already been talking about her for half an hour; but one minute of Henry's attention is all I can expect these days. Perhaps by tomorrow I may hope to increase it to two minutes."

"It would be much wiser for you to stop encouraging any friendship between Miss Brereton and Mr. Brudenall," Charlotte told him.

Sidney already knew Sir Edward was an admirer of Clara's and perhaps found amusement in provoking him. Had he known Sir Edward to be so serious a contender for her affections, he might have hesitated to promote further circumstances for rivalry; and with the likelihood of an actual elopement still vividly in her mind, Charlotte believed such interference from Sidney could lead to disastrous complications.

But she had no intention of giving this reason for her advice. Charlotte had not been so disloyal to her own sex as to impart her earlier suspicions of Miss Brereton to Sidney; she would have thought it equally unforgivable to do so now those suspicions had become a certainty. So she could think of nothing to add in support of her advice beyond a rather lame, "You would hardly wish to be entangling Mr. Brudenall's affections again during his last month in England."

171

Sidney protested this to be quite impossible. Even Henry's affectionate heart and talent for sentiment were incapable of so rapid a switch from one young lady to another. He had loved his cousin for ten years. The next ten years might prove he was not inconsolable. Ten months might even do it. But the ten days or so he now had at his disposal were inadequate to work such a change. All that could reasonably be expected was that they might prove to Henry that other charming young women existed in the world besides his cousin; and the more he saw of Miss Brereton now, the more speedy would be his eventual recovery.

Any objections which Charlotte produced only served to confirm him in the brilliance of his scheme. Certainly, there might be other young ladies in Sanditon who could console his friend quite successfully. But she must admit Henry's susceptibilities were blunted for the moment and there was no point in dividing them among several contenders. No, no, Miss Brereton had been the first to show an interest in him and that, she must also admit, already had a charm of its own. The simplicity of his deft little plot appealed to him more every time he considered it. And the impulsive nature of the plan seemed to Charlotte rather typical of Sidney Parker.

She tried again.

"But surely it is very wrong to be promoting any *particular* degree of friendship between Mr. Brudenall and Miss Brereton?" she persisted earnestly. "By throwing them together all day like this — "

"My dear Miss Heywood, I am not for a moment suggesting we become matchmakers," cried Sidney, pretending to look shocked at the idea. "Do *you* think Henry and Miss Brereton are suited for anything of a permanent nature? This is purely a temporary expedient — for my own convenience, I do admit. But I promise you no harm could possibly arise from it. Henry is certainly immune from any charms but his cousin's at the present time. And as for Miss Brereton — I know she pities him from the bottom of her heart; but she would have to be his cousin to find any attraction in such low spirits or any pleasure in such languid conversation."

Although Sidney ridiculed the notion that any dangers and evils could arise for either party from this drive, Charlotte would have continued to argue had it not occurred to her that Mr. Brudenall might indeed distract Clara in some way from her still hesitant plans to elope with Sir Edward. And though unwilling to become an active campaigner in Sidney's schemes, to either impel or assist them, she saw no harm in being a passive witness. Charlotte had done.

"Well, I would counsel caution rather than encouragement," she added only, in faint warning.

"Exactly," laughed Sidney. "That is exactly the advice I expected you to give. Caution and Miss Heywood go so well together. Would you very much object if I galloped my horses on this most tempting stretch of road?"

Charlotte smiled her permission — with no objection to his changing the subject. She was only sorry he regarded her as such a poor-spirited creature, and was not at all alarmed by the speed at which they were soon travelling. His horses were fresh and excited by the prospect of a gallop but he appeared to have them well under control, took full advantage of the fine straight stretch of good road to let them have their heads, then reined them in effortlessly.

"Whoa there, my beauties, this is no elopement, you know."

"Elopement?"

The word startled her. Charlotte stiffened and directed candid eyes of enquiry at Sidney Parker.

"Why yes, an elopement," he said easily. "Horses are supposed to travel fast on such occasions, you know: to escape enraged parents, add excitement to the adventure — thundering hooves — romance of the roadway — " He glanced at her face, rather surprised at the expression of disapproving gravity. "In an elopement or a race. Would you prefer me to have called, 'Whoa there, this is not a race'?"

Charlotte pulled herself together. Sidney, she decided, had no doubt been using the phrase very lightly. With *her* mind still half-engrossed by the recent more earnest reference, she realised she was reading a significance into the word he had not himself intended.

"Yes, I would prefer it," she said curtly.

"You do not approve of elopements?"

"Not at all."

"In no circumstances?"

"I cannot think of any where I would approve."

"You are extraordinarily consistent in your opinions, Miss Heywood. But cannot you allow the tiniest loophole for an elopement to be possible between two sincere and genuine people?"

Sidney was laughing at her again, she knew. But she had no intention of withdrawing from her position.

"An elopement," she said, choosing her words carefully, "appears to me as irresponsible conduct. It gives pain and apprehension to parents, undue worry to friends and altogether, in most cases, seems highly unnecessary."

"Unnecessary is a favourite word with you, I note. Lies are unnecessary. Elopements are unnecessary. But come, let us suppose there are circumstances — unreasonable guardians, unavoidable separations, persecuted lovers, over-strict parents, perhaps even a forced marriage being arranged — anything you like to imagine which might make an elopement the only way of uniting a couple very deeply in love, would you still disapprove?"

"The instances *you* like to imagine are certainly unnecessary.

Outside of library romances, whoever heard of such cases? What parents today are tyrannical enough to insist on an enforced marriage if their daughter is at all unwilling?"

"Then let us not bother with circumstances at all. Will you make no allowance for the instinctive guidance of the heart, for intensity of emotions? Or do you consider they are also unnecessary?"

"It is not really a subject I care to discuss," said Charlotte crossly. "And I cannot see it is of the slightest importance to establish what my opinions might be on a hypothetical elopement."

"Oh, but your opinions fascinate me," replied Sidney. "They are so very definite that I long to know if they will change — or how and when they will change. But there, if the subject vexes you, I will not press it. By all means let us talk about something which interests *you*."

Sidney's readiness to consider her wishes and her preference in any conversation was always one of his main charms. And they were soon talking easily again on a variety of topics with the familiarity of long-established acquaintance. London and Brighton, which she had never visited, came alive for her when he described them. Even his occasional teasing she had learned to meet with good humour. The subtle compliments he occasionally paid were not so extravagant as those Sir Edward laboured to produce; and she accepted them quietly and properly but with no pretence at all of believing them. They were obliged to sit together for two hours and she gave Sidney full credit for the simple, disinterested benevolence with which he carried out his duty to entertain her.

Charlotte was not vain enough to think it possible for Sidney to have any sort of partiality for her. He was pleasant and courteous to all young women. His manners, frank candour and high spirits must be a general recommendation to all; and to imagine that she could ever appropriate any particular regard

175

for herself from a good will so universally bestowed was clearly absurd.

Common sense having thus indicated to Charlotte that it would be most unwise of her to think too much about Sidney Parker, she continued to sit beside him, to listen to his engaging talk and to enjoy his company very thoroughly. And as the happy blend of reason and weakness in this conduct did not seem at all contradictory to her, the danger resulting from Sidney's plot for rearranging their positions was quite as serious to her as any she had ever apprehended for Mr. Brudenall.

In short, it can only be inferred that she was in a promising way to falling in love herself and would be well into the middle of it before she realised she had fairly begun. With all her level-headedness and all her sobriety, Charlotte was unaware of the pitfall opening up before her — the supreme folly of bestowing her regard without any certainty of its being returned; and like many a less sensible sister, she was behaving in the most normal and illogical way.

The only discovery she did make was that once again several hours spent with Sidney Parker sped by so quickly that Brinshore was reached before she had thought they could possibly have covered more than a quarter of the distance.

CHAPTER 20

BY THE TIME Sidney's carriage drew up at the inn, the rest of the party had already set out on foot to explore Brinshore; and no immediate explanations for their odd seating arrangements proved necessary. Charlotte, whose relief was pretty well equally divided between Sir Edward's not being at hand to comment on Clara Brereton's position nor Miss Denham to comment on her own, wondered if explanations would ever be made now at all. That Sidney was bent on giving his own apologies and thanks to Miss Brereton was obvious from the manner in which he walked hurriedly away with her on the pretext of finding the others.

"They are bound to be somewhere on the shore line," he called to Henry and Charlotte over his shoulder. "Come along, keep up."

"Come along, keep up, Miss Heywood," echoed Mr. Brudenall, with a light touch of mimicry Charlotte had hardly expected from him. "We must all do as Sidney dictates on these occasions. He decides what is for our own good and it is best to obey."

Charlotte was very much inclined to think Sidney was right and the morning's drive had had all the happy effect on Henry Brudenall which his friend intended. For though he was still rather serious and occasionally absent-minded, she was surprised to discover she could now extract an almost normal conversation from him. He agreed with her that the Brinshore surroundings seemed flatter than Sanditon's, that the village was not so immediately charming and, when they reached the beach, that there was indeed a remarkable quantity of seaweed.

As Charlotte always tried to avoid Henry Brudenall's company wherever possible, and had been particularly determined to do so on his cousin's wedding day, she found this sudden change in his spirits as welcome as it was perplexing.

They walked along the shingle, exchanging several more polite comments and perceiving and pointing out the main party to each other at almost the same time. They were all at the other end of the beach by the bathing machines, and Charlotte and Henry followed Sidney's lead towards them. The brittle brown fronds of seaweed, dried by the sun, crackled quite pleasantly underfoot the whole way along; but Charlotte had just announced — and Mr. Brudenall acquiesced — that such a profusion of seaweed must be ranked a distinct nuisance at any seaside resort, when all their views on the matter were overthrown by their meeting with the others.

The Miss Beauforts were ecstatic about the seaweed. It was, apparently, Brinshore's chief claim to fame — and had they seen the sweet seaweed pictures in the shop outside the library? Oh, then they must all come immediately to look at them. Seaweed, the Miss Beauforts insisted, was a very definite attraction at a resort; one could spend happy hours collecting prize pieces; one could trace them or press them and arrange them most artistically.

Even Arthur seemed to have caught something of their enthusiasm — though regarding it as a more scientific pastime. Released from Miss Beaufort and Miss Letitia and now getting near to Charlotte, he flourished a specimen of glossy olive-coloured seaweed he had picked up himself.

"What do you think of *that*?" he said proudly. "Not a tear or a bruise on it anywhere!"

"No," agreed Charlotte, poking it rather gingerly. "I suppose all that slime makes it yielding enough to prevent tearing."

"And think how absorbing it must be collecting and identifying all the varieties — there are hundreds of them. We have just come across a man on a naturalist's ramble; he had a basket in one hand and a prod in the other; and he was wading out on the low tide to look for more specimens. This one, he told me, was very common. But only look how beautiful it is with such jagged fronds and sweeping curves."

Charlotte looked at it but declined to take it. But Miss Lambe, who had also decided to walk with Miss Heywood, admired it so shyly and yet so sincerely that Arthur was very content to present it to her instead.

Charlotte herself remained unmoved by the charms of seaweed even when they reached the Miss Beauforts' shop and were entreated to admire the framed pictures. Dried and arranged carefully under glass, the seaweed appeared now in the form of baskets and bouquets of flowers, set above, below or around a set of obligatory verses in faultless copperplate:

> *Call us not weeds, we are flowers of the sea,*
> *For lovely and bright and gay-tinted are we,*
> *And quite independent of sunshine or showers;*
> *Then call us not weeds, we are ocean's gay flowers.*

or

> *We are nursed not like plants of a summer parterre,*
> *Where gales are but sighs of an evening air,*
> *Our exquisite, fragile and delicate forms*
> *Are nursed by the ocean and rocked by its storms.*

"Oh! I am quite enchanted with these seaweed pictures," exclaimed Miss Letitia. "As soon as we get back to Sanditon, we must try to find seaweed there. And then we could make our own pictures. At low tide, you know, I am sure we could discover patches of it somewhere."

"And perhaps we could also find some gentleman who would be willing to help us," cried Miss Beaufort archly. "One who would not mind sopping his shoes occasionally in sea water to bring us back a few trophies."

She sparkled a glance of such saucy appeal at Sidney Parker that he instinctively retreated a pace or two. He recovered however to reply with some resource.

"I am very sure you will. Arthur is exactly the man you want. He seems to have taken a great fancy to seaweed already. And what about you, Miss Heywood? Are you also enchanted by Brinshore's beautiful seaweed? Ah yes, I can read in your eyes that we are in complete agreement on the matter."

But the Miss Beauforts were not interested in Charlotte's opinion, still less in reading her eyes with Sidney Parker. If they had ever looked carefully into those clear grey eyes, they might have been disconcerted by the steady twinkle in their quite remarkable depth. But neither of the Miss Beauforts was in the habit of looking very carefully at members of their own sex — or at most not beyond their clothes. Miss Brereton's and Miss Denham's opinions they eagerly canvassed; they could not escape hearing Diana's; and even listened with attention to Miss Parker's: all of these had beaux or brothers to claim their respect and entitle them to form the core of the merry little group, gathered inside and outside the small curio shop.

And despite Sidney's efforts to include them in the general conversation, Charlotte found herself isolated with Miss Lambe over a counter of sea shells. They both stared down in silence at shell boxes, shell-work picture frames, shell boats and shell rondels; but finding nothing to comment on in this trumpery collection, Charlotte soon wearied of it and was about to turn away, when she became aware of the absorbed expression on Miss Lambe's face as she examined the shell-studded trinket trays. At that moment she glanced up and, conscious of being observed, gave Charlotte a smile of sudden brilliance.

"I love shells," she confided. "So fragile — so delicate —"

This was only the second sentence Charlotte had heard Miss Lambe utter. The first had been, "I love to watch the sea gulls." Charlotte found them an arresting combination and turned back to the trinket tray, wondering what she could find to say in its favour to encourage the conversation.

"Some of the shells have pretty shapes and colours," she conceded at last; but she spoke so kindly that Miss Lambe was emboldened to continue on her own.

"Oh! not these. I do not mean these. They are rather clumsy — and common. But all shells remind me of my childhood. At home, in Barbados, there were such beautiful shells. My father made a collection of them, and I have it now. Would you like to see it?"

Charlotte replied that she would like to see it very much and listened with attention as Miss Lambe described it. But she was far less interested in the shell collection than in this transformation of a timid young girl into a voluble enthusiast as she spoke about it. There was no longer any question of drawing Miss Lambe out. She went on happily talking about her exotic shells till they were interrupted again by Sidney, this time calling them across to admire a particularly tasteless shell box his sisters had just bought. It was entirely covered with what Miss Lambe had just described as clumsy and common shells and had "Brinshore" inscribed on the lid in tiny pebbles.

While Sir Edward talked of its "frangible appearance" camouflaging an "adamantine construction" and racked his brains for a suitable quotation about shells, Sidney silently passed the box around for inspection. The Miss Beauforts agreed it was exquisite; Miss Denham thought their own villagers should be encouraged to produce similar boxes with "Sanditon" on the lid. Miss Brereton allowed it to be pretty; Miss Lambe faltered and, whispering it was "very interesting," retreated into her usual silence. Charlotte, rejoicing in having avoided all comment on the box when it was dutifully praised by everyone else, realised rather too late that Sidney had not drawn Miss Lambe and herself into the group from motives of consideration alone.

"I do not think we have yet heard Miss Heywood's opinion," he said with a polite bow in her direction which informed her he had let her off over seaweed pictures merely to trap her more entertainingly over shell-work boxes.

Charlotte now heartily regretted she had missed the opportunity of emulating Miss Lambe's almost inaudible "very interesting." She began stammering that she was naturally, that of course she had given her opinion, but found she could no longer avoid doing so, Sidney having produced a lull in the general conversation by advancing towards her and holding out the box. She took a fleeting glance up at him, saw the gleam of amusement in his eyes and said with dignity,

"It is extremely pretty."

"You would not call it an — ah — unnecessary object?"

"Not at all, in this case," she replied, biting her lip to refrain from laughing. She was willing to concede Sidney had outwitted her; but she refused to look up at him in open acknowledgement of the victory. She kept her own eyes very firmly on the box, determined to reserve her right to that measure of independence at least. But Sidney, equally determined to impose his will on anyone with whom he chose to exert himself, continued to stand in front of her till in sudden embarrassment that everyone must be watching them — in a rush of confusion she was unable to control — Charlotte weakened and glanced up again.

She had frequently found the teasing expression of Sidney's eyes could be completely exasperating, and had every intention of meeting it with a blank look of innocent gravity. But before she could check herself, she discovered she was smiling back at him involuntarily and admitting that, exasperating or not, Sidney's teasing gleam had quite become irresistible to her.

182

In that moment, as they stood smiling at one another, Charlotte was conscious of several contradictory sensations, of which the chief were these: annoyance with herself for being incapable of governing her own actions, satisfaction that Sidney had won this very minor victory over her, amusement, embarrassment — an odd something between perturbation and pleasure — and, above all else, a flutter of singing, exclaiming, joyful spirits which made her feel she had strayed somehow into a most unfamiliar world.

And as Sidney turned away, a phrase he had used that morning drummed suddenly in her ears: "Will you make no allowance for the instinctive guidance of the heart?" Was *this* what he had meant? Could such a thing happen to someone as sober and sensible as herself? Could *she* have so little control over her own conduct that Sidney could make her behave according to his will and not hers?

She told herself that indulging in this train of thought was folly and tried to dispel the agitation such an idea had started up by setting the trivial little incident in its proper perspective. She may have been made to smile to order: it did not necessarily follow that Sidney could force her into doing anything else. On their homeward journey, for instance, if he were to suggest they adopt the same seating arrangements, if he were to stretch out an imperious hand to help her up on to the box — it was very possible she would instinctively obey him; and arguments and reasoning would occur to her far too late to be of any avail. Had not this already happened to her on their outward journey? She had certainly allowed Sidney to overrule her own judgement then although she neither respected his motives nor approved of his plans. But surely now she realised the weakness and inconsistency of such behaviour, it would be the easiest thing in the world to rectify it?

Studying herself with honesty and recognising the amazing

influence Sidney had somehow acquired over her before she was aware of it, Charlotte's next reaction was to try to counteract it by concentrating on his very obvious defects of character and reciting them over to herself: he was flippant, worldly, imprudent, impetuous, domineering, officious, unrepulsable, irresponsible and probably unreliable. But this catalogue of his faults only made her smile more broadly than ever. When the seed of this indulgence had been planted she could not say, but it had grown untended into a flourishing and hardy tree which now branched out to shelter every deficiency of his she could name: she was quite certain he told any lie which came into his head. He was also, she suspected, a most hardened flirt, who used compliments merely to get his own way. She caught herself smiling again and realised, with a reluctant but very sturdy regard for the truth, that her detachment over Sidney Parker's real character seemed to have vanished; and her estimation of his qualities — either good or bad — was now completely worthless.

The thought suddenly occurred to her that this was perhaps how Clara Brereton had managed to shut her eyes to all Sir Edward's many defects. She must have grown a similar tree of indulgence to shelter his foolishness, his pomposity, his conceit and his selfishness, shading them from her own view with thicker and thicker branches till they no longer mattered. Was this what people meant when they said love was blind? Was this some important key she herself had always missed in trying to understand strange relationships, odd partnerships and human beings in the generality?

Her astonishment increasing with every second at these unbidden thoughts and novel theories, Charlotte was obliged to turn aside, to lean over the counter of sea shells in pretended employment, while she scolded her senses back into their proper places. Her mind was now in too much confusion to think anything out clearly. She was uncertain of her own judgement, mistrustful of her own feelings and unwilling to think any more along these lines.

But her self-possession gradually returned and with it a heightened perception of all that was ridiculous in allowing herself to become engrossed in her own concerns in the midst of her present companions and present surroundings. She looked about her, struggling for composure. She was standing in a crowded little seaside curio shop, in broad daylight; and there were people chattering all round her with a buzz, a restlessness and an indecision as the large party began to split up in one of the inevitable divisions of such excursions.

"But we must see more of Brinshore," complained Miss Denham, tired of standing about in a group. "Who will join me on a walk of exploration?"

Sidney, to whom this was chiefly addressed, declared himself very willing and suggested Miss Denham sort out the walking party while he remained in the shop to complete his sisters' purchase.

"Oh yes, we must all return to the beach and search for seaweed" was Miss Beaufort's rejoiner and "Oh, certainly" was her sister's. "I simply cannot wait to make our collection and experiment over pressing seaweed for *our* pictures!"

Whether others besides Miss Denham disliked the prospect of travelling home in carriages full of seaweed or preferred more private inland routes, the principle of separation was now taken up and canvassed by many; and Miss Diana was energetic in promoting her own scheme for dividing up the party even further. Anxious to get back to the inn and organise a cold collation, she insisted both her sister and Miss Lambe should accompany her and have all the benefit of a short rest. "They could enjoy some leisure while she neglected herself for the convenience of everybody else."

And Miss Heywood also happening to fall under her scrutiny

just as this little party was setting off, Miss Diana was struck by her bewildered appearance; and Charlotte was so kindly pressed to join them that there was no refusing.

Despite her own preoccupation, she was able to render valuable service to Miss Diana when they reached the inn. The necessity for this arose from the unlikely circumstance of Miss Parker's being stung on the nose by a bee as they entered the inn yard.

"Oh, poor Susan, what is to be done? Take her, take her, Miss Heywood! No, no, catch Miss Lambe — I am sure she is about to faint."

Roused most unexpectedly from her reverie by the sudden commotion, Charlotte could not at first understand what had happened and Diana's exclamations made the situation no clearer.

"Oh, my poor Susan, how grieved I am for your nerves! Will they stand up to such a trial? But I must make myself useful. I must be off to fetch assistance," remaining, nevertheless, to stroke her sister's shoulders affectionately but rather helplessly. "Ah! what is to be done?"

As far as walking and talking went, Miss Diana was competent to deal with the everyday management of their affairs, but faced by an unexpected crisis, she only wrung her hands and talked on.

"Poor dear Susan is always so prone to such accidents. You would scarcely believe it — whenever she has a day's health, some insect attacks her or some obstacle trips her up. Something is always at hand to undermine her constitution. But what is to be done now? And was it a bee or a wasp?"

"It was a bee. I saw it," said Miss Lambe calmly and very definitely. "Wasps fly faster, they make more noise, have longer shapes and no yellow underneath." And Charlotte felt an immediate and implicit trust in both her claim to identify insects and her ability to refrain from fainting. She also had no hesitation in assuming command now she properly understood the nature of the crisis.

"My younger brothers have often been stung by bees," she told Miss Diana. "It *is* painful but there is no real cause for alarm. Lean on my arm, Miss Parker. We can do nothing till you sit down and allow me to examine it."

Between them, she and Miss Lambe led Miss Parker into the inn-parlour; and despatching the gaping landlord to find ammonia and a clean piece of linen, Charlotte coaxed their patient to the sofa.

"There, lie still and let me see. I can relieve the pain a little, if you will let me withdraw the sting. It is really only a very fine hair; but if I can pull it out, you will feel much better."

"Yes, yes," agreed Diana, hovering about. "Have you sent the landlord for a potion? I do not know at all what to suggest in this case. Rose water perhaps? Or a tincture of mallow leaves? Such an accident has never occurred to *us* before. But it is always best to take medicines lying down — much the best thing to adopt a posture that makes them slow in travelling through the body instead of hurrying them through post. Oh dear if only the bee had stung poor Susan in the ear, I could have made a suggestion — a roasted onion placed in the ear once cured Fanny Noyce of an ear-ache almost immediately. She wrote and told me; and I have been waiting ever since for one of us to get the ear-ache so we could test it out for ourselves. But a nose! I know little of noses!"

While she was talking, Charlotte managed to soothe Miss Parker sufficiently to extract the bee sting.

"I hope I have relieved her a little already," she said, straightening up. "If she can now lie quietly and we dab on some of the ammonia the landlord brings, she will be quite comfortable in a few hours. It is only a question of time and patience. There is nothing further we can do."

But Miss Diana continued to do a great deal in an ineffectual way, pestering the landlord about leaves of elder, red dock leaves, mallow leaves and mutton suet, intent on discovering if any or all of these were readily available in case they should suddenly prove useful. She was so obviously incapable of finding out at the same time what the inn larder could afford in the way of cold meat, that Charlotte quietly arranged that too before allowing her own thoughts to engross her again.

By this time her head had become so full of Sidney Parker (as it had been rather less consciously for the past week) she had lost the power to concentrate on anything but essentials. The incident of the bee-sting had revived her practical instincts for a brief period, but now they sank again under a weight of conflicting thoughts and emotions. And though common sense directed that she must not excite the suspicion of others by her silence and lack of spirits, her mind was so busily engaged that she was not always aware of her own behaviour. She also took little notice of her surroundings. She observed very little of Brinshore, the inn, or any of her companions; and the remainder of their stay there passed in a fever of growing impatience on her side to discover whether they would drive home in exactly the same way — and whether she should or should not object to this?

Nobody had yet noticed or commented upon the disappearance of one of their carriages; and so far as Charlotte could make out, neither Sidney, Henry Brudenall nor Clara Brereton intended to draw anybody's attention to it. Was it for *her* to involve them in the embarrassment of a general discussion on the subject? She could readily imagine Diana's exclamations, Sir Edward's objections and his sister's astonishment; and she did not blame Sidney for wishing to avoid explanations about Mr. Brudenall's personal circumstances with the entire party.

There was, Charlotte told herself, no serious impropriety in the mode of travel Sidney had chosen. There would be none at all if he discussed the whole incident openly, maintained that the Parker carriage had broken down, and submitted to new seating arrangements for the journey back. But Sidney appeared determined to support Henry Brudenall's spirits on the way home as well, Miss Brereton apparently did not object to travelling with him and while these three continued to preserve a reticent silence, Charlotte felt quite unequal to exposing them all to the curiosity of the others by raising the subject herself. But she dreaded lest some mischance should bring on discovery and had many more doubts and many misgivings as the afternoon advanced.

But she need not have worried. Diana was too concerned over her sister to put up any opposition to her brother's plans for the journey home, everyone else seemed too fatigued by their exertions in chasing walking partners for the day to pursue them further as driving companions; and nobody objected when Sidney began his usual ploy of hurrying them off to their destination before they had time to decide how they wished to travel there.

"We have overspent our day in Brinshore by an hour already," he began, raising the subject and consulting his watch at the same time. "And this evening there is not even a moon to help us. I have ordered the carriages to be brought round. It would be best — do you not agree, Diana? — if we travel back in the same order as we set out — a deal of time and trouble saved in discussing any rearrangement! And I am, in any case, determined to drive last."

It was done. He had despatched them all and was holding his hand down to Charlotte before she had let go her breath in suspense that he would not achieve it.

"Well, Miss Heywood," he said as he guided his horses carefully out of the inn yard. "What a fine day this has been for you. All the opportunities for observing people you could possibly want."

"Observing people?" Charlotte realised she had observed almost nothing throughout the entire day. She recollected now that the morning's drive had opened with the embarrassment of Clara Brereton's unexpected confession. Her chief wish then had been to avoid Miss Brereton for the remainder of the day — and she had scarcely given another thought to *that* problem! She could also dimly recall some surprise over Henry Brudenall's sudden change in spirits — and then her awakening interest in Miss Lambe. But all had been sunk in her own preoccupations.

"I do not really think — " she began slowly. "Was there something of great interest that I missed?"

The guarded glance of enquiry Sidney directed at her brought a quick blush to her cheeks; but she had the impression his mind must be very differently engaged.

"Oh come now, Miss Heywood, you are the observer. I am so busy directing, I often miss such details as you would inevitably notice. But surely it was a day of great promise for your powers."

He paused again, but Charlotte still could not trust herself to speak with sufficient composure.

"Well then, let me see what I had much amusement in observing myself," went on Sidney. "Sir Edward, for instance. Did he not give *you* the benefit of Lord Byron's "dark blue seas"? He did so with practically everyone else. And the Miss Beauforts so vociferous in proclaiming the latest craze, even though, in this case, it was as unprepossessing as seaweed. Susan, as usual, suffering from a ludicrous accident; Diana scolding, vapouring and organising everything into chaos. Miss Denham sulky because Henry and I kept our distance; and Arthur, like the immature youth he is, snuffing about everyone's heels in the manner of a joyful puppy. I thought we were all behaving very much in character and offering great scope for a detached observer like yourself to laugh at us all."

"No," admitted Charlotte. "The only people I observed closely were not behaving in character at all."

"Indeed! And whom were you observing so closely?"

Charlotte had, in fact, observed nobody but herself; but almost at random, she named Clara Brereton and Adela Lambe as the two people who had interested her most during the day. As soon as she had spoken, she regretted it, hoping Sidney would not enquire why Miss Brereton had excited her particular curiosity.

But he only laughed.

"Miss Brereton and Miss Lambe! What a blow that is to my vanity!" sighing in mock disappointment. "Here was I hoping that if you were overlooking everyone else today, you might at least have been concentrating in unravelling my character to your satisfaction."

Charlotte could not be made comfortable by this speech. That was impossible. Nor could she think of anything to say in reply.

"Ah well, I am afraid you have now missed your opportunity," Sidney said lightly. "And I must ask you to suspend any judgement on *me* till I return from London."

"Are you going to London?" Charlotte demanded; and the sudden stab of disappointment would have told her — if she had not admitted it to herself already — that Sidney's presence in Sanditon was of increasing importance to her. "When are you going?"

"Early tomorrow morning. Have I not mentioned it before?"

"No," said Charlotte. "I suppose there was no reason why you should."

The dissatisfaction she felt at his announcement of this sudden departure for London was almost as much over his character as his coming absence. Vanity, extravagance, love of change, that restlessness she had noted in all the Parkers, the family failing — to be always doing something, always moving about — heedlessness of others: he became liable to all these additional charges. It did not accord with the unselfish warmth of friendship towards Henry Brudenall she believed she had discerned in him. Now that his friend had survived his cousin's wedding day, was he intending to abandon him without further compunction? Would he abandon all his friends with the same ease and the same indifference?

Charlotte was conscious that her distress at this news was far too excessive and tried to overcome it. Her spirits were certainly depressed; but she could still exert herself to appear unconcerned. And though her complexion varied, she was soon able to say in a tolerably disengaged tone,

"And when will you be coming back?"

"Ah, that I cannot definitely say. My business in London is rather complicated — and has become more so from my having postponed it several days already. I dare say I might manage to come back and collect Henry within a week or ten days."

He did not sound particularly concerned over what Henry would do for entertainment during his absence. And when she tried to imagine what he himself would be doing during those ten days, her mind could only conjure up a vision of some unknown and fashionable world. She had inferred — from Sidney himself — that London was a world of glamour, excitement, activity, amusement and all the attractions of urbane wit and casual relationships; and she knew this was very far from the world of peaceful fixity and of stable rural values to which she herself belonged. For she had also inferred that London was a world of endlessly false appearances, in which manners were perhaps a substitute for morals: a place easily given over to cold deception, manipulation and exploitation. Why had it never occurred to her that Sidney's background — his natural values — were so totally dissimilar from her own?

She was extremely angry with herself for not having thought along these lines before; for not having realised that, all day, she had been unconsciously encouraging and indulging sentiments which she should have been repressing. She did not attempt to deny that Sidney stood very high in her esteem. But she had almost succeeded in convincing herself they could hardly share one opinion of any importance in common, when he turned to her and said cheerfully,

"And so, Miss Heywood, as this is to be our last meeting for some time, how shall we set about enjoying it? Do you want speed or rational conversation or a combination of both?"

And forgetting everything else in an instant, she determined to enjoy Sidney's company while it remained hers to enjoy; and though perhaps their journey back to Sanditon afforded not quite the same light-hearted pleasure as the journey out, she stored and treasured those two hours the more thoroughly in the foreknowledge that they would have to last her in memories for some time to come.

CHAPTER 21

A SLEEPLESS NIGHT spent examining her own conduct and coming to terms with her own feelings was so unusual an event for Charlotte that she expected the next day would exact its toll in reactions of lethargy and discontent — even perhaps in unwelcome second thoughts which were only bound to confuse her. And great was her surprise, when the morning sun at last crept into her room, to discover she was already wide-awake — and awake, moreover, with a very curious sense of beginning to live so intensely that she was a little frightened.

The main window of her bedroom overlooked the driveway; and, a sudden clatter of horses' hooves below drawing her to it while she was dressing, she looked down at an oblique angle through the gauze curtain to Sidney's neat carriage pausing for a moment outside the front porch. By craning her neck in an absurd and undignified way, she could even see part of Sidney's profile. He was talking to Morgan, leaning down to hand him something, laughing, turning his carriage and driving off again through the gates of Trafalgar House.

Standing tiptoe on her bare feet, she watched the top of his head recede into the distance till it disappeared from view over the downs. And although she smiled at herself in her folly of standing half-dressed behind a window curtain in the early morning breeze from the sea, not all her scolding at being such a simpleton could have made her turn away till she was certain no more distant hills might bring the carriage again into view.

She felt ridiculously light of heart as she finished dressing; and had to stop several times on the staircase to compose her looks into their normal sober pattern before she felt equal to showing herself to her hosts at the breakfast table.

On entering the room, she wondered if she had in fact succeeded. A certain constraint in the greetings of both Mr. and Mrs. Parker troubled her; and as she took her place at the table, she was uncomfortably aware that they seemed to be staring at her rather curiously. But this was almost immediately resolved by Mr. Parker's handing her a parcel and saying in his eager, inquisitive way,

"Well now, Miss Heywood, this is for you and we neither of us can imagine what is in it! Sidney called early this morning, took us in his way on setting out for town — and *he* left this packet for you. I was never more surprised in my life! Not even downstairs when I heard the commotion — shouting in the drive-way and Morgan rushing to the door in his shirt sleeves. 'I forgot to leave in this parcel,' calls Sidney from his carriage. 'Yes, sir,' says Morgan, 'I will give it to Mr. Parker as soon as he comes down.' 'No, no, not for my brother,' cries Sidney. 'For Miss Heywood. I am leaving the parcel for Miss Heywood. Only the small booklet is for my brother.' By that time, you know, I had reached the front steps and tried to ask him what he meant. But Sidney was turning his horses round and could not hear me. He would only laugh. 'Well, Tom, I am off. See that Miss Heywood gets her parcel.' So, of course, we have been wondering ever since what it could be that Sidney has left for you."

He held out the small parcel, carefully wrapped and tied, and accompanied by a letter thrust under the string. There could be no doubt of his burning curiosity with regard to the contents. Even Mrs. Parker, in quieter fashion, appeared wary and worried over this impulsive gesture of her brother-in-law in sending a letter and a gift to their young guest.

Very conscious of their intent observation, Charlotte accepted the parcel, laid it aside, extracted the letter and opened it. Knowing she would have to read it aloud to satisfy Mr. Parker, she had some misgivings herself; and from her still imperfect knowledge of Sidney's character, was dreading what it might prove to contain. She glanced over it.

Dear Miss Heywood,

Forgive this hurried note. I could not resist buying the accompanying gift in Brinshore yesterday. I believe I intended it at the time as a present for my brother, but on reflection, have decided he might not appreciate it, and will have to content himself with the "Guide to Watering Places" which I had already purchased for him. Moreover, as I was indeed lucky enough to find an exact replica of the object my sisters bought, it now occurs to me that my own family are well provided with mementoes of Brinshore. Your own admiration was so clearly expressed that I feel I can do no better than bestow my rash purchase on you. I cannot, in any case, take it to London, as it is too fragile to pack. And you, I am sure, will agree such an "extremely pretty" and "necessary" box deserves better than to be broken.

Yours etc. Sidney Parker.

Suppressing a smile, Charlotte handed the letter to Mrs. Parker, and cautiously unwrapping the layers of paper, revealed the small box, labelled "Brinshore."

"What's this? What's this?" cried Mr. Parker. "A box all covered with shells? And why does it have Brinshore on it in those little coloured pebbles? What does one do with it? And what can Sidney mean sending such a thing to Miss Heywood?"

"Sidney says he meant to give it to you," said Mrs. Parker, looking up from the letter. "It is clear enough what his intentions *were.* So exactly his sense of humour! He thinks it would have been very amusing to give you a box with Brinshore written on it." She handed the letter to her husband. "It is one of his jokes."

"Then why did he give it to Miss Heywood?" demanded Mr. Parker in bewilderment.

"Would you like it?" offered Charlotte a little fearfully. Quite suddenly she found she had become very possessive over the ugly little box.

"Me? Like a useless box labelled *Brinshore?* No, no. Sidney is quite in the right there. 'On reflection, I have decided he might not appreciate it.' Very proper. But let me see it. So this is the type of thing Brinshore goes in for! Do they think *that* will attract visitors? Yes, yes, I see it is one of Sidney's jokes, as Mary says. But good Lord! I would not have such a thing in the house. Ah! so Susan and Diana bought one too — precisely what they would do, of course. My sisters are very worthy women, Miss Heywood, but without a scrap of taste to share between them. You should see some of the knick-knacks they keep about their house — tables crammed with ornamental pill-boxes and extravagant gewgaws. It does not surprise me in the least to find them adding to the number. Well, it is funny, I suppose. 'Too fragile to pack.' And did you really call it an 'extremely pretty box'?"

"I believe I did *say* so," admitted Charlotte. "Your sisters had already bought one and the Miss Beauforts were admiring it — and Sir Edward — in short, out of politeness, I remember saying something of the sort because I could not very well avoid it."

"Ha! I see how it all was. Many a time have I been forced to admire some hideous thing Diana has bought and Sidney has teased me about it afterwards. He can never resist these little attempts to be humorous at other people's expense."

The Parkers had decided to laugh at Sidney's unexpected letter to Miss Heywood; and the box was now firmly established as one of Sidney's jokes, to be looked at and smiled at over their breakfast, but not given another thought. And Charlotte, who also smiled at it, was not really surprised to discover it meant far more than a joke to her. She was grateful the box had been presented in such a way that she could keep it without arousing anybody's suspicions. But she was forced to admit the Parkers' assessment of the incident came closer to Sidney's own intentions. He had bought the box on a sudden impulse without thinking of her at all; he had written the note in a hurry just as he was setting off for London; and provided the fun was enjoyed somewhere, he did not mind who in particular claimed ownership of the box.

"He has played another such joke on me," said Mr. Parker taking a small booklet from his pocket. "This *Guide to Watering Places* he has left for me — all heavily underscored in what Sidney considers the appropriate places. Well, of course, I knew such an annual handbook existed but have never bothered trying to get Sanditon included in it. And here, you see, he has turned down the corner to bring my attention to it — Brinshore, coming straight after Brighton. Two columns of it!"

"But perhaps it would be no bad idea to arrange for a mention of Sanditon in such a book," Mrs. Parker suggested. "Surely many people we cannot know of must consult a library or buy this book before deciding on a seaside holiday?"

"Nonsense, my dear Mary. The sort of people who consult such rubbish are not the sort we want encouraged at Sanditon. What facts, what truth can be expected from a publication like this? It shows no discrimination at all. Though they may be trying to puff up Brinshore, what have they actually found to praise? Listen to this," reading in a sarcastic tone: " 'The possibility of pleasant living without extortionate expense may, in this comparatively retired and humble spot, be secured in a manner more compatible with the rigid rules of economy than at places of more public and splendid resort.' "

"But I see nothing to censure in that," said Mrs. Parker mildly. "Brinshore knows it cannot attract the fashionable and is making a bid to secure the respectable invalid."

"Oh, undoubtedly," agreed Mr. Parker, still scanning his booklet. "And in almost illiterate language," reading again scornfully: " 'Another advantage particularly advantageous (*Who*, outside of Brinshore, would descend to so clumsy a phrase as that?) is the early hour at which public amusements commence and terminate —a matter of more importance than is generally imagined in preserving actual health and in promoting its restoration.' Ah! Sidney has added a marginal comment to that," turning the page at a right angle and trying to make out the scrawl. " 'Sanditon has, of course, an advantage even more advantageous to invalids in the complete absence of any public amusements at all.' Impudent young dog!"

He threw the booklet down on the table in disgust. Mrs. Parker picked it up and began searching the two columns for more factual information than her husband had read out. She soon found one item of interest.

"It says here that Brinshore has just developed the amenity of a new Marine Walk for its visitors. Now *that* is the sort of thing which might really attract visitors. Did you walk along it yesterday, Miss Heywood?"

"No, I — that is — I was not aware of it," said Charlotte in some confusion, rather ashamed to admit she had noticed so little of anything in Brinshore, and hoping she was not now to be called upon to confirm every statement set down to its credit in the booklet.

"There, you see!" crowed Mr. Parker triumphantly. "Brinshore boasts of one walk but nobody notices it. Sanditon abounds in walks — "

"Then you should let people know about them," Mrs. Parker advised him calmly. "Look, here is a list of Brinshore's chief attractions for anyone who likes to read: Good prospects for restored health and spirits; a resort physician and experienced apothecary always at hand; bathing highly favourable in six well-equipped bathing machines; pleasure boats kept for hire; sedan chairs, bath chairs, wheel chairs, horses, gigs and donkeys to be had upon reasonable terms; important aquatic and inland excursions; possibilities for geologists, fossilists, naturalists and collectors of seaweed and sea shells; Assembly Rooms — ball, billiard and card rooms — located in one compact group; regular fortnightly Assemblies held throughout the season. Sidney has underlined that amenity, naturally."

"Let me see, let me see," cried Mr. Parker. "As if Sanditon could not do better in listing attractions. I could fill at least four columns without having to huff and puff the way Brinshore does. I would start with one simple statement: 'There is no reason why Sanditon should not, in a little time, rank among the most attractive of watering places.' And then, you know, go on to list our own special advantages: Highly favoured situation, being defended by our own range of hills from every wind but the south, salubrity and mildness of our atmosphere, purity of water, rich fertility of the soil, diversity and beauty of our scenery. This would make Brinshore's list seem feeble indeed! And where are *their* important aquatic and inland excursions? No mention, of course, of what they are in detail! Have *they* anything like Fordcliff Abbey in the vicinity? Have *they* a Peak Hill or a chesil over their stream? Have they constructed tea rooms on *their* beach? They would never dare to construct tea rooms without a good dish of tea to be served in them. How was the tea at your inn yesterday, Miss Heywood? Brackish taste? Insupportable, no doubt?"

"I do not think I noticed anything amiss," confessed Charlotte. "The tea seemed, that is, I think — "

"Probably they import inland water for tea at the inn," Mr. Parker agreed comfortably. "You would certainly have noticed it otherwise. No sweet water to be had anywhere near Brinshore. However, I really must speak to Lady Denham about developing a Marine Walk. Though of course we shall call ours an Esplanade!"

And fired with sudden enthusiasm, Mr. Parker seized hold of the *Guide to Watering Places* and retired for the morning into his study to scan it for further ideas, and to compose a suitable entry on Sanditon for submission to the responsible editors.

Charlotte, finishing her breakfast, reflected on the peculiar satisfaction to be derived from witnessing a really clever director outwitting someone rather less gifted, and the delight with which Sidney would have greeted his success in manipulating his brother — even from a distance and without any persuasive arguments — into doing precisely the opposite of what he intended.

But when she picked up her own box and carefully carried it off to her room — not forgetting the accompanying letter — it never occurred to her that she, too, might be doing something which Sidney intended.

A young lady's exact estimate of her own charms would be a difficult matter to determine but Charlotte certainly never estimated hers as meriting the full treatment of one of Sidney's intricate little plots. If she could have brought herself to believe he had purchased the box especially for her, and devoted a great deal of thought to composing a seemingly hasty letter which made it possible for her to accept it, she would have valued the gift even more.

CHAPTER 22

CHARLOTTE had every intention of spending her day — and perhaps several succeeding days — with Mrs. Parker in her new greenhouse. Though lacking her husband's general enthusiasm, Mrs. Parker had developed a quiet fanaticism of her own in becoming a dedicated gardener. She grew all her own flowering plants from seed, experimented with new varieties, and was rarely content to hand anything over to the gardener till it became too large for her to house or for him to damage by ill-treatment.

She was always busy transplanting small seedlings from crowded boxes into a succession of ever larger pots, where she watered them, tended them and coaxed them into the flourishing bushes she was prepared to abandon.

Happy enough in her greenhouse to pass all her mornings in solitary cultivation, Mrs. Parker welcomed any genuine offers of useful assistance; but her mild countenance assumed its nearest approach to a frown whenever she was interrupted in her own labours.

Charlotte observed this frown and a gentle sigh, both being suppressed, as Lady Denham pushed open the greenhouse door that morning.

"Lord bless me, here you are at it again! Morgan told me I should find you here. No, no, leave your gardening gloves on, Mrs. Parker. I am not one to stand on ceremony with my neighbours. I will not have you regarding this as a morning call — just taking you in on my usual walk and come to pass the time of day; no need at all for me to sit down, I assure you. Miss Clara is off to change her books again, and I did not choose to walk so far. Well, it *is* a pity you have no room for a little bench or two in here! Oh, my dear Mrs. Parker, I can just as easily stand. Do not, I beg of you, come back to the house on my account."

But Mrs. Parker had already laid down her tools, taken off her gloves and nodding pleasantly to Charlotte to follow, was leading the way out of the greenhouse.

"Your young visitor is not such a gadabout, I see," said her ladyship approvingly as they walked towards the house. "Her head seems in no danger of being turned to giddy nonsense like others I could name. With all these young people making merry in Sanditon nowadays, Miss Clara is become so fidgetty and restless — never settling down properly at home as she ought. And where she finds time to read all these books she borrows from the library is beyond me! I declare one and twenty is a most trying age for young ladies — their minds full of nothing but clothes and social pleasures. The Miss Beauforts, I can see, are cut from exactly the same piece of cloth."

Mrs. Parker made one of her amiable remarks on the happiness and high spirits of young people in general which did nothing to distract Lady Denham from her own particular grievance.

"Oh aye, that's all very true, I dare say. But I tell you what Mrs. Parker, *some* young people consult nobody's pleasure but their own. However, I am not a woman who minds owning to making mistakes. I should have seen from the first that one of my older nieces would prove more of a steady companion to *me*. But it's clear enough now Miss Clara is too young and flighty to settle down with me forever. Still no harms' done that can't be mended. My original invitation to her was for six months only, you know; and you may be sure I mentioned the probability of one of the other girls coming to take her place after that. Yes, yes, it is high time I made the exchange."

"Indeed!" said Mrs. Parker with some surprise. "You are contemplating an actual exchange among your nieces? This is surely most unexpected. I had no notion Miss Brereton would be leaving you."

"Oh, that is still quite between ourselves. I have told *her* I will invite her cousin, Miss Elizabeth, for a few weeks. And then, you know, I am still free to make up my mind between them," with a self-satisfied smile at her own sagacity. "You may be sure, Mrs. Parker, I am not one to be pushed into anything against my will; and those persons who fancy they can pull the wool over my eyes will soon find they are mistaken! I can't be expected to be feeding and housing two nieces where one is enough for my own convenience. So if Miss Elizabeth makes herself useful and takes over all Miss Clara's little duties — well, then we shall see."

This sudden eagerness of Lady Denham's to exchange one niece for the other made Charlotte wonder if some inkling of Sir Edward's partiality for Miss Brereton had at last penetrated that suspicious but oddly insensible mind. Her keenest attention was aroused but she knew no useful purpose would be served by taking part in the conversation herself. She would have to rely on Mrs. Parker to extract all the particulars from her guest. But as Lady Denham had settled herself into a comfortable armchair for a lengthy visit, a full airing of both her suspicions and her selfish schemes seemed likely to follow without much encouragement.

"I had always understood Miss Brereton had now made her home with you," Mrs. Parker observed after a little hesitation. "Will she not perhaps be somewhat upset at being thus turned back on her relatives?"

"Oh, as to that, I cannot say. She may even be glad to make the change. She has hinted often enough Miss Elizabeth would suit me much better than herself. But I can't be worrying myself over Miss Clara's views on the matter. I am on the lookout for a fixed — a *permanent* — companion for myself; and who's to say Miss Clara may not even decide on marrying one of these days? And what shall I do then, I ask you, if I have made no other arrangements? I can't be left at a moment's notice to run all these errands and do all the tasks I have been busy teaching Miss Clara to perform."

Why the possibility of Clara's eventual marriage should never have occurred to Lady Denham before puzzled Charlotte as much as this tardy recognition of the problem now.

"Naturally, Miss Brereton is bound to marry some day," Mrs. Parker said very sensibly. "Good-natured and gentle as well as beautiful — who can doubt she will not be sought after as a wife?"

"I was certain *you* would think so," replied Lady Denham, with one of her shrewdest glances. "It was that brother-in-law of yours who first put me in mind of it. To be sure, Sir Edward plays at gallantry with Miss Clara too; but I know *he* can mean nothing by it. He must marry for money! But when a young man who can afford to marry where he chooses starts smirking in her direction — "

"You refer, I collect, to my brother-in-law, Sidney," said Mrs. Parker, who did not like this type of gossip. "I do not think you should refine too much on his behaviour. His manners, I am afraid, are sometimes over-insinuating but he seldom means anything by them. Can I offer you some refreshment, Lady Denham?" And she rang the bell as though putting an end to this subject.

"Well there may be nothing in it, as you say; but it put me in mind of the danger all the same," continued Lady Denham, impervious to hints of such subtlety. "And I have no scruple in owning I have taken a great fancy to Mr. Sidney — his manners do him no harm in *my* eyes. On no, his manners are very civil indeed, most obliging and respectful; he even insisted on stepping in to pay a farewell call on me last night when he drove Miss

Clara home. Upon my word, he always says and does everything that is proper. On my merely happening to mention my latest plan of writing to invite Miss Elizabeth to Sanditon, he most kindly offered to collect the letter on his way to London this morning. So many days saved in the usual correspondence by post! She will now receive my letter by this evening — may even be able to arrange her journey within a week or two. For as Mr. Sidney pointed out, he himself will be back in Sanditon before then and can bring me her reply."

Charlotte was interested to learn Sidney was still involved in this scheme of bringing Miss Elizabeth Brereton to Sanditon; and his connection with the affair intrigued her considerably. To what extent his determined sponsoring of Miss Elizabeth had weighed with Lady Denham she could only surmise; and she wondered whether this new amendment of allowing her to supplant Miss Clara entirely would take him by surprise. But she had observed enough of Sidney's methods by now to recognise his contriving hand in the whole arrangement of the visit.

Lady Denham, however, seemed unaware that Sidney had directed her in any way at all; her own views on his skill at management had taken quite a different turn, as became obvious a few moments later when she observed gleefully,

"Oh yes, Mr. Sidney has already been very useful to me. And I intend to turn his talents to even better account when he comes back to Sanditon! I honestly think I can rely on him to help me in carrying out any scheme I have in mind. That quickness he has of understanding any ticklish little situation has quite delighted me," dropping her voice and rushing on with an even greater burst of confidence. "For you know, between ourselves, the main reason I agreed to the use of my coach and horses yesterday on that excursion to Brinshore was to throw Sir Edward and Miss Lambe together for the whole day. He cannot afford to let

such an heiress slip through his fingers; and so I told him! Oh,
he knows well enough he must marry for money, but he has too
high an opinion of himself and thinks he can take his time about
it. *He* won't make a push and fix Miss Lambe in a hurry unless
I help him into it! So I just gave Mr. Sidney the merest hint of
my plans — told him I wanted Sir Edward to take charge of my
coach and suggested Miss Lambe as one of his passengers. And
now I hear from Miss Clara how discreetly it was all arranged —
not the slightest suspicion seems to have crossed *her* mind that
Sir Edward and Miss Lambe sat together by my arrangement or
that Mr. Sidney Parker was contriving it all to please me."

This additional complication in Sidney's seating arrangements
for the drive to Brinshore surprised Charlotte as well; and on
consideration, she was bound to admit it had been carried out
with such subtlety as to have aroused no curiosity at all. She
was not, however, inclined to think Lady Denham's schemes were
likely to have prospered by it. Neither at Brinshore nor anywhere
else had Miss Lambe or Sir Edward ever appeared to show the
slightest interest in each other.

"And I have another scheme in mind which is just as good,"
announced Lady Denham in a tone of great exultation. "But I
won't go dropping such broad hints about that to Mr. Sidney.
He is exactly the right age for settling down himself. And I have
decided he would do equally well for either Miss Clara or Miss
Esther. Both of them lack any fortune of their own so they need
to find a husband in comfortable circumstances. But" — very
generously — "I will leave him to make his own choice between
them. Young men in positions of easy independence like his do
not like to be guided to quite such an extent."

The trend of this conversation was now making Mrs. Parker
extremely impatient. She was used to humouring Lady Denham
and very much in the habit of allowing her to ramble on about all
her own petty concerns. But her forbearance towards near

207

neighbours stopped short of encouraging them in idle speculations about each other. After pointedly changing the subject several times, she was distinctly relieved when their visitor finally arose to depart.

"What a tiresome way of spending our morning!" she said to Charlotte as they walked back to the greenhouse. "Well, thank heaven she is gone and we can settle down to be comfortable again. For, between ourselves," with a gentle smile as she parodied Lady Denham. "I much prefer to talk about flowers than about people."

In perfect accord with one another, they pulled on their gardening gloves and aprons and resumed their stations at opposite ends of the long shelf, each busy with her own array of pots and her own arrangement of thoughts. Charlotte's were almost entirely given over to reflecting on what she had just heard. She regarded Lady Denham's plans for a marriage between Sidney and Miss Denham as ridiculous as her expectations for Sir Edward and Miss Lambe. But her discernment of some attachment between Sidney and Clara Brereton required more serious consideration.

There was certainly admiration on one side and a great wish to please on the other, but Charlotte herself had distinguished little beyond this. The rest appeared to her merely the suggestion of Lady Denham's interested wishes. And she was less inclined to believe in these from the very fact of their influence operating in a contrary direction when Lady Denham dismissed Sir Edward's much greater partiality for Miss Brereton in so arbitrary a manner. "I know *he* can mean nothing by it. He must marry for money!" Such wilful blindness in one direction did not encourage credibility in another.

Charlotte decided she was having rather less success in discounting her own interested wishes. Though rendered suspicious from the first by Sidney's warm commendation of Clara, she had not of late been observing them so intently whenever they were together. Her early surmises had all been on the side of Sidney's

208

developing a decided preference for Clara; but recently she had been content to accept his own explanation for the interest he had always shown in Clara, and to believe his own assertion that he was merely enlisting her sympathetic cooperation to console his friend.

She tried now, most resolutely, to remember what she had actually seen and to separate it from both his statements and her conjectures. There was that first walk through the woods to old Sanditon and the mutual understanding Sidney and Clara had very quickly established; his frequent calls during the following week at Sanditon House; Clara's readiness to oblige him in taking pains over Henry Brudenall; and the recurrent meetings and conversations both in Sanditon and Brinshore. But none of these offered conclusive proof for supposing any sincere and serious regard on one side or the other; and all had been openly conducted in full view of the entire Sanditon community.

Against this, and from her own private knowledge, Charlotte could produce one definite clue, which seemed to *disprove* the existence of any such attachment: Clara Brereton's confession to her of a possible elopement. So desperate a plan indicated little hope of Lady Denham approving her intended match — and she clearly had not the slightest objection to an engagement between Sidney and Clara.

Had Charlotte known nothing of Clara's plans for an elopement, she might have been inclined to agree with Lady Denham and the Miss Parkers. Even as it was, she was certain some connection — some secret understanding — between Sidney and Clara *did* exist. That they were somehow both concerned in persuading Lady Denham to invite Clara's cousin Elizabeth to Sanditon she could not doubt. Had Sidney perhaps promised Clara his cooperation in that direction in return for her services in respect to Henry Brudenall?

It was a subject on which reflection would be long indulged and must always be unavailing. And Charlotte determined she would think of something else as she set about her tasks under Mrs. Parker's directions. She enjoyed the monotony of this work and the soothing, desultory conversation which accompanied it.

"This new strain of dahlia, I am told, comes from Chile — or was it Peru? Next year, I will be able to start them off earlier from root cuttings."

"Yes, of course."

"I am so pleased with my fuchsias. How healthy they are looking already. Such a profusion of buds. Be careful of the leaves as you lift them."

"Yes, of course."

But Charlotte had scarcely got beyond deciding there must be something in the very air of Sanditon which — sooner or later — caused everyone's behaviour to be dominated by some wild, leading passion, and everyone else to ignore it in preoccupation with their own concerns — and had scarcely firmed the earth in two of the new pots — when Arthur's chubby features appeared round the door of the greenhouse.

"Ah, you are only gardening, I see, Mary, so you will not mind my interrupting you," he said, unwittingly offering Charlotte further confirmation of her new theory. "I have come to ask Miss Heywood if she will join myself and the Miss Beauforts on a seaweed-collecting expedition."

"Seaweed collecting? I have never seen any seaweed on our Sanditon shore."

"Not enough to wash up on the beaches," agreed Arthur, "but Miss Beaufort thinks there may be some over by the rocks if we search for it."

"But what does one do with it? You search, you collect, and then what?" This latest of seaside crazes bewildered Mrs. Parker. "Can you transplant it? Would it grow anywhere else but the sea?"

"The Miss Beauforts intend to frame it. And Sir Edward Denham has promised to write some verses for the seaweed pictures they are going to make. But I should like to identify it first," explained Arthur. "Everything is decided and we are all waiting to set out. But you see, I am supposed to wade out if it is under water, so of course I must take an extra pair of shoes — and some towels and dry socks. Miss Beaufort and Miss Letitia are very obliging over all this; but I *did* think as Miss Heywood — well, as she is staying with you — and we are already friends — "

Charlotte saw his anxiety. He wanted protection from the enthusiasm of the Miss Beauforts. Left to their direction alone, he might easily be persuaded into catching an unnecessary cold. But with her to watch over his interests, with her as a guarantee the expedition did not involve him in futile exertion or foolhardy enterprise, he would feel more comfortable.

"And I am sure Miss Heywood will be very glad to accompany you," said Mrs. Parker understandingly. "You are quite right, Arthur. A very sensible notion of yours. Miss Beaufort and Miss Letitia, from what I have observed, are very good-humoured, charming girls — but not perhaps very practical. Miss Heywood is exactly the addition you need to your party. And my plants are always here. She can help me with them another day."

So, rather unwillingly, Charlotte took off her gardening apron for the second time that morning and allowed Arthur to escort her down the hill to the Terrace.

CHAPTER 23

THE MISS BEAUFORTS, with considerable paraphernalia of collecting baskets, drawing paper, crayons, pressing boards, green eye shades and floating shawls, were eager to set off on their expedition; but while loudly proclaiming their zeal for seaweed, they were hesitant about leaving the Terrace before they had gathered up more admirers than Arthur.

Sir Edward Denham, his sister and Miss Brereton stood in an indecisive group, debating whether to join them. Miss Denham seemed to prefer awaiting suggestions for some more interesting pastime from the young men at the hotel. Miss Brereton gave no opinion at all; and Sir Edward was being very eloquent in favour of the seaweed excursion.

Charlotte, who now most sincerely wished to understand how Clara Brereton could favour his suit, was determined to regard Sir Edward with more sympathy than she had lately accorded him; and with this laudable object in view attended to his conversation with his sister.

"But, my dear Esther," he was concluding. "There is no certainty our present procrastinatory conjuncture will culminate in the authentication of your wishes. Our new friends seem disinclined for their morning perambulations today. Perhaps we may discover that, like Burns's Highland Mary, they have forsaken us."

This reference could equally and inappropriately have been applied to Burns's Jean, his Nancy or his Bonnie Lesley, Charlotte reflected. She had long since renounced any attempt to understand Sir Edward's quotations and reluctantly abandoned her new resolution to understand *him*. But as she doubted Henry Brudenall would put in an appearance without Sidney Parker there to insist on it, she hoped some activity might result from supporting Sir Edward.

"I understand Mr. Parker has gone to London on business this morning; and perhaps Mr. Brudenall finds occupation which keeps him indoors."

The announcement had very nearly all the effect she intended, broadening Sir Edward's smiles, deepening his sister's frowns and spreading disappointment among the Miss Beauforts. Clara Brereton alone took no share in the general surprise.

"Oh yes," she said calmly. "When I was telling you that Lady Denham had consented to invite my cousin Elizabeth to visit us for a few weeks, I forgot to mention it was Mr. Parker who was carrying our letters up to London today. This should prove a considerable help in speeding up the necessary arrangements."

There was a note of contentment in her voice, which spoke the serenity of a mind more at ease with itself, and convinced Charlotte that Miss Brereton had recovered from her little fever of the previous day and was prepared to postpone any decision over eloping with Sir Edward till after her cousin's arrival in Sanditon. While his reply of "Indeed yes, we are all eagerly anticipating Miss Elizabeth's introduction among us" seemed to indicate he still did not despair of a favourable outcome.

To Miss Denham however, the prospective arrival of another Miss Brereton made no amends for the present departure of a Sidney Parker; and she showed her ill-humour by exclaiming, —

"Well then! there is no point in standing about on the Terrace. We may just as well walk along the shore with Miss Beaufort and Miss Letitia," and relapsing into a silence of cold displeasure.

Sir Edward's delight was equally obvious as he contemplated

213

the unexpected felicity of a walk which would give him undisturbed monopoly — he did not count Arthur — over the entire
bevy of young ladies in Sanditon — for even Lady Denham's
broadest hints had not led him to count Miss Lambe either. And
offering Miss Brereton first claim on his arm, he hurried them all
off the Terrace before they could change their minds.

But Sir Edward was out of luck. They were passing the hotel
on their descent to the sands, when Henry Brudenall not only
appeared himself — but in the company of a most interesting
stranger, a young man so modishly dressed that the Miss
Beauforts both gaped. It was too much for Sir Edward to expect
any of his five young ladies to ignore this apparition. By
approaching Henry Brudenall immediately himself however, and
making a series of highly unnecessary enquiries about Sidney
Parker's journey to London, he did what he could to forestall any
introductions, hoping perhaps if he detained Mr. Brudenall for
long enough and left this new rival standing disconsolately about,
his own party would eventually walk on out of harm's way.

The stranger was not in the least deterred by this incivility.
Having run a swift eye over the group before him, he made directly
for Charlotte, who was standing by herself, a little to one side of it,
deriving much critical amusement from Sir Edward's graceless
behaviour.

"Henry is too busy to introduce me at the moment, so I see I
must do it for myself," he said with a friendly smile. "Reginald
Catton at your service. And *you* must be Miss Heywood."

A good deal of Charlotte's astonishment was evident in her
face and he laughed very heartily at it.

"Oh! I was easily able to pick you out from everyone else.
I arrived late last night — but not too late for Sidney to give me
a very thorough description of you. We sat up till midnight while
he went through the Sanditon notables and I yawned over every
Parker and Denham in the place. But it's as well Sidney insisted

on doing it then. He was away so early this morning I missed him completely. Never one for getting up at those hours myself."

Charlotte's pleasure in learning that Sidney had bothered to describe her to his friend far exceeded her surprise in being rated as a notable of Sanditon. She would have been very interested to hear what that description had been; and thinking it unlikely Mr. Catton would volunteer more information himself, she did her best to lead him back to the subject by saying smilingly,

"I hope Mr. Parker's description was not too uncomplimentary?"

"Uncomplimentary? No, indeed! How could it have been? I would most certainly repeat it all to you, if I could but remember the details," he said cheerfully. And she perceived he had much of his friend's frankness without his mental alertness. He seemed to be trying to concentrate, to recall something; but then he shrugged his shoulders and gave it up. "The part I do remember clearly, which was why I came straight towards you — just the one phrase that did stick in my mind — something Sidney said about 'smiling grey eyes.'"

This small compliment could not fail to gratify. That Sidney could have made such a remark without any idea of its being carried back to herself was a much greater source of pleasure than any of the compliments he had paid her in person. And though it was tantalising to know there were others details locked up in the recesses of Mr. Catton's mind, Charlotte was very satisfied to have extracted this single tribute and willing to turn the conversation on his own concerns.

"Your arrival in Sanditon seems to be most unexpected. Did you take a sudden idea into your head of visiting your friends?"

"It certainly was sudden," he agreed. "But scarcely my own idea. Sidney sent his brother's groom over to Brighton ordering me across. He wanted someone to keep Henry company while he was off to London."

"His brother's groom? Parsons?"

"Yes. That's the fellow's name. Drove over yesterday."

Charlotte stared. She found this piece of information difficult to fit in with any previous interpretation of Sidney's arrangements over the drive to Brinshore. His own explanation — or the several versions he had successively offered — had never attempted to include this new evidence. She herself had never believed his original and very flattering excuse that he wished to secure her company for the drive. She had *almost* believed his avowal that he wanted Henry to survive his cousin's wedding day as effortlessly as possible. And she had conceded the plot to involve Miss Brereton in the scheme was a very typical example of Sidney's thoughtless frivolity. Even Lady Denham's contribution to the day's arrangements she had regarded as mere fanciful embroidery of his own plans — a subsidiary trick Sidney was quite capable of engrafting on to his main purpose.

But now it seemed the entire affair could be covered by a much more simple explanation; and that he had invented a whole series of unlikely and even conflicting stories with no more serious object in view than freeing one carriage and despatching it on a message to Brighton! And Charlotte began to wonder if there had been anything more devious in it at all.

In retrospect the day in Brinshore offered a remarkable challenge to her powers of observation. The more she heard about it, the more or less she was able to read into it. But except for her own personal involvement in vividly memorable interludes at distinct and highlighted moments, the rest of the expedition was rapidly becoming too vague to hold any meaning for her at all. She had a sudden vision of Sidney's face and his quizzical, teasing expression: "Well, Miss Heywood, what a fine day this has been for you! All the opportunities for observing people you could possibly want." But her own thoughts and feelings had occupied and flurried her too much in Brinshore to permit taking proper notice of others or sorting out all the various and separate incidents of which the day had been composed.

She felt quite ashamed of her failure. That she, who prided herself on her observation, should have been thus blinded for a whole day — and a day on which so much seemed to have been happening. How humiliating to discover Sidney Parker had the power of driving reason and clarity so far out of her head as to render her own most prized abilities completely valueless! She decided the full day in Brinshore was something she would have to lie awake reconsidering for yet another evening. For the moment she would do better to concentrate on trying to understand Reginald Catton's own connection with it.

"You know, it is very strange," she said slowly, "but Mr. Parker gave quite a different reason for sending Parsons off in the carriage yesterday."

"Did he indeed? Oh well, there is no one like Sidney for inventing complications and making everything as confusing as possible for everyone else," said Mr. Catton, laughing a good deal more than Charlotte thought necessary at such whimsical behaviour. "Besides, he always has a score of reasons for everything he does. I doubt he is even capable of doing only one thing at a time! Oh! you may be sure Sidney never has less than four pots on the boil, three irons in the fire and as many sticks as he can find heaped into it as well."

Charlotte felt that both this jumble of metaphors and Mr. Catton's renewed laughter were rather excessive — preventing anything from being very clearly expressed — but persevered in her interrogation.

"It is also rather strange that Mr. Parker never mentioned your coming to any of us yesterday."

"Oh well, he may have been uncertain *then* whether I really would come," he admitted quite frankly. "He is always accusing me of being fickle. But I promised I would help out with Henry no matter what the inconvenience. And not many of Sidney's friends would refuse to do something he asked. So here I am. Must keep the horses harnessed up."

"The horses?" said Charlotte, considerably mystified.

"Why yes, the horses — keep them harnessed — a saying, you know," explained Mr. Catton, with a comic look of alarm which he quickly suppressed by beginning to laugh again even more immoderately. "Have you not heard Sidney using the same expression?"

"Indeed I have not. What does it mean?"

"Mean? Oh, nothing of great importance. Just a saying we have — for fellows in Henry's situation, you know."

"I see. But — "

They were here interrupted by Henry himself, whose approach Mr. Catton welcomed with obvious relief. For some time and with increasing chagrin Sir Edward had been observing the stranger making it impossible for him to obstruct his inclusion in the party, and had now resigned himself to allowing Henry to perform the general introductions, and to giving his sister, Miss Brereton, and the Miss Beauforts their share in these impertinent attentions.

But when they resumed their walk a few minutes later, Reginald Catton took the earliest opportunity of rejoining Charlotte, and almost immediately embarked on a series of highly indiscreet remarks.

"So that was Miss Denham! Predatory female — Sidney warned me. He said I would not be in the least danger from anyone else — could handle all the Miss Beauforts with ease — but Miss Denham would be hanging about me forever if once she caught sight of my barouche. I told the groom to keep it well out of sight in the stables."

Charlotte was very amused. The style of Reginald's conversation had a faint flavour of Sidney's, reminding her of the first evening she had spent in his company — the very frank and lighthearted comments he had passed on all his relations, and her own embarrassment over trying to make adequate replies. But she discovered that the consequences of keeping Sidney company for a brief period meant she did not even try to look disapprovingly at his friend. And although she still felt she should be delivering a reprimand, she could not help laughing outright at him instead. In return, he regarded her with great satisfaction.

"I can see we are going to deal famously together, Miss Heywood. You understand my position I am sure. Very happy to be of service to Henry, of course; but here I am marooned in Sanditon till Sidney returns — and what I shall do for my own amusement, I cannot make out at all. So you must let me know whenever I can be of assistance in any scheme you may have in mind. I will be delighted to help you in organising it — not that I have Sidney's finesse, but I shall do my best."

Charlotte was at a loss what to make of this speech and could only suppose Reginald bracketed her with Sidney as a person who derived amusement from organising all her acquaintance into schemes of one sort or another.

"How long do you expect to be in Sanditon?" she enquired.

"How long? Well, that depends I suppose. Sidney says it is not even certain yet when Henry's ship sails for Bengal."

"But is Mr. Brudenall planning to remain in Sanditon till then? I thought he would be returning to London fairly soon now his cousin's wedding is safely over."

"His cousin's wedding? But — " He broke off, an expression of such embarrassment on his face that Charlotte hastened to add, "It is quite safe to mention that to me. I do understand Mr. Brudenall did not want the exact date of the wedding generally known, but Mr. Parker told me about it yesterday."

"Did he indeed? Oh, well — " Reginald laughed again and confessed rather ingeniously. "You know it is amazingly difficult for me to decide exactly what Sidney has told anybody."

"I cannot guess how much he may have revealed to others,"

said Charlotte. "But, so far as I know, the wedding yesterday was mentioned only to myself and Miss Brereton."

"Oh yes, of course, Miss Brereton. Sidney told me about *her*," agreed Reginald. "And perhaps I was a little sleepy when he was explaining everything else. Or I dare say I was too busy trying to make him listen to me. You know how it is with Sidney — not the slightest notice did he take of my protests last night. It's always the same. When he has any serious business on hand, he rides roughshod over everything — disregards social engagements completely — his own and everyone else's. But I mean it was dashed inconvenient for me. Two parties cancelled — and he waves them aside as mere trifles. Great fellow for insisting his friends must dance to his tune."

"Yes," agreed Charlotte. "He manipulates people. He — "

"Oh! famous for it," interrupted Reginald cheerfully. "Always maintains he is doing it for our own good, of course. And in this case he says it is Henry's. But I told him last night — when he finished warning me about all these odd people and the hazards I was likely to fall into — I said I was dashed if I could get through a whole week of Sanditon without running into trouble somewhere. 'Oh, you will be perfectly all right, Reginald,' says he, 'You stick with my friend Miss Heywood and you cannot come to any harm.' Those were his very words."

They were words which Charlotte was happy to hear repeated at second hand; and yet she felt there was something derogatory in them as well. Why should Sidney be so certain his friend was safer in her company than in anyone else's? Clearly he was prone to indiscretion — which she had already sanctioned with indulgence. But was there something else he and Sidney wanted to hide? Something they expected her to overlook or condone? Again she had the uneasy feeling she was being far less of an acute observer than she had always believed herself. But Sidney's careless recommendation of her to his friend gave such a glow of satisfaction that she was almost prepared to disregard any other implications, and fully prepared to rank the compliment as high as her "smiling grey eyes."

It was these indirect and unconscious small presents Reginald occasionally dispensed which caused her to listen with a concentration his conversation as a whole scarcely merited. He seemed determined to adopt her as his confidante and talked gaily on without ever expecting a reply. But inevitably most of his conversation centred round Sidney; he took it for granted the possession of this mutual friend formed some definite bond of sympathy between them.

"Of course I quite understand Sidney had to go to London himself. Very busy fellow. Three urgent committee meetings, he says, and he could hardly have ordered me up to attend those. I would not have understood a word about gas, light and coal."

"Gas, light and coal?"

"Oh Lord! yes. Did he never mention them to you? Well maybe you have no money to invest but he is always trying to make me invest mine. Or perhaps he thinks it is not a subject which would interest females. I don't say it interests me a great deal but he goes on about it forever lately. 'Lighting London by gaslight, Reginald,' says he, 'is an enterprise you should be proud to support.' I told him I read in the papers somewhere that it would destroy the whale-oil trade; and that meant whale-fisheries, ropemakers, sailmakers and mastmakers — in fact one paper I read predicted the ultimate ruin of even the British Navy from the introduction of gaslight — but do you know what Sidney said? He said his company was doing more for the prevention of crime than any single body in England since the days of Alfred the Great. Oh, Sidney can produce very good arguments in favour of anything he wants you to do, but there is often too much risk involved for me to agree with him."

"I take it, then, that Mr. Parker himself does not approve of caution?"

"Sidney — cautious? I should say not. I remember him saying

to me once: 'Reginald,' says he, 'we are living in a reckless age. Those of us like you who are content to sit still on their capital will only lose it. There are hectic years ahead of us and we must all learn to keep pace with them.' He was trying at the time to make me invest in steam engines. But now he has gone completely off his head over gaslight — takes absolutely no notice of the derision and opposition there has been to it. Oh, Sidney is all for taking risks," pausing and considering this statement rather more carefully. "That is — well, only *some* risks. Because, on the other hand, I can remember his advising me against several of my favourite schemes. Why, when I first heard about his brother's development plans here in Sanditon — and it was Sidney himself who told me of them — I thought it would be the very thing for investment. But no, says Sidney, why venture your money in that? 'Sanditon,' he says, 'is even too much of a gamble for me. Why do you want to be involved in it?' Seaside resorts depend on fashion, he says, and fashion depends on tastes and who can ever predict those with any certainty? He said his brother was making a hobby out of Sanditon and combining commerce with pleasure, which was a good thing for *him*; but it was clearly no investment for an outsider. Well, here I am running on about money and investments which probably do not interest you in the least. You just stop me whenever you are bored with what I say. All my friends do."

"I am not in the least bored," said Charlotte, who had been so busy listening that she had to suppress several possible trains of thought which might have caused her to miss some of Reginald's revelations. For although he was clearly a rattle and one would hardly have expected much usefulness or information from him in the normal way, he had hit on the one topic of conversation which was, at present, of absorbing interest to his audience. Sometimes it might be a little difficult to follow the twists and bends of his grasshopper mind, but Charlotte was finding ample repayment in her rapt attention; and in many small ways, she was learning more about Sidney's true character in one morning than Sidney had told her about himself in the course of a week.

Where Sidney evaded and joked, Reginald, left to himself with perhaps only an encouraging word or two, revealed everything he knew on any subject at all; and in cheerful acceptance of his friend's superior talents, he was ready to be guided by him without exercising any further thought over the matter.

In fact, she was inclined to doubt whether Reginald exercised much thought in any direction. He often began sentences which seemed to lead nowhere; and a great deal of what he said was not very clear to her. But on the few occasions when she did interrupt with some query which might have helped her understand some of his remarks rather better, a wary expression would come over his face as though he was suddenly conscious of saying too much. And then he would give one of his loud bursts of laughter and immediately change the subject.

His general imprudence was plainly shown in the shout of derision he gave on hearing he had become a member of a seaweed-collecting party.

"Good God! Have they all taken leave of their senses? Who can possibly go collecting that slimy stuff? Miss Heywood, surely you are not serious?"

She assured him three of the collectors at least were perfectly serious, laughed at his undisguised incredulity and attempted to moderate some of his disastrous frankness; but he continued to pour waspish scorn on the whole enterprise in a series of incautious asides at intervals throughout the morning.

He firmly declined to help Arthur in wading out for the seaweed; and at first resisted even the Miss Beauforts' entreaties to admire it. But he became a more enthusiastic member of the party as soon as he realised the graver risk he faced of falling victim to Miss Denham. She was always on hand to appropriate him whenever Arthur called Charlotte away to look after his dry towels, his socks and his shoes; and she never despaired of coaxing him to sit on the "comfortable rock" she had discovered while everyone else clustered about such specimens of seaweed as Sanditon could grow and Arthur could find.

But Reginald was quite practised enough in social graces to slide away from the Miss Denham Sidney had warned him about; and Charlotte was frequently amused to overhear him proclaiming a sudden passionate interest in examining the latest specimen and occasional minor effusions on seaweed in general, which provided him with the excuse of remaining within the orbit of the harmless Miss Beauforts.

Towards the end of the morning, Charlotte became almost fully occupied with Arthur, whose pride in being the only gentleman to risk getting his feet wet almost equalled his anxiety to suffer no ill consequences from it. And Reginald then appended himself to Miss Letitia entirely, standing behind her as she drew outlandish and complicated patterns with seaweed overtones. She had left her easel behind and was constantly heard bemoaning the fact, protesting it was impossible for her to make faithful sketches of seaweed without an easel. But Reginald gallantly defended even the most unsuccessful of her attempts, politely insisting it looked just like seaweed to him; and though nobody else agreed with him, Miss Letitia was flattered enough to go on sketching industriously.

Charlotte did not grudge Arthur his full share in her attention; and in handing him his towels, wringing out his socks and commenting on his finds, felt she was making some return for the confidence he reposed in her.

The morning had added so considerably to her knowledge of Sidney that she was already well satisfied with it — though she hardly knew where to begin in cataloguing all Reginald's scraps of information. Most prominent among those which demanded a period of meditation was his scornful "Sidney — cautious? I should say not." This had been stored away in her mind alongside the memory of Sidney's own remark: "Caution and Miss Heywood go so well together." But she postponed any development on that theme till she could be alone to reason it all out.

How differently did everything now appear in which Sidney was concerned! Heedlessness of his friends, flippancy, shallowness and improvidence — she could no longer accuse him of these. And that he thought very seriously indeed about some subjects she could no longer doubt. But she was no nearer to understanding his character; and after restoring Arthur to his sisters' care, she looked forward to regaining her own room, unwrapping her shellwork box, rereading Sidney's letter and thinking over all she had heard about him that day.

"Ah, there you are," cried Mr. Parker catching her on the way upstairs. "Now I want your comments — and Mary's — on this piece I have been writing about Sanditon. Facts, hard facts, are what I have put down. No exaggeration about them at all. I have said we have a capital set of Assembly Rooms but made no boasts like Brinshore of holding fortnightly Assemblies. For of course, I do not believe that, you know. They may *intend* to hold fortnightly Assemblies, but I am very sure they do not. Now I have only claimed we hold *occasional* Assemblies — perfectly legitimate, would you not agree? In fact, I believe I will start organising one directly. So long as we manage *one* Assembly this season, we can be said to hold occasional Assemblies. I shall set about it immediately — finding out how many couples we may count on, cards, candles, chairs, musicians and so forth and so on. Oh, there will be enough to do over the business; but I dare say we shall be able to arrange it all very speedily. So I shall write to Sidney and tell him we are about to hold one of our occasional Assemblies! *That* will bring him back to Sanditon fast enough. Sidney can never resist any entertainment that is going — idle fellow that he is. Well, and have you time to read my notes on Sanditon now? I can fetch them in a moment from the study. No, on second thoughts, it might be as well to give them to Mary first. A much better plan, now I come to think about it. She has been out in that greenhouse all day and must be longing for some excuse to leave off. I will go and relieve her boredom for her first."

And with this happy thought, Mr. Parker went off to interrupt his contented wife, leaving Charlotte to resolve against ever trusting to his judgement again where even the interests of his own family were concerned.

CHAPTER 24

ONCE MR. PARKER had reached his impetuous decision to hold an Assembly in Sanditon, his impatience to carry it out swept away his own former objections; and nobody else's were even consulted. By the time he sat down to dinner that evening he had already fixed on Thursday, August the 27th, as a definite date; and, full of energy and infectious enthusiasm, had mentally engaged the musicians, ordered the candles, hired extra chairs and calculated the probable cost of the supper.

To his wife's protests that she had no time to arrange an Assembly, that Sanditon was too thin of company and that a week was not long enough to complete all the necessary planning, he paid no attention.

"Now you are talking nonsense, my dear. If one plans something a fortnight ahead, it takes a fortnight. If one only allows a week, then that is always sufficient too. These details of supper dishes and card tables — what do they amount to? All speedily settled once you give your mind to it. And have you forgotten, my dear Mary, that Diana is with us at the present time? You have only to ask Diana; she will give all the help and advice you could need."

Had Mrs. Parker been interested in organising the Assembly herself, she would have found it difficult to prevent her sister-in-law from giving far more help and advice than she cared to receive; but as she much preferred to run her own household efficiently and continue her gardening undisturbed, by the following morning she had accepted Diana's obliging offer to take over entire responsibility for arranging the Assembly.

If she had any little vanity, boasted Miss Diana, it was in her belief that she knew how to organise large-scale entertainments of this kind and how to supervise people successfully. Everyone was always ready to work under her direction. Servants — her own or other people's — were always devoted to her. Even such disappointing material as their Sally could be turned into a good servant under her management. And organising an Assembly was, of course, but an extension in magnitude of those precepts that rule the ordered management of a household. It required only a clear mind, the ability to issue simple concise orders and the selfless expenditure of a great deal of energy to make sure they were carried out. Mrs. Parker must not disturb herself trying to acquire such very necessary qualities within the next week when she, Miss Diana, already possessed them. She would be extremely happy to be of service to them all.

And, consequently, Miss Diana was very soon most busily occupied striding between the Terrace and the Assembly rooms at the hotel, toiling up the hill to Trafalgar House to consult her brother over every minor point, and disorganising the Woodcocks and their staff in ordering windows to be cleaned, chandeliers to be washed and floors to be polished by servants she had already despatched elsewhere on unnecessary errands.

With all this talk of dates and plans, Charlotte came to the reluctant decision she herself should be making plans for a return to Willingden. No date had so far been mentioned — no limit had ever been set to her seaside holiday; but on the day fixed for the Assembly, she would already have been a full month in Sanditon, which seemed an appropriate time to raise the subject of departure with her kind hosts.

The suggestion was met with all the concern and hospitality she had come to expect from them. But did she wish to leave them so soon? They had been hoping she would stay the whole summer. She could not be meaning to fix on so early a departure. Charlotte was warm in her gratitude but remained firm in her intentions. Perhaps no precise date could be settled, but certain things must be thought of; she must write to her father and arrange a convenient day when the family coach could meet her at Hailsham. And though Mr. Parker protested she could be driven the whole way in his carriage whenever she liked — any morning at all she "woke up feeling homesick" — she smilingly insisted on giving her parents due notice and arranging her homecoming in advance.

On one point only did she waver — allowing herself to be persuaded this could all be discussed "after the Assembly." There was too much else to be thought of now, Mr. Parker claimed. Diana, for one, could not be distracted by such proposals. Diana was forever saying Miss Heywood was the greatest help in all her little arrangements. Oh no, Diana could never spare her.

It was true that for the past two days Charlotte had carried many urgent messages for Miss Diana and had been summoned by her so many times that the Parkers could be excused for believing she was greatly involved in all their sister's bustling activities. But it was also true that she had spent most of those two days sitting in the drawing room of Number Four doing nothing whatsoever except wait for Miss Diana to return with fresh orders.

She was very kindly received there by Miss Parker, with whom she had become something of a favourite since the excursion to Brinshore, where her calm good sense had recommended her to Miss Parker's particular notice. And though they had very little in common beyond the episode of the bee sting, Miss Parker could never grow tired of discussing that. She now looked back on the incident with the utmost complacence, quite proud of the consequence it had given her. Of all the people and all the bees in Brinshore on that day, it was really most extraordinary she should have been singled out for so marked a distinction!

Charlotte always listened very patiently to the repeated and detailed descriptions of the varying degrees of pain experienced in the process of receiving and recovering from a bee sting. Miss Parker would never forget those hours of agony on the sofa, the nervous spasms she had endured; and although she never neglected to mention Miss Heywood's very great kindness on the occasion, it was clear that her mind was chiefly preoccupied with a sense of her own heroism in the face of sudden crisis.

From the window of Number Four, Charlotte occasionally caught sight of the customary morning party assembling on the Terrace and strolling along the shore line, but felt no resentment at being unable to join them.

The Miss Beauforts no doubt often congratulated themselves on the success they were enjoying over their seaweed excursions. Arthur remained their only serious convert to the collecting mania. But for want of anything better to do, Reginald Catton and Henry Brudenall had at least become regular members of the party. Clara Brereton clearly regarded these organised meetings as excellent pretexts for escaping regularly from Sanditon House. Sir Edward was still promising the Miss Beauforts his verses and using them as an excuse for his daily encounters with Miss Brereton; and his sister always accompanied him, though Charlotte often wondered how she was able to justify her continued presence when she professed such open disdain for seaweed and merely sat on her comfortable rock taking no active part in the proceedings. Miss Denham was scarcely in a position to acknowledge her real motive to anyone, whether this was to make headway for herself with the visitors from the hotel or to keep a watchful eye on her brother's conduct towards Miss Brereton.

How the latter affair was progressing, Charlotte could make only distant surmises. From her vantage point at the window, she had once observed Sir Edward trying to detach Clara from the main group and liked to imagine the firm shake of the head he had been given on this occasion was worth more than the complacent smiles he was given at other times.

There were other sources of speculation for Charlotte too as she sat listening to Miss Parker recount her impressions of Brinshore; and she often tried to imagine how very differently each member of the party would consider the day of that visit in retrospect. For Henry Brudenall, it was his cousin's wedding day; for Arthur and the Miss Beauforts, their introduction to seaweed; for Clara Brereton a day of unhappy indecision, which had ended in Lady Denham's invitation to the very cousin who might sensibly advise her; for Sir Edward, perhaps a day of frustration when Clara postponed the elopement he was now urging her to reconsider; for Sidney Parker it was certainly an occasion for displaying his powers of organisation, for duping everybody and playing practical jokes; for the Miss Parkers, this noteworthy adventure of the bee-sting. And for herself? It had been an unforgettable day on which she was confronted by problems whose existence she had never recognised, and struggled with emotions she had not believed herself to possess.

It was calming to sit with Miss Parker, sorting out these memories of Brinshore; and Charlotte was never seriously disturbed, on arriving at Number Four following an urgent summons, to discover Miss Diana had walked off on even more urgent business, leaving instructions for her to but "wait a few minutes," which invariably stretched into half the morning.

She was on her way there for the third successive day, escorted by Arthur who had conveyed Miss Diana's latest message to Trafalgar House, when she caught sight of the pale features of Miss Lambe, peering wistfully from a half-open window of the corner house. A smile and a wave in passing would have been enough. But Charlotte, who had not seen Miss Lambe since their day in Brinshore, had overheard several careless remarks of the Miss Beauforts that "poor Adela was quite done up with so much travelling" and "her migraines are the most horrid thing, you know — the slightest exertion seems to bring one on." Though she would have hesitated to call and put Mrs. Griffiths to the inconvenience of entertaining her, she was determined to make proper enquiries now an opportunity presented itself; and stopping beneath the window to call a cheerful greeting, she was rewarded by seeing Miss Lambe's face light up with sudden pleasure. Letting down the window-sash to its fullest extent, she leaned eagerly forward.

"Oh Miss Heywood, I was hoping so much to see you. Mrs. Griffiths does not think I should venture out of doors yet. But I would be so happy if you could find the time — if you could spare even a few moments — to come in and see my shell collection."

Charlotte had almost forgotten Miss Lambe's shell collection; she had no particular wish to see it herself, but could not ignore a request where her acceptance appeared likely to give such satisfaction.

"Of course I have time," was therefore her warm reply. "I am only going along to Number Four on some errand or other; but" — turning to Arthur, — "perhaps you could go ahead and discover if your sister is waiting for me?"

"You mean Miss Diana Parker?" asked Miss Lambe. "I saw her go past on the way to the hotel not five minutes ago. Perhaps if we keep an eye on the window, we can see when she returns. Looking at my shells will take no time at all and," speaking very earnestly, "I have been longing to show them to you."

Such a plea could not be resisted. Charlotte turned immediately towards the front door, followed by an unwilling Arthur, who was fairly certain he had not been included in the invitation but uncertain how he could now avoid being so, and more dubious still over intruding on what promised to become a distinctly feminine tête-à-tête.

He shifted from one foot to the other, unable to decide whether to escape while he could or remain to make some apology.

"Now if it had been bonnets, I would know, of course — but shells! What do *you* think I should do?" he demanded of Charlotte. "No, no! leave the bell for a moment."

But Miss Lambe must have flown down the stairs and had the door open before Charlotte touched the bell. She looked very slight and frail but showed no sign of the nervousness which usually overcame her when confronted by more than one person. The consciousness of now being their hostess may have added to her self-possession, or perhaps she was so happy to have these visitors to entertain that she forgot her shyness. Whatever the cause, she recognised Arthur's quandary at a glance and earned his gratitude by exclaiming tactfully, —

"Oh, I do hope you will step upstairs too, Mr. Parker. You will not be very interested in my shell collection, I imagine; but if you would be so kind as to watch for your sister through the window, it would be extremely useful to us."

And Arthur followed them both upstairs, feeling much less awkward, indeed quite flattered by this persuasion of his extreme usefulness on the occasion.

Miss Lambe had her own private sitting room on the second floor, a pleasant, airy chamber facing the sea; into this, she had crowded a number of private treasures which Charlotte would have thought it possible to travel without. Prominent among these was a brass-bound wooden chest, fitted up with a succession of little drawers, each with its own small brass handle; and towards this they were now led.

"Perhaps you think me very stupid to bring so many personal possessions on a short summer stay," said Miss Lambe as if aware of Charlotte's impressions. "But I spend so much time on my own and it gives me pleasure to look at beautiful things — and Mrs. Griffiths is so understanding about it — "

In her embarrassment, she pulled open one of the drawers and neither Charlotte nor Arthur listened any longer to these stumbling apologies. They were staring down at a rainbow profusion of shells such as they had never known to exist: fragile heaps of pink, blue and mauve, carefully sorted into cotton-lined nests. Each shell was exquisite in itself — round or elongated, striped, speckled or plain — whether it belonged to a pile of the same variety or was isolated in the proud possession of a nest of its own.

Pulling out more drawers as though fearful her visitors would not appreciate the collection unless they saw it all at once and in a great hurry, Miss Lambe made further explanations.

"Down here at the bottom, I keep the larger ones. See, here is the biggest conch. And this one is a pinnidae. These mother-of-pearl molluscs have such wonderful grey lights, I always think. And this is just an ordinary oyster shell but it has the pearl still in it. Did you know," she added inconsequentially, "that an oyster changes sex every time a cloud passes over?"

"Who told you that?" demanded Arthur, much struck.

"My father. He knew everything about shells and sea creatures — about nature altogether. He read and he studied and sometimes he talked to me."

Then, all at once, she retreated back into shyness; and, stammering again, turned to Charlotte with an air of timid appeal. "I hope you did not mind my pressing you so much to come in — that you feel my shell collection is deserving?"

"It is the most beautiful thing I have ever seen," said Charlotte with such undoubted sincerity that Miss Lambe went quite pink with pleasure and gave her a quick, bright look — almost of adoration; she said nothing, however, only touched a few of her shells lightly and affectionately before turning away. And although they had not exchanged more than half a dozen sentences, Charlotte suddenly felt they knew each other intimately; the shell collection was an odd vignette which had illuminated for her Miss Lambe's whole personality.

"Would you like to see some of my water-colour sketches of the shells?" Miss Lambe was asking now, pulling open the drawer of a small table. The success of the shells seemed to have emboldened her to reveal all her treasures; and she lifted a pile of drawings on to the table top and began turning them over very quickly. At least half a dozen had already been discarded before Charlotte and Arthur could move near enough to see them, when they immediately begged to be allowed examine each one more closely.

Miss Lambe's sketches were not of a type to skim over casually — as unlike Miss Letitia's dashed-off impressions as it was possible to imagine. More the drawings of a naturalist than an artist, these were painstaking, life-like reproductions of the original shells, each vein and each shadow clearly delineated, the true colour washed in with careful exactitude. At the bottom of the pile was her most recent drawing — that of the seaweed Arthur had presented to her in Brinshore.

"My word!" he said, picking this up, turning it this way and that, and finally holding it at arm's length while Miss Lambe blushed in sudden apprehension. "But this is brilliant! This is admirable indeed! Those greens and browns so exactly the colour. A truly excellent representation of an enteromorpha."

"A what?" said Charlotte.

It was Arthur's turn to blush.

"An enteromorpha — at least I am fairly sure that is what it must be," he said, rather less emphatically. "But the problem is, since I have been trying to collect and identify all this seaweed, I have had to rely on description alone — and enteromorphas sound much the same as cladophoras if you cannot *see* the colour. Pressing specimens is no great help either — they warp and discolour so quickly when taken out of the sea water. To catalogue scientifically, one should have life-like reproductions such as this. I suppose," appealing to Miss Lambe rather diffidently, "you would not be interested in drawing more pictures of seaweed?"

"But of course — if you bring it to me," she offered with the utmost readiness. "I have drawn all my own shells and tried to capture their colours over and over again; and the English shells, I am afraid, do not interest me. But seaweed colours are so subtle and delicate — so many shades of green and olive, all those different hues of brown and red — oh! I could experiment forever trying to reproduce them exactly."

Charlotte, who found seaweed far less interesting than shells, carried some of Miss Lambe's water colours to the window to look through them in the better light; while Arthur, who had become quite animated, began making plans to supply fresh seaweed at the corner house every morning.

"For if you paint it the same day I collect it, we will have the very best opportunity of preserving the correct colours — "

"And perhaps, in a few days, if the weather remains warm, I can come down to the shore myself," cried Miss Lambe. "And then I could mix the colours on the spot."

They both became so absorbed in their new plans and so engrossed in their discussion of seaweed, that it was Charlotte who remained at the window on the look-out for Miss Diana. And it was a full ten minutes after she had seen her through the front door of Number Four before she could prevail on Arthur to accompany her.

CHAPTER 25

MISS LAMBE'S INTEREST in seaweed proved more durable than the Miss Beauforts'. They had been enthusiastic in praising it, energetic in promoting their collecting parties for it, and ecstatic about each other's pressed arrangements of it; but their ardour cooled most abruptly.

As the date of the Assembly drew nearer, seaweed gave way to social concerns; and seaside-promenading clothes had to take second place to ball dress. They stopped pestering Sir Edward to finish his seaweed verses for them to frame and no longer entreated Arthur's services in wading out among the rocks at low tide. Closeting themselves away with patterns, trimmings, ribbons and flounces, they were even prepared to forgo their daily meetings with Henry Brudenall and Reginald Catton in their preparations to dazzle them on the night of the Assembly.

But for Miss Lambe, waging a quiet but persistent battle with her own constitution — and Mrs. Griffiths' apprehensions for it — the shore line had become a goal she was determined to reach. For several rainy mornings she had to be content to stay indoors sketching pieces of seaweed Arthur delivered after his own damp and solitary rambles. And when, on a particularly fine, windless day, she managed to achieve her objective and sit, wrapped in shawls, for a few hours in the most sheltered cove, her delight and her diligence were both highly gratifying to Arthur.

Charlotte was again most earnestly petitioned to rejoin the collecting parties; but now, she noted with interest, Arthur was no longer requesting her assistance with his own towels, socks and shoes. These were tucked into a convenient bundle, pulled out, put back and scarcely mentioned the whole morning. And although his preoccupation with comfort and his anxiety about health remained considerable, all his solicitude in these matters was now entirely at Miss Lambe's disposal.

He himself must carry her folding chair, her easel and her drawing paper. Charlotte was required to look after her shawls and her paintbox, her cushions and hartshorn. In Miss Lambe, she decided, Arthur had encountered someone quite unique in his experience — a genuine invalid, who despised her own weakness, disliked talking about her symptoms, and overtaxed her strength in her eagerness to lead a normal life whenever she was capable of it.

And Arthur, who did not usually spare much thought for anybody's comfort but his own, had lately been forced into recognising the difference between selfish indulgence and necessary prudence. *He* wanted Miss Lambe's sketches of seaweed and *she* was very willing to execute them; but he had begun to realise that health, which he had always regarded as an excuse for behaving exactly as he liked, could also intervene in one's pleasures and prevent one from carrying out a favourite scheme.

His sisters had always encouraged Arthur to discuss his minor ailments at such length that it astonished him when Miss Lambe denied having a headache, pretended to feel better than she really did and made so few complaints as to seem almost ashamed of her condition. But one day's exhaustion could mean several days' recuperation. And from being protective about the progress of his seaweed sketches and watchful for warning signs of fatigue on their behalf, Arthur naturally enough became protective about Miss Lambe herself.

It was he who decided how long their collecting expedition should last; it was he who decided if the sea breeze was too strong, the clouds threatening or Miss Lambe exerting herself beyond her own strength; and in making these decisions and insisting they were acted upon, Arthur was also outgrowing a little of his own immaturity. The change was as yet barely perceptible but, on several occasions, Charlotte noted and welcomed it.

She was the only person (with the possible exception of Mrs. Griffiths) to observe this interesting development in Arthur's character; and she often wished Sidney would return to Sanditon to discuss it with her and confirm the improvement she fancied in his younger brother's outlook. But beyond one short note to his elder brother with ironic congratulations on the plans for an Assembly, there was no further news of Sidney.

It was not, however, till the actual day of the Assembly that Charlotte gave up all expectation of seeing him present at it. She had been relying on that impetuous streak, so prominent in the Parker family, and believing Sidney would arrive without notice, late at night on the eve of the Assembly, and walk in to surprise them all that very morning.

The sound of the doorbell while they were at breakfast seemed to confirm this guess, and though Miss Diana's appearance banished the first flutter of her spirits, she still expected every moment to hear her announce his arrival. But Miss Diana, most perversely, would talk only of blackberries.

"The most abundant crop of blackberries this year on the downs! I have never seen anything like it — it would take scarcely an hour to fill a basket. Two baskets, Duckworth and I have decided would be enough for a fair-sized syllabub. And I had it all arranged so well; indeed nothing could be clearer — if four of the young ladies spent only one half-hour each — "

"Well, and is he come?" Mr. Parker eagerly interrupted.

"What are you talking of, my dear Tom? Who is come?"

"Sidney, to be sure. Are you not come to tell us he has arrived? Drove down late last night I dare say?"

"Oh Sidney! No, no, I know nothing of Sidney — or at least

239

I can tell you he has definitely *not* arrived because I have just come from the hotel myself. But what difference will Sidney make to our arrangements for the Assembly? I am here on purpose to tell you and Mary about the blackberries for the syllabub this evening. Can you not give your attention to what I am saying?"

Charlotte's disappointment was so intense that she was unable to comply with this request herself; and though Miss Diana's strict disregard for anyone else's concerns often diverted her, it was some time before she felt equal to appreciating this latest example of her absurdity.

Diana's original and optimistic plan had apparently been that all the young ladies of Sanditon could employ themselves on the day of the Assembly picking wild berries for a blackberry syllabub to be made by Duckworth, the hotel cook, at the very last moment — the freshness of the fruit being the most important ingredient in Miss Diana's special recipe. And she had been astonished by the selfishness of these young ladies, when they pointed out they did not wish to tire themselves stretching and bending, exposing their complexions to the hot sun, nor to attend the Assembly with blackberry stains on their fingers and scratches across their arms.

"So what is to be done now?" she cried despairingly. "Duckworth has no time to pick the blackberries himself. That man is a positive treasure — a born cook, most willing to cooperate and quite devoted to me — would do anything I asked — but of course I would not dream of suggesting he should pick the blackberries. Oh no! Duckworth and his kitchen staff are fully occupied today with preparations for the rest of the supper. And nobody could expect me to go picking all those blackberries — as it is I shall be busy till sunset supervising last minute details. The success of the entire evening depends on *me*. I am wearing myself out in the service of these same young people! Incredible! quite incredible they will not do something for me in return!"

Mrs. Parker's mild suggestion that the absence of one black-berry syllabub would make little difference to everyone's pleasure in the evening met with all the scorn Miss Diana felt it deserved. On the contrary, the blackberry syllabub would form the main attraction of the sideboard — no Assembly was complete without one — and, in short, Miss Diana was determined to have her own way, her obstinate resolution of providing a syllabub which nobody else particularly wished to eat only increasing with the opposition she encountered.

Charlotte's offer to tramp from one blackberry bush to another till she had collected the two baskets by herself was made less to please Miss Diana than to spare the others her complaints. Every prospect of her own pleasure in the evening now seemed most unlikely; and she felt it no great sacrifice to undertake what any sensible person must regard as a most ridiculous quest. Nor was it part of her disposition to imagine she was being imposed upon, so she was able to reply to Miss Diana's effusive thanks by saying, with perfect sincerity, that she would honestly enjoy two hours' ramble in search of blackberries on so sunny a morning.

Her wishes for the evening now centred almost entirely on Miss Lambe in hoping that she, at any rate, would be in spirits enough to enjoy the Assembly. And as she was persuaded Mrs. Griffiths' wishes must be the same, she was not at all surprised, on joining Arthur on the Terrace at midday, after delivering her two baskets of blackberries to the hotel, to discover his proposal for a seaweed expedition that morning had been firmly rejected.

"It is all such nonsense," complained Arthur. "I have just been calling on them and Miss Lambe is in better health than I have ever seen her. She begged Mrs. Griffiths to let her come down to the beach. And I am quite sure she would prefer sketching seaweed this morning to attending a ball this evening."

Charlotte, with some amusement at the Parkers' tenacity in their own selfish projects, attempted to convince him an Assembly would rate as the more agreeable alternative with most females.

But Arthur obstinately insisted Miss Lambe's propensity as a naturalist had been developed so early in life, and her knowledge of such subjects so extensive, that it would be a great pity to squander her talents in any other direction.

"Do you know what she told me today?" he cried, still rather awed by the disclosure. "Goats are the only animals which can eat arsenic without ill effects. Now what do you think of that?"

These odd and irrelevant scraps of information, always imparted suddenly, shyly and quite gratuitously, were of absorbing interest to Arthur; and in exclaiming over this latest example of Miss Lambe's erudition and wishing for the twentieth time he could have met her remarkable father, he was some time in recollecting he had a message for Charlotte herself.

"Well, I will walk with you now as far as the tea rooms," he said at last. "You will find everyone there."

Charlotte thanked him for this kind offer but denied her intention of joining any party in the tea rooms.

"Oh, but you must," Arthur said simply. "Sidney told me to take you there."

The surprise of this announcement made her quite speechless for a moment. And even when she had scolded back her self-possession, she was grateful there was only an unobservant Arthur present to overlook her stuttering.

"Has S-s-s — your brother — returned to S-sanditon then?"

"Oh yes. More than an hour ago. It was before I went in to call on Mrs. Griffiths. They were all standing here on the Terrace at the time, even the Miss Beauforts. Miss Letitia was telling Miss Brereton how busy she was over some new hair style and had only stepped out for a minute to greet everyone. And my sisters were here too talking to Lady Denham about some tart cases her cook had promised for the supper tonight. And Sir Edward, Mr. Catton and Mr. Brudenall — you can imagine how delighted they all were when Sidney drove up — jumped straight down from the carriage and left his groom to turn it into the hotel. 'I am in luck,' says he. 'Here is all Sanditon out to welcome me. But where is Miss Heywood?' "

Charlotte, only half-attending to what Arthur was saying, was arrested by the sound of her own name and listened more carefully while he repeated all the commonplace observations everyone had made about her absence. How Diana had boasted of the blackberry syllabub she would supervise the hotel cook in making as soon as Miss Heywood had kindly picked all the berries; how Susan had argued Miss Heywood could not possibly still be doing it now the sun had grown so hot and maintained she must be helping Mrs. Parker in her greenhouse; and how Arthur (as soon as he could make himself heard) had settled the matter by announcing Miss Heywood would be joining him at noon for a seaweed excursion.

Although the charm of her own name was likewise present in all of this, Charlotte found it no longer pleased her. It was quite a long time before Arthur worked his way back to Sidney again, but she was finally rewarded by hearing that he had charged his brother with the office of escorting Miss Heywood to join the whole party in the tea rooms.

"Even Diana has gone off there, though she says she still has a thousand things to do. And do you know why?" smiling broadly. "She has taken a notion into her head that Sidney has come down to the Assembly on purpose to see Miss Brereton," Arthur confided. "Oh, I saw myself he made straight for her directly he arrived and handed her some note, which he *said* was a letter from some cousin of hers. But as he said the same thing and gave another letter to Lady Denham, I dare say it was."

Charlotte had recovered herself sufficiently by now to treat these suppositions with what she hoped was no more than a proper degree of interest.

"You yourself, I take it, do not think there are serious grounds for your sister's suspicions?"

Oh well, as to that, he could not definitely say, was Arthur's unsatisfactory reply. Diana always *had* been wrong in any of her previous conjectures about Sidney. "She goes on this way whenever he takes particular notice of anyone at all. She will pry and gossip! But my belief is that half the time Sidney only pretends to have flirtations to tease her. However, when it came out he was only down for the one night, I overheard Diana telling Susan he must be serious. If he had travelled all the way from London just to dance with Miss Brereton, they had best go as far as the tea rooms to observe them together."

Arthur then reverted once more to his own concerns and she was left to recover her composure while he talked on about seaweed and Miss Lambe. Charlotte was glad he had warned her of Miss Diana's suspicions. She was ashamed of being so nervous in meeting Sidney again herself; and Arthur's words were of a sobering tendency which helped allay this agitation and determine her on appearing detached and unmoved by any attentions Sidney might decide to pay her. The fact that these attentions were more likely to be directed to Miss Brereton should — indeed must — relieve some of her anxiety.

In their walk across the shingle she tried to arrange her own feelings a little better, to tell herself how unaccountable and absurd it was to be thrown into such confusion by the very natural arrival of Sidney Parker on the day of the Assembly. She had even predicted it herself. A few hours ago it would not have surprised her in the least! But she was extremely grateful for the few moments of preparation she was being granted now before entering the tea rooms and seeing Sidney himself.

The few moments were over far too soon; and Charlotte was bitterly conscious how slight a control she exercised over her own heart, when the faces which turned towards herself and Arthur in the doorway all became blurred and indistinct. For one second she distinguished Sidney's but moved her eyes quickly and resolutely away from it, fixing at last on Miss Diana Parker's.

She was further indebted to Miss Diana for the first words she could distinguish from the babble confronting her.

". . . and here at last is Arthur with Miss Heywood. Have you picked all the blackberries, my dear? Oh yes, I can see your hands are all stained and — oh! what a pity! — the brambles have pulled so many threads in your gown!"

Charlotte, who had forgotten all about her dress, was now made miserably aware of its being the oldest one she possessed — a faded, shabby blue cotton she had chosen specially to pick black-berries in and not bothered to change for Arthur's seaweed collecting.

"You must come and join our table, my dear. But where will Arthur sit?"

Charlotte had already sunk thankfully into the nearest chair at this nearest table before registering that the other occupants were Miss Denham and Miss Parker; and two further tables were likewise fully occupied. While Arthur was gravely explaining he needed no place for himself and preferred to wade out at this low tide for his seaweed, she managed a fleeting glance round the room and once again caught Sidney's eye. He was sitting with Lady Denham on one side, Miss Brereton on the other, and Mr. Brudenall opposite.

The attention of the others being politely directed towards Arthur, Sidney took advantage of it to raise his teacup in the mock-manner of toasting her with a wine glass; and to smile very warmly at her over the rim. Charlotte felt herself blushing and turned away quickly as she realised that in this single, simple gesture he had succeeded in demolishing all her carefully con-structed defences. She could no longer attend to anything that was said and felt herself the greatest simpleton in the world to be affected by so harmless and friendly a greeting.

When she had criticised herself back into being sensible again, she discovered Arthur had already gone, and Miss Diana needed no assistance in conversation at their own table; she had returned to a theme she had been expounding on before Charlotte's arrival: an account of her transactions with local musicians.

"Two violins, I said, were quite enough for a small Assembly — with the piano and violoncello as well; for I dare say there will be no more than sixteen couples. Now if we could have counted on twenty or twenty five, I might have added a harp — "

Like Miss Denham, who was yawning, and Miss Parker, who was daydreaming, Charlotte gave up attending and tried to overhear what was going on at the next table. Miss Letitia and Miss Beaufort were both competing there for the attentions of Sir Edward and Reginald Catton. But Sir Edward, at least, was in full flow about cottages ornés and ignored all their remarks about the Assembly and their broadest hints on the modern fashion of securing partners for the first two dances in advance.

"A friend of mine," he was telling them, "has lately requested my advice on converting his little hunting lodge into a cottage orné similar to my own."

"It is always done in London these days, I believe," said Miss Beaufort. "And Miss Nicholls tells me it is quite the thing in Ramsgate."

"But a conversion, you know, is never as satisfactory as building in the original style. You can, of course, throw out a few canopied porches with ironwork trellising; and nothing easier than to add barge-boards, verandahs and Gothic-pointed windows — "

"Well, Ramsgate is a more fashionable place than Sanditon, you know," tittered Miss Letitia. "But I agree with you, Lydia, there are great advantages to some of these modern customs — one hates arriving insupportably early at any Assembly merely to secure a partner before the music strikes up — "

"Oh really? That is quite easy, is it, Sir Edward?" cried Reginald, feigning as much interest as he could in a similar attempt to remain deaf to the Miss Beauforts.

"Easy enough — but it has not the same effect as if it was *planned* into the main structure. Not the same effect at all. Careful planning is an essential of so intricate a style."

Charlotte, relieved that this conversation could amuse her, and beginning to feel quite normal again now she was surrounded by such banal topics, relaxed her determined effort at concentration; and she was just resolving to steal another glance in the direction of Sidney's table, when Sir Edward reclaimed her attention by uttering a very familiar place-name.

"Willingden Abbots — not much above five or six hours' drive, I should imagine. My friend Atwell has gone to Switzerland for the summer and left me his keys. So one of these days, I shall drive over there and draw up some plans for his conversion. Somewhere due east of Hailsham, I believe."

Very pleased to discover she was at last capable of forming and pronouncing a complete sentence, Charlotte was on the point of interrupting Sir Edward with the correction that Willingden Abbots lay seventeen miles south east of Hailsham, when she realised from a sudden scraping of chairs at her own table how far her attention had indeed wandered.

Sidney and his table companions were already at the door. Miss Diana, with a significant look at Miss Parker, hurried across to join them; and Miss Denham, who seemed equally determined to eavesdrop on any conversation between Sidney and Clara Brereton, darted so quickly after them that their table had been deserted before Charlotte collected her wits sufficiently to realise what was happening.

"Oh! Miss Heywood," cried Diana, remembering her with reluctance and turning back from the door. "Perhaps you are not yet ready to walk with us to the Terrace?"

"Yes, of course, I — " began Charlotte in some confusion, starting to rise but scarcely noticing she still held her cup and saucer.

"No, of course not," Sidney contradicted. He took a few swift steps across the room and, removing the saucer from her hand, placed it on the table again. "How thoughtless you are, Diana! Naturally Miss Heywood wants to stay and finish her tea." He sat down at the table. "And I will stay to keep her company."

"Oh, but — I am not — the tea — really — " Once again she was overwhelmed with shame in being so nervous; despite all her careful resolutions of maintaining detachment over any friendly notice from Sidney, she had become almost tongue-tied with embarrassment at finding herself now sitting alone with him. But her legs seemed to fail her at the same moment as her tongue; and though she could see everyone moving past her to the door, she felt incapable of any movement whatsoever.

Miss Diana marched back, inquisitive and perplexed.

"Well, Sidney! it is all very well for you to say so. But I am sure Miss Heywood herself would prefer — "

"Of course," Charlotte repeated again, mechanically beginning to rise for the second time.

"Miss Heywood prefers to stay here," said Sidney with authority. Charlotte's hand had been gripping the table as she prepared to rise and he placed one of his over it as though to emphasise the command. "I do say so, Diana," half-turning towards his sister. "We will catch you up before you reach the Terrace. Now, off you go and join the others."

Without removing his hand from Charlotte's, he swung back again to the table. She tried to convince herself that this circumstance — this contact between them, so precious to her — meant nothing to him beyond a rather absent-minded kindness. And yet it was difficult to maintain such a belief when Diana was regarding them both with unrestrained wonder. Charlotte caught a glimpse of her face and the startled glance she gave the two linked hands, in full view on the table top, before she whisked herself out of the tea rooms as quickly as possible.

She left Charlotte staring shyly at Sidney, and Sidney smiling back at her in a half-teasing but wholly enigmatic fashion. For a moment neither of them spoke. Then Sidney withdrew his hand from hers and laughed.

"Do you know what Diana has gone off to tell Susan?" he said in a tone of evident satisfaction. " 'Sidney and Miss Heywood are flirting prodigiously together in the tea rooms.' Would you take it amiss?"

The idea darted through her mind that there had been nothing absent-minded after all in Sidney's prolonged retention of her hand. It had been coolly deliberate. He wanted Diana to report this incident to his relations, to mislead them into believing she, Charlotte, was his ostensible object on this journey to Sanditon. With his quick perception, it could not have escaped him Diana was following everything that passed between himself and Miss Brereton. And this interlude with her was nothing but a ruse to assist him in concealing some more essential purpose. The conviction helped Charlotte considerably as she struggled for speech.

"I do not think I would mind," she said very carefully, "if that is what you want her to tell Miss Parker. But all the same, I do not think she will report it quite like that."

"No," said Sidney with a great sigh. "You are quite right. She will only say 'Sidney is flirting prodigiously with Miss Heywood in the tea rooms. Miss Heywood is being as sensible as ever.' "

Charlotte was fully aware of being less at ease with him than formerly, but it heartened her that he could still believe she was as sensible as ever. She made a great effort and tried to make herself so.

"Your return seems to have been most unexpected," she said in a firmer and more prosaic voice than usual. "Will you be staying long in Sanditon this time, Mr. Parker?"

"Only for the Assembly, Miss Heywood," he replied in accents of solemn mimicry; and then relaxing into his normal tone, "I hope you have saved me the first two dances, as that, I assure you, is my only reason for driving all this way from London."

"Or so you would like everyone to believe," agreed Charlotte pleasantly. "But you cannot really expect *me* to believe it."

For a moment he looked at her with smiling penetration before replying,

"Would you believe it was half the reason then? If you are so unwilling to accept the compliments I give you, I shall try to remember to halve them in future. And if in return you will agree to double yours, I will promise to believe them too. Have you missed me at all, Miss Heywood? I have missed you exactly half the time I have been away. Now will you believe that or do I still sound too much like Sir Edward?"

"You could never sound like Sir Edward," said Charlotte, completely forgetting the cheerful unconcern she had fully intended to convey.

"No? Well I sound very much to myself as though I am trying to sound like Sir Edward. Gallantry is truly a fine virtue to practise. A pity the coin has become so debased in Sanditon one hardly dares use it. But no, why should Sir Edward frighten me off from saying something I very much want to say to a pretty girl? Miss Heywood — oh, are you indeed ready to go?"

"We must," said Charlotte rather reluctantly. "The others will have nearly reached the Terrace by now."

"We shall walk very quickly," he said, rising and tucking her arm into his. "But I am not going to be cheated of my compliment. Miss Heywood, as my brother Tom would say, the Sanditon breezes have brought your beauty to perfection.

"And you see how cunning I have been," he added gaily as they walked across the shingle. "By putting the words into Tom's mouth, I can get away with a full compliment. Half perfection would not sound nearly so well."

Half would have been quite enough for Charlotte. She dared
not even hope Sidney meant as much; she well knew that such
beauty as she herself possessed was unlikely to tempt so popular,
polished and lively a young man, that her fortune was non-
existent and her personality a trifle narrow and over-decorous for
his tastes. But for the purposes of his present schemes and their
present acquaintance, she was also willing to believe he found her
a more sympathetic friend than the remainder of Sanditon's
limited society afforded. He could scarcely be blamed because a
simple country girl, who had scarcely travelled beyond the borders
of her own parish, should have been reckless enough to fall in
love with him on such very slight encouragement. She told
herself she should at least retain sufficient pride not to allow
Sidney or anyone else to realise it; but she had thrown even this
last instinct of caution aside before she was conscious of having
done so.

"Caution and Miss Heywood go so well together." But why
should they go together any longer? What harm could there be in
returning smile for smile and in allowing the most charming man
she had ever met to conquer the few remaining corners of her
heart where common sense retained a last fleeting hold? She
wished he would remain stationary long enough for her to behave
towards him with the restraint she knew was required; but it had
been her fate, on every occasion they had met recently, that
another announcement of a speedy departure panicked her into
acting exactly as she felt and not as she knew she ought. Had
Sidney intended to remain in Sanditon, she might have had time
to pause and consider, to try and check her feelings, her delight
in his high spirits and her indulgence of his faults. But now,
once again, there seemed only time to enjoy his company; and for
a brief period, Charlotte chose to be happy rather than wise.

She felt herself in good humour with all, paid no attention
whatsoever to anything that anybody except Sidney said, knew

not how she parted from the group on the Terrace, was scarcely aware of Miss Diana accompanying her up the hill, and walked on towards Trafalgar House, seeing nothing of the view, feeling nothing of the sun's heat and smiling to herself repeatedly.

"I will just look in at the greenhouse for a moment and talk with Mary," announced Miss Diana. "No need for you to come with me, my dear. So many matters as we still have to discuss together before the Assembly this evening," she added — but not very convincingly.

"Oh, yes — the Assembly," said Charlotte, smiling absently at Miss Diana too. Such of her thoughts as she could understand made her feel kindly towards the whole world and to pity everyone she saw as being less happy than herself. But as Diana so clearly did not want her in the greenhouse, she wandered in a bemused way into the garden, where she found little Mary, seated on a swing with her new parasol; and on a sudden impulse ran towards her and picked her up in a warm, swift hug and embrace.

"Oh! Miss Heywood. You made me drop my parasol," complained Mary.

"I am very sorry," said Charlotte, setting her on her feet again and picking up the parasol, a little embarrassed by her own outburst. She decided she had perhaps gone far enough in indulging this heady emotion of happiness. "Did not you like being kissed?"

"Oh, yes. I liked that," said Mary, still looking surprised. "But it is so very strange. You have never done anything like that before."

"No," said Charlotte, properly humbled now. "I am sorry if I startled you."

"But I did like it," repeated Mary, slipping her hand into Charlotte's. "Now I am used to it, I liked it very much," regarding her speculatively for a moment. "You do *look* different today too, Miss Heywood. Much prettier than before."

This involuntary tribute from Mary restored Charlotte to all the early enjoyment of her happiness. They strolled about the garden very contendedly together, picked a daisy chain out of the side lawn and waved Miss Diana down the drive with the same artless pleasure. And Charlotte then had to stand a full minute outside the greenhouse door before she reined in her smiles enough to present herself in front of Mrs. Parker. But the tranquillity she sought still eluded her.

"Dear ma'am," she exclaimed in her new and uncharacteristic manner of impetuosity. "You have been working here all day! How tired you will be for the Assembly tonight."

"Yes," agreed Mrs. Parker easily. "But I shall be very contented. And it is because of the Assembly, you know, that I have been able to finish these new primrose seedlings. Except for Diana stepping in for a few minutes just now, nobody has come to interrupt me all day."

"But let me help you finish this last box," Charlotte offered eagerly. "You will want to see to your dress and arrange your hair — oh! are not you looking forward to the Assembly? Now that it is so near, I am beginning to enjoy the thought of it, I own, to an extraordinary degree. What very great pleasure a meeting of this kind, with music and dancing, can give even in a circle accustomed to seeing each other every day." She seized a flower pot and began filling it with earth. "I suppose Miss Diana Parker told you her brother has arrived back in Sanditon?"

"Yes," agreed Mrs. Parker even more easily; and it seemed to Charlotte she was subjecting her to the same speculative look Mary had given. "And that he is staying only the one day. They are all surprised by that and cannot imagine why he comes for so short a time. But usually, you know, there is a very good reason for everything Sidney does. He may joke and pretend he moves about for his own amusement, but it is seldom really the case. I myself am quite sure that this time his business has something to do with Mr. Brudenall which he wants none of us to guess."

Mrs. Parker was bending down to firm one of her plants into

position; and it may have been because of this exertion that her face looked flushed when she straightened up.

"I am very fond of Sidney," she said with candour. "He has been the kindest of brothers to me since my marriage. But I must confess I have never fully understood him. There is such a mixture of levity and seriousness in his nature that it is always difficult to know what he intends. But what he says and what he means are sometimes very different; and from what Diana said of his high spirits this morning, I gather he is determined to mislead us all very thoroughly during this visit."

This was quite a long speech for Mrs. Parker and, vague as it was, Charlotte felt it was meant to contain several hints to guide her own behaviour.

"He is always a very pleasant companion," she said, carefully untangling the roots of two interlocked seedlings and trying to assume a detached expression.

"Yes," agreed Mrs. Parker again. "Clever people can always make themselves agreeable when they wish it. And Sidney is certainly the cleverest by far of any of his family. He knows how to amuse; and in the main he has integrity and good principles too — but what are these if steadiness and decorum are both absent? People can be hurt as much by thoughtlessness as by heartlessness." She paused as though she might have added something more; but the mingled expressions in her young guest's face made her change her mind and decide she had said quite enough already. "There! We have finished the box and now we shall both go to our rooms and rest. Tom proposes we should dress for the Assembly after dinner; and as we have only ourselves and our own comfort to consider, it seems to me a very good plan."

For Charlotte there was much cause for reflection in this conversation. Her mind was in a state of wonder and agitation which made it impossible for her to be collected. The dancing, singing, exclaiming spirits were still there; but now she also felt a measure of fear, though she knew not of what. She wanted to be alone and to be with people, both at the same time. But till she had spent a period of quiet, serious reflection, she knew she was unfit to talk to anybody at all.

She went to her room to indulge in this very necessary interval of meditation. But two hours later, when summoned to an early dinner, she discovered she had done nothing but sit holding an ugly little shell box in her hand, reliving a few moments in a curio shop and a few others in some tea rooms.

CHAPTER 26

MR. PARKER was in a buoyant mood as they sat down at table and could scarcely restrain his impatience for Morgan to leave the room before revealing some secret, of which he had already dropped several broad hints.

"Now," he said importantly as soon as the butler disappeared. "I have something very interesting to tell you. Shall I make you guess what it is?"

Mrs. Parker protested she had been doing that quite long enough already and added, with a worried glance at Charlotte and a warning one to her husband, that she knew he had been gossiping with Diana and Susan for the past hour.

"Yes, I have been down at Number Four," admitted Mr. Parker. "And they are all guessing away there too, trying to puzzle out why Sidney should have come all the way from London just to attend our little Assembly. Arthur says one thing and Susan another; and Diana, to be sure, has the best intelligence of all and is trying again to make the rest of us believe it," laughing heartily. "No, no, it would be very nice if it *were* true," with a significant look at his wife as if they had discussed this particular story in private, "but we all know Diana is inclined to let her imagination run away with her; and then she rushes here and rushes there, making enquiries and uncovering details which will bolster her own ideas. Do you know she has been talking to Sidney's groom and discovered he is not even spending the night here? John says they are driving straight back to London from the Assembly; he has already paid their toll dues to save time waking up gatekeepers on the return journey. Driving all night! They have even arranged the postings in advance and will pick up Sidney's own horses at Croydon by nine o'clock to cover the last stage. John says they must be in London by midday for some unknown meeting Sidney sets great store by. And of course Diana insists only her theory would explain why he should have come all this way for one evening."

"I thought you had decided Diana's theories were not worth discussing," interrupted Mrs. Parker, beginning to look anxious again. "You said you had something interesting to tell us."

"So I have, so I have," rejoined her husband in high good humour. "I know something Diana does *not* because I called in to see Sidney at the hotel on my way back. My plan was to try, if I could, to worm the truth out of him. Well, at first he refused to tell me anything — you know the way Sidney laughs and evades when you ask him a direct question. So I put it to him very earnestly — showed I was really concerned over the matter — that these rumours of Diana's were not the sort of thing he should countenance — not the sort of thing at all. And in the end, he agreed to tell me. Observe, he said it was to be a secret, but I am sure he would not have the least objection to my own family knowing it."

"If it was to be a secret," said Mrs. Parker, "perhaps you had better not tell us."

By this time Charlotte was very curious to know what this mysterious secret of Sidney's could be. Several wild and rapid conjectures had already occurred to her; and though she could hardly bear the suspense of waiting to hear whether she would be let into the secret, she went on slicing an apple into smaller and smaller sections with what she hoped was a fine show of indifference.

"Oh! as to that, Sidney as good as told me I might mention

the matter freely at home. 'Let Susan and Diana go on believing what they like,' said he, 'but I agree you and Mary are in rather a different position; and it might relieve *her* mind a little if you reveal my real object in visiting Sanditon today.' "

If Mr. Parker was quoting his brother's exact words, Charlotte reflected, there was no mention of herself in this permission of Sidney's. And from several eloquent looks being exchanged between husband and wife, she gathered this very point was now being debated in silence between them. But Mr. Parker had evidently decided the licence extended also to their guest; and with a final reassuring nod to his wife, he began in an impressive tone,

"When I selected today for the date of our Assembly, little did I realise its importance for Sidney's friend, Mr. Brudenall. But Sidney has just been congratulating me on such uncanny sense of timing. If he himself could have chosen one day out of any others for our Assembly, he would have fixed on today — the very thing he would have wished for, he says, to take his friend's mind off his present miseries and help him to survive this particular evening as effortlessly as possible. Today, Sidney has just informed me, is the wedding day of Henry Brudenall's cousin."

Charlotte was so near to laughing at this anti-climax that she cut up her apple again with even greater concentration. Such an explanation might appear wholly credible to Mr. Parker. Such judicious flattery from his brother over the random selection of an important date might have added the final corroborating touch to compel his belief. But this particular wedding day was becoming so mobile an event that she herself was beginning to doubt its very existence. She could well understand now why Sidney had purposely excluded her name from inclusion in his latest secret.

"So you see, Mary," Mr. Parker added comfortingly, "there was quite a simple explanation of the mystery after all. I as good as told you that this morning. I was sure, when we discovered the truth, it would prove more prosaic than Diana's fanciful notions. And, you know, Sidney's good nature in seeing his friend through this difficult period is so praiseworthy that we must lend him all the support we can. He was always determined, he tells me, to be in Sanditon this evening if he could. And he is grateful to me for furnishing the additional excuse of the Assembly. Never, he says, would he like Mr. Brudenall or anyone else to suspect he travelled down here for a more serious reason than that."

Charlotte could scarcely be blamed for concluding there must indeed be some very serious reason for Sidney Parker's presence in Sanditon. She was also convinced she would never discover the truth from listening to any of his relations; she even had some sympathy with him in his persistent efforts to mislead them. The Parkers were so inquisitive a family that she could readily believe he found the greatest amusement in deceiving them all. It must have been a source of high entertainment to him all his life: to be constantly making his brothers and sisters waste their time in impertinent guesses and futile discussions, as he invented one story after another and watched them being taken in by each deception in turn.

If it helped him to confuse his family, Charlotte even forgave him the pretence of his gentle flirtation with herself. These light-hearted attentions to her — what, in fact, did they amount to, when she considered them rationally? Nothing more than an easy, friendly playfulness; and she would indeed be a fool in imagining they meant anything else. It was hardly Sidney's fault that she had given him her heart long before his lively brain hit upon such a scheme for teasing his sister Diana; and that her own feelings were now complicating his little plot far beyond his own conception of it. She knew it was her behaviour and not Sidney's which was causing Mrs. Parker's anxiety; and with a sturdy resolution to be level-headed and sober-minded the whole evening, she went upstairs to dress for the Assembly.

If any further proof was necessary to enforce this resolution before she left Trafalgar House, she overheard it in descending the stairs again an hour later. Mr. and Mrs. Parker were still debating the matter in their hallway as she came to the first bend of the staircase.

"My dear Mary, do not give it another thought," Mr. Parker was saying. "You must allow me to know best; and I am quite sure I did the right thing. Miss Heywood is a sensible girl, but she does not know Sidney as we do. That liveliness of his is often misplaced, so it was as well to let her know Mr. Brudenall and not herself was his main concern this evening. I hope I have given her a little hint not to take these attentions of his too seriously. It is quite clear to me now that he was mainly intent on hoaxing Diana."

"That is all very well — but is it clear to Miss Heywood?" said Mrs. Parker unhappily. "He should take care not to deceive our guest at the same time as his sister. Besides, you now have Arthur's account to confirm what these attentions have been. Sidney was most insistent he should escort Miss Heywood to the tea rooms. Susan too — her story about speaking to Miss Heywood twice at the table and three times on the Terrace, and never once getting any reply, convinces me of the danger almost more than all the rest. Even the most sensible girls can be misled by attentions as marked as these seem to have been. Oh, I am sure Sidney means no ill, but it is really bad of him to behave in this thoughtless way."

"I will speak again with him," promised Mr. Parker. "Only high spirits, we know — but shhhh," at last catching the sounds Charlotte had been at considerable pains to make on the stairs. "Well — and here we all are ready to set off! I am sorry I must insist we arrive down at the Assembly rooms at so early an hour. But you know somebody always has to be the first. Somebody has to lead the way."

Mr. Parker was, however, by no means the only one in Sanditon to covet this distinction; for Lady Denham, attended by Miss Brereton, and Miss Diana Parker, flanked by Arthur and Susan, were all standing in the broad entrance passage when they arrived.

"Ah! my dear Tom, I am so glad you are here at last," cried Miss Diana. "Here is Lady Denham saying we should have the candles lit in the main rooms and settle ourselves upstairs. But it is a good half-hour before we can expect anyone else to arrive."

"How do you do, Lady Denham — a capital idea of yours," Mr. Parker agreed. "We shall all catch colds in this draught downstairs. Ha! the musicians have arrived too, I hear. Splendid, splendid. Let us all go and listen to them tuning up." And with as much noise and bustle as he could contrive, he urged them up the stairs.

Charlotte found herself beside Miss Brereton who, unlike herself, seemed under no constraint to dissemble her excitement at the prospect of the evening of dancing before them. Her eyes sparkled in anticipation, as with more open-hearted animation than she normally displayed, she confessed,

"Oh, Miss Heywood! I am convinced this is going to be the most delightful evening we have yet spent in Sanditon. I have been practising Scottish steps for the last hour in my impatience to begin dancing. I can hardly wait for everyone to arrive and the music to start up. Do you not feel the same?"

"Why yes — yes, of course," Charlotte smiled. She and Clara Brereton had been diligently avoiding each other since their drive to Brinshore. The uneasy awareness between them of the confidence offered and rejected had precluded any further attempts towards intimacy. But Charlotte had long ago repented her lack of warmth on that occasion and willingly responded to this friendly overture. Feeling, however, that their roles had suddenly been reversed and it was she and not Miss Brereton who now had something to hide, she searched for a reply passing over herself. "It is a pity your cousin should not have arrived in Sanditon before this Assembly."

"Ah, but she is coming a week from next Tuesday," exclaimed Miss Brereton, speaking in a low but excited voice. "This is another circumstance which adds to my happiness. I heard from her this morning and it is now all settled — there is to be no more delay and uncertainty. My dear Elizabeth, in her letter to me today, writes that she will be coming by the mail coach as far as Hailsham on September the eighth; and Lady Denham has already agreed to let me meet her there in the coach. I am so happy about such definite and decided arrangements. Elizabeth's coming will solve everything for me."

And then perhaps wondering if she had spoken too openly about her private difficulties, to which Charlotte had once turned a deaf ear, Miss Brereton moved away to exchange civilities with Mrs. Parker. But Charlotte was left with the impression that Clara Brereton had solved most of her problems to her own satisfaction already, that no confidante was now necessary to her, and she was quite certain of her own judgement in reaching any decision.

Envying so contented an air of self-possession, sadly lacking in herself that evening, Charlotte decided she must at all costs preserve a decent show of composure in front of the Parkers; she was determined that not by one word or one look would she betray what she was feeling; and the resolution of maintaining a staid demeanour formed her main preoccupation as the Assembly rooms began to fill.

Their cold and empty appearance soon gave way as the Mathews and the Browns, the Fishers, the Miss Scroggs, the Mrs. Davis and Miss Merryweathers of the library subscription list began making a hesitant appearance; to be greeted by Miss Diana as old friends, and to dissipate some of their first stiffness by recognising all the other faces as ones which had long been familiar to them on daily walks along the shore line.

262

Sir Edward and his sister managed to time their arrival with that of the three young men from the hotel. Mrs. Griffiths, showing great solicitude for Miss Lambe, and carefully intent on seating her well away from the draughty passage into the card room, scarcely noticed that the Miss Beauforts had eluded her chaperonage. They dallied on the staircase, twitching each other's gowns and pinning up each other's trains till, resolutely stylish and fashionably late, they could make their entrance with the orchestra's first strains of a favourite air; and were thus on hand to engage the knot of young men still standing by the door before they could escape to choose their own partners.

Sir Edward and Mr. Catton offered themselves up with good grace as the first sacrifices of the evening; and Sidney Parker left Henry Brudenall no choice but to engage Miss Denham for the first two dances, by walking away from them both and coming to claim Charlotte's hand. She was by now not very well pleased by this distinction; and well aware the suspicions of the entire Parker family were directed towards them, had been regretting for some time that she had allowed Sidney to form this engagement in advance.

However, the five pairs of eyes watching her made her more determined than ever to appear perfectly easy and unembarrassed; and as Sidney made this quite feasible by chatting to her in his most sensible, unaffected manner, she began to feel she was really managing very well in hiding her own confusion. They were half way down the first set before he made one of his devastating asides.

"Both Diana and Susan are looking another way at the moment," he whispered. "I do think it would be quite safe for you to smile just once."

Charlotte found herself doing so involuntarily.

"It has gone a lot further than your sisters," she said frankly. "You have Mr. and Mrs. Parker and Arthur to contend with now as well."

"Oh, you may be sure I have had that impressed on me! But I hoped they had sufficient tact to spare you. However, your prudent conduct towards me for the last ten minutes has set all their minds at ease again. Even Mary is now convinced her guest is in no danger of falling victim to her unscrupulous brother-in-law's shameless intrigues. Look — she is quite comfortable over in that corner with Lady Denham. And Arthur is entirely engrossed with his dear little Miss Lambe. How long has that been afoot?"

"All this last week," said Charlotte, very pleased to be able to discuss this topic with him. "I was sure you would approve. It is making such a difference in Arthur's outlook already. I remember your once saying some buried inclination of his own might stimulate him into exertion. And it has. He has forgotten his own health completely in his passion for collecting seaweed and his concern for Miss Lambe's comfort."

"And which of these inclinations has been lying dormant in poor Arthur all these years?" wondered Sidney, looking across at his brother. "There they sit, oblivious of nearly everyone else in the room; and nobody except ourselves seems to notice what has happened to them. They remind me of two babes in the wood — or perhaps I should say, their forest of seaweed? I agree the change in Arthur is so striking that I am more amazed than ever Diana does not see what is in front of her eyes. According to Tom, she is too busy concentrating on the vagaries of her imagination." He paused for a moment, and after a little thoughtfulness, added, "Do *you* think it is only Diana's imagination, Miss Heywood?"

The question revived all Charlotte's agitation. To her dismay she discovered she was beginning to breathe far too quickly; and though she felt the necessity of speaking, she felt the impossibility of entering on such a subject even more.

"I am sorry — that is — my attention must have been wandering — it appears — I am afraid I was thinking of something else," she finished lamely.

Her eyes were fixed on the ground and she wished for a movement of the dance to separate them for the present. But there was no such fortunate interruption; and after waiting a few moments in an agony of apprehension, she heard Sidney say with some amusement in his voice.

"Exactly what were you thinking, Miss Heywood?"

The absolute compulsion of replying and continuing the conversation produced an immediate struggle and lent Charlotte the courage she required. Raising her head with renewed spirit, she said the first thing that came into her mind.

"I was thinking how very strange it was that you should have just abandoned Mr. Brudenall to Miss Denham if you wished him to survive his cousin's wedding night as effortlessly as possible."

The sudden frown which flitted across Sidney's face was enough to convince her he had certainly not intended she should share this intelligence. But Sidney was always very quick to recover from any reverse.

"Oh, Sanditon has been working wonders with Henry. He is making a splendid recovery. But I do agree I must be more methodical about those wedding days. I should have noted down in my diary which date separate people have in mind."

"Then you do admit you have been misleading everyone about Mr. Brudenall and his cousin?" Charlotte demanded defiantly. "I wonder if there was actually any wedding day at all."

"One day I shall tell you," Sidney promised her. "Believe me, there is nothing I should like better than to take you fully into my confidence now. But in a ballroom lengthy explanations are impossible. All I will beg at the moment is that you trust me a little longer, and never believe *any* of the stories my family may tell you." And he said this so solemnly that Charlotte was once again flustered into silence. It was only when their dance was over, and she had time to think about it later, that she realised Sidney Parker had succeeded both in reading her thoughts and evading her questions.

She hardly knew how the remainder of her own evening wore away. She began not to understand a word anyone said and scarcely to distinguish between her partners. She danced and chatted and pretended everything was normal but her eyes seemed to follow Sidney of their own accord and she envied every one of his partners. They covered a wide selection; and she had no difficulty in distinguishing between *them* at all — the Miss Beauforts, Miss Denham and Miss Brereton. He even persuaded Miss Lambe to dance with him for half a set before he returned her to Arthur and sat with them both for half an hour. He then took both his sisters in to supper; and finally sat out another dance with Lady Denham — with whom he appeared to be on the best of terms — before returning to Charlotte to claim the last dance of the evening.

"Come, Miss Heywood," he said, holding out his hand. "I have taken the greatest compassion on your position all evening; you cannot refuse to dance with me again now. Diana will be so disappointed if we do not give her a little more to talk about; and you can keep your eyes on the floor for the whole set if that makes you feel Mary will not censure your conduct."

Charlotte could not have refused him. When she told herself that this might be the last time she would dance with him — perhaps even the last time she would see him — she felt hot tears pricking at the back of her eyelids; and his very kindness to her made self-possession more difficult than ever to maintain. Her heart was now too heavy and her thoughts too painful for much dissemblance; to keep her eyes downcast on the floor had become more a necessity than a ruse.

Sidney talked away easily on indifferent subjects as though he never expected her to reply; but at one point he did introduce a note of sympathetic understanding.

"I am indeed sorry I cannot stay behind in Sanditon to protect you from my family, Miss Heywood. But if I were you, I would behave very coldly to Diana for the next few days. It should at least keep *her* in her place if you make it clear how offended you are over the blackberry syllabub." Charlotte did look up, once, rather blankly. "Well, surely you must have noticed at supper what a disaster that was? I admit it seemed like any ordinary syllabub to me too; but according to Diana it was a very inferior variety indeed. Some villain called Duckworth seems to have been responsible for it. She has been entirely deceived in him and he turns out to have no talent for cooking at all. No lemons to bring out the flavour! Who could have expected such an omission merely because she forgot to go along and supervise this Duckworth making it up? Her own special recipe was completely ignored. The poor man could not find where she had put it so used his own initiative and did what he could: sack instead of Rhenish and a glass bowl instead of an earthenware pot. Diana says the result was deplorable."

Charlotte had eaten nothing at supper, had not even seen the syllabub and had forgotten her exertions in collecting the baskets of blackberries that morning. She was reminded of them only when Sidney ran a finger lightly across a scratch on the back of her hand.

"So all these bramble marks were earned for nothing! You must show Diana how much you resent being tricked into collecting a lot of unnecessary blackberries. It is all her fault — though, of course, being Diana, she is busily dividing the blame between the unfortunate Duckworth and myself. In fact I am honoured with a very liberal share in the business! She says it was my arrival and my nonsense which put everything else out of her head. Oh, Diana is so vexed — her syllabub was a failure, the Assembly is ruined and she does not know what she has ever done to be inflicted with such a tiresome brother!"

He talked on in this playful style; but Charlotte would have gone through their whole dance in silence if he had not, towards the very end, given her hand a light pressure and said kindly,

"Do not look so worried, Miss Heywood. By this time my folly of the morning has been well driven home to me by my entire family; and I sincerely apologise for all the embarrassment it has caused you. At least say you forgive me."

"There is nothing to forgive," said Charlotte simply, feeling a constriction in her throat. It was not possible for her to say more but she managed to glance up with a smile of reassurance. She thought she understood him, and was very much affected by the view of his disposition which this appeal indicated: it was an impulse of good nature and a proof of his own warm and amiable heart, which she could not contemplate without emotions so compounded of pleasure and pain that she knew not which prevailed. But the remembrance of his appeal would at least remain a pleasure to her, comprising as it did his perception of her embarrassment and his resolution of parting with her on friendly terms.

"Thank you," he said, smiling back at her. "That gives me hope that my journey to Sanditon has not been the complete disaster I feared."

She was glad Sidney felt he could now drive back to London with a clear conscience; she was glad she had done nothing which might have betrayed her too obviously. But the evening had seemed to her almost endless; and she was convinced at least one person in Sanditon, whom she had always suspected of conspiracy and deceit, now bore a more satisfied and complacent mind than her own, when Miss Brereton said on the way downstairs, with the same happy sparkle she had shown on the way up,

"Oh! my dear Miss Heywood! How soon it is all at an end! I wish we could have it all over again!"

CHAPTER 27

CHARLOTTE had by no means exhausted all the emotions possible in a young woman who has the misfortune to fall in love without any assurance her affections are returned. Happiness and pain, agitation and uncertainties had been lived through in a state of alternating dreams and doubt. For many mornings she had awoken with thoughts of Sidney, had relaxed against her pillows for the first half hour of every day, remembering sentences he had spoken, jokes they had shared, fleeting expressions which had crossed his face as he listened to others talking. And then one day had been crowded with so many events, to which she responded with such intensity, that the blankness of the days which followed caught her unawares. She was not prepared for the reaction of numb misery which now set in.

Common sense had at last reasserted itself: it told her all was now at an end: it warned her that she must teach herself to be insensible towards Sidney Parker; and though her heart still dictated periods of abstraction, they were no longer so heedless and never pleasant. She could only hope this single-minded obsession, which occupied all her thoughts, clouded every present prospect of enjoyment and deadened all her earlier interest in the Sanditon scene, would be softened by time and change. The remembrance of this interlude might become happy and natural again, when some of her peculiar attachment to him had faded, when she could look back on it all from the security of her own quiet home. Then she would at least have the recollection that such things had been, which could never be looked for again, and which could never cease to be dear to her.

The morning after the Assembly, Charlotte broached anew the subject of her departure from Sanditon as the best and most effective cure she could devise for herself. She had relinquished any hope that she would see Sidney again before she left, and was now only anxious to remove herself from this background which carried too many associations.

The Parkers were still reluctant to lose their young guest, said a great many kind things in protest, and offered her their carriage to drive the whole way whenever she wished; and finally agreed with her suggestion that she write to her father proposing a date in the second week of September for her removal.

Once Charlotte had written her letter and gained her point, the remaining days she was to spend in Sanditon became precious to her again, with all the gentle melancholy of something she was about to lose. From stretching emptily ahead of her, as they had done immediately after the Assembly, her days began to fill up with little incidents, with sights and sounds and impressions of a peaceful, sunlit beauty in sea and sky, which never wearied her as she sat in contemplation of them.

She continued to spend part of her time rambling about the countryside with regular walking parties the young people of Sanditon were still eagerly promoting. The Miss Beauforts were to be found on the Terrace every morning with suggestions of yet another route for the party to explore, another lane they had discovered and with more vivacious conversation to engage their walking partners. Sir Edward was still at hand to keep his usual proprietary eye on Miss Brereton, who seemed equally determined to continue the daily encounters; and even without Sidney Parker, Miss Denham evidently found the young men from the hotel still worthy of her attention.

Charlotte was always happy to walk with Reginald on these

excursions and listen to his ready jumble of chatter, laced with an occasional spice of wisdom — invariably prefaced by "Sidney says." He made few claims to any opinions of his own, and Charlotte soon learned to distinguish between his usual muddle of conversation and the pungent remarks of Sidney, even when he failed to attribute them. She also learned how useless it was to ask Reginald any direct questions about his stay in Sanditon. His vagueness and his laughter only increased whenever she tried to discover how long he and Henry Brudenall intended to remain there. Well, of course, he had no immediate plans — fortunately his time was his own — no real point in making definite decisions for a while — it all depended on Sidney — then of course Henry's sailing date was unsettled — his own friends in Brighton could wait a little longer — and, in short, it was very agreeable to be staying on among such pleasant company in so quiet a resort.

Charlotte listened, but without quite understanding it. Here was a complete reversal of Reginald's opinions since his first day in Sanditon when he was impatient to return to Brighton as soon as possible! She smiled at his lack of method in now professing opinions in absolute contradiction to those originally expressed, but forbore to tease him by pointing out this inconsistency. But she could not be satisfied, and had the sensation of there being something quite curious in his present arrangements.

Charlotte also spent many of her mornings on the shore line with Arthur and Miss Lambe. She watched the sea gulls wheeling and swooping, while Miss Lambe busily sketched her seaweed specimens and Arthur paddled happily about among the rocks. None of them spoke a great deal on these occasions. A few comments of sincere admiration from Charlotte when she inspected the latest drawings, and a few pensive remarks in reply often comprised the whole of the ladies' morning conversation, their silent companionship being interrupted only by a few gleeful shouts from Arthur whenever his prod emerged successful from

271

a rocky pool. The little that Miss Lambe did say was always to the point; but sometimes she surprised Charlotte by beginning in the middle of her thoughts with some shy and ingenuous statement.

"If I could spend my whole life by the sea, I would be perfectly happy," she had said one day after sketching for half an hour in silence.

On another,

"How fortunate you are to have sisters and brothers of your own. You need never be lonely."

And finally,

"I wish you would call me Adela."

These remarks were never adorned by the extravagant embellishments the Miss Beauforts would have found it necessary to add. And Charlotte responded to them in the same simple terms, appreciating the bright quality of warmth Adela so often hid before strangers and her unfailingly sensitive awareness to even the unspoken opinions of the few friends she valued.

One morning when Charlotte called at the corner house to meet her, she found Adela silently assembling her drawing materials, more intent than ever on her own thoughts. She barely uttered a greeting, could scarcely raise a smile, and, turning away quickly to select her paint brushes, said very suddenly with her back towards Charlotte,

"Before we go down to the beach, there is something I should like to tell you," pausing in a rather nervous way. "Arthur has asked me to marry him and I have agreed." She glanced round with a brief look of appeal. "I hope you will not think it very wrong in me. I will never be strong and healthy but I am not a complete invalid; and fortunately I have inherited quite enough money never to be any sort of burden on a husband." And then, with a great rush of words to cover up a mounting embarrassment. "We intend to build a house for ourselves here in Sanditon, to invite Mrs. Griffiths to live with us and look after us both — oh! please say you do not think it is such a foolish idea of ours."

Charlotte heard the quiver in her voice, could imagine the tears in Adela's eyes, and feeling words inadequate at that moment, went to her immediately and embraced her. But even on this emotional occasion, Adela could not express her feelings directly.

"You, I hope, can understand how such a thing could have happened. But do you think — would you help us by explaining it to his brothers and sisters? Can you make them *see* that Arthur will never have any cause to regret taking such a step? I am sure — in short — I know he will be happy. We are both so very fond of seaweed."

Once Charlotte might have wanted to laugh at such a conclusion. But the deep regard Arthur and Adela had for each other was so apparent to her that she could understand their reserve, their constraint to discuss it before others. She had grown very fond of them both, and was herself quite confident of the perfect compatibility of the match; but they lacked the assurance to admit their mutual affection even to her. Even before her, they spoke not of their attachment but of their apprehensions — Arthur thinking his sisters would find it very odd in *him* to be wanting to marry, and Adela positive they would disapprove.

They were, indeed, so bashful about their plans, so nervous of everyone's reaction to their engagement, that all Charlotte's persuasion was required before they would even reveal it to Mrs. Griffiths. Arthur's stumbling avowal and Adela's apologetic explanations were then met with such calm good sense that they both began to feel their plans were not so outlandish after all, and to hope their acquaintance in general might even regard a marriage between them as quite normal.

But Charlotte and Mrs. Griffiths were perhaps the only people in Sanditon who were not surprised by the engagement. To everyone else it was more than the proverbial nine days' wonder — it was the sensation of the season. Various combinations of various names had occurred to various people, but never this one.

The Miss Parkers repeated "Impossible!" with great vigour to each other many times before they could be brought to modify it to "Most extraordinary!" in front of Arthur and a mere "Quite remarkable!" before Adela. It was still the oddest thing that ever was, and neither of them could understand it. Arthur to be getting married! Arthur in the role of a husband!

Mr. Parker did his optimistic best in persuading them both it was a very desirable match. He was certain Arthur could learn to look after himself in time. Arthur's needs were simple and he had never been in danger of overspending his own small income. But had his sisters considered this large fortune of Miss Lambe's which would now make everything easy for him? The existence of the fortune had been taken for granted for so long that Adela's modest style of living and diffident behaviour had, in fact, led the Miss Parkers to overlook it in their first reactions to the engagement. When its full extent now became known to them, they were so awed by its amount they had not another word to add in dissent. Who would ever have believed *Arthur* capable of doing so well for himself?

Within twenty-four hours the "Impossible!" had been transformed into the feasible. All highly desirable! Most delightful! The most sensible thing Arthur had ever done!

The Parkers were not a mercenary family; but a fortune, though they had not sought it, they naturally considered a very good thing to have in any family. And yet this fortune, which was an afterthought to them, and almost an irrelevance to Arthur and Adela themselves, was immediately assumed by the rest of Sanditon to be the entire reason for the match.

Lady Denham, mourning it on Sir Edward's behalf, had always been certain somebody would make a determined effort to seize hold of it before the end of the season.

"Lord bless me, such chances do not often occur! If I told Sir Edward once, I told him a thousand times not to be letting the grass grow under his feet; but I observed how pitiful were his efforts. The few smirks he gave in Miss Lambe's direction were not likely to profit him. And so I told him. But, between ourselves, this reverse may set him down a peg or two. He is far too fond of strutting about and thinking to himself what a fine young man he is! Oh, you may be sure I gave him many a hint that any of those three young men from the hotel could walk off with our heiress under his very nose. And now even Mr. Arthur Parker has done it! Oh well, if Miss Esther still manages to fix Mr. Sidney Parker, I will not regard the season as completely wasted."

Though neither Miss Beaufort nor Miss Letitia had ever elevated Arthur Parker to the status of a real beau, they were sorry to lose him as an elegible bachelor and their earliest admirer in Sanditon. But they were philosophic about the match — the fortune, of course, explained it all. And it was better to lose Arthur in such a cause than any of the four other candidates. They outdid each other in extravagant and insincere compliments to "dear Adela" on her "conquest," while satisfying their own vanity by the persuasion that Arthur still admired them a great deal more than his chosen bride; and that if they had fifty thousand pounds apiece, they would never throw themselves away on such a pudding.

To Mr. Parker, Miss Lambe's determination to settle in Sanditon outweighed almost everything else. For although she was unwilling to speak of her affection for Arthur, Adela was fortunately not so inhibited in expressing her warm admiration of Sanditon. Her praise was enough to make her a first favourite with Mr. Parker; and he was amazed that Arthur should have had the sense to choose such an intelligent wife.

Mrs. Parker's quiet acceptance of her new sister-in-law was

everything that it should be. She sought her frequent company, kindly offered her assistance in all her plans, and was as pleased as her husband to feel they could soon number near relations as near neighbours.

"Well, this news makes some amends to us for losing our own dear guest," she said on the evening of the Monday which had revealed the engagement to her. Charlotte had heard from her father that same morning: he proposed sending the family coach to meet her in Hailsham the following Thursday. "And perhaps, my dear, as you and Adela have become such firm friends, we may often expect you here again at Sanditon. You will always be very welcome at Trafalgar House; but I am sure Arthur and Adela will claim you as one of their first guests when they build their new home."

Charlotte smiled rather sadly at these plans for future visits, which only succeeded in depressing her. She knew her friendship with Arthur and Adela would always give some sweetness to the memory of her stay in Sanditon, though it could take only a very minor place among her recollections of that summer; a summer such as she could seldom remember — scarcely any rain and no storm of consequence.

It was with a certain relief that she greeted a clap of thunder that evening, as though proving to her the weather could be less than perfect even in Sanditon. But the summer storm which this heralded was so violent that by tea-time she was sharing her host's fears for his tiles, his canopy and his new plantation. A cold stormy rain set in, accompanied by such tempestuous gales that it seemed everything outside the house must be despoiled as everything inside was being rattled and shaken.

The storm continued with unabated fury all night; and Charlotte, lying sleepless for many hours, could hear the waves pounding along the beach and the rain lashing against the windows, with every now and then a crash of thunder which eclipsed even these powerful sounds.

The winds seemed to hurl themselves at Trafalgar House, whistling through the young plantation, down the chimneys, raging against this stubborn block of resistance on the top of the hill, tearing Mr. Parker's gay canvas awning from its stanchions in protest, and ripping it into shreds as a violent proof of displeasure.

CHAPTER 28

IT WAS SUMMER again when Charlotte awoke; the sea was calm, the clouds had all been carried away and the sun shone down on the havoc caused by the storm of the previous night.

The Parkers' first object, after breakfast, was to inspect the damage the wind and rain had wrought in all their favourite corners. Mr. Parker, with three uprooted trees to mourn in his plantation, could only shake his head at the canvas awning completely beyond repair. Mrs. Parker, rejoicing in only one broken pane in her greenhouse, helped Mary to disentangle her swing from overhanging branches, consoled her boys for the loss of their tree house and scolded them soundly for two sodden books and a coat found lying in a puddle of mud.

Charlotte shared and sympathised in all these family concerns; but having walked all round the shrubbery to report upon hydrangeas and rhododendrons, pointed out two tiles missing from the roof and a lopsided weather vane, she paused for a moment on the edge of the lawn, wondering how much farther afield to wander in search of fresh disaster.

And as she stood there, surveying the distant flotsam washed up on the beach, she saw Reginald Catton and Henry Brudenall pass through the entrance gates, change direction on perceiving her and walk towards her instead of the house. The gravity of both their faces surprised her; and she had no need of their constrained "How-do-you-dos" to inform her that they intended something out of the ordinary in this morning call.

But though neither of them looked or spoke cheerfully enough to make the encounter appear normal, they seemed unwilling to venture beyond a few vague comments on the storm, the wind and the despoiled trees across the down; and both soon fell into an uneasy silence.

Convinced as she was that each was waiting for the other to begin, Charlotte made no attempt at conversation herself. She glanced only from one to the other, trying to guess their purpose, while the conviction grew in her that they had heard something from Sidney which caused concern to them both. She was sure whatever they had to impart would be disagreeable and the reluctance to tell her arose from their uncertainty over the extent of her own friendship with him. She did not feel equal to opening any such subject herself, but looked anxiously towards Reginald, expecting he would be the most likely of the two friends to lead the way. But it was Henry Brudenall who finally cleared his throat and began,

"Miss Heywood, if you have time to spare us, there is something of great importance we should like to tell you."

The belief that it was indeed Sidney — that he had met with some accident during the previous night's storm, had taken part in a duel or been overturned in his carriage — flashed one after another through her mind: all immediately suggested by her fears as possible causes for so solemn a communication.

Scarcely knowing what she did or how she spoke, she had faltered no more than his name, when Reginald impetuously interrupted his friend.

"No, no — it is not Sidney," he cried, taking her hand with a ready understanding which showed more feeling than sense. "How hopeless you are, Henry. It has nothing to do with Sidney, I swear it, Miss Heywood."

A good deal surprised by his warmth and a good deal ashamed of her sudden weakness, Charlotte mastered enough of her agitation to beg him to speak and tell her the reason for such wretched suspense. The seriousness of his manner had by now prepared her, quite as much as his words, for something extraordinary. But Reginald, having made this one rapid outburst seemed to consider any further communication would be best made by Mr. Brudenall; and looking impatiently towards his friend, urged him to continue; while he, with a heightened colour and a hurried manner, floundered into yet another beginning.

"Miss Heywood, the fact is that we — that I — have come to ask your help. Believe me, if there was another person in Sanditon at this moment to whom I could appeal, I would prefer to approach them. I know you will not wish to be consulted; I know you will not approve of what I shall ask — "

Charlotte could only stare at him in utter amazement while Reginald Catton, throwing up his hands in despair, said bluntly,

"He means Miss Brereton has told him you would not approve of their elopement."

"*Their* elopement? Is Miss Brereton planning to elope with *Mr. Brudenall?*"

A sudden wave of relief swept over her; and Charlotte instantly recognised this was not merely relief that Clara Brereton had no intention of eloping with Sir Edward. The real possibility she dreaded had never done more than cross the confines of her imagination to be instantly dismissed again. But she was honest enough with herself to recognise it had always been there to haunt her from the background. She had dreaded it so much she had never admitted or allowed herself to dwell on the possibility: that it was Sidney himself who was involved with Clara.

"Only thing to be done now," said Reginald with a certain gloomy satisfaction. "Henry sails on Friday and it is too late to do anything else. What is the use in going on talking and contriving and achieving nothing? For weeks they have been trying to work out some better solution. Henry always wanted straightforward action: simply to tell Lady Denham he had come to take Clara away; but the Breretons were so determined to keep their foothold with her, so frightened she would leave all her money to these Hollises or Denhams instead of to them, that they begged Clara to get her cousin installed in the place before upsetting the old lady. But Clara must be made to see there is no time for such fingle-fangling now."

Charlotte looked her astonishment at these surprising and somewhat sketchy revelations, feeling she should at least phrase a few questions which would make Reginald's confused sentences more intelligible to her. But before she could exert herself, he had rushed on.

"If Sidney were here, he might be able to get round the old lady and make her consent to it all reasonably enough. But she's much too selfish and set in her ways to be talked into sense by any of us before Henry's ship sails. She hates anything to upset her routine. The performance she gave and the fidgets she went through before Sidney could get her to invite Elizabeth Brereton to Sanditon! He thought he had arranged all that in time. But now we seem to be a day or two behind in our calculations. This *is* the Tuesday Clara is supposed to be meeting her cousin at Hailsham!"

"Yes, of course, I remember Miss Brereton's cousin was due to arrive in Sanditon today," Charlotte said slowly, wondering where all these details were expected to connect. "But what about Mr. Brudenall's cousin?" she added, still groping to separate new facts from old fiction.

"Clara Brereton is his cousin," insisted Reginald firmly. "Distant cousin on mother's side; and they *have* been devoted to each other since childhood. Sidney did spread a lot of moonshine about a broken romance to confuse all the Parkers, but he stuck to the truth whenever he could. They are cousins and they always intended to marry before Henry left for Bengal. There was never any secrecy about it among the Breretons; but they had not yet spoken of the engagement to outsiders when Lady Denham interfered and complicated all their plans. *She* took an instant liking to Clara and settled on inviting her to Sanditon House. The entire Brereton family entreated her to invite Elizabeth to stay with her instead. But no! She was certain there was some trick in it somewhere. The more they tried to put her off Clara, the more she insisted on having her; and she had become so suspicious by this time, they decided the plain truth was too much for her to accept without ill-will and disbelief. And as *she* was so unreasonable, and *they* were so anxious to keep on good terms with her, they persuaded Clara to put up with the arrangement for six months. Six months! It could be six years if nobody does anything more about it. Sidney has been arguing with Henry for months to come down and take Clara away from Sanditon. And for weeks now he has argued with Clara that there is no point in stretching this all out any longer. Let the old lady leave her money to the Denhams instead of the Breretons. Why should Henry and Clara have to suffer for it?"

"Why indeed?" cried Charlotte; and she spoke with such warmth that Reginald, turning to his friend, cried triumphantly,

"There, what did I say, Henry? I told you Miss Heywood would see everything the same way as we do. It's not as though Lady Denham were Clara's guardian. If both your families approve of her engagement to you, I have my doubts you can even call this an elopement. Miss Heywood is sensible enough to understand how it all is. You can see that for yourself, surely? And, pray, Henry, do you now proceed."

Charlotte was only surprised that there still remained something left to get on with. Reginald's own style of communication might be rapid, diffuse and disconnected, but the sentiments expressed were plain and matter-of-fact enough. He did not think very clearly and seldom gave himself the trouble of doing so when he could rely on Sidney to advise him; but the few opinions he did form were unshakable in both their honesty and common sense. And as she listened to his recital, if it did not perfectly justify an elopement, it proved Lady Denham to have been very unfeeling and selfish in her conduct towards Clara, deficient alike in sympathy and discernment. But Reginald had told her nothing which did not accord with her own observation and what she could imagine of Lady Denham. Her manoeuvres of selfishness and cunning had always been offensive and her reactions to any new suggestions had always been unpredictable.

Henry Brudenall had none of Reginald's gift for frank outbursts and, in Charlotte's estimation, had always been a romantic and rather sombre figure. But now, as she faced him with an encouraging smile, he suddenly transformed himself in front of her eyes from a shadowy caricature into a real person. Confronting her, deeply earnest and full of some sensitive emotion, he said,

"Miss Heywood, do you remember the stream?"

"The stream?" echoed Charlotte in some bewilderment.

"The stream that flows from old Sanditon and is blocked by the chesil where it reaches the open sea? I have been walking along that path this morning. Do you remember the first day we walked there and I said it was a poor stream to creep between pebbles instead of driving them left and right in front of it?"

"And Mr. Parker agreed with you," cried Charlotte as a sudden shaft of light revealed the key to that commonplace conversation. "But Miss Brereton — "

"Clara said it could not do that before the winter," said Mr. Brudenall. "But it has broken through its ridge of pebbles this morning. After the storm last night, the stream has swept everything before it and is now flowing straight and unhampered into the open sea. Do you not think this is a good omen for us? Will you try and help me convince Clara this is so?"

"Really, Henry!" Reginald interrupted with exasperation. "What have all these streams and omens got to do with the case? Show Miss Heywood that letter you had in the post this morning to say your ship has sailing orders from Hull instead of London. Tell her you now have to spend three days travelling there instead of one. Explain that Sidney is not yet back with his carriage to take you there, that Clara will have to leave with you this morning instead of meeting her cousin at Hailsham. And for heaven's sake, stop wasting precious time with streams flowing to the open sea."

Charlotte laughed at such a typical outcry; Reginald's prosaic manner might never have won him the hand of so romantic and fascinating a heroine as Clara Brereton; but having won it, she felt he would have carried her off with more resolution and less fastidiousness than his friend. His blunt announcement that an elopement which had the blessing of both their families could scarcely even merit the term had convinced Charlotte that some of the scruples over such proceedings could more easily be waived. If Lady Denham's eccentricity was the only obstacle to the match, she felt she should offer what help might be required towards overcoming it.

"Tell me what you are expecting me to do?" she asked Henry. But she was not at all surprised when it was Reginald who rapidly unfolded their present plans. His barouche, he explained, could hardly carry the fugitives all the way to Hull. They must drive with him to Brighton and hire a postchaise for the longer journey. Would she agree to accompany himself and Henry immediately and waylay Clara Brereton as she set off for Hailsham to meet her cousin? Clara could then write a brief note of explanation to Lady Denham for her cousin Elisabeth to deliver. Charlotte would take her place in Lady Denham's coach and meet Elizabeth Brereton in Hailsham; and Elizabeth — sensible, good-humoured and well aware of the whole situation — could competently be left to deal with the tangle once she had been allowed inside Sanditon House.

"But what," said Charlotte with some hesitation, "if Miss Brereton does not agree to all this? If she has been unwilling to consent to an elopement, and waiting till her cousin arrives before entering on any explanations with Lady Denham, do you think she will now throw all caution to the winds and risk her disapproval at the last minute?"

"She must," said Reginald with childlike simplicity. "Henry has already postponed his departure for India three times. He cannot be kept dangling about forever in England doing nothing. Oh, his father has promised to arrange Clara's passage and have her follow him; his family will do all they can to send her out to join Henry whenever she may. But surely she will see that more delays and postponements are hardly worth the risk? It is a long way to Bengal and many things may happen during such a separation. If she loves Henry, she must now trust him to decide their future. Sidney told her himself," he added impressively, "that their whole chance of happiness might depend on her seizing one particular moment and acting on it before it was too late. Why spend a lifetime, as Sidney says, regretting wasted opportunities?"

Sidney's opinion carried even more conviction to Charlotte. For him, these sudden plans would have brought no element of surprise. He had been advising his friends how they should act for many weeks now and had been able to decide on their future without haste and without confusion; and she was all at once quite certain that Sidney's principles could be relied on.

"I will be with you in a moment," she said, beginning to dart away, but not so impetuously that several very practical suggestions had not already raced through her mind. "I will need a wrap for the journey to Hailsham; and I must give some excuse to Mrs. Parker for being absent the whole day."

285

It also occurred to her that she was the first of this little group to be committing herself to carrying through this deception, when she appeared round the greenhouse door a few moments later and told Mrs. Parker a downright lie in a steady voice.

"I hope you will not mind, ma'am. Miss Brereton has just come to beg for my company on her journey to Hailsham. We would be away the whole day meeting her cousin there — have you any objection to this?"

Should she have complicated the whole story by a stammering long-winded explanation that Miss Brereton had not come herself but sent two young men, seemingly unconnected with this journey, as her emissaries? Unused to taking risks and intimidated by her own bravado, Charlotte held her breath at the possibility that Mrs. Parker might put down her gardening fork and hospitably decide to greet Miss Brereton in person. The pause which followed was very dreadful to her; and she could only command an outward composure by trying to look as unruffled as she knew Sidney would have been in the same circumstances.

"What, my dear? No, no — not at all — if you would like to go," replied Mrs. Parker at last, raising her eyes from her flower-pots and bedding trays but leaving her mind resting behind on them. "Of course it will be more pleasant for Miss Brereton to have company on the journey. The carnation cuttings are coming along beautifully, you see. Only two plants damaged by that broken pane — I have cleared away all the bits of glass already. What a pity she did not suggest this earlier! Be sure to take something warm — the weather seems so changeable at the moment. No good at all letting old Andrew transplant anything out of doors. Well my dear, we shall expect you back by dinner then?"

And Charlotte, making good her escape, realised she had gravely misled an open-hearted person for the first time in her life; and also that she felt not the slightest guilt in having done so. Because Mrs. Parker *was* guileless, her task had been easier;

but it did not follow that such innocent people should against their will be involved in a similar predicament to her own. Mrs. Parker would be much more contented for the moment to know nothing whatsoever about an elopement; and Charlotte could honestly believe that in suppressing the truth, she was protecting her.

This comforting theory remained with her as she accompanied the young men down to the hotel; and helped console her further when she encountered the curious stares of the Miss Beauforts from the balcony of the corner house, as they drove in the barouche out of the hotel yard. She voiced only a mild protest to Reginald.

"Do you not think all that luggage at the back must present rather an odd appearance to anyone who sees us?"

"Henry can hardly set out for India without clean shirts," he replied sagely. "And do you blame me for packing up my few things too? No sense at all in my staying in Sanditon now and facing up to that old lady's tantrums. I am very sorry, of course, that you may come in for some of them yourself. But it would scarcely help *you* if I remained behind too, you know. Bound to be uncomfortable whichever way you look at it."

Charlotte had no quarrel to find with the soundness of this reasoning; and though still amazed to find herself taking part in so unlikely an adventure, was perfectly willing to bear the consequences on her own return. She felt some curiosity, however, to meet Miss Elizabeth Brereton, who appeared destined for the role of her fellow scapegoat. A few enquiries of Mr. Brudenall elicited the information that Miss Elizabeth was thirtyish, kind and resourceful — the very companion who should suit Lady Denham admirably if she could only step over her threshold — a companion chosen long ago by her relatives as much more to her tastes than Clara, and far more capable of standing up for herself in any given situation.

Charlotte began to hope the whole incident might turn out

more pleasantly and more satisfactorily for everybody than she had first imagined. She had several uneasy moments, some twinges of doubt and a good deal of apprehension as they waited on the Hailsham road for Lady Denham's carriage to appear; but Reginald's cheerful certainty in the journey's being no elopement at all, and Henry's steady trust in Clara's own reactions to this sudden wild proposal had already made her believe his plans were far less preposterous than they had seemed only an hour before. She had been willing to help him then from instinct alone; but logic witheld its approval of her decision till she had witnessed the scene of meeting between Henry and Clara.

She could then have no further doubts. Once she had seen them together, she was determined they should stay together. She was only astonished she had never noticed their complete absorption in each other before. How could she have missed that soft glow of warmth in Clara's eyes when she looked at him? Or that unmistakably tender quality which crept into Henry's voice when he spoke to her? True, they were no longer dissembling before strangers but discussing their most intimate affairs before proven friends. But in failing to recognise something of this devotion to each other, Charlotte realised her powers of observation must indeed have been severely clouded for the past month. Had she ever, in fact, seen them *together* before? Connecting Clara with Sir Edward and Henry with his fictitious cousin, she had *looked* at them together but *seen* them apart. And they had been acting their parts to preserve this illusion. But now all reserve was at an end, and with it any pretence on Clara's side that she would be unwilling to elope with Henry at any time he decided such a measure was essential to their happiness. Indeed her only concern, after staring and listening and agreeing with a now animated Henry Brudenall, was voiced in one feeble and very feminine objection.

"But Henry — after all this time — to be leaving Sanditon

without any preparation at all! Nothing with me for the journey! My clothes, books — possessions — " in some confusion, "it must seem ridiculous to you but — "

"Oh, we have prepared for all that!" cried Reginald with another of his completely practical interruptions. "Sidney said he knew just how it would be once we ever reached this point. He said your own things could be sent after you when he managed to prise them out of Lady Denham; but in the meantime he sent my sisters on a shopping expedition last time he was in London. Very good taste, my sisters. Shrewd too. Laura writes that none of the clothes you have now would have been a bit of use to you in India anyway. Whalebone stays for instance — they rot in the heat. Did you know that? Well, you must have solid silver ones when you become a memsahib, Laura tells me. I dare say you would never have planned out these details for yourself — but your new wardrobe is all in that black trunk at the back; and Sidney says it is to be our wedding present — his and mine."

Miss Brereton smiled her appreciation of this admirable foresight and, taking Henry's hand, climbed into the barouche without further argument.

"Perhaps you and Mr. Parker would also like to write the letter I should leave for Lady Denham," she suggested with gentle irony.

"No, no," disclaimed Reginald. "Henry can dictate a letter much better than I. But it must be done now. Miss Heywood will hand it to your cousin Elizabeth at Hailsham — and she will be able to give it to Lady Denham when she arrives at Sanditon House. Much the best plan all round! A few sentences will do — but you and Henry can word them best."

All the same, Charlotte noticed, it was Reginald who had provided himself with paper and ink for the purpose; and having extracted them from his travelling case and handed them into the barouche, he walked with Charlotte a little way down the road to allow them to compose the letter.

"As you can plainly see now, Miss Heywood, Henry is a romantic idiot — and Clara not a great deal better," he said with affectionate tolerance. "Sidney says they are both like characters who just stepped out of fairy tales instead of houses. Any fairy tale at all, he says. Clara, he decided, could be Cinderella, Snow White or Sleeping Beauty and Henry could be any of the princes. And they have about as much idea how to manage things for themselves as any such hero and heroine. Unless a fairy godmother or a lilac fairy comes along and makes everything right for them, they would go on dreaming impossible fantasies and never get anything done at all. They have both been so compliant towards everyone else for so long that nothing was ever resolved upon for themselves. Far more feeling than common sense. Their hearts have belonged to each other for years — but would *they* ever have united them without our interference? As Sidney says, meddling is a talent he was born with but had to start teaching me from our first term at school when we both met Henry."

"You have known each other as long as that?"

"Forever," said Reginald simply. "We are going to miss Henry in Bengal. He will have to learn to look after Clara but whom will we practise our skills upon in future?"

"Perhaps you will find a Clara of your own," Charlotte said lightly and was only conscious after she had said it that, whereas Reginald spoke in the plural, she had confined herself to the singular. She coloured a little at this slip but he appeared to accept it quite naturally.

"Ah, but perhaps it is only the romantic Henrys who call forth such devotion," he sighed. "Do you think any Clara would run half across the world with me if I asked her? No, there are people who can inspire dreams and other people who can carry them out. And on the whole I feel more comfortable with the second best choice, though Sidney says — " But Charlotte was not fated to hear what Sidney had to say on this interesting subject. "Hullo, have they finished their letter already? Yes, Henry, we are coming."

Now all their preparations were complete and all her anxieties over, Clara Brereton wanted only a few last words with Charlotte before they set off. There was a new glow of animation on her face and her eyes were alight with excitement and anticipation: that total lack of constraint and radiant delight Charlotte had first noticed in her on the morning of their sea bathe. She remembered now that had been the morning of Henry Brudenall's arrival in Sanditon. Clara spoke very quickly — in a great rush — as though she would never be able to finish all that she had to say.

"I can never thank you enough, dear, dear Miss Heywood. I could never have left Sanditon without knowing Elizabeth would soon be here. In agreeing to drive with Saunders in the coach to Hailsham, you will finish what I have been trying to do here. Tell Elizabeth I would have liked to wait for her — so much kindness I owe her family, I would have been glad to repay as best I could — but Elizabeth will understand. She will make all right with Lady Denham if anybody could."

"I wish," said Charlotte impulsively holding out her hand, "that I had let you complete your explanation about this elopement the day we drove to Brinshore. Did you ever realise I thought it was Sir Edward you had in mind?"

"Sir Edward?" cried Clara in tones of genuine astonishment. "You could have believed *that* of me? It is a pity we never got to know each other well enough to exchange opinions about Sir Edward! Oh, his selfishness, his persistence! I never dared tell Lady Denham how often he waylaid me without her knowledge! And what stupid speeches and muddled proposals he continually made! Lady Denham's fondness for him — how could I have undermined it? Had I told her of his foolishness, she would only have suspected me of setting her purposely against the Denhams. But Sir Edward and his sister have complicated everything for me as much as Lady Denham herself," with a sigh of regret and a shrug of relief. "The more I came to know both the Denhams, the more unpleasant I found them. Both of them so grasping and servile and determined to ingratiate themselves with Lady Denham. But I have never risked offending either of them — I am sure Elizabeth will handle that situation more easily too. Now that I am really going with Henry, I begin to see I should have done so long ago. I am not very clever at managing people and should leave it to the Sidneys and the Elizabeths of the world."

"And the Reginalds," interposed Mr. Catton with mock jealousy as he took over the reins from his groom. "Just what I have been telling Miss Heywood myself. Now then, we must be off."

"And thank you, Miss Heywood, again and again," cried Clara.

Henry Brudenall was even more effusive. Leaning down from the barouche at the last moment, he took both Charlotte's hands in his, and with a great deal of genuine feeling but a trifle dramatically nevertheless, cried,

"We may never meet again but Clara and I will remember all our lives what you have done for us today. I wish we had known earlier we could trust you so well. But I should have known — I should have guessed what to expect from any friend of Sidney's. God bless you, dear Charlotte."

Reginald, flourishing his whip on the box, was more prosaic in his parting.

"Our regards to Sidney when you see him," he called cheerfully. "He will be happy to learn how we all danced so merrily to his tune in the end. Goodbye, goodbye."

Charlotte was left standing in the road. She watched the barouche disappear out of sight before turning back to Lady Denham's coach and the waiting coachman; and in the long journey to Hailsham found time enough to indulge the thoughts and reflections such a morning of unexpected activity had helped her to resolve. She felt how improbable it was that she would ever meet any of them again. Within a few days she herself would have gone from Sanditon; and if Sidney Parker wished to steer clear of trouble with the same natural inclination as his friend Reginald, he would be wise to postpone his return there for several weeks. This was not, however, a reaction she expected from him. The disclosures of the morning had brought her a lot closer to an understanding of his character; and she really believed he would be prepared to face any amount of trouble and inconvenience on behalf of his friends.

She realised now how well he had kept this secret, confounded his family and done everything he could to help Henry and Clara — and all with that light-hearted gaiety which seemed to mean nothing, but only hid everything. At last she could also understand the reasons behind his pretence of a flirtation with herself, readily acknowledged its usefulness in distracting the Parkers from the real situation and forgave him for it without rancour.

She was perfectly convinced now that he never had any serious design of engaging her affection. But with a strong desire to please, lively powers of address and a great deal of charm, Sidney had probably never realised how little he need do to captivate a heart like hers which had known no such previous temptations.

And what in fact had he done which was not essential to his main purpose of bringing Henry and Clara together? He had insisted that Charlotte sit beside him on the drive to Brinshore so that Henry and Clara could be granted several long and necessary hours together to discuss their future. He had required an excuse to return to Sanditon with Elizabeth Brereton's reply,

Clara's sea trunk and a final reassurance that all was in readiness for Henry's sailing date. And what better excuse could he offer to his inquisitive family than a mild flirtation? Diana's lively imagination had already credited him with this — but as usual, she had muddled matters and selected Clara herself as his object. To correct this mistaken impression, Sidney had tried to lead her fantasies in a different direction.

Even then, he had been careful to do no more than place his hand over Charlotte's in full view of his sister after everyone else had left the tea rooms. He had practised no deceit; he had frankly acknowledged his object to her immediately afterwards and, confronted by an expostulating brother, had glibly produced yet another excuse to account for his trip to Sanditon.

At the Assembly he had shown his good sense and his awareness that the scheme had been carried far enough for his own purposes and too far for her comfort by dancing with her just enough to keep Diana guessing, leaving her alone for the rest of the evening and apologising handsomely for his conduct.

Charlotte had her own suspicions that Sidney may have realised by then that the prudence and common sense he teased her about were no longer sufficient barriers to her falling in love if he persisted in his attentions. Perhaps he had guessed it even earlier in the tea rooms? But his kindness, frankness and cheerfulness towards her had never varied. Beyond paying her a few charming compliments and amusing her with gay conversation, had he done anything at all to try and gain her affection? He had, Charlotte remembered rather wryly, done nothing except — in a burst of typical high spirits — bought and bestowed on her a hideous little shell box, which she would keep as a treasured memento. And she smiled to herself a little sadly when she reflected that this — her most precious souvenir of Sanditon — was, in fact, labelled Brinshore.

The morning had indeed provided her with very full and detailed reasons for any attentions Sidney had ever paid her; and this rational explanation of them, which ended any hope she may have had that they could ever have been serious, at least brought her the consolation of being able to feel proud of him. She had always admitted his charm but doubted his integrity; but now, in finally losing what had never been hers, she found some comfort in this new pride she could take in Sidney. His principles were as steady as her own — and he had a great deal more audacity in practising them.

She had often compared him with his sister Diana and believed his interference was as officious and improper as hers. It had seemed that both of them took a delight in trying to modify the course of other people's lives. Meddling or helping — it came to the same thing. But Sidney's solicitude for others had now been proved beyond any doubt to be legitimate and open, entirely prompted by genuine good will. He had no love of power for its own sake, no conceit in doing more than anybody else, no sentimentality about his duty to be useful to others. He merely helped his friends when they were in need.

Of course Sidney could never have loved her! It had been presumptuous of her ever to have imagined it. But he had liked her, respected her and trusted her. At least, Charlotte decided a little wistfully, at least she could be grateful for that.

CHAPTER 29

DRIVING INTO HAILSHAM in Lady Denham's carriage, Charlotte felt anxious and uneasy as she contemplated her approaching meeting with Miss Elizabeth Brereton. The two hours of her journey had been occupied solely with her own concerns; but now she thrust these resolutely aside and began considering the explanations she would soon be called upon to make, and hoping Clara's reliance on her cousin's sympathetic response would be quite justified. The stormier explanations, another two hours hence, to an intolerant, suspicious — perhaps even unreasonable — Lady Denham would lose some of their terror if her new accomplice did indeed possess those virtues of calmness, common sense and resource with which Charlotte had already endowed her.

The sight of Clara's letter to Lady Denham lying beside her on the seat of the coach conjured up visions of the same letter being opened on their return to Sanditon — the exclamations, accusations and scenes of anger which might follow! Would she be required to take the lead in this drama or would Miss Elizabeth Brereton agree to handle it all? And what would the Parkers say when they realised the part their guest had played that morning in straining their relations with their most important neighbour? Charlotte's courage was still high and her belief in the necessity for such measures still unshaken; but she was beginning to dread the consequences of her own complicity as the time for closer involvement drew nearer.

She was, therefore, considerably relieved to discover, from Saunders' enquiries at the coaching-inn, that the London mail was not expected for nearly an hour; and she had leisure to stroll about the outskirts of the town, to walk to recover her spirits and order her thoughts, before hurrying into this important first encounter with an entire stranger.

Clara's letter now being discovered as too large for either reticule or pocket, Charlotte left it in the temporary charge of Saunders; and with the illogical feeling that she was shelving a heavy responsibility, walked briskly out of the inn yard and along several tidy streets which led her almost into the countryside. A signpost pointing south east to Willingden was a comforting sight: she remembered her own family and reflected that, whatever the unpleasantness — how many distressing scenes — she might have to face in Sanditon in the next few days, her return home was already determined. On Thursday, she would be here in Hailsham once again, the family coach to meet her, at least some of her brothers and sisters to greet her; and within three hours, they would have conveyed her safe back to her own dear world.

For the first time since leaving home, Charlotte felt a longing to return. The novelty of Sanditon, the kindness of the Parkers, her pleasure in their society — all now seemed to count for nothing; and as she walked along the road that would soon be taking her there, Charlotte almost wished she could anticipate the intervening days and the warm security of her family's welcome — all the blessings of stability and those peaceful, unchanging rural values which formed the accepted pattern of existence in Willingden.

So intent was she on her own thoughts that the sound of a carriage behind her scarcely broke through her reverie. Even when the rhythm changed from a trot to a walk and ceased as the carriage drew alongside her, Charlotte did not trouble to glance round. And she was considerably startled to hear a low laugh behind her and a masculine voice declaiming melodramatically,

"You have walked away from me once too often, my fair charmer. But this time you will not find me so complaisant. This time — "

Charlotte spun round in astonishment to find herself confronting Sir Edward Denham in his gig. A bewildered look of complete stupefaction, which replaced the sardonic and impassioned expression Sir Edward had been trying to assume, immediately made it plain to *her* that her pelisse, her bonnet and her presence in Hailsham had led him to mistake her identity from behind; and his immediate exclamation — "Good God! But where is Miss Brereton?" though ludicrously inadequate in accounting for the very great difference in their height, colouring and mode of dress proved this conjecture beyond all doubt.

Charlotte was so fascinated by Sir Edward's range of facial contortions that she found it almost impossible to reply for a few moments to either of his very singular outbursts. It was clear to her he must have planned such an assignation in Hailsham without Clara Brereton's knowledge and that, in his usual absurd style of gallantry, his intentions towards Clara at this meeting were as muddled as ever. Deciding her best course was to behave as conventionally as possible, she mastered a very strong inclination to laugh and said coolly,

"Good morning, Sir Edward. I had not the least expectation of seeing you in Hailsham. What business has brought you here?"

"Where is Miss Brereton?" Sir Edward only repeated through clenched teeth.

"I do not at all know," said Charlotte with perfect truth. "I have not seen Miss Brereton since this morning when she asked me to take her place in meeting her cousin at Hailsham today."

"You are lying," cried Sir Edward, almost beside himself with rage. "I have just been speaking to Saunders and he told me Miss Brereton had walked out of the inn yard scarcely ten minutes ago in this direction — "

"Then I am afraid you were mistaken," Charlotte replied pleasantly. "Are you sure you did not use some such phrase as "your young mistress" or "your passenger" which Saunders could have misunderstood as relating to me? There is no need for this confusion, I assure you, Sir Edward. I am very willing to accompany you back to the inn where Saunders may clear the matter up within a few seconds."

Another facial contortion as Sir Edward's mind ran swiftly over his brief conversation with Saunders told Charlotte her guess was correct and he was now acknowledging his own mistake to himself. Dropping the reins so suddenly that his horse shied and kicked, covering his face with both hands, groaning, cursing and venting his temper, Sir Edward presented a most distasteful spectacle to Charlotte's critical eye. She did not even pity him. His own conceit and his own preposterous conduct had led him into this ridiculous adventure — where he had betrayed his intentions by his first remarkably foolish utterance and now in a most inglorious fit of temper — and she felt no desire at all to make his recovery any easier for him.

She realised, however, that it would be better to overlook the implications of the incident and to pretend Sir Edward's violation of all social canons to this lavish extent was not quite so obvious to an outsider. He stood revealed to her as a very shallow character pretending to be a romantic hero, but she did her best to treat him as a common acquaintance.

"Come, Sir Edward. Let us drive back into Hailsham and find Saunders. I believe it is almost time I was turning back in any case to meet the mail coach."

As he made no reply but continued only to groan and lament in the most incoherent manner, Charlotte climbed sensibly on to the vacant seat beside him, picked up the reins and began to turn the gig back towards the town.

"Too late! You are too late," cried Sir Edward with an almost hysterical laugh. "It is done — the die is cast. Inevitable ruin stares me in the face. Nothing is left now but to lose myself in a vortex of dissipation."

"What?" said Charlotte, considerably taken aback. "What die is cast?"

"Saunders! He is on the road back to Sanditon. With four horses. We cannot hope to catch him up with one. I was three hours in driving here yesterday, rested my horse overnight and planned — how, oh! *how* can my schemes be thus tragically overthrown?"

Though Charlotte had been trying to ignore these schemes of his and remain on terms of civility with him, her sense of proportion was now strained to its limits. She halted the gig astride the road.

"On what pretext and whose orders did you send Saunders back to Sanditon?" she enquired coldly. For once, Sir Edward seemed capable of a more intelligible reply.

"I told him his services were no longer required; that I had learned Miss Elizabeth Brereton would not be arriving on the mail coach, and I would drive his passenger back to Sanditon myself. But I gave him a letter to deliver to Lady Denham on arrival which explained everything — I cannot now halt it. I cannot intercept it. All, all is now undone. You see before you, Miss Heywood, a doomed man!"

In the midst of her vexation with Sir Edward, Charlotte could still summon up some amusement at the thought of the two discordant letters, addressed to Lady Denham, which Saunders was now carrying back to Sanditon. Sir Edward's account of the day's events at such cross purposes to Clara Brereton's! She bit back the retort that, if doomed he was, then it was his own idiotic fault, and said calmly,

"Sir Edward, I can no longer pretend that I do not understand you. Am I to take it you have written a letter to Lady Denham announcing your intention of eloping with Miss Brereton to-day?"

"Five pages," nodded Sir Edward. "Throwing myself on her mercy, begging her to forgive us both, proudly and finally declaring my unbounded passion — driven by sublimities of such intense feeling that I was at last ready to dare all and hazard all — even *her* displeasure — in the unlimited ardour of this overruling fire in my breast. To what suffering, to what depths of depravity has it led me!"

Charlotte was perfectly convinced that Sir Edward was quite incapable of either truth or suffering. And if he had not brains enough in his head to realise that Clara Brereton would never have consented to such an elopement, and that a one-horse gig was a completely unsuitable vehicle for carrying it through, then he thoroughly deserved his present ruin. She sighed. He did not really merit her compassion but she hoped he could be talked into some semblance of reason by kindly treatment. Why, he was a child — not a very nice child — and his faults were bragging, childish pinpricks without any real power to inflict hurt on anybody. He was a man of straw, but she felt she should do her best with this very poor material available and try to make Sir Edward behave sensibly.

"I do not think you have yet considered your present situation quite rationally, Sir Edward," she said with admirable patience. "I am sure we shall be able to retrieve your letter — or even perhaps pass it off as a joke. Now, is it indeed true Miss Elizabeth Brereton is not arriving on the mail coach?"

"How should I know that?" cried Sir Edward with such a burst of irritation as dismayed her of making him listen to her with any lucidity. "I suppose she is arriving. But *her* presence in Sanditon is quite unacceptable to *me*. I have left her a letter too — at the coaching-inn — that will send her straight back to London where she belongs. I told her nobody would be meeting her from Sanditon — she was not wanted there, neither by her cousin, nor Lady Denham nor anybody else."

"And why should you have done that?"

"Why should I *not?* I planned this day's adventure very thoroughly, let me tell you. Down to the very last detail — disposing of one cousin at the same time as I gained the other — "

"Yes, yes," agreed Charlotte. "I can see you planned it very well indeed. But your plans have gone wrong now. Can you not realise we must *now* think of some alternative? Sir Edward — please listen to me carefully for a moment." It had occurred to her that the revelation of Clara's long-standing attachment to Henry Brudenall and her elopement with him that very day might have a salutary and sobering effect on Sir Edward and bring him under reasonable control. "I believe I should perhaps tell you that your chances of success were a great deal less than you imagined. When I told you some minutes ago I did not know where Miss Brereton was, it was only true in a literal sense. I do, in fact, know that she is somewhere on the road between Brighton and Hull. She did indeed leave Sanditon today, but in quite a different direction. She will not be returning — she is already on her way to India. She has eloped with her cousin, Henry Brudenall, to whom she has been sincerely attached since childhood."

She spoke very slowly and very distinctly as to a backward child; and he seemed to be listening with a solemn concentration which gave some hope that her words were having the moderating effect she intended. "I am very sorry to tell you there was never any hope of your gaining Miss Brereton's affections. She would never have eloped with you."

"Eloped?" cried Sir Edward, suddenly infuriated. "Who talked of elopements? I wrote in my letter to Lady Denham that we were eloping — but I never considered that for one moment. Mine was to be an abduction, not an elopement," he shouted, as though proud of this superior boast. "Clara Brereton spurned my noble passion, my generous emotion — she paralysed my heart with her indifference. This day was to have been her ruin and not mine!"

Charlotte almost gasped at the effrontery and the violence of this loud bragging. Sir Edward was sunk indeed. He was cheap and impudent and so puffed up by vanity that it had injured what little intelligence he had ever possessed. She still believed him manageable by adult understanding, still thought she had only to find and press the right spring and Sir Edward would respond; but she counted without his present unusual excess of rage. Beneath his glossy and handsome surface, Sir Edward was a petty tyrant, to whom rational conduct meant nothing whatsoever when he found his will crossed.

He seized the reins from her hands, and whipping and backing his poor horse, set it at a gallop along the Willingden road.

"*What* do you think you are doing now?" cried Charlotte in alarm as the gig lurched and bumped, forcing her to clutch at the seat for support. For a moment she believed the horse had bolted with them; but although she was not over-impressed by Sir Edward's reckless style of driving, she soon realised he had his horse under control. On his whipping it even further, she recognised that he was only trying to frighten her. And this had the odd effect of calming her instead.

"Thwarted of one fair charmer, why should I not take another?" shouted Sir Edward with a savage laugh. Glancing up at his profile on the first occasion their erratic progress would allow her, Charlotte saw that his features were again becoming set in that sardonic and impassioned expression he had been doing his best to assume at the outset of this very peculiar encounter.

Charlotte was by now very angry, much more angry than alarmed. Sir Edward's last action — this wild and theatrical charge into the countryside — released her from any remaining obligations of civility towards him. And she spoke quite as sharply as she felt.

"Sir Edward, rein your horse this instant and set me down. I have had quite enough of this nonsense."

For answer, he gave another of his hollow, seductive laughs and tried to look more dangerous than ever.

"Rein my horse indeed! You are now my captive, my hostage, and there is no chance of escape. Have you not yet realised it is *you* who is now being abducted?"

"In a *gig*?" cried Charlotte scornfully. But sarcasm was too subtle a weapon to have any effect on her companion. When he had cooled off and abated some of his fury in a headlong dash down the road, she could not fail to believe some shreds of sanity would return to him. She had scarcely needed this present, rather dramatic illustration to be convinced that Sir Edward was a mountain of conceit and selfishness. But she wondered why — without violently caring, or even pretending to care, for her — he had chosen to abduct her. She imagined he must have talked himself into some semblance of real passion for Clara Brereton. But it made little sense that he should set out on this particular morning to abduct one young lady and then, quite illogically, seize another instead. From various spiteful and fatuous sentences which he threw over his shoulder from time to time, she could only conclude that the muddled state of his mind only equalled his extremely bad temper; and if this were the case, she decided he was not a companion she could endure for many miles longer.

As the direction they were travelling could eventually take them to almost any channel port, her first rapid conjecture was that Sir Edward had planned to abduct Clara Brereton to France. But a very few seconds sufficed to make her decide that even Sir Edward could never have hoped to accomplish such a protracted and complicated journey with a reluctant companion. He had, moreover, taken the trouble to drive his one horse from Sanditon to Hailsham the day before, and it would seem unlikely that he was planning to cover more than a similar distance today. It required very few more seconds for her to hit upon their most probable destination, as the memory of little snatches of conversation overheard in the tea room came into her mind. "A friend of mine has a little hunting lodge he wants to convert into a cottage orné." "My friend Atwell has gone to Switzerland for the summer and left me his keys." "Willingden Abbots." "Somewhere due east of Hailsham, I believe."

How typical of Sir Edward's careful planning, Charlotte reflected, to be now intent on abducting a young lady to within a few miles of her own home! But having reached this very comfortable conclusion, she found the few remaining inconveniences of this abduction (for Charlotte had never regarded them as terrors) vanished completely; and she was left only with a strong curiosity to observe in what manner Sir Edward would at last be brought to his senses.

She was forced to admit she had not yet found any successful method of handling this conceited, stupid braggart herself. His behaviour was quite outrageous; but expostulation and wrath would not help her. And although she remained in a high state of indignation, she was not at all frightened to be careering across the country on a summer day in an open gig. She had no intention of either jumping out or of shouting at Sir Edward; and she would have thought it unpardonable weakness to begin crying, even as a means of gaining her own way. Common sense told her that, however much Sir Edward might whip up his one fairly staid horse in an effort to appear villainous, sooner or later he would be forced to reduce its present pace to a point where conversation would again become possible. So she merely sat, clutching at the seat till the horse dropped into a canter.

Some of his ill humour being dissipated in enjoyment of the

unusual burst of speed he had extracted from his gig, Sir Edward was in a slightly better frame of mind. Though not yet sufficiently discriminating to think matters out clearly, he was at least cheerful enough to essay one of his quotations, declaimed with typical inaccuracy and equal perversity of interpretation.

"Assuaging your alarm, my fair one, must now become my chief aim. Those lines of the poet will be my guide to our future brief life of adventure together —

> *When lovely woman stoops to folly*
> *And finds too late that men betray*
> *What charms shall soothe her melancholy*
> *What arts will wash her tears away?*

Delicious! Delicious! Dryden has stated my case with such unrivalled, immortal sublimity that I can accept him as my guide and mentor."

"Goldsmith," Charlotte contradicted bluntly. Sir Edward, she felt, no longer merited even the compliment of politeness from herself. And although she believed judicious flattery might have been a very good method to adopt — probably an excellent device in pulling the marionette strings by which Sir Edward might be expected to behave — scorn was a technique which held more appeal for her at the moment.

"And your quotation in this case is even more inaccurate and inappropriate than usual, Sir Edward," she pursued, surprising herself by the waspishness of her own spite. " 'What charm *can* soothe' and 'what art *can* wash' is the correct version. And to what tears do you refer? No doubt it has entirely escaped your attention that I have none; and I am scarcely the one who has stooped to folly either!"

Sir Edward was not clever enough to employ a sarcastic tongue in return. He merely shouted veiled threats, lost his temper again for several more miles and cut viciously at his flagging horse with the selfish tantrum of a spoilt child. Charlotte now perceived a very great resemblance between himself and his sister and, under the new license of freedom she had granted to herself, said so. This provoked another outburst, which Charlotte met with the greatest indifference, discovering she much preferred dealing with Sir Edward in a temper than when he was effusively amiable. He could be obnoxiously polished in compliment, but his innate manners were shocking indeed; and she found it quite a relief to have him revealed in his true character.

As they covered mile after mile, and the pace of the gig slowed as the afternoon wore on, she said a great many more things, which she hoped Sir Edward might remember when he finally came to his senses.

The landscape was becoming more and more familiar to her; and as she gained in confidence, she began lecturing him on his folly, pointing out the consequences he could expect from the course of action he had embarked on so histrionically and with so little forethought. Indeed, at several points on their journey Charlotte was almost ashamed of her own lack of charity towards him; but she consoled herself with the reflection that forbearance would scarcely restore the moral strength Sir Edward lacked.

He still replied occasionally with some confused and impassioned outbursts; but she could see her policy of withering scorn was at last having some effect; and that he was already heartily regretting having selected her for his companion in this adventure.

"You will find yourself very isolated at Denham Park on your return to Sanditon, Sir Edward," she observed. "Had you considered that? Or is it yet another of the drawbacks you have overlooked? I fear you will be quite an outcast when the story of today's events becomes known. Your abduction of their guest is most unlikely to improve your relations with the Parkers."

"What care I for the Parkers?" cried Sir Edward with one of

his sweeping gestures of disdain. "But even if I worried about their opinion, it is *you* they will condemn. Naturally, they will believe you came with me willingly. I am Sir Edward Denham and my word will be listened to in Sanditon before yours."

"Very true," agreed Charlotte. "We are always in a far better position to uphold our respectability on our own home ground," smiling at the familiar landmarks they were now passing on both sides of the road.

Both Sir Edward and his horse were showing definite signs of fatigue by this time; and as the gig began climbing a long hill, the tired horse slowed his walking pace even further. Charlotte could have descended from it with ease at almost any point over the last few miles. But she saw no reason to start walking sooner than necessary. Any part of the present slope would be convenient for her but she decided she might as well wait till they were farther up the crest of the hill.

She was also determined to avoid any undignified scuffling and recrimination; so she watched the figures of two yeomen-labourers advancing through the slanting rays of the setting sun downhill towards them. She chose her moment very carefully: the figures were almost abreast of the gig when she sprang nimbly down into the road.

"Good evening, Thomas. I hope the children have recovered from their whooping cough, John?"

The weary horse had stopped involuntarily, adding a final corroborating touch of normality to this seemingly prosaic home-coming. Sir Edward stared down from the gig, too stupefied to interfere. Even to his weak understanding, it was clear that Miss Heywood, pleasantly greeting two stalwart farm labourers, was a personage of some note in this district. He heard cheerful words passing between them; he even heard words addressed to himself; but they were directed, he knew, to this audience — an audience who had known Miss Heywood of Willingden all their lives, but to whom he was a complete stranger.

"I thank you for your kindness, sir," Charlotte was saying, turning back to the gig and regarding Sir Edward calmly. "It was extremely kind of you to come so far out of your way on my account. But I need not trouble you any further. It is only a step for me from here. I will be home in a very few minutes now. I wish you good evening."

Nodding a final smile at her audience and dropping him a very slight curtsy, Charlotte turned on her heel; and without one backward glance, either of triumph or trepidation, she walked off across the fields.

CHAPTER 30

MR. AND MRS. HEYWOOD'S RECEPTION of their daughter on
her unexpected arrival home was greatly to their credit as sensible
parents. Their surprise, when she walked in across the fields
to join the family party at tea, without an escort, a trunk or
advance notice of her intentions, can be readily imagined; but
after their first exclamations, they were willing to listen to her
explanations, which were delivered in so collected a manner as to
cause more astonishment than alarm.

In walking from the road, Charlotte had plenty of time to
rehearse what she had to tell them; and though in everything
which related to herself, she witheld nothing and spoke only the
simple truth, she felt she could be forgiven for omitting both
Clara Brereton and Henry Brudenall from her tale. If her
parents had ever seen Clara, they might perhaps have recognised
her as the beautiful and bewitching heroine of a romance, and
expected her to provide them with all the entertainment of a
fairy tale come to life; but even to Charlotte, who did know her,
it still appeared slightly incredible that two young men should have
planned to elope with her on the same day.

She had very quickly reached the conclusion that Clara and
Henry would only add to the complications of her own story; so
she limited the account to her own uneventful trip to Hailsham,
where she had driven in Lady Denham's carriage to meet Lady
Denham's niece; and where she had been — so strangely and
unexpectedly — abducted by Lady Denham's nephew by marriage.

Reduced to its essential elements and told with no inflated representation of her own first reactions of panic and anger, it sounded, nevertheless, a very shocking business to her sympathetic family audience.

However, their Charlotte was certainly home and unharmed now, once again seated at her normal place at table, pouring out tea for her younger brothers and sisters; and her plain, unvarnished account of the villainous conduct, immoral behaviour and unprincipled selfishness she had met with seemed too far-fetched to concern her parents to any marked extent. Indeed, had it not been their own honest, straightforward Charlotte telling the story, Mr. and Mrs. Heywood could scarcely have been blamed for disbelieving it. Her daughter's adventure was of a type Mrs. Heywood had sometimes encountered in novels set in far distant countries but would never have associated with the safe counties of England. As for Mr. Heywood, it had never previously occurred to him that such folly could have been contemplated — much less carried out; and it was clear from his bemused questions that Sir Edward's conduct struck him as improbable rather than dangerous.

"You say this young man actually tried to abduct you in broad daylight in an open gig?"

"Yes, sir."

"And drove you at walking pace within a mile of your own home?"

"I hardly think he could have been aware of that fact when he chose his route, sir," said Charlotte. "He struck me from the first as not possessing a particularly strong head, so I doubt if it was ever clear to him exactly where I lived. And perhaps Sir Edward had little choice in the matter of his destination. He had been offered the use of a friend's hunting lodge, which probably played a decisive part in his plans. I gather his own financial resources are fairly limited."

Charlotte was rather amused by her attempts to apologise for Sir Edward's woolliness.

"Ah! that would explain the gig and the one horse too," agreed her father, shaking his head in amazement at such preposterous arrangements. "But it sounds quite muddle-headed to me. Very strange indeed! No money to afford such adventures either! Bless my soul! Quite extraordinary! Well, Charlotte, you have certainly shown your usual good sense and I am only sorry your holiday has ended thus abruptly. But it is only by two days. For my part I am glad to see you returned home, and you must write to Mr. and Mrs. Parker directly. It is quite likely they may be worried over your disappearance."

"To be sure, as they are not so well acquainted with your character as ourselves, such a very shocking story will be bound to alarm them," agreed Mrs. Heywood comfortably.

"I will write first thing in the morning," promised Charlotte; and discovering her parents had nothing further to add on the subject, she escaped to her own room to hide the attack of nerves she felt only too imminent. Her courage had remained steady throughout the events of the day and the long tense drive with Sir Edward; but despite her composure, the sensation of anti-climax in this happy conclusion to her improbable adventure gave some evidence that she was suffering symptoms of shock. Her exertions that day had been considerable, and were now beginning to depress her — the more so from not having overpowered her at the time. She was home and she was safe; but her spirits had never been so low nor her thoughts so hopeless.

After a disturbed night, Charlotte arose early to write her letter to the Parkers. She did not doubt her kind friends would be distressed to learn what had happened to her while under their care. And as she wanted to make it very clear that no shadow of blame attached itself to them, to relieve them of the anxiety they must be feeling about her, and to attempt some explanation of Sir Edward's conduct — which was still not very clear to herself — her task was indeed a difficult one.

She wrote and rewrote painstakingly, her mind cool and active; and it was only when she came to that paragraph in her letter, in which she thanked them for her holiday, expressed her sincere pleasure in the visit, and asked for her trunk to be returned, that her pen began to slacken and she allowed her thoughts to wander.

"I will never forget Sanditon," she wrote, after long consideration, "and the summer I spent there will always remain one of my happiest memories."

And discovering there were tears in her eyes, she quickly signed her name, sealed the letter hurriedly without rereading it, and leaving it on her father's desk, escaped into the shrubbery.

It was over. It was indeed only a memory. And although she walked up and down the tidy walks trying to convince herself that she could never have hoped for anything more, she sighed many times and wished the ending had been less abrupt, and that there had been a few more days to prepare herself for it.

From such reflections she was aroused by her youngest sister, Margaret, calling from the lawn in high excitement.

"Charlotte, where are you? Charlotte! Charlotte! are you there? Mr. Parker has come. Mr. Parker has come."

Not a little distressed to hear her good friends had been so concerned about her that Mr. Parker should have found it necessary to drive all the way to Willingden to see her parents, Charlotte ran to join Margaret on the lawn and saw Mr. Parker's carriage standing in the driveway.

"Is he in the drawing room?" she called, overtaking her sister on her way to the open french windows.

"No, no. He *was* in the breakfast room. John showed him in while mama was giving me my history lesson. We were so surprised! He seemed most upset about something; and when mama told him you were here, he just said "Thank God!" and sat down in a chair for so long, without saying anything at all, that mama said she would go and find papa, leaving me all alone with him. And then — "

"Where is he now?"

"I'm *telling* you," said Margaret very importantly. "Then he suddenly woke up out of his daze and asked where you were; and so I took him to look in the study but you weren't there, so then he asked for papa — "

"Dear Margaret — just tell me where he has gone now."

"The second meadow behind the hayfield," said Margaret crossly. "The one the hedge-cutters are working on. I directed him round by the road but I am not so sure now papa *is* there this morning. If you take the path near the copse — "

But Charlotte had already run on ahead across the garden, and gathering speed down the grassy slope on the far side of it, was soon out of sight behind the small wood. Skirting this wood by a small path, she arrived at the hedge which bounded the field to the road and was rewarded by the sight of a gentleman's hat beyond it. In her anxiety to reach Mr. Parker and beg him not to complicate her story by any mention of Miss Brereton and Mr. Brudenall, not to confuse her parents by acknowledging this successful elopement from Sanditon, she panted to a stop, rather out of breath, and called his name. The hat paused, turned and Mr. Parker seemed to be seeking the gap for a stile in the hedge. She had taken only a few more steps along the path towards it, when he must have caught sight of the opening himself, and a few strides brought him abreast of it. But to Charlotte's very great astonishment, the head which came through the hedge belonged not to Mr. Parker but to Sidney.

"Oh! But my sister said Mr. Parker had come," she said, staring at him foolishly. "I wanted to see Mr. Parker first — before he spoke to my father. I hope they were not too upset — how strange they must have — no blame to them. But it *was* Mr.

Parker's carriage in the drive. Indeed, I thought it must have been Mr. Parker. Not you. This is — I mean — "

Dimly aware that she was speaking entirely at random, that her words had very little connection, and were making so little sense to herself that they probably conveyed none at all to him, Charlotte withdrew her fascinated gaze from Sidney Parker's face and stared down at a point near her feet. Her thoughts became more coherent when she was no longer looking at him. Was it *this* Mr. Parker who had said "Thank God" and sat down in a daze without saying anything further at all? A very queer sort of breathlessness, which had nothing to do with having run so fast and so far, seemed to have constricted her throat; and the colour which had been driven from her face returned with an additional glow; but so long as she did not look at him, her mind at least remained perfectly clear.

"There are other Mr. Parkers besides my brother," said Sidney and she heard him brushing against the bushes as he walked towards her. "And at ten years old, you know, it may not seem very important to make distinctions between them. I also agree it is my brother's carriage in the driveway. His horses were quite fresh, you see; and my last pair of post horses were blown on the final stage down from London. I could not hope to exchange them for another good pair till I drove back to Hailsham."

He paused after each of these trivial sentences to discover if she was yet ready to reply; and deciding she was not, went on talking in the same politely effortless manner.

"And yes, Tom and my sister-in-law have certainly been concerned about you; though I did my best to convince them, during the short time I was at Trafalgar House, that the sensible Miss Heywood would very soon outwit a paltry suitor like Sir Edward."

"How did they know Sir Edward had anything to do with my disappearance?" Charlotte demanded, her embarrassment momentarily overcome by surprise. She managed a fleeting glance up at him, saw that he was laughing at her, and quickly looked down again. That familiar teasing smile was more than she had powers to contend with at present.

"Oh, it was *most* confusing at first! By the time I arrived, Lady Denham had read her two letters from Hailsham, both of which announced their writers' intentions of eloping with quite different people. She had also rushed here and there, spreading their contents around Sanditon and hearing all sorts of conflicting stories in return. Mary told her you had gone to Hailsham at Miss Brereton's special invitation; Miss Beaufort told her you had driven off with Henry in a barouche loaded heavily with luggage; Hodges told her Sir Edward had left for Hailsham the previous day; and Saunders told her it was Miss Heywood and not Miss Brereton Sir Edward had met there. All very contradictory, as you see. It took the combined efforts of Miss Elizabeth Brereton and myself to produce any sort of order out of such chaos."

"Miss Elizabeth Brereton?" exclaimed Charlotte. "But how did she come to be in Sanditon?"

"Well, naturally, I drove her there. I found her at the inn in Hailsham some hours after the mail coach had left her there. She was a little distressed, wondering what she should do — whether to wait for the return mail to London or to try and hire some conveyance for Sanditon. All this because of a letter Sir Edward had written her. What a fellow he is for words — always writing letters or making speeches! And all of them so long-winded and incomprehensible! This one was full of malice and dire warnings — but otherwise so vague one could scarcely make head or tail of it. Never having met Sir Edward, Miss Elizabeth was in some confusion, hesitating whether to take his letter seriously and abandon her journey, or to ignore both that and the discourtesy of not being met and continue her way to Sanditon. I was soon able to convince her what nonsense it all was and explain that Sir Edward's speeches, letters, quotations, compliments or threats would never be taken seriously by any normal person. So we continued the journey together, depositing Miss Elizabeth at Sanditon House, where she has already become the prop and pivot of Lady Denham's household."

"Oh! I am so glad," Charlotte said thankfully. Even in her present agitation, she could experience some relief at this news.

In addition to her other anxieties, she had not ceased to worry about her failure to carry out Clara's plans for her cousin. "But I still do not quite understand how — "

"How we could guess what really happened at Hailsham? Well once Miss Elizabeth and I had added our testimony to support Clara's letter — and Saunders had backed it up by describing the meeting of coach and barouche on the Hailsham road — none of us had any difficulty in concluding Sir Edward had taken leave of his senses and attempted to console himself elsewhere. I assure you your fate is being mourned throughout Sanditon at this moment. I did my best to convince them Miss Heywood was no feeble character; and Mary agreed she was certainly more equal to dealing with such a situation than most young women would have been. But, you know, I was the only one who really believed you could rescue yourself from the clutches of our village villain."

This was all spoken very lightly. But while she heard the amusement in Sidney's voice, Charlotte was remembering Margaret's description of his arrival in Willingden: "Mr. Parker seemed most upset about something; and when mama told him you were here — " She had derived a delightful conviction from these words; but she felt a reluctance to repeat them to him, to look up at him or do anything at all which might make his real feelings apparent to her. And though impatient to know everything at once, she tried to be calm and leave things to take their natural course. Had she been able to encounter his eye, she might have read his sentiments for herself; but she was scarcely in a humour to wait while Sidney went on amusing himself at her expense, and went rushing into sentences she had not properly thought out.

"Oh, it was all such thick-headed nonsense! I could make nothing of Sir Edward! Miss Brereton, of course, is so beautiful and romantic that I can understand why he should want to elope with her — she is exactly the sort of heroine one can imagine something of the kind happening to — but Sir Edward must indeed have been out of his mind in thinking that I — I mean — that is — "

"You feel the same thing could never happen to a sensible young woman like you?"

"Certainly not," Charlotte said, the more decisively because she envied Clara the power of inspiring such illogical actions. "It is most unlikely. No normal person would ever dream of such folly. Only someone as scatterbrained as Sir Edward could — "

"The devil take Sir Edward!" cried Sidney between exasperation and amusement. "It seems always my fate to be having to adjust my conduct to avoid any comparison with his. After his compliments, you never believed any of mine! And now will you ever believe that long before such an idea entered Sir Edward's muddled head I had decided to behave exactly as he did yesterday?"

"To elope with Miss Brereton? But you knew that — "

"Let us put aside Miss Brereton for the moment. My plans had nothing to do with her either. Oh, I have met many young ladies in London far more beautiful and romantic than Miss Brereton, but I have never imagined eloping with any of them. Shall I tell you the only sort of young woman who could inspire such thoughts in me?"

Charlotte discovered she had lost the power of speech; but her silence seemed sufficient encouragement to Sidney.

"I have always wanted to find someone with so much common sense that an elopement would not appeal to her at all. Such a thing would never enter her head, except perhaps when she was reading a romantic novel. At the very suggestion of it, all the practical objections would immediately occur — the lack of consideration to her parents, the folly of the entire proceedings, the inconvenience of so unnecessary a journey. You see, I am a very prosaic, unromantic, sensible sort of fellow myself; and I have always had my heart set on finding the most sensible, prudent, level-headed wife in the world. But, on the other hand, it is very important to me that she possess one very particular flaw: she must have no sense whatsoever where I myself am concerned. She would only have to take one look at me and — no matter what her steadiness of mind — she would lose it in the space of seconds. She would be willing to elope with *me* — without another thought — the moment I asked her. This is the only way I can ever hope to be certain I have found exactly what I am looking for. If someone insists their feet are always firmly on the ground, how else can you discover if their head is sometimes in the clouds? Just lately, I have sometimes thought I may have found what I have always wanted. But just lately I have also noticed she has developed a most irritating habit of looking at the ground whenever we are together. Do you think she could try to overcome it? Well, Charlotte, *are* you going to look at me now?"

It was the first time he had used her name. Like the touch of his hand in the tea rooms, it made her heart begin to pound with a happiness so heady, so immediate and so violent that she could not have spoken a word. She raised her eyes to his face, however, and what she read in his was almost too wonderful for her to believe.

"Well, my Charlotte?" he said again.

"You know very well I could never refuse anything you asked," she replied, hardly knowing what she said.

"All the same, I want you to say it," Sidney insisted, smiling down at her and holding out his hand. "Will you elope with me, instantly, without one more second's thought?"

"Yes," said Charlotte, putting her hand in his and moving towards him without realising what she did.

"Even though it may turn into an abduction and I take you to a remote farm-house in a gig straight past your own home?"

"Yes," repeated Charlotte. "You know perfectly well that I will. And you have known it for weeks."

"I only hoped," said Sidney modestly. "But now I am quite certain you have not a particle of common sense where I alone am concerned, let us go and find your father."

"Then we are not going to elope?"

"Certainly not," he said with his old commanding air of authority. "I have far too much respect for convention and decorum to consider such a ridiculous course of action."

But he was heedless enough of conventions to make Charlotte very happy strolling through woods, down lanes and across fields without any attempt to discover the direction Mr. Heywood had taken with his hedge-cutters.

This was an hour of such high-wrought felicity for Charlotte as made her awed to discover so perfect, exquisite and unalloyed happiness could really exist for anybody. All the little variations of their meetings and conversations were gone through, and of the progress of their attachment, there could scarcely be an end.

As Charlotte could date the exact moment of her falling in love — or, to be more precise, the exact moment of realising she had done so — she was very interested to learn if Sidney could do the same. At first he disclaimed there had been any such moment of revelation for him, protesting it had been far too gradual a process to recognise any beginning at all. But as he had no dislike of the subject and a strong curiosity to know which particular moment held such importance for Charlotte, he had soon persuaded her to describe her sensations in the curio shop at Brinshore.

"Ah, but you were miserably behind hand," he cried. "I may not be able to date a beginning but I had certainly begun long before that. The very first evening of meeting, when you rebuked me so very correctly for my levity, I was struck by the firmness of your opinions and caught by their sincerity. And I distinctly remember the first time I had an overwhelming desire to take you in my arms — we were sitting on a green bench on the Terrace with Miss Beaufort in between us. And though you always refused to believe it, I *did* arrange the seating on the drive to Brinshore to have four hours of your company. There were, of course, several other motives to combine as well; but the balance was certainly in your favour."

These details were of absorbing interest to Charlotte; and the dread of being awakened from the happiest of dreams made her stifle any objections and any inconsistencies which occurred to her, and allow Sidney to have all his own way, quite unchallenged.

"And I can date another precise moment too," he added triumphantly. "When you told me you disapproved of elopements, I made up my mind I would make you consent to elope with *me* within a month."

But Sidney's final assurance that his main purpose in attending the Assembly *was* to dance with her finally strained Charlotte's credulity to such an extent that she blushed, disclaimed and openly doubted. She absolutely refused to believe him, murmuring something incoherent about delivering Clara Brereton's new trunk.

"As if I could not have arranged some other way of sending that trunk down to her!" cried Sidney scornfully. "And surely my manner to you that day must have made my feelings plain enough? I told you — I distinctly remember it — that I had driven all the way from London only to dance with you, that I had missed you all the week. It was *you* who made me pause in my madness and decide I was proceeding too quickly for you to keep pace with me."

"I thought you were only paying me compliments to tease your sister Diana," Charlotte confessed.

"But Diana was not there when I paid you compliments."

"She was there when you held my hand in the tea rooms."

"Oh yes — I scarcely noticed her at first. But she was quite determined to get in the way. The complications she introduced for the rest of the day! I could see her prying and gossiping was making you uncomfortable; and though my original plan had been to seek out some opportunity that day to put my proposals and offer you my hand and my heart, between them my maddening relations certainly succeeded in turning it all upside down. Diana upsetting Mary by telling her I was paying you too much attention! Tom demanding an explanation of my conduct — and when I satisfied him with one, what must he do but immediately go repeating the nonsense to you! Oh, I could see you were never going to take me seriously once Tom had got in first with that rigmarole about Henry's cousin's wedding day! I knew that would make you doubt I had meant anything I said to you! I realised then that I had bungled the whole business; and that I would have to restrain my impatience and try again another time."

"How I wish I could have known what was in your mind!" sighed Charlotte. "It seemed to me you were only ashamed of your behaviour in the tea rooms and trying to part with me on friendly terms."

"To part? Surely you could not have misconstrued my meaning to that extent? At least I told you at the Assembly that I wanted to take you fully into my confidence. I begged you never to believe anything my family said about me; and I apologised for causing you such embarrassment. What more could I do then? I hoped I was making the situation plain to you and preparing my way for taking a second chance."

"I thought you were merely being kind," said Charlotte. "Treating me as a friend and making it clear you never wished to be anything more."

Sidney could only repeat that he had long wished for a great deal more; and he now made this so clear that Charlotte had no more excuse for doubts. But she was still encouraging him to repeat such very satisfactory explanations when Mr. Heywood found them.

On being applied to by Sidney for permission to marry his daughter, Mr. Heywood gave his most willing consent. The good sense and good manners of his future son-in-law were immediately apparent to him: he could see at a glance he was not a young man who would go about abducting females in gigs. Sidney's sincere regard for his daughter and his steady principles were self-evident recommendations; and Mr. Heywood was confident this judgement would be confirmed by further acquaintance with him.

But for the moment, Sidney could not stay in Willingden as long as he would have liked. The Parkers were anxiously awaiting news of Charlotte; and he felt he should drive to and from Sanditon yet again before accepting the Heywoods' pressing invitation to remain as their guest.

When he returned, he brought back all the warmest wishes of his family; for though he had stayed only the one night in Sanditon, he had been energetic enough in his calls to collect congratulations for himself and messages for Charlotte from both relations and friends.

The joy with which Adela received the information that she and Charlotte were to be sisters perhaps surpassed all the rest. She wrote five pages expressing her delight and decorating the margins with sketches of shells and seaweed.

This made some amends for the empty professions and insipid sentences of the Miss Beauforts, who could not quite disguise their astonishment that the staid and sensible Charlotte had walked off with the most eligible bachelor of the season under their elegant and disdainful noses.

Even Lady Denham sent a kindly greeting and a downright

condemnation of her nephew's folly. Sir Edward had sunk himself indeed with Lady Denham — to the point where she would no longer allow even his sister to be admitted to Sanditon House; and the news of Sidney Parker's engagement to Miss Heywood affected her only as it gave gleeful satisfaction for the setback it would be to Miss Esther and the chagrin it might cause her brother, when she wrote to him at his friend Atwell's hunting lodge. Sir Edward, Lady Denham trusted, was now experiencing the first labour pains of common sense and would never again allow his conceit to undermine his morality.

It was not possible that the outcome of this one disastrous adventure could turn him, overnight, into a well-judging, rational unselfish creature for the rest of his life, but some improvement was inevitable. Removed for some time from the influence of each other, both he and his sister improved in temper; and though their real characters underwent no revolution, they at least learned to hide them more successfully from others.

Miss Parker and Miss Diana decided their constitutions had weathered a summer in Sanditon in rather more robust style than they had ever imagined; and they soon began making plans to remove themselves there for good: to be close enough to the rest of the family to interfere in all their concerns, and to provide themselves with a receptive audience for all their nervous spasms. They tried to persuade Sidney to settle there with Charlotte, but he was easily able to evade that suggestion, and would never promise more than the occasional visit they were both happy to make every summer. For although Charlotte knew Sidney could only have lived in London, she had a great attachment to Sanditon, which held so many fond memories and good friends.

Sanditon itself, to the greater comfort of most of its inhabitants and all of its summer visitors, never prospered into the smart seaside resort Lady Denham and Mr. Parker had wished to make it. An Esplanade, a Waterloo Crescent and even a Wellington

Square were added in time, a few more visitors came each year, but it retained its peaceful, secluded character long after the introduction of Sidney's gaslight, which his brother resisted as a vulgar outrage for as long as he possibly could.

An Apology from the Collaborator

THE FIRST ELEVEN chapters of *Sanditon* were written between January 27 and March 18, 1817. By that time, after writing 26,000 words, it was clear that Jane Austen was gravely ill and physically unable to pick up the work again. She died on July 18, 1817.

The fragment was bequeathed to her niece, Anna Austen Lefroy, and now belongs to King's College, Cambridge. Only brief extracts from it were quoted in Austen Leigh's Memoir, published in 1870; and it had to wait more than a hundred years after the author's death for its first edition by Dr. Chapman in 1925.

Another fifty years have now passed, nobody has yet attempted to finish the story and the general public has tended to ignore it. Like all Jane Austen's minor works, *Sanditon* has of course attracted critical attention. But unlike *The Watsons* (of which no less than three completed versions exist) *Lady Susan* or *Catharine*, there could be no learned theories advanced about when it was written or why it was abandoned. Nobody could suggest it was a forerunner of *Emma* or *Mansfield Park*. Nobody could write other articles contradicting them. The only profitable line was to assess the fragment on its own merits as an isolated example of Jane Austen's "probable development."

As such, *Sanditon* has long been familiar to literary critics; I would like to emphasise, however, that neither this apology nor my completion of the manuscript is intended for them, but for the lay readers of Jane Austen. Ever increasing numbers, seeking to escape the shoddy values and cheap garishness of our own age, are turning to the past to catch glimpses of life in what appear to be far more leisured times.

In rereading Jane Austen, we are able to experience something of that age of elegance which too often eludes us in the twentieth century. We are unrepentant about this form of escapism and turn to her six novels for relaxation on plane journeys, in family crises and after the sheer physical exhaustion of our own servant-less world. Like Mr. Woodhouse, we enjoy the company of these old friends best; and though we prefer their actual company to secondhand discussions and speculations about them, anything concerning them will always hold a fascination for us. *Sanditon* and its gallery of characters have been exerting this fascination over me since I found myself broken off short of my first acquaint-ance with them.

The actual join in the present narrative takes place half way through Chapter 11 following that last typically Austen sentence: "Poor Mr. Hollis! It was impossible not to feel him hardly used; to be obliged to stand back in his own house and see the best place by the fire constantly occupied by Sir Henry Denham."

How did Jane Austen intend to continue the novel after that?

Her intentions over plot presented no great stumbling block. Many eminent critics have commented on Jane Austen's limited range. They have pointed out — frequently — that she only has one plot at her disposal, that her social range is tiny, that nobody dies on stage and there are no calamities. She knew nothing of politics, disregarded the Napoleonic wars and never revealed a conversation unless a woman was present. Her choice of subject matter was as limited as her range of patterns and background. In five of the six novels, the heroine lives in a country village until a financially eligible bachelor arrives on the scene. (In *Emma* and *Mansfield Park*, Mr. Knightley and Edmund Bertram have been living there all the time, thus confusing us at first with the

misleading bachelors, Frank Churchill and Henry Crawford.)
Only in *Northanger Abbey* does Catherine set out for Bath to
meet Henry Tilney halfway. Each heroine usually has a foil or
rival. But happy endings are always in store.

So why depart from such a well-worn and ready-to-hand
formula? Why should anyone feel Jane Austen herself intended
to do so in her seventh novel if it had already taken her so
triumphantly through six? None of her readers object to the
monotony of her plots. Had they happened to other people, it
is true, nobody would have taken much interest in them. But
Jane Austen had already introduced all the necessary characters
in *Sanditon*. Henry Brudenall, Reginald Catton and an off-
stage Elizabeth Brereton are my only additions.

Charlotte was clearly intended as the heroine in the original
manuscript. We have, moreover, the author's own testimony
that someday she would call a heroine Charlotte. On Monday,
October 11, 1813, she had written to her sister Cassandra: "I
admire the sagacity and taste of Charlotte Williams. Those large
dark eyes always judge well. I will compliment her by naming
a heroine after her."

Sidney has also been introduced and marked out for the hero
as early as Chapter 2, when Jane Austen explains that Mr. Parker
had two brothers, of whom the eldest was "by collateral inheritance, quite as well provided for as himself." This is the sort of
information Jane Austen's faithful readers immediately register
as a clue. It is, in fact, quite unnecessary information to include
at this stage, as Sidney is not even to appear for another ten
chapters. The next reference to him is dropped so carelessly into
Chapter 4 that surely Jane Austen would have disguised her
intentions more in any final revision? I have left the paragraph
as it is, so that readers may make their own early deductions and
enter Sidney firmly on the list of eligible suitors for Charlotte.

Jane Austen's intentions over place and atmosphere raised no difficulties either. Her own descriptions of Sanditon in the opening chapters almost exactly fit Sidmouth, as it would have been in the summer of 1817. She probably visited it herself in 1801. (Letter to Cassandra, Thursday, January 8, 1801: "Sidmouth is now talked of as our summer abode; get all the information therefore about it that you can from Mrs. C. Cage.") And though no later visit is recorded, she may have been given more up-to-date information by other members of her family.

There is certainly a Trafalgar House at nearby Branscombe (Brinshore?) and for those who wonder where Jane Austen collects her names of places and people, there is a Barton Cottage in Sidmouth, there were Dashwoods, Elliots and Willoughbys registered as living there in 1817; and a William Larkins and a Frederick Woodhouse are buried side by side in the cemetery of the local Church of St. Nicholas and St. Giles. Jane Austen has merely shifted Sidmouth to the Sussex coast, which she never visited, christened it Sanditon and placed it somewhere near Peacehaven.

So what was there left to worry about in completing Jane Austen's last manuscript? Only the way she wrote it. Her language, her integrity and her painstaking methods of work — that terrifyingly accurate and meticulous technique — combine to give us the same sense of serenity and assurance in the six novels in which she brought her world to life and made it real for us. None of these things can be faithfully copied. And for their deficiencies in this seventh novel, I do apologise.

DATE DUE

DATE DUE			
JUN 1 9 1993			
FEB 2 0 1998			
FEB 2 9 2000			
JUN 2 1 2001			
JUL 1 0 2007			
JUL 2 4 2007			
JAN 2 7 2009			
			Printed in USA